THE
DENOUNCER

THE DENOUNCER

A NOVEL

PAUL M. LEVITT

TAYLOR TRADE PUBLISHING

LANHAM • BOULDER • NEW YORK • TORONTO • PLYMOUTH, UK

Published by Taylor Trade Publishing
An imprint of Rowman & Littlefield
4501 Forbes Boulevard, Suite 200, Lanham, Maryland 20706
www.rowman.com

10 Thornbury Road, Plymouth PL6 7PP, United Kingdom

Distributed by NATIONAL BOOK NETWORK

British Library Cataloguing in Publication Information Available

Library of Congress Cataloging-in-Publication Data

Levitt, Paul M.
  The denouncer : a novel / Paul M. Levitt.
    pages cm
  ISBN 978-1-58979-967-7 (cloth : alk. paper) — ISBN 978-1-58979-968-4 (electronic) 1. Soviet Union—Social conditions—1917–1945—Fiction.
I. Title.
  PS3612.E935D45 2014
  813'.6—dc23

                                                    2014002181

∞™ The paper used in this publication meets the minimum requirements of American National Standard for Information Sciences—Permanence of Paper for Printed Library Materials,
ANSI/NISO Z39.48-1992.

Printed in the United States of America

Acknowledgments

John Donne, in 1624, wrote: "No man is an island entire of itself; every man is a piece of the continent, a part of the main." Every one of us is indebted: to other people, to country, to language, to faith, and even to fashions. We are all, like the double helix, intertwined.

Similarly, no book is written free of influence and help. The writer, consciously or not, draws on books and articles, past and present. Friends lend a hand. Foundations and institutions fund a project. Family keeps one sober, literally and figuratively. A publisher, like mine, stands by the work and offers whatever assistance it can. Not to thank those from whom I have drawn sustenance would be to suggest that I live in a vacuum. I therefore wish to express my indebtedness to the many who have made this book possible.

For their moral support, I owe a world of hugs to my wife, Nancy, and children, Scot, Daniel, and Andrea; my sister, Sandra; and my colleagues Elissa Guralnick, Victoria Tuttle, Paul Murphy, Don Eron, Tim Lyons, and William Kuskin.

For his ongoing encouragement, I cannot measure the worth of Frank Delaney.

For her scholarly help, I owe more than I can express to Susan Weissman, professor of politics at Saint Mary's College of California.

For her illuminating scholarship on denunciation, without which I could not have written this book, I am grateful to Professor Sheila Fitzpatrick, formerly from the University of Chicago and currently at the University of Sydney, Australia.

For their financial support, I appreciate enormously the Kayden Research Grant Committee at the University of Colorado, and Chancellor Philip DiStefano.

For their wondrous generosity to my scholarship students, I thank Martin and Gloria Trotsky.

For their expertise in bringing this book to press and promoting it, I am immensely grateful to Jehanne Schweitzer, senior production editor; Gene Margaritondo, copyeditor and plot doctor; Kalen Landow, marketing; Sam Caggiula, public relations; Karie Simpson, assistant editor; A. J. Kazlouski, proofreader; and Clare Cox, translation rights.

A special appreciation is reserved for Marcus Brauchli, friend and newspaperman extraordinaire.

And as always, I applaud Rick Rinehart for having the courage to publish literary fiction about a dark side of Russian history, especially given that some publishers shied away from my former novel, *Stalin's Barber*, with the explanation that few American readers would know the name "Stalin" or have any idea what transpired during the Soviet period.

Paul Levitt
Boulder, Colorado

When the military light truck arrived at the elderly couple's farm, deep mud greeted the sergeant as he slid from the cab and left his intoxicated companion behind. The Parskys nearly collapsed on learning that they had been denounced as "exploiters and parasites."

"Who . . . who would accuse us?" sobbed Mrs. Parsky.

"Five minutes. Then into the truck. If I was you, I'd take a few valuables to trade and a heavy coat for the winter."

Overhearing the sergeant, the Parskys' son fled to his childhood hideaway, the haystack. A thousand times as a child, Sasha had burrowed into the stack to escape monsters, giants, witches, evil spirits, and ghouls. He knew the permeable part of the hay and how to lose himself in it. Sasha noted that the policeman spoke Russian badly, using the crude colloquialisms of the whorehouse and the inn. Like so many young men who had left their subsistence farms for work in the OGPU (secret police) and other defense forces, his language and behavior betokened "I am a faithful son of the state, a dependable Bolshevik." These social misfits, often stationed in towns as public officials, had been waiting years to settle scores with landowners and the literate. Among the resentful, literacy functioned as a divining rod to identify enemies of the people, though, ironically, the benighted wanted their children to read and write.

Yes, the Bolsheviks knew how to exploit differences. With one decree they condemned landowners and the educated classes, and with another they promised drunkards, thieves, and wife beaters that the government would school their children.

Sasha watched as the policeman herded his parents toward the lorry. Mikhail Parsky, still energetic at sixty-five, vaulted onto the truck bed. But Sasha's mother, nursing a bad knee, fell as she reached for her husband's outstretched hand. Sasha would have remained hidden had the man not lifted her from the ground by the beautiful braid that hung down her back, causing her to cry out in pain. Leaving his place of concealment, Sasha bolted into the barn, grabbed a sickle, and fell upon the man, decapitating him with one slash of the blade. The other policeman could not believe what he briefly glimpsed in the side-view mirror: a headless torso. Climbing down from his seat to investigate, he stared in shock at his comrade and then at the Parskys. His primal scream reached back across the centuries, across the steppes, to Kazan and the khanate, to those innocents pleading for mercy before the conquering Mongol hordes. He unholstered his pistol. But Sasha, who had stolen around the other side of the truck, came up behind him. This time the blade failed to pass through the neck. The man's head dangled like a slack puppet. The Parskys stared wordlessly. He who had never hurt another person, who had never caused his parents a moment's trouble from his birth in 1915 to this moment in 1935, had become a monster.

Was this the same Sasha who had frequently brought from the field injured birds and nursed them back to health? Other children used slingshots to wound or kill wildlife. He hated hunting. With his gentle hands he often cradled sick animals, and when a creature died he was inconsolable. His kindness extended to beggars on the road, whom he brought to the kitchen door and implored his mother to feed. His principles and honesty were not of the straitened Soviet type: unbending, blind to the individual, and devoid of allowance for the dissenter and the weak. His behavior exemplified his belief that the seats of justice should be filled with good people but not so absolute in justice as to forget what human frailty is. Imbued with this idea, Sasha had saved Pavel Zimmerman, a young man of fourteen, subjected to continual abuse at the hands of his drunken father, who beat him for any infraction of his rules. One night, the father threatened to shoot his son and brandished his Winchester 10 rifle that he had brought back from the war with Germany. The son tried to wrestle the weapon from his father. During the skirmish it discharged, wounding the father in the leg. Pavel fled.

While police and peasants searched the countryside, the boy took refuge in the Parsky barn, where Sasha found him asleep in the hay and promised his protection. Although questioned by the gendarmerie, Sasha said he knew nothing of the boy's whereabouts. In a few days the searchers disbanded, declaring that the boy was no longer in the oblast. In reply to Sasha's questions, Pavel said that he would be safe if he could reach his grandmother, but she lived 120 kilometers distant. Sasha prevailed upon his family to pay for the boy's transportation and saw him off on the train.

But who really was this Sasha? For that matter, who was any Russian, so many of whom were part European and part Asian? And what of the Russian characteristics that writers and rulers so often invoked? In Sasha, the Parskys saw some of the same traits: pride and emotion, longing for the unknown, unpredictability, spontaneity, lack of moderation, and, like the land, a spacious soul. His generosity was unrivaled, to family and friends, and also to strangers. He preferred working with others to working alone, a trait handed down from Old Rus and the Orthodox Church. When he had money, he lent it; if the borrower couldn't repay, he ignored the debt. The Russian proverb applied to him: "Give, spend, and God will send." He genuinely believed in the common good, sharing and exchanging with others, and he addressed soul mates with the most intimate word in the Russian vocabulary: *rodnoy*, kinship. Most Russians, the Parskys believed, harbored in them "Yemelya," the great idler, a fairy-tale hero who never wishes to leave his favorite place—his bed or seat above a warm stove. Sasha, though contemplative, was not lazy. Long on thought and academically suspicious of extreme feelings, he was typically slow to act, enduring grievances with resigned patience. Like other Russians, he knew what his country had lived through: centuries of the Tatar yoke, a world war, revolution, a civil war, repression, and now Stalin. But once he saw the OGPU agent grab his mother's braid, he was like an icy current driven by a compulsive course. His acute sense of justice, which transcended any law or Russian habit, raced from his head to his hand, leaving him no choice other than to kill the two policemen who embodied a government that wished to confiscate his parents' farm without any regard for the age or health of the owners. Sasha had, unbeknownst to himself, been gripped by madness.

Without a word of regret or the sign of the cross, Sasha said to his parents, "You must leave at once for uncle's farm in Perm. Given the incompetence of Bolshevik bookkeeping, they'll never trace you. Return to the house and pack what you hold dear. We'll drive to the Kamyshlov Station. From there you can take a train to Yekaterinburg and then Perm. If asked, I will say that you have gone to Sochi."

His mute parents retreated into the house, where they filled two suitcases with clothing and stowed their most treasured belongings in three flour sacks, all of which Sasha put in the back of the military truck under a tarpaulin. In a field behind the barn, he buried the two men and the sickle, but not before he removed the personal contents from their pockets and from the truck. Setting out for the station by a circuitous route to avoid any villagers, Sasha questioned his parents' silence. What could they say? His father wondered if ten years in a labor camp wouldn't have been preferable to seeing his son commit murder. And his mother cried softly, unable to believe the scene that she replayed in her mind. Had she actually given suck to a boy who had beheaded two men as easily as he might have harvested wheat?

At the station, Sasha bought train tickets. Although fear and disbelief had rendered them speechless, his parents paused briefly on the platform to embrace him with an energy that bespoke their terror. Sasha started to leave and then paused. Behind him, a train

4

exuded great clouds of steam that briefly enveloped him. His parents, who later spoke of this moment, treated it as an omen signifying a cloud of unknowing.

As the steam faded, the first part of him to reappear was his face, then his hands, and finally his body. As he moved toward his parents, intending to embrace them a second time, they backed away, frightened by this son who had several hours before figuratively vanished into a fallen world to serve as an avenging, satanic angel, and who now emerged from a white mist.

Mr. Parsky, more worldly than his wife, summoned enough sense to say, "If they come for you, denounce us. We'll understand."

"Just speak of me kindly," Sasha said, "in the years to come."

His parents obliged their son, whom they never saw again.

Outside of town, Sasha wiped the steering wheel, abandoned the truck, and hailed a ride on a hay cart to the next station. In the icy drizzle, the lantern hanging from the cart cast pools of light in the puddles, which seemed like underground portals beckoning Sasha to enter. He took a train west to Tula, the site of his college studies in history. Several days later, two secret policemen, Rockoff and Zoditch, arrived at his dormitory to question him about the "slaughter." The police had learned from the Parskys' neighbors that Sasha had traveled to his village for Easter. He was questioned interminably. On what date had he returned to the school? Who had seen him return? Witnesses? Where were his parents? The local stationmasters swore that they had not taken train tickets from him, and, at the Yekaterinburg terminal, the ticket sellers explained that they hardly had time to stare at travelers' faces.

"Did you drive the truck to a distant city?"

"No."

"We can examine the truck for fingerprints, so you would be well advised to tell the truth. Our records show you have a license to drive. Correct?"

"Correct."

The questions seemed endless. Yes, he had visited his home, but left a day before the "event in question" and was as shocked as the secret police. His parents had written him from Sochi, but omitted a return address. They had said they'd keep in touch. Did he have the letter? The police wished to look at the postmark. No, he had thrown it away. Had he any suspicion that his parents harbored ill feelings toward the government, that they would desert their home, that they would reside in Sochi? None. He was as amazed as the agents.

"Surely," he asked, "you don't think my parents murdered two policemen and then disappeared?"

"Come with us," said Zoditch, and the two policemen led him to a car.

Rockoff took the wheel and drove to a distant police station of unpainted cinder blocks and a roof sprouting antennae. The building resembled a large insect, surrounded by a gray, featureless landscape shrouded in the melancholy of madness. In the distance lay a soccer field. Trash littered the vacancy between station and field, and a raw wind blew out of the east, tossing papers in the air like a whimsical juggler. Rockoff entered the station, behind which stood several police cars protected from vandals by a chain-link fence. Zoditch and Sasha remained outside. The former lit a cigarette. His stained fingers resembled orange tentacles. He suggested they walk, leading Sasha past stalks and field grass crushed from the morning frosts. Water squished underfoot. Zoditch stopped to watch two soccer players, one defending the goal and the other trying to pass him.

"I played midfield good," said Zoditch, "but my father he beat me for running off from farmwork to kick a ball. That was his words."

A small, cunning fellow with a narrow forehead and yellow eyes jaundiced from drink, he had grown a goatee, in the manner of Lenin, but his beard was spotty, bare in places. He ran a hand over his pocked face, exhibited decaying teeth, and spat through a gap between them. His other hand he kept running over his wrinkled uniform as if he wished to correct its disorder. Unlike his unkempt appearance, the policeman spoke in straight lines, briskly and to the point, even if his remarks were frequently ungrammatical.

"You are under a cloud," he said, "and to come out . . ."

"Yes?"

"You must denounce your parents."

Sasha and Zoditch approached the goal as the kicker lined up a shot.

Mr. Parsky's advice echoed in Sasha's head. After pausing a moment, he said, "Here and now, Comrade Zoditch, in your presence, I denounce them."

The goalie blocked the shot. Zoditch mocked without mirth. "Not good enough. In *Pravda*, you denounce them by the words 'traitors' and 'murderers.' You swear them enemies of the people, and you say those hiding them, unless they turn them in, love the Tsar."

Sasha fingered the netting of the goal, which reminded him of fishing with his father in a favorite river and Mr. Parsky's hook net, which he had bought from a *nepman*. His father, adept with a rod and reel, put his son in charge of netting the fish. Without facing Zoditch, Sasha asked, "Do I write the denunciation or do you?"

Strident laughter greeted his question. "We have people who these kinds of things they like to do."

For a few minutes, the kicker had a good run. He beat the goalie four times in a row. Then they exchanged places. Zoditch and Sasha walked toward the station over the decaying bronze leaves.

"First, I am a Pioneer," said Zoditch, referring to a Communist children's group. "Second, I am a Komosol," he said, citing the acronym for the Communist Union of Youth. "And you?"

Sasha Parsky had never shown any interest in politics, but rather in books. As a youngster, he had tried to imitate Pushkin, writing verse and short stories, but quickly decided that he had no talent for literature and turned to history, which captivated him even more than fiction. His decision became final once he had read Lord Byron's lines from *Don Juan*: "'Tis strange—but true; for truth is always strange; Stranger than fiction." Those words, he had decided, were written for him, because he loved nothing more than he loved the different, the strange, the eerie, the outré.

"I entered poetry contests but never won," Sasha mused.

Zoditch spat between his teeth. "Poetry," he scoffed, "that's a long time ago what the court wrote—and not in Russian."

He was referring, of course, to the successors of Peter the Great, the Tsar who admired the West and built Saint Petersburg, a city looking toward Europe. Those who served the subsequent Tsars, and the numbers were thousands, spoke and wrote in French. Russian was considered a doggerel language. Not until Pushkin wrote poetry in the idiom of the people, and eschewed stilted Church Slavonic, did Russian literature come alive. The most avid readers of poetry were women, a fact that did not escape Zoditch's contempt.

"Women, they read poetry, not men."

Dark clouds massed overhead, and a few snowflakes began to fall. Soon the poplars and beeches would be leafless, and bleak winter would blanket the land.

"They read everything more than men. Writers depend on them. If women didn't buy literary subscriptions and journals, no bookseller could survive." The policeman seemed unready to give up the argument. "I don't like make-believe, women do."

"And yet you're a Bolshevik."

Zoditch eyed him suspiciously. "You are suggesting what?"

"Self-improvement, the new man, the paradise to come . . . are these not all fictions? And yet you embrace them."

The policeman, feeling that his imperfect command of language put him at a disadvantage, decided not to detain Sasha in the police station but rather to take him for further questioning to the chief of the bureau, Major Boris Filatov, who was a certified engineer with his own office and a college degree.

"Into the car! I'll get the key."

Major Filatov, head of the Tula oblast OGPU, fervently believed that the future would be socialist and just. He had invested too much of his life in the Party to believe otherwise. All the denunciations and sacrifices that had earned him his current position . . . had they not been in the service of the common good? Why else would he have lent himself to prisons and torture and shooting squads? To maintain his sanity, he had to accept that the investment in blood was worth the price, and that the ends justified the means. The logic was inescapable. If the ends didn't justify the means, what did? To make an omelet, the Soviets loved to repeat, you have to break eggs. A future paradise requires effort. The soil must be tilled, weeds and tares removed. If bloodshed provides the fertilizer for Eden, then let it leave no place untouched.

At the unmarked building that housed Filatov's office, a guard met Zoditch and took Sasha to a cold basement cell, where he waited several hours, reading and rereading the poignant graffiti declaring the innocence of the occupant. Sasha surmised that his treatment was all part of the "method" used to gain a confession—or make a convert. Before long, the guard brought a young man to the cell, a suspected murderer. He was about twenty, well-dressed, with handsome features and straight teeth. His dark hair, parted down the middle, had been recently cut, and his pink face newly shaved. The fellow even had about him a slight whiff of cologne. Introducing himself as Goran Youzhny, he garrulously asked Sasha his name. But when Sasha failed to respond, the man, in well-spoken phrases, said:

"You're probably wondering why I am here. But I could ask you the same." Sasha refrained from replying, and Goran continued. "I killed two policemen, decapitated them and then trod through the sticky blood to bury them."

In the half-dark light, Sasha groped for one of the boards and sat. He tried to sort out his riotous thoughts. Was this man an OGPU "plant"; was he, like so many others, a religious fanatic who took upon himself the sins of the world; or was he a coincidental murderer? Lest he appear skeptical, Sasha took the young man at his word.

"Why did you kill the policemen?"

Goran sat down next to him and answered softly, "They had come to expel my parents from their farm. Kulaks, that was the charge."

Don't lower your guard, Sasha told himself. Be wary. Feign horror and disgust at the young man's story. "What a detestable crime!" said Sasha. "I am accused, falsely I might add, of a similar one. Now I see why they put you in a cell with me."

Goran then recounted the location of the farm and the name of the family, Parsky. Sasha could only conclude that Goran Youzhny was either a spy or a member of a forest community of religious zealots who feel that they are born with primordial guilt and must assume responsibility for the world's sins, even if such behavior includes confessing to crimes they didn't commit. But the forest priests dressed in disheveled robes, never shaved, and wore their hair long. Perhaps they had spawned a new breed of zealots. In any case, surely Filatov could see that this man was not a double murderer; but then, based on appearances, the same could be said about Sasha.

"Why did you kill them?" Sasha asked impassively.

"Given the absence of justice and fairness, I acted to right a wrong. The laws we live under, as you know, have nothing to do with justice and fairness, so I acted according to my own moral law."

"Even at the expense of your life?"

"Human history is littered with the bodies of the just."

"Perhaps an appeal to the local Soviet might have helped. Murder is an admission of failure, moral and legal."

"The local Soviets are elected; they are not moral arbiters."

"Tell me, Citizen Youzhny, in your opinion, which comes first, guilt or the crime? I mean, do we feel guilty for plotting a crime or for committing it or both?"

"If you believe in original sin, the answer is both. But whether or not one believes in original sin, one may feel equally guilty."

Sasha warmed to the subject. Here was a chance to mentally exercise. Even if Goran was a plant and the cell bugged, he had said nothing amiss. This discussion would ready him for Major Filatov. If the police chief wanted to argue about the number of angels that could dance on the head of a pin, he would be ready.

"And if one feels no guilt at all, what then?"

Goran sucked air through his clenched teeth and issued a low whistle. "Such a person would be devoid of conscience and merely a creature of instinct. Sin is punished, one way or another."

"A minute ago, you decried the law. So I assume you believe that transgressing the law is justifiable. Would refusing to denounce a friend qualify?"

Goran's silence betokened his moral quandary.

Sasha goaded him. "Isn't it a fact that some sinners escape judgment?"

"Perhaps here, but not in the afterlife. And don't underestimate conscience. Thank God, I am not one of those who make up all manner of excuses to explain their felonies. I do not blame my own on Soviet arrogance or the confiscation of private property."

Sasha smiled, knowing full well that Goran was preparing to recite a litany of Soviet sins—in order to draw him out.

"They promised religious freedom and then closed the churches. They promised the different nationalities the right to continue their cultures and then suppressed them. They gagged the writers and promulgated their own form of art. They restricted the right to travel. They promoted hacks and exiled genius. They introduced the cult of personality—Stalin's—and imprisoned the Vozhd's former comrades. It's intolerable. Don't you agree?"

Sasha knew not to agree with criticisms of the government. Once you agreed, the trap sprung shut. Goran was undoubtedly an OGPU stooge told what to say. And even if Sasha couldn't prove that Goran's list of Soviet sins was rehearsed, why take the chance of assenting? The rule was "Never agree or disagree, even with a friend. The walls have ears."

"How did you kill the policemen?" Sasha asked.

"With a sickle. I cut off their heads cleanly. Swipe. Swipe."

At that moment, Sasha knew that his cell mate was a plant. One of the heads had failed to come free. Goran's factual error was small, but just large enough to brand him a liar. You can never be too careful.

When the guard finally led Sasha upstairs, he entered a carpeted room with a desk and sofa and three chairs. On the wall behind the desk hung a large portrait of Stalin. Affixed to another wall was a colored map of the Soviet Union, covered with red and yellow pins, indicating the major war zones during the Great War and the civil war. Two windows looked out on a wooded area. Behind the desk, Boris Filatov, ramrod straight, wore not a uniform or a tunic but a beige suit. In front of the desk, a woman sat with legs planted firmly on the floor, a pad in her lap, and a mechanical pencil at the ready, waiting in a totally impersonal manner to record the proceedings.

"Please make yourself comfortable on the couch," said Filatov. "Comrade Olga is our secret service stenographer."

Sasha leaned back on the couch and stretched his legs, now cold and cramped. He noted that while Filatov was a handsome man who exuded energy and strength, the woman was pale and dispirited. Her flaxen hair, pulled back carelessly, revealed a lifeless face with black holes for eyes. She nervously tapped one foot on the floor and then rubbed a thigh, revealing more leg than one would have expected from a lady commissar. Her drab officer's dress accentuated her flat chest. Sasha looked at her hands but saw no rings. Was she married? Did she always look so absent? Perhaps she had liver trouble and smoked too much.

"How are your parents?" asked Filatov, breaking the spell of Sasha's thoughts.

"My parents?" Sasha repeated. The question had taken him by surprise. "I thought you knew."

"Knew what?" asked Filatov, stroking his ample well-barbered mustache that bore a striking resemblance to Stalin's.

"They left for Sochi and haven't yet sent me their address."

Filatov shook his head sympathetically. "No news. It's a shame how badly our postal service works. Or perhaps I should say doesn't work. Our people ought to investigate."

"I'm rather surprised myself," said Sasha, rubbing his hands to dispel the lingering cold.

Filatov came from behind his desk and extended a hand to Sasha. "Such poor manners on my part. I am Boris Filatov, and you are Citizen Sasha Parsky." They shook hands. "I hope you are well."

"Just chilled from your basement apartment."

"I like irony, Citizen Parsky. It shows wit. I will have to tell my people to install central heating downstairs." Filatov returned to his desk. Zoditch knocked, entered, handed him a note, and left. "My apologies as well," added Filatov, "for the clumsy attempt of one of our agents to induce you to talk about a crime you didn't commit." He left his desk and repaired to the couch with a folder in hand.

Sasha remembered what his professors had told him, albeit in whispers, as well as the many students interrogated by the secret police. Avoid garrulousness. Exercise caution. Reject friendship. Folders like Filatov's were often stage props. The contents? Perhaps damning, perhaps nothing. To escape OGPU traps, be doubly deceptive.

"Comrade Parsky," Filatov said, eliciting a smile from Sasha, who noticed the shift in diction from "Citizen" to "Comrade." "According to our files . . ." He rustled some papers.

For the first time, Sasha noticed Filatov's hands. The nails were polished, the mark of a dandy. "Comrade Parsky," Filatov repeated and pointed at the map. "The red pins signify the important Russian fronts during the Great War." He paused. "Are you any relation to General Parsky?" Sasha shook his head no. Filatov then rattled off a number of facts about Sasha's personal life. "While you were waiting," said Filatov, "Comrade Zoditch dictated to our typist. It says here that you are a cooperative witness and that you are willing to see your parents denounced." He paused. "Not so much as a demurral? Most children take convincing. But you are ready and willing, as the saying is. Are you familiar with their crime? Were you told?"

"Murder."

"Two policemen . . . we recovered the remains . . . and the murder weapon, a sickle. They were buried in a shallow grave, freshly dug."

"Sounds awful," said Sasha, wiping his perspiring forehead with his sleeve.

"Inconceivable is what I would call it: two elderly people with the strength to overcome two policemen and behead them, or almost." He paused. "Do you suppose a third party could have been present?"

"We have no paid workers except at harvest time."

"I was thinking of you."

Sasha decided to play Filatov's game and come to the same conclusion, thus weakening Boris's argument. Protestations of innocence were to be expected, not agreement. "If I were you, I would think the same thing. But I was not present. Perhaps a bandit or runaway *zek* was in the area. Have you checked?"

Filatov nodded sagely, as if he had expected this line of reasoning, and answered, "As a matter of fact, we have."

"A sickle, you say? A great many itinerant farmworkers come through our area carrying sickles. Scythes, too. Or perhaps it was someone who ran away from a collective farm."

Studying his hands, Filatov said without looking up, "I return to the point that two elderly people were unlikely to have the physical strength to decapitate two men. Do you agree?"

"Absolutely."

"Good. Then what are we to conclude?"

"They are innocent and someone else is guilty."

"And yet you are willing to denounce them."

It took very little for Sasha to realize that in Filatov he was facing a different kind of policeman. To make light of his acquiescence and elicit a smile, Sasha rejoined, "If you'd like me to resist, I can say no and protest loudly."

Filatov's gentle face turned hard. "Don't jest about betrayals. To denounce a parent is a life-altering decision. No one should ever be put in that position."

Sasha saw that he was not wrong about this inquisitor. He had been selected for his cunning. Filatov had the brains to side with his adversary, and the personality to insinuate himself into the prisoner's trust. His comments had the effect of causing Sasha to remember a spring day in school, with the fragrance of lilacs drifting through the open windows. All the children were asked to stand as the teacher related the story of a wife who denounced her husband for making comments critical of Lenin. A gentle sort, the teacher, who had grown up in an educated family, impressed upon the children the importance of motives. The husband, related the teacher, was removed by the Cheka and, in front of the villagers, made to kneel and ask for forgiveness. Hoping to save his life, the poor man confessed to the crime of undermining morale. But a soldier stepped forward and shot the man in the back of the head.

Alas, events are not always as they seem. The villagers subsequently learned that the man's wife had been conducting an affair with a young fellow from another village and wanted her husband out of the way. When her motives were reported to the police, they shrugged and did nothing. So the villagers took matters into their own hands and drowned the woman in a nearby river. The teacher's conclusion was not that one should remain silent in the presence of a crime, though he was quick to point out that the disparagement of Lenin was allowed by the guarantees of free speech in the Soviet Constitution, but that before rushing to judgment, one should have all the facts or as many as possible, given the self-interest of people who supply "truth" in excess of demand. The teacher's lesson might have been forgotten in the farrago of childhood experiences had not a boy in his class denounced the poor man for saying that it was acceptable to criticize Lenin, with the result that the teacher was removed from the school and never seen again.

"You are finishing your degree," said Filatov, shuffling some papers. "In this area of the country, we have need of secondary-school directors." He paused, admired his fingernails, which glinted in the light, and glanced at Sasha's hands, which Filatov rightly marked as those of a scholar. "I trust that you would like such an assignment, which is not possible without someone like myself signing off on your loyalty." He opened a silver case, removed a cigarette, lit it, and offered Sasha one.

"I don't smoke."

After a few puffs, Filatov quit and exclaimed that tobacco was a filthy habit. Sasha guessed that Filatov cared more about his stained fingers than whether smoking was de rigueur. After all, Stalin smoked, and it was whispered that his fingers and teeth were yellow.

"A secondary school would suit me perfectly," replied Sasha, and instinctively turned toward the window to gain a better view of the autumn leaves and the whispers of ground fog. Like so many Russians, he found comfort in the landscape.

Filatov, ever observant, commented, "At this time of year, so often the sun resembles a dying patient. It grows increasingly pallid, and of course eventually dies, as do our citizens who drink profusely to escape the dreary darkness."

Sasha found the medical analogy unsuited to the scene—unless Filatov was trying to link Sasha's ashen face to sickness and guilt.

"Having grown up in the country," Sasha remarked, "I have experienced the pain of loneliness and the absence of culture."

"In Moscow, they die in doorways, drunken and diseased." Before Sasha could reply, Filatov rose and pulled down another map. This one detailed the topography of Tula Province. He pointed to a spot on the outskirts of Tula, not far from Tolstoy's estate, Yasnaya Poliana.

"The neighboring villages once enjoyed the patronage of the great writer himself. Will this area suit you? It's a choice location and only 120 miles from Moscow."

Sasha excitedly asked, "You can arrange it?"

Without moving his facial muscles, Filatov sighed wearily, as if Sasha's question was hardly worth the answering. Sasha feared that Filatov found him taxing. "The secret police can arrange whatever is in the best interests of the country." For the first and only time, the stenographer smiled. "You graduate in a few months. I'll see to it that you receive a position as director of a secondary school. I have in mind a particularly good one in need of reform. Repetition is good for some things but cannot eclipse reasoning. Russians love learning. The written word is sacred. A book makes you a pilgrim at the gates of a new city."

Sasha, who had expected the knout, not a niche in the world of education, felt his face redden. Was it from appreciation or fear of a trap? He put a hand to his forehead and stuttered his thanks.

"The murdered policemen had families, one, a wife and child, the other, a brother who writes political polemics. Visit them! Here are their files. I regret we have no photographs."

A bewildered Sasha fingered them awkwardly. Should he open them at once or later? He waited for a signal from Filatov, but the major was now staring silently out the window. Sasha knew that of all the forms of human communication, silence speaks loudest. He thought of his parents' neighbor Mr. Zaslavsky, who would move his queen but not release his hand to indicate that the move was complete. All the while, he would study Sasha's face to see his response. Sometimes he returned the queen to its original position, sometimes not. Filatov at last spoke but without turning round. His words were strangely strangled. He seemed to be choking on grief. Perhaps Filatov had met the dead men, knew their families, maybe even worked with them, or shared a cigarette.

"You are no doubt asking yourself why you, a stranger, should be making condolence calls? On what pretense?"

"It did occur to me."

"When the time comes I will give you a letter of introduction explaining that you work for the police, and that you are calling on behalf of the government. We have already awarded the survivors a financial settlement. You are simply following up."

Sasha had by now regained his composure. This Filatov was a sly one. The chief obviously felt that Sasha was implicated in the murders and wanted to render him vulnerable with the offer of a plum position and the request that he visit the families. Well, if Filatov thought that Sasha would drop his guard and succumb to sentiment, thus putting his head in a noose, he was underestimating Sasha's resolve and determination to survive.

But when Filatov finally turned to face Sasha, his moist eyes had an immediate effect on young Parsky, who could feel his own throat tighten and his breath shorten. "Their names are Galina Selivanova and Viktor Harkov. The child's name is Alya. She's adopted. Both families live in Ryazan. I would suggest that you write them first and give them ample notice of your visit. At the moment they are in mourning, so I would wait, perhaps until summer, when the weather will favor you."

Fighting against his own humane impulses, Sasha wondered whether Filatov's tears were real or confected. A second later he upbraided himself for his cynicism. His next thought was how does a slayer condole with his victims' families? He felt strangely as if he were observing the murders both as an outsider and as the perpetrator. Until a minute ago, the dead policemen meant nothing to him; and then he saw Filatov's sorrowful eyes. Perhaps, on further reflection, Sasha was closer to these men than he imagined. If creation and destruction are two poles of the same arc, then he had merely completed a nexus that others had started. He would assuage his guilt through kindness and care. He would take the woman and child on a boat ride or a picnic or maybe a trip to the fair, with a ride on the carousel. But first he would bring the mother a box of candy, and the child a nested doll. And the brother? A fine fountain pen might please him. He was, after all, a writer. In the meantime, he had only a few days to prepare to defend his honors thesis before a group of fractious university examiners.

2

Sasha rented a small room within walking distance to the university. As he strolled to class, he used the time to review his lessons. Autumn had arrived early this year and with it ruminations about life. The trees, shedding their foliage, fractured the sparse sunlight into geometric shadows on the roads. What did the figures portend: his fate, his fortune? Some of his schoolmates delayed their exams; some failed; some passed; some simply disappeared, usually the outspoken ones or those who had something to hide.

Under a floorboard of his room lay the papers—unread—that he had found on the policemen and in the truck. Although he had initially saved them out of a morbid curiosity to know something about whom he had killed, he found it too painful to disturb the dead. After leaving his family, he had boarded a train and sat staring out the window. A railroad vendor had asked if he wanted tea, but even though the samovar whistled and he felt an insatiable thirst, he lacked the energy to reply. An old woman sitting across from him asked if he felt unwell. Her words came to him as if through water. On having heard the one soldier scream back through history, he had defensively rearranged his mind to muffle all sound.

He now stared at the ominous plank board covering the papers. In his dreams he could hear the board squeak, as if someone was suspiciously examining it. Other times he tried to dispel the phantasm of dream to interpret the Morse code that the board seemed to be sending, a farrago of dots and dashes. The longer he had left the papers untouched, the harder he'd found it to read them. But the night before, he had dreamed that his university examiners knew the contents and asked him why he hadn't studied or burned them. His indecision, they said, called into question his readiness for his honors exam, an exhausting exercise to be held the next day.

Once awake, he scolded himself for his timidity. Perhaps the papers contained information about his parents having been "unmasked" as kulaks and the name of the denouncer. But that discovery was what he feared most: learning the name of the person who had betrayed them. The villagers were like family. They took meals together and, side by side, walked to church. In times of sickness and want, they aided each other. What if he learned, for example, that the Judas was the Chumachenkos, who shared a thresher and a plow horse with his family, and whose son, Sergei, pitched horseshoes with him; or the Sharatovs, who had helped build the Parsky barn; or the Bulgakovs, who famously invited the neighbors' children to sit around a fire on a summer night and listen to fairy tales and ghost stories; or the one-legged Gregori, who showed the children his souvenirs from the Great War and regaled them with his exploits on the German front; or the Krichefskis, who raised chickens and, until their younger son died of polio, never failed to give the poor a stewing hen; or the Ezhovs? Having played with the Ezhov children, three boys and two girls, he regarded them as his own brothers and sisters. One August day, he had even kissed Natasha Ezhova on the cheek, in the apple orchard. At the time, she had said that Sasha was now promised to her and made him kiss the crucifix that she removed from around her neck.

Down the road lived the Nazarovs. On warm August nights, the two families would take their meals in the Parsky garden, at a long table covered with a white linen tablecloth. Although the dishes were cracked and the silverware common, the food would have suited a boyar: pheasant and partridge, carp and herring, mushroom soup, hot bread fresh from the oven, boiling water for *chai* thanks to the samovar that the Nazarov family carted by horse to the Parsky house. Pavel Nazarov had generously offered his samovar when Mr. Parsky complained that his was too small for ten people and needed repair. In the long summer light, the children would play tag and catch fireflies and read poetry while the parents sipped a cordial and reminisced about traveling operas and ballets that used to come to the theaters of the great estates and perform for the locals. Sasha wondered whether his parents actually saw such performances or lived them vicariously through the memories of their parents.

The Zaslavsky family, Ida and Naum, lived to the south of the Parsky farm. They had no children. After years of medical advice, Ida was told she was barren. A Jewish family—the only one for miles around—they kept to themselves. If they observed any religious practices, it was in the quiet and security of their own dwelling. Sasha would often visit them on his way home from school. The road passed their farm. They treated him as a surrogate son and called him their little David. During Passover, Sasha liked seeing their candle holders glowing with tapers and never ceased to stare at the mezuzahs on the outside doorposts, but best of all was the ivory chess set on which Naum taught Sasha to play. He would occasionally let the lad win, but they both knew that he could have swept Sasha any time that he wished.

Infrequently, Sasha would stay for a meal, and then return home to tell his mother that Ida Zaslavsky made strange foods with odd names, like gefilte fish and knishes and kugel and cholent and babka and charoset and hamantaschen. Mrs. Parsky worried that Sasha was being poisoned. But he assured her that the Zaslavskys ate the same food. The Parskys never invited the "Yids" to dinner, and the latter never invited Sasha's parents. Such was life in their village.

If Naum had denounced Mr. Parsky . . . no, that was impossible. Yes, the two families had once quarreled over property lines, but any man who talked about the Talmud with Naum's reverence could never betray his neighbor. Although the other farmers were rabidly anti-Semitic, Sasha's parents, other than sometimes using the word "Yid" and repeating some jokes about Jewish economy, never repeated phrases like "the Christ killers." To learn that Naum had been the denouncer would have elevated all the local prejudices to the status of truth. And since he couldn't think poorly of the Zaslavskys, he adopted Winnie Verloc's view in *The Secret Agent* that "life doesn't stand much looking into."

When he thought of the papers under the plank board, what tormented him most was the fear that his examiners might ask him about the murders. Personal digressions were common during honors thesis exams. His mouth suddenly tasted of bile, and his forehead oozed sweat. He breathed deeply. His body seemed to be acting independently of his mind, signaling him, telling him to read the hidden papers and dispel all his fears. He went to the door and fastened the bolt; then he slowly dressed in preparation for the examination—and the unveiling. He removed from the small mahogany armoire a black suit, his only one. From a bottom drawer, he took a white shirt, a blue tie, and his lone pair of dress shoes, which a former tenant of the house had left behind and which fit him. Now suitably attired in a funereal manner, he used the same knife as before to raise the plank board, extricating a wallet, a brown morocco notebook, and some incidental papers. Spreading them on his bed, he pulled up a chair and studied the contents. The first man he had killed, the one with the wallet, was Alexander Harkov, almost thirty-three years old. His birthday would have taken place in two weeks. A lock of hair in his wallet must have come from some former or current girlfriend. It exhibited a ringlet. Sasha ignored the few rubles. The notebook, actually a diary, belonged to the other man, Petr Selivanov, twenty-nine. Although he had found it in the glove compartment of the truck, Sasha concluded that the frayed and broken corners resulted from its having been carried in the owner's pants and not in his jacket or shirt pocket. With shaking hands, Sasha ventured into Petr Selivanov's private life.

Inside the front cover were birth dates. A photograph of his wife and daughter showed a pretty woman whose dark, Jezebel eyes exuded excitement, and a child with a bright face and pigtails. The pages were covered with rather elaborate sloping handwriting. Although short, the notebook was telling. One could see in an instant that the author had received a good education. On the wave of words, Sasha read:

12 May

Galina has given me this small brown morocco notebook. We have recently been arguing, usually over our differing views of life. I bought her a jar of caviar, and now she has given me this cahier. Two years ago, when we first met, I thought her the most beautiful woman in all Russia. She is passionate and sentimental and has wild Cossack blood. Her family comes from the region of the Don. Our first disagreement occurred over my joining the secret police. In the quiet of our bedroom, she called Stalin a limping leech. I told her the walls have ears and to watch what she says. (I shouldn't even be writing this down.) She accused me of joining the wrong side, the Bolsheviks, instead of the Left Opposition. We both come from political families that fought in the civil war, hers on the side of the Whites and mine on the Reds. And yet she has taken a middle ground: that of the Social Democrats. I fear trouble will ensue.

20 May

We continue to disagree but now our differences have affected the bed. She tells me I am unworthy of her love. We met outside of Ryazan in August 1934, a stifling day. The sunbaked roads were hard as oak. A runaway horse, copiously dripping foam from its silken lips, came thundering down the lane. She grabbed the pommel, and swung into the saddle as effortlessly as if she were mounting a horse at rest. A rotund fellow with a sweaty red face, puffing from the exertion of chasing his mare, took the reins from her and opened his purse. She refused the reward. So taken was I by her courage and courtesy—yes, her handsome face also—I crossed the lane and boldly spoke to her. Although it is not my custom to speak to strangers, especially women, I could feel her magnetism from across the road. In these Soviet times, women have become fiercer than men. Give them boots, a uniform, a shoulder strap, and they behave like the Praetorian Guard. She smiled and we entered a shop for a cup of chai. I asked if I could see her again, and she said not likely. Only grudgingly did she tell me her name, Galina, and that she lived twelve versts from town on her parents' farm. I told her mine were Kalmyk sheepherders. I had the impression that she disdained Mongols, but my family's blood is so mixed with European that I could pass one way or the other. She repeatedly rebuffed my advances. But a chance meeting between her and my mother took place in a shop. Only *then did she begin to treat my overtures seriously, I think because of my mother's remarkable beauty.*

27 May

They say a long courting period is best. We saw each other wherever we could, and whenever we made love she was always sensuous and tender. Finally in March, she agreed to live with me, and last June we married. Unlike some women, she never becomes hysterical over love. She is physically robust and shares in the pleasures of sex. But I am not without worry. She likes men and especially well-educated ones who excite her with ideas and shower her with praise. I suspect I have failed her in this regard. My own college education was rather conventional, though from time to time she does compliment my courage and compassion. She seems to be saying, "For now you will do."

20 June

Less than a month ago, Galina was all loving and sweetness. I know she is moody, but of late also overtly flirtatious. How can this clever young woman, blessed with a college degree and wise to the guiles of young men, so naively accept their flattery? Does she sincerely believe it when they say that not beauty but wit makes her shine in their eyes? Does she pretend not to see their oily designs just to incite my jealousy? When it comes to love, her powers of self-delusion border on the irrational. I swear she suffers from "uterine frenzies," which she always manages to dress up in some romantic locution, the better to abandon herself. She needs to have at her side a young man who is constantly singing her praises. And that man never changes. He is always morose, daring, and willing to ignore her outbursts of temper. She claims that these men are only friends and charming conversationalists. But more often than not, they are childlike, so she can soothe and console them.

1 July

From the OGPU training I am receiving, I have developed a nose for wrongdoing. Whenever I return from a field trip, the flat smells different and the furniture looks as if it has been moved, not much, but slightly. Of late, Galina has been colder than ever.

8 July

I arrived home early from headquarters and found Galina making the bed. She usually has it in order by the time I leave in the morning.

I asked her why she was just now straightening up, and she said that she had been out. When I asked where, she flew into a fury and said that she would not stand to be questioned as if she were some criminal interrogated by the police. *You have changed,* she cried. *You have become the enemy.* Alya was standing at the door, watching.

19 July

My neighbor Alexander Harkov was recently assigned to the same police group as me. He left school at an early age to work in a metal shop. He may be rough around the edges, but he's a good sort. Alexander and I often talk. He showed me a family picture. His sister, now dead, was quite beautiful. I was once friendly with his brother, Viktor, but he prefers his own company—and his political pamphlets. He's obsessed with how dictatorially our Soviet commissar, Vladimir Lukashenko, runs the oblast. The two brothers are unmarried, but, as Alexander says, he's not opposed though Viktor is. We ride in the same truck. He drives and I roll his cigarettes for him. Our current assignments have been to apprehend kulaks and confiscate their properties. I am more affected than him by the tears and the pleas of the women and children, but I take courage from following his example. Recently, a Jewish family threw themselves at our feet and begged to keep their small plot of land. Alexander called them Christ killers and roughly shoved them into the back of the truck. I tiptoed lightly through the house and saw religious objects of silver and gold, all of which I took for the state, including an antique menorah.

30 July

Galina's training as a nurse has landed her a job at the local hospital, which has child minding. No more working at home as an editor and translator. I wonder whether the new job will affect her elegant writing style and mastery of French. Although I liked political history and writing analytical papers, if I had my university education to do over again, I think I would study archeology. Perhaps that's why I like police work. It enables me to uncover the past and re-create a crime from the evidence, little as it may be.

11 August

Today was Galina's birthday, and although we are still spatting, we had friends over to share several bottles of vodka and cake. Galina drew up the guest list: the Harkov brothers, her parents, the Tchai-kovskys, and the Antipovas. We sang songs, toasted Galina, and read some Pushkin poems. Alya had happily painted a picture for her mother, but by the end of the evening, when Viktor Harkov and Galina were dancing cheek to cheek, Alya grew sullen. We all teased her, and took her aside to explain that Viktor was nothing more than a friend.

22 August

Alexander asked how Galina and I were faring. In the past, he only listened when I complained but never questioned me or com-mented. I told him that the marriage was failing, and that I could see an end in sight. Of late, she has selfishly started spending money on fashionable clothing, money we don't have. Alya, she dresses in hand-me-downs. He murmured that Galina was a fine woman. Is he thinking of her for romantic reasons? But recently he's been seeing a widow with two children.

31 August

I can smell fall in the air and see it in the lilac darkness. The dust motes have virtually disappeared from the sunlight, and the trees are already turning. My almanac says that it will be a cold winter and an early one. Today, for the first time in my police service I had to draw my pistol. A farmer refused to leave his farm. He and his family boarded themselves inside the house. I shot my pistol in the air. Alexander taunted me. He shot his pistol into the house. The family immediately abandoned the premises and boarded the truck.

10 September

The Harkov brothers came to us for dinner. It was Galina's idea. They brought pastries, and we supplied the chicken and lentil soup. Galina asked Viktor to read some poems from Lermontov, but he said he was in no mood. Everyone could see that he was out of sorts. He complained angrily about the Soviet commissar for our region. He swore that the man was a tyrant and that someday he would kill him. I tried to settle Viktor down, but he was outraged because Lu-kashenko insisted that our district would have to undergo a chistka to determine who was faithful to the state and who was not. It's criminal, Viktor swore, that we should have to live through a purge. This is 1935!

15 September

Another day, another action against kulaks. I am beginning to wonder about the wisdom of these arrests. This time we encountered a scene we had only heard about from other reports but had never witnessed for ourselves. The owner of the farm, rather than allow us to confiscate his animals, hid his three cows in the woods, where we found them under a thatched roof supported by four poles. Lying in a ditch near the house was a roan horse, shot through the head. One of its hind legs was sticking up in the air and the shoe was glittering in the sunlight. In the distance was a whitewashed church. The leg of the horse, bent at the knee, made me think of a broken cross. A small cloud momentarily blocked the sun. A minute later, the sunlight illuminated the smooth reddish fur of the horse's leg, which blossomed like some magical leafless branch into orange splendor.

24 September

I ran into Viktor as I walked toward the river to fish. He refused my offer to join me and said that he had a pamphlet to print. His polemics have reached the ears of the city officials, as well as Galina, who strongly defends him against any criticism. Alexander can't be sure, but he thinks that his brother has acquired a pistol. He found a manual and several bullets for a TT 30.

28 September

Galina was in a good mood this evening. She prepared a fat salmon for dinner that Viktor brought to the flat this afternoon in appreciation for her support of his views. I played the gramophone—Beethoven— and then suggested that Galina and I let love enfold us. But to my annoyance, no, fury, she said she was bleeding. I knew damn well she was lying. She had said the same thing two weeks ago. Either she was deceiving me then or she is now. I am sick of her excuses. I stormed out of the house and walked the streets for hours. When I returned I knew she was feigning sleep, so I audibly grumbled that love is a flower that wilts after marriage.

3 October

After days of silence, Galina and I finally spoke. She apologized for her behavior and said it was because Alya had been throwing tantrums after I left for work. The child seems troubled. She probably remembers her parents and the other orphaned children, all of whom prayed to be adopted by some kind family. We had both agreed at the time of our marriage that we would wait to have a child until we could afford one. But Mrs. Platonov's pleas changed everything. After Alya went to sleep, we reminisced about the incident. Later we made love, but without the feeling of former days. As we lay in bed, she asked about the people, the kulaks we arrest, and how they react. I gave her a few examples. She turned her head away from me and said: Why do you still work for them?

10 October

The weather has turned unseasonably cold. Alexander and I have been ordered to travel a hundred versts to confiscate a farm. I usually make it a point never to remember the names of the families, but in this case the family name, Parsky, gave me pause. Dimitri Pavlovich Parsky was the first Tsarist general with battle experience to offer his services to the Red Army. No Bolshevik, he fought, he said, to save Russia from German slavery.

18 October

Alexander wanted to nap, so I agreed to drive. The roads were abominably muddy and slow. We stopped at a state-run roadside inn. I ordered tea, Alexander, vodka. Across the room we saw an old comrade, Martyn Lipnoski. He said that during a night of reveling, some whore had lifted his wallet, which held his papers and identity card. He looked as if he'd slept in his uniform. At least she hadn't stolen his sidearm. Outside, it was pissing rain. Alexander offered him a lift, and I gave Martyn the extra slicker we kept under the seat, all the time wishing we could trade places, he in the truck and me in the tavern. When we reached a rise in the road above the Parsky house, Alexander stopped long enough for him and Martyn to take a quick swig from Martyn's flask and for me to jot down a few notes. Sitting here listening to them guffawing uproariously at my scribbling, as they call it, I can't help but think that perhaps Galina is right.

3

The cramped university exam room, normally a smoking lounge for faculty, exuded the stale smell of nicotine. From the two couches and dusty drapes, in particular, came a foul odor. To achieve a bonhomous effect, the chairs formed a semicircle facing the one for the candidate. A coffee table, in the middle, held several ashtrays, a water pitcher, and five glasses. The examiners, less inclined to talk about the forthcoming examination than the price of onions, insouciantly flipped through their red folders. While Sasha paced in the hall, so too did Igor Likhachov, a security officer nicknamed Chick-Chick, who nodded at Sasha, and for no apparent reason put his briefcase under his arm and started to remove pieces of flaking plaster from the faded green walls. When a secretary opened the door and said that the committee was ready, Sasha had an urge to retreat to the men's lavatory, but suppressed his need. Likhachov followed Sasha into the room and sat apart from the group, in a corner, next to a rubbish bin, slowly peeling a hard-boiled egg.

Sasha stood at attention and waited for his adviser to start the proceedings. The examiners, all men dressed in drab black suits, sat passively, giving no indication of their disposition toward Sasha's work. Each red folder included Sasha's thesis and academic record. His dissertation director, Feodor Simyonski, a rotund fellow with droopy eyelids and pince-nez attached to his vest by a black ribbon, pointed to the empty chair and told him to sit. Sasha pondered whether to extend his hand in greeting to the examiners now or after the oral. He chose to wait. But he did greet each man by his formal title. Once Sasha was seated, Simyonski cleared his throat and began. "Sasha Parsky, candidate for history honors, thesis 'A Marxist Interpretation of the Russian Civil War.' You have all read the paper, and I am sure that my colleagues here have questions that they would like to ask Citizen Parsky."

A clean-shaven, balding expert on military history, Simyonski nervously fingered his glasses, which he frequently removed and polished with a dirty handkerchief. Unlike the other men, he had a certificate from a military academy and treated university degrees with suspicion. Strategy forged under fire, he felt, eclipsed classroom theory. To ground the discussion in geography, he had mounted on a stand behind him a large map of Eastern and Central Europe, including the Baltics and Scandinavia, with black arrows pointing to the major fronts of the Russian Civil War. To Simyonski's way of thinking the Upper and Lower Don had been the key to Bolshevik success. If the Cossacks had been allowed to distance themselves from both the Reds and the Whites to form their own nation, what was to prevent Ukraine and the Caucasus and Georgia and Latvia from following suit? Although he had not himself fought in the war, he had shared the nationalists' fears of fragmentation.

Artur Krasnov chain-smoked. A tall, elderly man, poorly barbered, with thin lips, furtive eyes, a beaked nose, long curved fingernails, and a sickly yellow complexion, he coughed so often that his chest rattled like loose change. A former Tsarist officer who had initially fought with the Whites, he had early in the war changed sides, and therefore regarded himself as an expert on matters touching upon the Bolshevik military, the Volunteer Army, and the Cossack rebellion. Pointing to the Don River and the steppe lands marked on the map, he asked:

"How great a role in the war do you think pillaging played, especially in Ukraine and the Don?"

Sasha pondered the question, which was a minefield. All sides had engaged in unlawful acts against citizens, though the Bolsheviks were inclined to minimize their rapaciousness and emphasize that of the Cossacks and Whites.

"It would be hard to measure, but we do know that such behavior was counterproductive, because the local populations would readily change sides when mistreated. How else can we explain the desire on the part of the Cossacks to have their own nation?"

Lighting a fresh cigarette from the former, Krasnov greedily devoured the smoke and exhaled a stream through his nose. Extending the pack of cigarettes toward Sasha, he paused, tapped a fingernail on his folder, and remarked, "I'd forgotten. You don't enjoy the habit."

Sasha forced a smile and acknowledged his abstemiousness.

"On the basis of social class," asked Krasnov, "do you think the Bolshevik officers or the White officers were more inclined to steal?"

Again, the question was fraught with danger. The Bolsheviks had argued that they represented the exploited classes, while the Whites had contended that their officers came from the upper classes and would never stoop to plundering. Of course, both sides had forcibly recruited in their service misfits and miscreants and could not account for their behavior.

Knowing that Krasnov took pride in his having once served in the Tsar's officer corps, which he regarded as the height of military service, Sasha replied, "The qualities of fairness and mercy can be found in any class. Where people evinced such qualities, brigandage was not a problem."

"Are you saying, then," Krasnov probed, toying with his cigarette, "that royalty is an innate quality and not bestowed by education or rank?"

Again trying to walk a fine line, Sasha replied, "The privileges of money often lead to education and good manners, but not necessarily to a good heart. The poor may be deficient in education but rich in feeling for their fellow man."

When his coughing subsided, Krasnov snorted and nodded to Simyonski to call on someone else. The chairman, seeing that Pavel Polyakov was keen to speak, called on him.

"Do you think, Sasha Parsky, that if Petrograd had fallen to the Whites, we'd still be living under a Tsar; or do you think a revolution was inevitable and the monarchy, in any case, doomed?"

Simyonski grimaced and poured himself a glass of water. The question was precisely the kind he despised, academic and theoretical. And whatever answer Sasha gave, what would it matter? Theory, he mused, was all gray, and the golden tree of life green.

Outside the one window, which looked into a courtyard, the sky remained bright, even though the afternoon was eroding. The glorious hours of honeyed Russian sunshine were all too ephemeral, and the dreary cold all too lasting. At that moment, Sasha wished to be running through the fields behind his parents' house and flushing quail from the wheat fields. He could picture the bustards and crows overhead, and he could see the wide stream in which he and his father fished. In May, the sound of the melting ice resembled the report of a gun, as the melting floes hiccupped and heaved. His mind wandered to Tolstoy and Sholokhov. Who could describe better than they the Russian countryside, the fields and the rivers?

"It's always easier to fight in the countryside than in the city. Had the Whites actually entered Petrograd, the guerilla street fighting might have kept the city safely in Bolshevik hands."

Polyakov sucked on the shiny hairs under his lower lip, a clump that resembled the ones on the backs of his small brown hands. Leaning forward, he peered out of his sunken eyes, made all the deeper by his high cheekbones, and objected.

"That's not what I asked. My question concerned historical inevitability. As a good Marxist, you should understand the meaning of Marx's statement that men make history 'under circumstances directly encountered, given, and transmitted from the past.'" He studied Sasha's face for a sign of weakness, but seeing none, lipped his clump of hair and pondered his next step. Famous for intimidating students with his black stares and cheerless demeanor, he barked, "Inevitable or not? One word!"

"Inevitable."

"Quite so."

Polyakov leaned back in his chair satisfied that he had just taught this honors student a lesson in Marxist theory.

Dimitri Nikiforov, a lady's man, though his drab clothing would have argued otherwise, spoke with a nasal voice. He whined, "Although you say in your thesis that the intervention of Britain, France, the United States, and the eleven other foreign countries was in great part to stop the spread of Bolshevism to the Baltics and Finland and other countries, you seem to neglect the nefarious role played by Germany. Is this omission not a serious oversight?" But before Sasha could reply, Nikiforov said, "I would remind you that many Russians thought—erroneously—that since Germany's own socialist revolution had failed, then Russia, a far less industrialized country, had no chance of succeeding."

As Sasha considered his reply, Dimitri took a comb to his fine hair and pointed beard. His long, elegant fingers, with which he stroked the air, tended to divert one's attention from his slightly drooping eyes and captiousness. Placing his fingers in a prayerful attitude, he pressed his mouth against them and murmured:

"Well?" But Nikiforov had no intention of listening to the explanation of a student. He wanted to confer on Sasha his expertise. "Trotsky and the Left Opposition were wrong. Stalin was right. You can have revolution in a single country. Isn't that so?" Sasha, who had barely uttered a sentence, was again interrupted. "Admittedly, for a socialist country to be surrounded by capitalist ones is a problem, but hostile borders do not mean ipso facto that socialism cannot succeed in a nation like ours. Right?" Realizing that he would have little chance to respond, Sasha simply nodded. Professor Nikiforov continued. "Moreover, surrounded as we currently are by enemies of socialism unites the country. Correct?" Sasha nodded. "For example, an invasion of our motherland would bring out the best in people. Don't you agree?"

Quickly Sasha interjected, "Yes."

Nikiforov sighed audibly. "The naiveté that some people display about politics is simply incredible." He inspected his well-groomed nails and then removed from his vest an unsmoked briar pipe that he used, like his fingers, to poke the vacant air when punctuating a point. Unwilling to be gainsaid in any argument, and especially not by students, he protected himself by refusing to let anyone else utter a word. Had Sasha tried to speak over Nikiforov, the professor would have told him that one had to earn the right to hold forth on such matters, and that Sasha's modest learning did not qualify him.

At this juncture, with Nikiforov waving his pipe and others taking issue with Dimitri on fine points, the committee members began to debate among themselves, an ideal situation for a candidate sitting exams, because attention is diverted from the student to the examiners. Irrespective of the speaker or his position, Sasha shook his head in agreement, hoping to encourage his professors to continue their parsing of sentences and squaring of circles: Who did and did not engage in reprisals and theft? Who provoked whom? Who was more to blame: kulaks, Cossacks, or commissars?

Eventually, Ivan Vyazemskiy, a stolid, chunky man with a pencil mustache and a mole on his right eyelid, exclaimed, as he lit a cigarette and delicately blew the smoke in the air, that he had not yet examined the honors candidate. Displaying a full set of white teeth except for one gold incisor, he revealed just the slightest aroma of spirits.

Running one finger over his mustache, he pursed his lips and began. "The intervention of the fourteen other nations unnecessarily prolonged the conflict. Their expeditionary landings in Archangel and Murmansk and Vladivostok, to say nothing of incursions from Finland, Estonia, Latvia, Poland, and Ukraine, brought with them the necessaries of war: troops, money, and supplies. I would go so far as to argue that without foreign intervention, the Whites would have been crushed by early 1918. Instead, the terrible conflict dragged into 1923. Just consider the results: millions dead through fighting, disease, and starvation; social revolutions in other countries thwarted . . . Finland, Hungary, and the Baltic states; devastating pogroms; the near loss of Siberia to Japan. I could go on but will rest my case there. Anyone who thinks that the so-called Allied Intervention did not change the course of history and stifle democratic movements in Eastern and Central Europe is unfamiliar with the historical sources. Yes, Germany was a major player, but not as major as some think." He inhaled, forced a smile, and, through the smoke flowing from his mouth, said, "But then I am speaking for you, Sasha Mikhailovich Parsky. What do you think?" A persuasive speaker, though not an eloquent one, Ivan Vyazemskiy had silenced the other examiners, except for Feodor Simyonski.

"I would direct my colleagues' attention," Feodor said, "to the fact that Sasha Parsky's thesis neither trumpets nor slights the German role in the civil war. Rather he argues that for far too long the role of the Central Powers and their allies has been misread, and that the intervention exacerbated the carnage and accelerated the financial bankruptcy of Russia." Feodor shook his head. "And to what end? Principally to keep the revolution from spreading, as Professor Vyazemskiy said."

Ivan smiled contentedly.

Simyonski concluded, "I would add, though Mr. Parsky does not, that we are suffering the repercussions of the civil war to this day."

A somber quiet pervaded the room. Feodor looked around the table and, not seeing in his colleagues any wish to continue the discussion, was prepared to ask Sasha to wait in the hall while the committee deliberated. But at that moment, the security officer, Igor Likhachov, pulled his chair up to the circle.

"Professor Simyonski, in my capacity as chief of security for the college, permit me to question the candidate."

Everyone present knew Chick-Chick, one moment jolly, the next lugubrious. A veteran of the civil war, he had returned from the Upper Don with a lame arm and a gimpy leg. A short man and a strong one, he could, even with his disabilities, have wrestled larger men to the ground. His dark skin suggested Kalmyk blood, as did his wide, black eyebrows that ran straight across the bridge of his nose. He opened his large mouth and from its recesses came the words that Sasha feared most: kulaks, parents, arrests, murder, police, alibi, and accusations.

With all the examiners silently tensed, Chick-Chick paused, reveling in the effect of his pronouncements, and then, to everyone's amusement, hatched from a pocket another hard-boiled egg, which he shelled, arranging the detritus on the table in a letter S. Reaching into a second pocket, he drew out a schoolboy's pen-knife, a bent nail, a ceramic water faucet handle, a key chain, a comb with greasy hairs, a pencil stub, and an old-fashioned inlaid pinch box that, in place of tobacco, held salt, which he liberally sprinkled on his egg. After putting away all his belongings, he bit into the egg, reducing it by half. Still no one spoke, bewitched by the scene. When he had finished, he pointed to the shells, said, "Sorry for the mess," swept them into his briefcase, wiped his hands on his pants, reached into his vest, and produced a small pad. Gently flipping back the cover, he fumbled a pair of glasses onto his face and opined:

"You know, people are a lot like eggs, white on the outside, yellow on the inside." He smiled at Sasha and said simply, "Your family was denounced . . . as kulaks."

"I never have understood that term," Sasha replied courageously, prompting Simyonski to shake his head in agreement.

"A rich farmer," said Chick-Chick.

"Comfortable maybe, but my parents were never rich."

"Cows, horses, goats, sheep, chickens, land, a house. What do you call these?"

"Possessions gained through several generations of Parsky family toil."

"Your parents hired laborers."

"For carpentry and during the harvest, but they never exploited them."

"So you say. Others say differently."

"Facts should weigh more than gossip."

Likhachov flicked over a page with his thumb. "Where is your family samovar?"

An incredulous Sasha, temporarily taken aback, answered, "My parents must have taken it with them when they left for Sochi. Why?"

Ignoring the question, Likhachov asked, "How often was it used?"

"Daily. I fail to understand . . ." Sasha looked round the group hoping to find support, but except for the lingering smile on his director's face, he met cold stares.

"It was smaller than the usual type."

"True."

"And could not service a large number of people."

"I guess so."

Bolshevik interrogators had mastered the technique of eroding the victim's confidence and sanity with small pricks. Taking the initiative, Sasha said, "Chick-Chick, if you are trying to worm information out of me, you needn't waste everyone's time. Just ask me directly. I will be perfectly truthful."

Looking at his notebook, Igor tapped the page. "Someone has accused your family of hiding jewels and rubles in the samovar." He stared coldly at Sasha. "Isn't that why your family never used it?"

"We used it at home, for the three of us, all the time."

"Tell that to your neighbors."

"I have no idea what you are talking about."

"Your family never entertained neighbors around the samovar. Apparently it had another purpose."

An angry Sasha ground his teeth and began to shake.

"I see that you do understand," said Likhachov.

"But . . ."

"No buts. You wanted facts. The facts are that one of your neighbors has done the country a patriotic service."

Having recovered from his initial shock, Sasha replied, "And in return, I am sure the country will reward the family with all or part of my parents' holdings."

"Part," Likhachov said. "The rest will be divided equally among the land poor."

With a stroke of daring, Sasha pounded the coffee table and said, "And that's just as it should be in a democratic socialist country!"

Simyonski clapped, leading the other examiners to applaud.

The radically changed atmosphere led Chick-Chick to see that nothing more could be gained from the investigation, so he stood and thanked the examiners for permitting him to speak. He then removed a Lenin-like cap from his briefcase, donned it, and made for the door, pausing just long enough to say, "Comrade Parsky, I wish you well. No hard feelings. I was only doing my job. But remember that the Soviet state is always vigilant, and so should you be."

Likhachov's cross-examination had earned Sasha, now waiting in the hall, the sympathy of the examiners, who took only ten minutes to come to a decision. When he returned to the room, Sasha was told that his thesis had passed, though certain errors of fact and style would have to be remedied, and that he would be graduating with honors in history.

"Sadly," added Simyonski, "your parents will not be on hand to see the ceremony."

Sasha stared at the floor, thanked the examiners for all their help and their illuminating comments during the thesis defense, shook their hands, and followed Feodor out the door. But before joining him in his office for a drink of schnapps, Sasha stopped at the men's lavatory.

4

Ryazan, a city divided by the Oka River and situated on the border of forests and steppelands, looked as if it had yet to recover from the devastation of 1237 when the Mongol hordes of Batu Khan sacked it. The Communists had boarded the churches and monasteries, though they had left intact the colorful, albeit fading, onion domes. Configured as a triangle, the town was originally surrounded by bow-shaped ramparts that conformed to the landscape, undulating and blending with the rise and fall of the land. Invaders could approach from three directions: through the yellow clay fields and by river, either the Oka or Serebryanka. When Sasha arrived at the Ryazan Station, he exited the train carrying a small valise and followed the nearly abandoned passenger platform to a faded yellow building with a red metal roof. Inside, after an official checked his papers, he passed into a small square, where two ancient Fiat taxis waited for fares. Flagging one, he could hardly fail to notice the plume of exhaust that the old car expelled.

Boris Filatov had told Sasha to write ahead to Galina Selivanova and Viktor Harkov. They had both answered. Galina lived near a park, on Ulitsa Pushkina, and Viktor, a short distance away, on Ulitsa Tatarskaya. In each case, they shared a flat with another family, but owing to the fact that their deceased kin had worked for the government, they had been awarded two rooms, with a lavatory and bath down the hall. Sasha, on the advice of the taxi driver, rented a bed in a sports hostel, with all its attendant body and cooking odors, noise, and lumpy mattresses, and a nine p.m. curfew, at which time the attendant turned off the electricity. As Sasha closed his eyes, he saw the family farm, with its pond and ducks and wooded borderland, and smelled the leather tack and harnesses of the work animals. He wondered why anyone would choose to live in a city when village life, for all its hardships and crudeness, offered rolling meadows, grasslands, yellow camomile, red lotus flowers, mushrooms, and fir and cedar and larch trees. At five a.m., one of the athletic coaches blew a whistle and summoned his charges to the field for soccer practice. Sasha buried his head in the skimpy pillow and slept for another hour.

He dreamed a fairy tale in which the princess Anilaga, while riding through the countryside in a gilded coach, saw a handsome young lad working in the fields. She ordered her driver to stop, summoned the boy to her side, and asked him his name. "Ahsas," he said. "It's Hungarian." Even with his face dripping sweat, she could not help but admire his handsome features. She invited him to join her for tea in her father's castle, the home of King Vokrah, and gave him a ring from her finger for purposes of identification. On arriving at the castle gate, he was stopped. Although dressed in his finest clothes, the guard regarded him as a beggar. When he held up the ring, the man fell to his knees, sought his pardon, and ushered him into the castle, where another servant, in livery, led him through acres of halls and rooms to the princess's quarters. She was sitting on silken pillows and petting a white furry lapdog. With a snap of her fingers, a woman servant appeared and was directed to bring the princess and her guest tea and biscuits.

"Now you must tell me about yourself. So handsome a lad as you must have lovers by the dozens." He explained that because he was a poor peasant, hardly a single young woman stopped to talk to him. And the ones in the field had been burned by the sun, and had gnarled and wrinkled limbs. "Then you have never lain with a lady?" she asked. He lowered his eyes and admitted to having paid a tart, on several occasions, for that pleasure. "Do you love her?" she asked. He replied, "I have slept with a woman, but I have never loved one."

The princess Anilaga invited him to stay with her in the castle. "I will feed and clothe you and then bed you." Ahsas asked, "And in return, what must I do?" She answered, "You are a man and, like all mortals, you will die, only sooner. But think of what you receive in return."

Later that morning, he found his way to Galina Selivanova's flat, which was just one of hundreds in a complex of poorly constructed cement blocks. The elevator displayed a sign, "Out of Order," and the staircase was strewn with litter. Cooking smells assailed Sasha's nose as he climbed the four flights of stairs to number 411, Galina's flat, which she shared with a Kalmyk family, the Baturins: mother, father, and two children. A note on the broken bell directed callers to knock. Rapping on the door, Sasha waited and surveyed his clothes. His pants, which had shrunk, ended at the top of his socks, and his jacket sleeves barely reached his wrist. Not yet in a position to afford tailored clothing, he was reduced to buying used wares on the black market. His shoes, though worn, had been purchased in better days and could still hold a shine. He had showered in cold water at the sports hostel—the hot water boiler, he was told, had failed a month before—and had shaved in a ceramic basin clogged with hair. His own trimmed locks, blond and parted down the middle, resembled a commissar's: shiny, stiff, and Stalinist. Tall and thin, with high cheekbones, he brought to mind those Ukrainians descended from Scandinavia. A former girlfriend had told him that his narrow lips, nose, and chin made him look like a scarecrow. Fortunately, Filatov had ignored his appearance, and had decided that his advanced college degree could benefit the Soviet state. But he knew not to gloat about his mental accomplishments. Too many made you an enemy of the people; too few made you fodder for a factory. As a result, Sasha always measured his speech carefully, using among workers a common diction and among the well-educated a learned one. He wondered about Galina's status and expectations. It would take only a few sentences to know.

A short, dark man answered the door, undoubtedly Mr. Baturin. His flared nose, oblique eyes, and dark hair demarked his Mongolian blood; and his accented Russian reinforced the impression of a nomad who had left the steppes for the city. He politely greeted Sasha, led him through the flat to the back, where a curtain separated the Baturin living area from Galina's, and called to her, announcing her visitor. A dulcet voice told him to enter. At a table sat the handsome woman of the photograph and the shining child. The mother was teaching her daughter how to calculate with an abacus. Mr. Baturin excused himself.

Rising from her chair and sweeping back her yellow hair, Galina Selivanova confidently walked to Sasha and extended her hand, smiling at him as he took it. "Citizen Parsky, I presume."

He presented her with a box of candy, and the child with a *matryoshka* doll, elegantly hand painted. Alya took the gift and repeatedly thanked the stranger.

"Tea?" asked Galina.

"I'd be delighted," Sasha replied, noting that the pretty face in the photograph had failed to capture Galina's electric energy. Having read Petr's diary, with its unsettling information, he had gained an advantage, but he had to tread carefully lest he reveal what he knew. Whatever she said, Sasha weighed in light of the diary. He suddenly wished that he were meeting this woman for the first time, without any prior knowledge. Ignorance, in this case, would have been a defense against bias. Unwittingly, Petr Selivanov, whose photograph was nowhere to be seen in the flat, had made Sasha an ally in his struggle with the selfish, undoubtedly wise, Galina. From her first words, he recognized her analytical intelligence, which she skillfully used to effect her own purposes.

"The government settlement I expected," she said, "but the belated condolence call suggests there is more here than meets the eye. Whom do you represent? Your letter says the OGPU. Are you a policeman? If so, I must confess: I never heard Petr mention your name."

Sasha could feign a friendship that never existed between him and Petr, but the pretense would leave him open to questions about

Petr that he couldn't answer, even though he had studied Petr's files and diary. Better, he decided, to represent himself on grounds he could actually defend.

"I have been appointed the director of a secondary school," he said honestly, "and we will . . ." Suddenly unbidden words tumbled out of his mouth, ". . . need a nurse, as well as someone who can teach Russian grammar and French literature—for the spring term."

Although he had made her an offer of employment that he'd never intended, he felt perfectly satisfied, and he knew that his posture expressed the same ease. He then told her about the school, which he had recently visited for a fortnight, meeting the teachers, hearing their concerns, discussing the curriculum, outlining his plans to focus on science and letters and to improve academic standards. In preparation for the visit, he had read about the history of the school and knew the records of all the teachers on staff. It had once been devoted to agriculture, hence the farmhouse and stables nearby. But after farms were collectivized, the school slowly evolved from its original mission toward becoming an institution dedicated to educating future managers, engineers, and, yes, Soviet commissars. In short, the students were to be trained as leaders.

But in the neighboring villages, where superstition and religion still governed family life, learning was treated suspiciously. By inducing some of the local children to enroll, he hoped to persuade the locals to value schooling.

"But what will happen," Galina asked, "when science and religion clash, and when children learn to read? Won't the illiterate parents complain?"

He admitted that the question of whom to admit and whom to exclude would be a problem. But Galina anticipated another.

"What if a great many villagers feel their children should be enrolled, what then? After all, they'll say, Ivan down the road was accepted, and he is no smarter or not much smarter than my own Ivan." Sasha had to agree—no fool, she—but he remained optimistic that he could raise the school's academic standards. In fact, even before meeting with his teaching staff, he had decided against "leveling," the Soviet means of treating all children equally.

Galina studied him for a moment and came to the conclusion that the OGPU, no doubt for perfidious purposes, had decided to use its gravitational pull to bring her into their orbit. It therefore made perfect sense that Sasha, a newly appointed school director, would be the bearer of the good news. As much as she liked working in a hospital, she found little occasion to exercise her critical mind. The doctors gave the orders, and the nurses carried them out. She took the box of candy, expressed her appreciation, and offered him and Alya a chocolate-covered cherry.

Sasha waited until they had all savored the sweets before he approached Alya, who had begun to disengage the doll's different levels. To enable him to look into the child's eyes on an equal plain, he knelt and asked:

"Are you well behaved?"

"Oh yes," she replied, her black, braided ponytail swinging back and forth in response to her shaking head.

"Is it any fun?" Sasha asked.

The child lowered her eyes, stole a glance at her mother, and said, "Sometimes, but not always."

"I think misbehaving is the most fun," said Sasha.

She held up the handsome matryoshka doll representing the different characters in Pushkin's *Ruslan and Liudmila*. "I know them all," she said proudly. "Mamma has read the book to me many times." And she threw her arms around the neck of the kneeling Sasha thanking him yet again for his gift.

Galina watched, initially with a wary eye, and then with a sympathetic one. This fellow had a way with children, and such people, she felt, were endowed with a natural playfulness. She again thanked him for his generosity and asked teasingly:

"And what form does your misbehavior take?"

Sasha chose to treat her question seriously. "I hate rules."

"Hmm. And why is that?"

He stood. "They are the last refuge of the unimaginative."

Galina reflected for a moment. "Then you approve of Rasputin's behavior?"

With her mother preoccupied, Alya took another chocolate, a breach of etiquette that brought a smile to Sasha's face. "No, but I can understand it."

"And yet you are a policeman."

He shook his head no and looked around the modestly furnished flat. Whatever financial settlement the government had made with her, it could not have been generous, judging from her worn parlor chair and old Primus stove. "In return for the position at the school, I agreed, among other things, to call on you."

"Am I to assume, then, that the decision to hire me was yours, and not the government's? But until you arrived a minute ago, you had no idea whether I'd be suitable for the position. In fact, you still don't know."

Caught off guard, Sasha mumbled that he had read the file and found her well qualified.

"Without an interview? You don't even know the extent of my French."

Here was his chance to respond substantively. "I read some of your translations."

Galina asked him to sit. "Would you like your tea with sugar?" He nodded yes. "Which of my books did you read?"

He remembered one author from the file. "Romain Rolland." He paused hoping that Galina would take Rolland as her cue to fill the void. Luckily, she did, remarking:

"*Annette and Sylvie* was the last one I translated . . . in fact, I think, rather well. You do know it?"

"Who doesn't?"

Alya had retreated to a corner of the room to play with her new doll. Galina poured two cups of tea and opened the cupboard, removing a sugar bowl. Looking over her shoulder, she said:

"I had hoped to translate all seven volumes but only had time for the first."

She brought the tea to the table, sat across from Sasha, and lit a cigarette, which she inhaled sensuously.

"Working for me you'll have time to translate the other volumes."

Thinking he had escaped the trap of book titles, he feigned reflection, which crumbled when she asked:

"Do you think *The Enchanted Soul* is equal to *Jean-Christophe*? You do realize that he conceived the later works as companion pieces to the former?"

Fortunately, he had read *Jean-Christophe* and immediately began to review the argument in the novel about Brahms and Beethoven.

"Surely," she said, "you are not a Brahmin?"

"Beethoven is the greater composer."

She inhaled contentedly and eyed Sasha with just the slightest contempt. Her look unsettled him. Although she didn't question his appointment to a position for which he had never apprenticed, he tried to justify it. "With all the poorly educated people being promoted to administrative positions, I think the OGPU felt that I, as a college graduate, would make a promising director, maybe even better than most." The instant he said "college graduate," the words sounded immature and immodest. "What I mean is," he awkwardly corrected himself, "the police wanted someone who would not, in the company of educated people like you, sound . . ." He paused.

"Gauche," she added.

"Yes."

As they sipped their tea, she continued to study him carefully. He was younger than she, though not by much. His education was apparent, as was hers. Could he, she wondered, be trusted? It was the eternal question that every Soviet citizen pondered in the presence of a stranger.

"You knew my husband?"

"Caravan tea," he said, hoping to sidestep her question. "You know why they call it that? The Chinese brought it by caravan, and their campfires infused it with a smoky flavor."

She smelled the tea and looked over the head of her guest to some indefinite point.

"In the seventeenth century," Sasha said, "a Mongolian ruler brought tea to Tsar Michael I, but he scoffed at what he called 'dead leaves.'"

Galina's eyes listlessly migrated to his face. Sasha, having come to the end of his digression about tea, weakly smiled hoping that Galina would resume the conversation, but take it in another direction.

"My husband's belongings were never recovered, including a diary I gave him." Clearly, she would not be deterred. "Perhaps the killer or killers thought that these possessions had no value and disposed of them. Have you any knowledge of their whereabouts?" Before Sasha could reply, she waved her hand dismissively and added, "But why should you know about such things, a mere emissary of the police."

Although her statement seemed to suggest that her questions had come to an end, her fixed stare, which held his face like a skewed butterfly, said otherwise. Sasha turned to the child at play in the corner. Perhaps Alya could provide a chance for Sasha to elude any further mention of Petr Selivanov. He called to Alya and asked her which person in Pushkin's story she liked best.

"The headless man who talks. I like him the best, the very best."

"He doesn't scare you?"

"No, I feel sorry for him. He knows the truth but can't say it."

"My favorite is the evil sorcerer Chernomor."

"I hate him. He makes good people bad."

With Galina's eyes riveted on him, Sasha turned from the child to his teacup and chuckled. "Dead leaves, indeed. That's a Tsar for you." Wordlessly, she rose and went to her larder. Most people who shared flats also shared kitchens. Galina, having one of her own, was fortunate. She returned to the table with a loaf of black rye bread, a knife, a spoon, and a pot of honey. She put the items on the table, sat, and folded her hands. He worried that any further attempts to turn the discussion away from Petr Selivanov would only heighten her suspicions. So he tried to gain her confidence with sentimentality.

"You did receive his remains?"

She walked to a bookcase and from the top shelf removed a white ceramic urn. "This is what they sent me . . . his ashes."

Sensible that the police, given Petr's decapitation, had little choice but cremation. Sasha considered, for the first time, the possibility that Galina had never been told about the condition of the body. Did he dare tell her? No.

"I think it's standard practice," said Sasha, having no idea what rules governed the transport of the dead.

She glanced at her daughter and whispered, "Had he been put in a coffin, I could have at least raised the lid for a last look."

Sasha began to perspire. Noticing his discomfort, Galina added, "When the ashes arrived, I felt the same way, in a sweat."

Her comment intimated that she had no suspicions about him. His unease was being interpreted as sympathy. "If you wish to find a proper resting place for the ashes," he said, "I'll be glad to help in any way that I can."

She reached across the table and touched his hand. "Just your coming here has helped."

Studying him she saw an intelligent, reasonable man, not a Bolshevik bully. Not a militant, opinionated, self-satisfied ideologue. He gave no indication of wanting to control people and tell them how to live. Unlike her friend Viktor, he didn't state a position and belligerently dare you to oppose it. She supposed he could be testy, like anyone else, but not to the degree of ridiculing another or raising an eyebrow or tapping a finger that said, in effect, you are an imbecile. She had grown up with strong men. Her father was one. Any time he thought her lacking in judgment or behavior, he made clear her error. Unlike her mother, who allowed for frailty, her father believed that any concession made to her own ideas was weakness and would lead to further, and worse, transgressions. In her view, men like her father had become the Soviet government, which forbade dissenting views. Her husband, Petr, was the polar opposite of her father and the oppressive government. Although physically strong, he leaked moral cowardice and confusion. His willingness to turn a blind eye to the injustice around him and to equivocate about his work made her want to scream, "What kind of man are you?"

She recognized, of course, the possibility that she was endowing Sasha with the qualities she wanted him to exhibit. Unfamiliar men didn't normally turn up in her life, not at work and not at home; in fact, this was the first time, and he was educated. The cretins she worked with and who ran the local Soviet could barely write their names. If this was rule by the proletariat, she would gladly settle for Plato's philosopher king. Sasha might not be a philosopher or a king, but he had the manners of a gentleman and the speech of a person who valued language, without superciliousness and pedanticism. She was no romantic, but she did wish for a man equal to her hopes.

The longer Sasha sat in Galina's presence the greater was his insight into Petr's diary and initial attraction to this Cossack woman: the feral spirit that infused the room with energy, the stubborn independence that radiated from her posture, the handsome countenance, the kind of strength that enabled the Bolsheviks to achieve victory in the revolution and civil war. Sasha had known a few such women in college. They were a breed apart. You felt drawn not only to their maternal, protective bosom, but also to the attar of their sensuality. Petr must have felt like Raffaello, the Renaissance painter, who was so taken with his model that his hands shook, preventing him from completing her painting until she slept with him.

Galina's face, not round or square-jawed like most Cossack women but perfectly proportioned, her eyes, not limpid blue but dark, her cheekbones, subtle not sharp, her yellow curly hair, almost white, and her perfect body, which she moved balletically without appearing seductive, entranced Sasha. Then, too, there were her coruscating insights. Astonished by his feelings, Sasha attributed them wrongly to Galina's witchery rather than to his loneliness.

Untiring Soviet careerist women of fierce passions, quick intelligence, and stout heart had usually graduated from Komosol into university and then into government, with the knowledge of how to maintain the necessary distance between themselves and the men who desired them, and of how to inflame desires and increase their own value. They played with the smitten, like a torero with a bull, and quickly learned that most men were immature sentimentalists. With superiors, they gave up their bodies but not their spirits. With equals or those below them, they tamed every fury and blunted every demand with their great cunning and ruthless daring, and by the inexplicable play of their bodies.

Sasha had known such a woman, Tatiana Sokolsky, who promised much and gave little, or rather nothing at all. For she knew that Sasha's desires were, of their very nature, impossible to satisfy, and in the end he had to content himself with crumbs. Was Galina another Tatiana? Petr's diary seemed to suggest so. Well, he had learned from the chilled love of Tatiana not to wear his heart on his sleeve. Like all good Soviet citizens, he had been schooled in the art of *vranyo*, pretense, and knew to say that Russia was the golden future and America the corrupt past, and that citizens of the Soviet Union, having grown up in paradise, were imbued with honesty and candor. But with Tatiana he had let down his guard. He would not allow the same to happen with Galina.

The ruminations of both Sasha and Galina were interrupted by Alya, who asked if they could feed the ducks on the lake. "We could call Uncle Viktor; maybe he would like to go with us. The sun is shining."

"I'm sure he's occupied," said Galina, but Alya persisted.

Was this Viktor the same Viktor Harkov that Sasha had been directed to visit? He was at a loss whether to ask. Not having told Galina at the outset that he was on a mission of condolence to her *and* Viktor Harkov, he worried about being tied to both murders. His initial reticence was a product of Soviet life. Never volunteer information. But although silence never betrays, it sometimes confirms the suspicions of others. Sasha decided to bide his time.

After repeated requests from Alya, Galina went to the hall telephone to call Viktor. In her absence, Sasha questioned the child.

"Who is Viktor?"

"A friend of Mamma's."

The child was walking on her toes in anticipation of good news.

"He must live in the neighborhood."

"A few blocks from here. If you want, we can take the tram."

Sasha's questions at best were producing only superficialities. He wanted to probe deeper without alarming the child. All Soviet children knew to beware of strangers and never disclose personal knowledge. He therefore tried a different tack, a riskier one, but with greater rewards. "I believe your father and Viktor Harkov were friends," he said, showing some of his cards, though not all.

"You mean Papa and Uncle Alexander."

"Of course. How silly of me to have mixed up their names."

He had just learned that this Viktor Harkov was the very man he was to visit. Sasha offered to show her a trick and told her to stand with her back to him. He lifted and seated her on his arms. Then he reached under her, took her hands, and flipped her. Alya squealed with joy and asked him to do it again, offering the unsolicited comment that Sasha ought to teach Uncle Viktor that trick.

"Does he visit often?"

"Mamochka mostly goes there, and I eat with the Baturins."

The death of both Petr and Alexander had understandably strengthened the ties between the survivors, who had known each other before the killings. Presumably, Viktor's reputation for iconoclasm and reclusiveness had kept him and Galina from becoming more than close friends, if that. Friends feel bound by sedulous fidelities; emotional anarchists do not. And yet . . .

"Did you know that I'm eight?" said Alya, as she held up five fingers on one hand and three on the other.

"Why, you're old enough to be married."

"I am not!" she insisted. "I don't even know how to cook."

From a distance, Sasha could hear a door open and close. A moment later, Galina appeared. She smiled at Alya, who cried:

"Sasha taught me a trick!"

"You can show me at the river. Viktor will meet us there."

The child clapped her hands and ran off, returning with a fishing pole in hand. "Do you know anything about fishing and digging for worms?" she asked Sasha.

"Actually, a great deal."

With this admission, Sasha flexed Alya's pole, observing that she could use a new reel and line, both of which he volunteered to buy, if such items could be found in Ryazan.

"Not in the stores," said Galina, "but Viktor knows a man who makes his own, and you can buy equipment from him."

Viktor seemed to hover over the family. Was he a lover, a friend, a secret agent, a freeloader: What? In the short time that Sasha had been in the flat, he had decided that Alya was the straightest path to Galina—and her friendship with Viktor. He would therefore have to think of some way to gain the child's confidence. But first he would have to take Viktor aside to express his condolences. A river outing lacked the formality the occasion demanded.

"Viktor already knows you're coming with us. I told him."

With their knapsacks holding fishing gear, bait, bathing suits, towels, and a change of clothes, they carried wicker baskets to the tram stop. A trolley trailing sparks took them to within walking distance of the Ryazan Fortress, its fading onion domes and crumbling walls exuding neglect. The cloudless sky promised good swimming, if not fishing. A path led from the hill to the river. They could see Viktor, a tall man, readying a boat to row to one of the small river islands, where they would picnic. As the party approached across the rocky shore, Viktor looked up and made a loud alveolar clicking noise by way of a greeting. From twenty feet away, Sasha could see his drooping mustache and careless barbering, his sharp slanting Kalmyk eyes, and glasses hanging from a string around his neck. His repeated movements exuded nervous energy: checking the oarlocks, adjusting the tiller, baling, positioning the cushions, and twitching his bushy eyebrows that spread like dark wings across his forehead.

After Galina introduced the two men, she and Viktor formally touched cheeks. Sasha expressed his condolences and impetuously hugged Viktor as an expression of comradeship. In the boat, he sat facing Viktor, who surveyed him with beady eyes.

"Do you have any further details about my brother?"

The water gently licked the side of the boat, which stood fixed to the shoreline. Viktor sat stooped, his foraging face appearing wolflike.

"I never met him . . ."

Viktor interrupted. "Then who sent you?"

"Didn't my letter of introduction explain that my position as director of a school came under the authority of the police, and it was they who asked me to see you?"

"Yes, but I still thought it odd that a complete stranger was being sent as an emissary of the government, a teacher and not a police officer . . . hmm, strange."

Wordlessly, Viktor pushed off and pulled on the oars. Although painfully thin, he had sinewy arms and legs that moved the boat quickly. Alya chatted to herself and dipped her fingers in the water. Sasha studied Viktor's face, and Galina his. On reaching the island, they beached the boat and carried the food baskets through tall reeds to a grassy clearing with a fire pit. The spot provided a dramatic view of the river. Sasha gathered that this was not the first time Viktor had rowed his friends here. As Galina spread a blanket, Viktor opened a can of worms and skewered one on Alya's fishing hook. She immediately darted for the water to cast her line. Viktor took a swig of vodka, and put away the bottle. Galina looked dismayed. Sasha pondered the cause of her annoyance. Was it because he did not offer any to them or because he began the picnic with vodka? Or was she troubled about something else? He felt as if Viktor and Galina were speaking in code.

Viktor kicked the ground. "Dead leaves. We'll need a basketful later to start a fire. I forgot the kindling."

As Galina explained that young people came to this island for parties and cookouts, Viktor lay in the grass, leaned on an elbow, and with unruffled confidence, eyed the newcomer. He had the manner of a man in whom years of defying authority and escaping punishment had led to a haughty bearing, a way of tilting his head, a special walk. Viktor's lips moved but said nothing audible. Sasha stood, intending to start for the water. Suddenly, at his back, Viktor shouted:

"I'll kill the bastard!"

Terrified, Sasha turned. Galina took his arm and said, "Pay no attention. It's not you, it's the *oprichnik* who runs the oblast. Viktor hates him. They've had numerous run-ins. His name is Vladimir Lukashenko. He treats the area like his personal estate. He never pays for anything: restaurants, clothes, shoes, furniture, flowers, holidays. Numerous times Viktor has written to Moscow to complain, but the authorities do nothing. Their attitude is that as long as Ryazan is quiet, except of course for Viktor, Lukashenko can do what he wants. Until now Lukashenko has ignored Viktor, because Viktor's brother, Alexander, was OGPU. Then came the murder. But I kept telling Viktor as soon as the period of mourning ends, watch out! Lukashenko's police and bodyguards have begun to harass him."

Alya shouted from the edge of the island that she had caught a fish, and ran up to the party with a small trout hanging from her hook. Galina disengaged it and, to the child's dismay, told her to throw it back in the water. Viktor sardonically commented:

"Everyone wants the big fish, not the small fry. But when all the big ones are caught, then the small fish become fair game."

They ate a lunch of boiled eggs, herring, brown bread, hummus, and black tea, which Galina served from a thermos. Later, Sasha washed the dishes and silverware in the river, and Viktor snorted:

"Women's work."

Galina ignored Viktor's questionable manners, but Sasha was annoyed and asked, "And what do you consider man's work?"

Viktor sat upright in the grass. "Resisting the tyranny of the state. And if that sounds too grand, then let me say simply: questioning the judgment of the Party."

Feeling as if Viktor's indictment was directed at him, Sasha defensively remarked, "The school that I have been assigned will run on democratic principles and teach the truth, not propaganda."

"Oh, my god," cried Viktor, putting his hands on his head in a gesture of incredulity, "listen to that rot! I can smell the awful odor of idealism hanging in the air. Spare me, please! You will do what the state commands—or else. Stronger men than you have initially resisted, and subsequently confessed to crimes against the people—crimes they never committed. And you want to know why? To further the work of the Party, and to preserve their faith in the Soviet Union. They had sacrificed too much not to believe. It was beyond their powers. To relinquish hope in Stalin was to admit that all their sacrifices had been for nothing."

For a few freighted seconds no one spoke.

Viktor then launched into a diatribe against compliant Soviet citizens, contending that most of his countrymen believed in Party truth, not truth based on evidence and experience. "Millions of fools every day are heard to say that the government wouldn't dare to execute men and women without conclusive proof that the condemned were enemies of the people. Even Stalin's enemies believe that wreckers have overrun the country. Wreckers?" He laughed captiously. "I'll tell you the vermin who have swamped the country: denouncers! Not a minute passes when people aren't denouncing their bosses and neighbors simply to get ahead or to settle scores. The result? A great many innocent people are being jailed, deported, and killed. When the accused say there's been a mistake, the imbeciles among us say only wrongdoers are jailed; therefore, the arrested must have committed some crime. At this very moment hundreds of thousands of guiltless people are languishing in jails and camps. But does anyone speak out? No. They are either blind to the truth or afraid of endangering themselves. And when some of the arrested do confess, you hear people smugly say, 'See, I told you. Their arrest was necessary.' Take that mendacious maggot Lukashenko. He lives in a spacious flat; in fact he occupies the top floor of the building. Now how did that happen? Simple. He arranged through his toadies for the former tenants—a teacher, an engineer, and a theater director—to be denounced and removed. Good people have to suffer so that our commissar can live in splendor. For the likes of Lukashenko we made a revolution and endured a civil war?

"Denunciation is ripping this country apart. In those families visited by the conspiracy virus, children come to hate their parents for bringing misfortune on them—and for making them orphans. This is socialism? This is paradise? No, Sasha Parsky, this is madness. Before the firing squad, some even cry, 'Long live the Party, Long live Stalin.' In this country we have laws, but no legality."

Sasha, speechless, could only ponder the terrible truth that he lived in a country where people justified torture and murder with the glib and dismissive comment "You can't make an omelet without breaking eggs." The problem was that both the breakers and the eggs were his fellow human beings. His Jewish neighbor, Mr. Zaslavsky, used to say, "Who can protest and does not is an accomplice." Was Sasha an accomplice? Viktor seemed to be implying as much. But Sasha also knew himself to be a murderer.

Had Viktor not reached for the vodka bottle, allowing Sasha to escape, the sulfuric lecture might have continued. Making his way to the river, Sasha stood watching Alya troll for a big fish.

"They're probably playing chess," she said.

"Who?" Sasha asked.

"Mamma and Viktor. She often goes to his house to play."

"Do you tag along?"

"No, I don't know how to play." She paused and looked around. "I like it here on the island. No one can see us. It's quiet, isn't it? Just the sound of the wind and the water."

An island, Sasha thought, is what the Soviets tried to create, an island paradise in the midst of a capitalist sea, a profit-free country surrounded by rapacious money-grubbers. Trotsky had said it couldn't be done. The socialists needed the economic know-how of the West. But would the propinquity of capitalism corrupt socialism? After all, differences invite comparison. The Western countries were wealthy, Russia poor. But Alya had certainly touched upon a personal truth. To exist in the Soviet Union you had to live internally, inside your own head, exiled from the madness around you.

Chirping sounds drifted to the river, the voices of Galina and Viktor. As Alya said, they were playing chess. When Sasha caught sight of them lying in the grass, he saw Viktor take Galina's hand to keep her from making a bad move, but he seemed to hold it for an unduly long time. Or was that simply Viktor's way of keeping her from further mistakes? On seeing Sasha, he released her hand and asked whether Sasha might like to play. Fancying himself a rather good tactician, Sasha agreed. Galina immediately relinquished the board, with the too coy observation, "Not for the first time he had me pinned down."

Although about evenly matched, Viktor attacked ruthlessly; Sasha played defensively. Meanwhile, Galina glided among the island's tall grass and flora, collecting armfuls. When she returned, she sat between the two men weaving a garland of reeds and long grass, a Clotho, Sasha thought, spinning the thread of human life. Would she also be able to indicate the darkness and obscurity of human destiny? Kneeling behind Viktor, she briefly rested a hand on his shoulder; then she sat beside Sasha, their bodies occasionally touching. Was she playing the fair damsel, displaying her charms for both sides to see, and would she then reward the winner of the chess match with her silk scarf or with some other guerdon? Sasha's wandering mind caused him to misplay his bishop to earn a pawn, leaving an opening for Viktor to take his queen and the game. Galina crowned Viktor with her garland of grass.

The Complete Secondary School that Sasha directed, called the "Michael School" after the poet Mikhail Lermontov, formally welcomed Sasha in August 1936. Located in Tula oblast in the village of Balyk, once home to a family of famous salmon fishermen, it enrolled about ninety promising students between the ages of fifteen and seventeen, for a two-year program. Although Sasha would have to contend with the unruly hormones and genes of teenagers, he had escaped the most difficult group of all, thirteen- and fourteen-year-olds, just coming into heat. On the far side of the village, a "literacy school" bore the brunt of a thousand years of provincial ignorance. And still further along, perhaps ten minutes distance by motorcar, stood Leo Tolstoy's estate, with its birch-lined approach.

Sasha's position as director of the Michael School entitled him to live on the grounds, in the state-owned farmhouse, which abutted an empty barn with stables that once held fine Caucasian horses. The shingled, whitewashed farmhouse had housed an animal tender and his family when the school, in the days of the Tsar, was dedicated to equine care and breeding. A ramshackle place, the house had numerous rooms, none of them large or handsome. After the school's conversion from animal husbandry to academic work, the farmhouse had functioned as a dormitory for indigent students. Their graffiti, since painted over, could still be seen in outline on the walls. For several years the structure stood empty because the authorities intended to raze it and plant a garden for the use of the school. But when some official objected to the destruction of a "perfectly good" building, it was left standing, abandoned, to become home to mice, birds, bugs, stray dogs, and the occasional lovers who nocturnally nested there.

Sasha promised himself and others that the first chance he had, he would marshal the students to restore the farmhouse to its original state. Many of his students came from families in which they had been taught carpentry and roofing and flooring and plastering. He would make use of those skills to improve the property. In return, he would see to it that the students received free tutoring and an extra day off for holidays, to say nothing of an occasional dinner with the director on an outside porch that provided incomparable views of grasslands and woods.

Tula oblast, in the western part of the country, was a nature lover's delight. Through his office window, Sasha could see rolling hills of cedar, birch, and pine. Glaciers and rivers had sculpted the landscape into valleys and lakes; and buried in the mixed forest-steppe lands were wooded paths. A few farms drew Sasha to them when he yearned for a fresh tomato or cucumber or onion. In many ways Balyk and the surrounding countryside reminded him of John Constable's paintings. The farms were not as prosperous as the ones that the English painter had depicted in England, but a haystack in one country looked the same as in another, as did a field of rapeseed or a wooden bridge spanning a creek. Willows shaded the water, and the brickwork in the milldams and the green riverbanks and the mossy posts all exuded a nineteenth-century charm. The millponds, home to ducks and surrounded by gooseberry bushes, brought to mind Chekhov's wonderful story of that name. Cornfields ran as far as the eye could see, and cattle lowed in the meadows. Rough wooden railings fenced the fields that the government seemed to have forgotten or overlooked in this small valley.

Sasha quickly discovered the marshes, where he could hide himself in the bushes and watch the waterfowl and their young, carried along on the water, suddenly dive to capture a fish. Kissing gates could be found in a few fields, though most of the farmers had little time for romance, which seemed to take place in the village square where young people danced to accordions and old people sat sipping tea. Although the church on the square had been closed years before, some couples still found their way to the altar to have Father Zossima marry them, though if asked, not a villager would confess to such a ceremony having taken place, and certainly not in Balyk.

Two ramshackle trucks, owned by a veteran of the civil war, constituted the town's transportation, except for one at the Michael School. When a farmer needed to transport his food or silage, the veteran, for a nominal fee, carried the produce. Most people either walked or rode bicycles, and the same man who owned and maintained the old Fords kept the bicycles in working condition.

After a week, the locals knew Sasha Parsky and treated the new director of the school with reverence. In former times, only priests would have commanded the respect shown to Sasha, but of course priests were now pariahs. Father Zossima, in fact, lived a short distance from the school, and, but for his former status, Sasha would have employed the shy and amiable man to teach Latin and Greek. After the school year had started, to assist the poor fellow, who resembled a pole streaming rags, Sasha surreptitiously paid him for tutoring students struggling with declensions and other academic demons.

The former director of the school also lived in Balyk, which was barely a village, much less a town. His name was Avram Brodsky. He had been denounced by one of his students for speaking favorably about the Left Opposition, a group formed in 1923 by Leon Trotsky in response to the rising tide of Stalinism. After the death of Vladimir Lenin, various men had vied for power, each of whom represented a trend in the Communist Party: right, left, and center. The Right (Nikolai Bukharin) argued for private ownership and capitalist policies in agriculture, retail trade, and light industry, with the state controlling heavy industry. The collectivization of farms, the Right contended, would be especially injurious to the peasants. The Center (Stalin) put their faith in the state and Party bureaucracy to forge a new country and economics. The Left (Trotsky) contended that Communism could succeed only if the Russian working class made common cause with workers and economists from across Europe. This group felt that revolution in one country was destined to fail, and thus promoted the internationalist traditions of all working classes.

Even with Stalin's iron grip on power, the Left and Right Opposition, though often at odds, worked for his downfall. At the mere mention of Stalin's long-standing nemesis, Trotsky, the Vozhd would froth at the mouth. When Trotsky fled the country, Stalin swore to hunt him down. Nikolai Bukharin, like Trotsky, a Jew, earned the Boss's contempt for his softness. Stalin was convinced that both splinter groups had to be cut down and, like chaff, thrown to the winds. But first, Sergei Kirov, Stalin's principal competition in the Politburo, would have to be killed. On December 1, 1934, an assassin shot Kirov outside his office. The murder became the justification for subsequent purges and show trials. Stalin led the nation to believe that a conspiracy was behind Kirov's death; but the arrests were actually designed to destroy all opposition to Stalin. Dissenters on both the left and the right were jailed in Moscow's infamous Lubyanka Prison, tortured, and made to confess, though some refused. Trials ensued and shortly thereafter executions or exile.

Brodsky, exiled for a year to a Kolyma work camp, returned with stories of the beastly conditions. He could be found in fair weather sitting in the small square of Balyk, next to the pond, with its low circling wall. The village elders plied him with cigarettes in return for his Kolyma tales. No one doubted his stories about the skeletal prisoners wrapped in rags from head to foot, nor his recounting of the hungry driven to eat tree roots and bark, but some of his descriptions seemed too horrific to believe: the women raped in the forest, the forced abortions, the lack of food, medicine, and blankets, the plank-board beds, the daily roll calls in which unruly prisoners were made to stand naked and barefoot in the below-zero weather, the daily prostitution of men and women, the hatred of the criminal prisoners for the political ones, the suicides, the rampant tuberculosis, and in general the treachery, as well as the goodness, of prisoners.

Bogdan Dolin, a Balyk kulak, so-called because he had at one time employed laborers on his land and lent money at interest, had actually served time in Kolyma for counterfeiting rubles and forging documents that ostensibly came from the Supreme Soviet exempting his farm from appropriation. He never failed to glare when Brodsky would sit on the low wall of the pond, recounting his experiences to men and boys sitting cross-legged in the dirt. A squat, sinewy man, Dolin had a halo of wild white hair, which the locals referred to as his death cap, because it resembled the top of a poisonous mushroom. His steely torso—he had worked field and forge both—made him a formidable foe. Unlike most bronzed farmers, Dolin had an ashen face. His detractors attributed his coloring to his icy behavior, particularly toward Brodsky, whom he clearly and mysteriously disliked.

For his part, Brodsky lived alone in a small state-owned cottage, with numerous books and a lovely garden of lilacs and lindens. Boris Filatov had advised Sasha to call on the erstwhile director to learn about the area, the school, the students, and the government's academic expectations.

Before the start of school, Sasha invited Avram to join him for a day of fishing. But Avram replied that "a proper chat required a proper setting." Sasha had thought a lakeside would do, but found himself one afternoon in Avram's sitting room having tea.

The man resembled a Dostoyevskian intellectual. He had a narrow face with sunken cheeks that exaggerated his orbital bones and gave his pale-blue eyes a melancholy sadness. His thick, gray hair fell across a broad forehead, deeply lined from years of squinting and skepticism. His nose, scarred from a childhood fall that resulted in a nail piercing his septum, resembled a dried fig. His thin lips, light-blue eyes, tulip-stemmed, rooster-thin neck, and peculiarly lined hands suggested he had Scandinavian roots. But his large ears, spotty beard, and wispy chin hairs argued for a mix of Nordic and Asiatic genes. He smoked constantly, and his long fingers bore the telltale nicotine stains. His painfully thin, gangly body seemed to be trying to keep a step ahead of malnutrition, which gave his skin a parchment-like quality. To assuage the discomfort of cracked lips and knuckles, he frequently applied a petroleum jelly pomade. Like many serious readers, he had pince-nez hanging from a chain around his neck. In his case, the thick lenses indicated poor eyesight. He was wearing, as he did on most days, wrinkled brown corduroy pants and a black turtle-neck shirt that exhibited a few food stains.

His sitting room, encountered immediately when one entered the front door of the cottage (there was no back door), had a low ceiling, papered to keep the cracked plaster from falling. The wallpaper, a gloomy brown-on-brown lined design, was the type sold in state stores and seen in a million flats. Avram's heavy walnut furniture, upholstered in a dark red, rough Mohair, looked as if several generations had used it. The cottage also included three other rooms: the bathroom, with its zinc tub and taps in the shape of antlers; a kitchen, with a small coal stove, a table and four chairs, and a badly pitted soapstone sink; and a bedroom, with a single cot, an armoire, and a rickety cane chair.

Avram understandably loved the sitting room, with its small fireplace and lined bookcases that held finely tooled leather volumes in several languages. Sasha noted works by Victor Hugo, Alphonse Lamartine, Louis Musset, Alfred Vigny, and Voltaire. Brodsky also had a good collection of German writers: Engels, Fichte, Hegel, Heine, Marx. And of course there were the great Russian writers: Pushkin, Lermontov, Dostoevski, Tolstoy, Turgenev, and Chekhov, as well as the modernists, Akhmatova, Blok, Mandelstam, Pasternak, Tsvetaeva, and dozens of others, all or most on the forbidden list. Filatov had said that Brodsky was a gifted linguist who could read all the foreign languages of his collected books.

"I like a strong, smoky tea," said Brodsky, "the kind that comes from Malaysia. Did you know that Kenya has good teas? Would you like some milk in yours?"

"Please." After Avram fetched his ewer of fresh milk, Sasha told him about the Tsar who scoffed at the very idea of tea.

"Dead leaves!" exclaimed Brodsky, lighting a cigarette. "In this country we have thousands of them, perhaps millions, and they are not tea. They are apparatchiks and *oprichniki*, bootlickers trained to parrot the current Soviet line, with all its jargon and ideological phrases that reduce the functionaries to unfeeling automatons."

Sasha, aware that Filatov had wanted him to befriend Avram to gain information useful for the police, could have easily encouraged the former schoolmaster to continue, but he rather liked the man and knew that eschewing political conversations was in Avram's best interests. So Sasha steered their talk to the school.

Brodsky told him that none of the ten teachers could be trusted, and that he needed a good administrator who would report faithfully to him. "They all wished to succeed me as director. When you received your appointment, I knew they'd be unhappy. And as we both know, an unhappy Soviet citizen is an ideal informer. So watch your step." He had consumed the first cigarette and was now devouring another.

What was there to watch, thought Sasha? Learning was factually based. The school, Sasha explained, would not be teaching philosophy or ethics; he had already told his staff that he wanted a rigorous curriculum based on science, history, language, and literature.

Nearly choking on his tea, Brodsky sputtered, "Whose science, Mendel's or Lysenko's? History, from whose standpoint, the West or Stalin's? Which literature, that of the masters or of the favored authors who kowtow to the Vozhd? One wrong step and you'll be reported."

At that moment Sasha decided that Galina Selivanova could not only teach Russian grammar and French literature but also serve as his chief assistant. As for her promised position as a nurse, to hell with it. An extra pair of eyes was more important.

"In your history classes," asked Avram, "do you intend to cover the civil war and Trotsky's prominent role in it? As you know, Stalin was absent from the fighting."

Yes, the civil war would be a minefield, but so, too, would be the revolution. Any events contemporaneous with Stalin would have to feature him and, whether true or not, extol his heroic presence and glorious effect on socialism.

"The person who teaches Russian history at the school is a Stalinist," said Brodsky. "I wouldn't cross him if I were you. Let him teach whatever rubbish they poured into his head at teacher's college." He paused, lit another cigarette from the former, inhaled deeply, and sighed as he expelled the smoke. "Teachers' colleges! Now there's an oxymoron. Such places don't teach; they engage in soul murder. What's their subject matter? Pedagogy? Utter nonsense. The thousands of books and essays on the subject can be reduced to one good monograph, nothing more. These schools are fraudulent, wherever they occur, here or in the West. Unfortunately, a majority of your teaching staff come from them. The few who are actually knowledgeable hold degrees in science, mathematics, and linguistics. In the entire school there isn't a single teacher of literature who knows how to read a novel or a play or a poem. All they do is summarize plots and talk foolishness about rounded characters and class struggle. And even if a book is imbued with class struggle, once you point it out, what more is there to say? Are you going to use the book as an occasion to hold forth on the divinity of Marx and Lenin, and to lecture on the defects of capitalism and the virtues of socialism? And supposing all your pronouncements are true, what have they to do with the book? A book is its own truth."

The inadequate lighting from the two floor lamps in the sitting room was made all the dimmer by the tobacco smoke suspended in the airless room. Sasha could smell the nicotine on his skin and clothes. He wanted to run outside and feel the cleansing wind pass over him. When he heard rain spattering the small cottage windows, he relished the thought of standing in a downpour and having his clothes washed by what his mother used to call heaven's tears. Instead, he stood and examined some of the books in the room, turning pages and noting some of Avram's marginalia. At last, enough time had elapsed for him to make a polite exit, which he did, putting his face up to the rain and thinking of the adage: Anyone who says sunshine brings happiness has never danced in the rain.

That evening, he requested the train master send a cable to Galina: "Come at once. The school needs you." Although he had initially offered her a job for the spring, the fall term would shortly begin, and he knew he could use her immediately. If the other teachers wondered about this hasty appointment, he could win them over with the promise of lightened clerical work. In the fall, Galina could manage the front office and, in the spring, move into a classroom. He would arrange a school for Alya and lodging for Galina. In fact, she could, if she wished, share his farmhouse. He would gladly partition it, giving her an equal amount of space. The important thing was that she function as his eyes and ears, write the numerous reports required by the local Soviet, and relieve the current secretary, a sickly woman, ambient with anxiety over her many tasks. He asked Galina to respond at once. Fearing she would say no to his importunate request, perhaps because of her having to estrange herself from Viktor, he was delighted to receive a response the next day that said: "Will arrive Saturday next. Bring a wagon to the station. We have baggage. Appreciatively, Galina."

She had neglected to say whether she would be arriving on the morning or afternoon train. So Sasha paced the platform from 9:30 a.m. to 4:22 p.m. It was a velvet day, with the leaves already starting to paint the forest in fiery yellows, oranges, and golds, the fall colors that brought travelers from afar to see the trees ablaze in chlorophyll wonder. Galina exited with bags and her daughter in a shower of sunshine, as if descending from heaven in a halo of light. Sasha hoped it was a good augury.

Hugging them both, he helped carry their bags past the small station house to the clearing behind, where he had parked the school's old Model T truck that was mostly garaged because it suffered from age and a shortage of parts. Sasha crossed his fingers that the vehicle would make it back to the school without incident. The three of them strapped the luggage on the flatbed and climbed into the open cab. An accommodating farmer cranked the motor, knowing to cup the crank in his palm so that if the engine kicked back, the violent twisting would not break his wrist or his thumb. Sasha handed the farmer a few coins, honked the horn, winked at Alya, and took off in a cloud of blue exhaust. Drat! He had neglected to bring goggles for his guests to protect them from the dust of the roads. He wore a pair that made him look like a deep-sea diver. The dusty roads were also deeply rutted, and tested the springs of any vehicle. Sasha made it a point to ease around the furrows and drive with one side of the car on the smooth sides of the embankments.

They passed a lake that assured good fishing, but that would come later, Sasha promised. Avoiding any blowouts—the tires were bare!—Sasha made it back to the school in record time. He explained the housing situation, dire as it was throughout the Soviet Union, and offered to give Galina and Alya the farmhouse while he slept in a classroom that had, for some inexplicable reason, been home to an adipose couch. Galina seemed conflicted, but Alya begged that he join them in the farmhouse so that he could teach her how to play chess and could flip her in the air.

"We'll see," he said, "but first we have to carry the luggage inside, and you have to unpack."

He had told Galina about his willingness to divide the house, especially in light of her smoking. She said she was quitting. He frowned skeptically. Once the family had unpacked, Galina offered to make everyone dinner. Sasha readily accepted, given his execrable cooking. He showed her the larder, which was more plentifully stocked than her own flat in Ryazan, and opened a bottle of wine, of a local manufacture. They clicked glasses, toasted her new life, and watched Alya run off to the barn and the hayloft.

Grudgingly, Galina remarked, "She'll love it here."

"And you?"

"We'll just have to see."

She donned an apron he kept in the kitchen, sliced cucumbers and tomatoes, and prepared the trout that he had bought for the occasion. He watched as she deftly salted, peppered, and dipped the fishes in a mixture of eggs and milk, and rolled them gently in bread crumbs. Then she made black tea. For dessert they had blackberries and yogurt.

"I must admit," he said aimlessly stirring his tea, "I didn't think you'd come . . . not now . . . not until spring." Pause. "Why did you?" Pause. "My saying I needed you wasn't the reason, was it?"

Through the kitchen window they could see Alya agilely climbing down a rope from the hayloft. Galina pointed and replied, "That's the reason. I grew up in the country . . . among horses. . . . I wanted the same for Alya." She looked imploringly at Sasha. "You won't mind if we have a horse?"

In Ryazan, he had talked about the school and its former mission . . . and of course about the horses. Now she wanted one for her daughter. "Would a pony do?" Sasha asked. It would require less work and feed. But Galina knew equines. She would use her free time to look over the pasturage in the countryside, where she could both acquaint herself with the environs and evaluate the horseflesh. Then she'd decide. Her independence both frightened and excited Sasha, but where would it all lead?

When he introduced Galina to the teaching staff—five men, five women—they were seated in the smoking lounge, arrayed in a semicircle, with Sasha and his "woman," as she soon came to be called, at the front. Sergei Putin, the groundskeeper and handyman, was also present. A factotum, he immediately smiled ingratiatingly at Galina. The instructors, all but one graduates of teaching colleges, were filled with theories about "active" learning, class indoctrination, love of the motherland, alternation of subjects to keep boredom to a minimum, weekly testing, circular seating, and the use of printed questions (which never changed from one semester to the next) to ready students for each class. Writing assignments were usually descriptive—"How I spent May Day"—rather than analytical or argumentative. His staff would have to be schooled in writing arguments, not plot summaries.

The teachers lodged in Balyk, some with other families, some in their own modest homes. Filatov had mentioned the advantages of housing the faculty in a single building, but given the shortage of funds, that project would have to wait. All but one of the male teachers were married, and their spouses self-employed: in stitchery, baking, wine making, and the like. Semen Sestrov's wife was a painter specializing in miniature watercolors. None of the women teachers had married. Sasha's roster read as follows.

Men	Women
Astafurov, Leonid (Greek and Latin)	Chernikova, Vera (Chemistry)
Budian, Mikhail (Marxism)	Levanda, Elena (Fine Arts)
Glinski, Pavel (World History)	Oborskaia, Olga (Physics/Math)
Kotko, Benedik (Russian Literature)	Petrowa, Irina (Biology)
Sestrov, Semen (Russian History)	Rusakova, Anna (French/ German)

Sasha pictured his faculty as animals and plants. Leonid was anything but leonine. He was a hunched prairie dog with two large front teeth. Mikhail taught and looked like a wolf. Pavel's fat cheeks reminded him of an inflated frog, and Benedik, with his unruly beard and nose sprouting black hairs, brought to mind a porcupine. Semen, who fastidiously attended to his dress and appearance, was called "the rose." The women, too, resembled fauna and flora. Vera, tall and thin, recalled a giraffe; Elena, she of the delicate hands, an orchid; Olga, he swore, could have passed for a wild boar, including the protruding tusks; Irina Petrowa, the dissecting artist, had the instincts of a hyena, always scavenging; and sweet Anna, the lilac, always arrived at school pickled in perfume.

Reading the expressions and posture of his staff, Sasha saw a range of emotions regarding Galina, from "She's here to spy on us" to "I'll just wait and watch"; from "She's quite a pretty woman" to "Clearly, she's a harlot." To relieve the tension, Sasha explained that the current secretary, Mrs. Berberova, had long needed help in the office. Galina would oversee enrollment applications, student transcripts, state financial aid, housing arrangements (most of the students boarded with local families or commuted), and counseling. In the spring, she would assume additional responsibilities, academic ones, as she was qualified to teach Russian grammar, which staff members found onerous, and French language and literature.

Anna, currently teaching French, asked, with downcast eyes, "In the spring, am I to give up my spot for *her*?"

"No, Galina will teach beginning French, and you the advanced courses. I am sure Galina can learn a great deal from you."

A satisfied Anna relaxed her shoulders and settled back into her chair. She even swept her wispy hair from her face.

Vera sat stiffly and pouted. Never one to speak directly, she struck poses. Sasha asked her to state her concern.

"Will the teaching staff still have the final say about admissions or will *she*?"

"The staff."

Vera conspicuously sighed in relief.

Sergei, he of the oily smile and bad breath, wanted to know whether Devora Berberova would still be in charge of the financial transfers that came from the state to the school. He seemed to be in her thrall. Sasha suspected that she occasionally dipped into money that belonged to the school. How else to explain the costly gifts that the gossipers said she showered on Sergei?

"I am introducing a new accounting system," replied Sasha, "one that Galina is familiar with."

She glanced at him skeptically but did not question his statement, though she did remark that she regarded the school as exceptional owing to the outstanding qualifications and dedication of the teaching staff. Sasha suppressed an ironic cough, since he had already told Galina that both the staff and curriculum needed overhauling.

"Where will you be living?" asked Semen, who always had an eye for a pretty woman.

When Galina glanced at him, Sasha feared that he'd have to answer the question mincingly, but a second later she bravely spoke up:

"At the moment, as you know, I am staying in the farmhouse, which is not a satisfactory arrangement. But the director intends to have a wall built and make two living quarters out of one, for privacy and decency. Have you a better suggestion?"

A flustered Semen, not expecting a question in return, acknowledged the shortage of housing and said that the director's plan sounded reasonable to him.

"Any further questions?" asked Sasha.

"Just one," replied Elena. "Will my counseling duties be curtailed? I am, after all, the only one on staff, who holds three degrees, in psychology, art history, and education."

Whatever the occasion, Elena never failed to tout her three degrees, even though her sclerotic personality made her an ineffective counselor. The students much preferred talking to Devora Berberova, who had about her a genuine warmth. Teachers and students alike often lodged complaints; thus the eventual announcement that Galina would be sharing the counseling was greeted enthusiastically.

The group then recessed for tea and biscuits, after which Galina absented herself, and Sasha took the occasion to revisit his ideas about academic standards.

"When classes begin, I trust that we can overcome our old habits. Instead of asking the question 'how,' we should be asking the question 'why.' Why, for example, does Macbeth fall prey to the inducements of his wife? The how question can lead only to summary, not analysis. In science, for example, instead of asking for the names of phyla and taxonomies, give the students that information, and then make them apply it. Take vertebrates, five classes of them, right, Irina?"

"Right!"

"Asking students to repeat fish, amphibians, reptiles, birds, and mammals accomplishes little. Better to give them the list and ask why reptiles are included. We would, then, be testing not whether they had memorized the list, but whether they could apply to snakes the characteristics of vertebrates: spinal cord, central nervous system, internal skeleton, muscular system, and brain case." Sasha paused and looked around, noting his colleagues' discomfort. "I realize it's a seismic shift to move from how to why, but unless you have a better suggestion, I can see no other way to teach our students to extrapolate and think critically. Can you?"

Mikhail reminded the assembly that Soviet education had always proceeded on the principle of rote learning. "In fact, I can repeat *Eugene Onegin* word for word because of the training I had. Memory is more important than . . ."

Before he could finish, Sasha interrupted him. "No one is disparaging memory. I am merely adding another level: analysis. Surely, you don't object to that?"

But the teachers knew that once the camel gets his nose in the tent, the body will soon follow. Give an inch, and then it's a mile. Students trained in critical thinking would soon be asking questions that could endanger everyone. Instead of the usual Soviet catechism, students would ask why this form of government and not another; why this leader and not someone else; why this approach to learning and not the old way or the Talmudic way or the Socratic way? As John Donne had said, "A new philosophy calls all in doubt."

Sasha encouraged his colleagues to talk openly about the history of the school and the staff. He wished to avoid the pitfalls of the past, and feared falling into a trap similar to the one that had ensnared Avram Brodsky. But his colleagues spoke only grudgingly. The best he could elicit from them was the observation that he should let common sense be his guide. But common sense without historical memory is virtually useless. From whence comes the sense? If it's common, then it must have a track record. What Sasha wanted to know did not issue from common wisdom. For example: Why had some teachers and students failed in the past while others succeeded? Could one discern trends or patterns?

Reminded that the school office had several filing cabinets of old records, Sasha replied that he had diligently read them and not a one bore on the history of the school, staff, and students. They had been purged. By whom? His colleagues merely shrugged, although Elena had a vague memory of two men using a dolly to wheel boxed files out of the office. Their destination? She had no idea. Looking around for help, Elena met only cold stares.

"If not for my counseling duties," she said, delicately stroking the air, "I would never have seen the files being removed."

To reinvent the wheel simply wasted everyone's time, Sasha observed. All of the current staff had served under Avram Brodsky. Surely, they could tell the new director "something" about the former one. "He lives within walking distance of the school," said Sasha. "It's not as if he disappeared."

"Oh," remarked Benedik Kotko, "he disappeared all right. For over a year. And no one in this room wants to touch the subject. It's poison."

Sasha let the subject drop.

When the staff left the meeting, they were not inflamed with the spirit of discovery but rather with the desirability of denunciation. This new director was challenging old truths and settled habits. To no one's surprise, Comrade Boris Filatov soon arrived. Wearing a neatly pressed military tunic, he wanted to discuss the direction of instruction at the school. But first he would meet with the staff, including Galina, and then Sasha. If forewarned is forearmed, Galina would tell Sasha about the encounter with Filatov, who would undoubtedly employ his usual candid style.

"Citizen Parsky!" said Filatov, spreading a newspaper before he sat on the stained and ragged couch in Sasha's office. "I received your report about meeting with Galina Selivanova and Viktor Harkov. In light of your initial reticence to visit these people, or should I say reluctance, I would never have guessed that you would offer Galina Selivanova a position. Viktor Harkov, too?"

"No, Comrade Filatov, just Galina."

"So, you're already on a first-name basis, but why wouldn't you be, since she is living with you." Pause. "Pretty woman."

"Looks can be deceiving."

"Are you punning? Do you mean the living arrangements or the woman's appearance?" Filatov removed his silver cigarette case, and then remembered that Sasha abstained from nicotine. He decided as a courtesy to deny himself the pleasure.

Sasha smiled in appreciation. "You raise several issues, Comrade Filatov: Galina's hiring, our living arrangements, and her attractiveness. As a matter of fact, the three are related. When I met the mother and daughter, I was much taken with the little girl and depressed by their living conditions. I knew that if I offered Galina Selivanova a job at the school, she could improve her standard of living—and the child's. Her good looks are an added bonus. By the way, did you know that she has a superb singing voice? She has started a choir. The students adore her." Sasha, who had been sitting behind his modest desk, with three wall portraits looking down on him—Marx, Lenin, and Stalin—went to his bookcase and removed a volume. He rustled through several pages and then quoted:

"'Music hath charms to soothe a savage breast.' Do you know the author of those words, Comrade Filatov?"

Although a cultured man, Filatov was not often asked questions of this kind. "Shakespeare."

"William Congreve, Act 1, Scene 1, from *The Mourning Bride*."

A bit annoyed, Filatov asked, "And the point of this exercise?"

"I knew you'd say Shakespeare. Everyone does. But it only goes to prove that majority thinking is not always right."

Filatov removed a cigarette and lit up. Would he now excoriate Sasha for his forwardness? Through a mouthful of smoke, he said, "Point well taken." Yet again Filatov had proved he was a different kind of OGPU officer, a more sophisticated and cunning one.

"With the deplorable state of housing in Balyk, I decided that since the farmhouse needed renovation and was large enough for two families, I would move in mother and child. Our living arrangement is perfectly innocent, irrespective of the whispers you hear."

Filatov looked around for a place to tip his ashes and decided on the palm of his hand. "I have heard nothing."

"That's good, if true."

"*True* that I've heard nothing or *good* that I've heard nothing?"

"I hope both."

Filatov appropriated the metal trash bin next to Sasha's desk, tipped in the ashes, and snuffed out his cigarette, leaving behind the stub, which now exuded a foul smell. "You are a clever lad, Citizen Parsky, perhaps too clever for your own good. I think we need to talk about education, Soviet education, and how you are expected to disseminate Party truths."

What followed was a stock speech that Filatov had given to a hundred schoolmasters in his lifetime. He, in fact, liked this part of his police work, "instructing instructors about proper Party instruction," as he liked to phrase it, convinced that the repetitions were not only witty but also pedagogically useful. He droned on about why the world functions as it does, and how it ought to function. He explained how ideologies became dominant and grew into systems based on religious, legal, and political beliefs.

"But where does the class struggle and the working man fit in? They don't, because the needs of the laborer are always ignored. Soviet education has to fill that omission in every discipline, from economics to literature to science. Social class is the crucible in which all else is forged. Since every class has its values, we should not be surprised to find that self-interest and selfishness are paramount. Take the example of commodities. The ruling classes have convinced us that *value* inheres in the product itself, when actually the value is external, added to it through labor. But does the worker receive his fair share of the profits? No. The ruling classes argue that if not for their investments, the product would never have come to market. So money trumps labor. This truism can be found in every aspect of society, and every student must be taught to see it."

In response to Sasha's question, Filatov said that Avram Brodsky had been allowed to return to Balyk after his year in Kolyma but could not leave the area. "Internal exile," said Filatov. "You would be doing us all a great favor if you could draw the man out. I fear he may still be secretly active in the Left Opposition. Learn what you can. The three R's: What is he reading, ruminating about, and 'riting?"

Sasha explained that he had no taste for politics, and that he and Brodsky talked mostly about literature. If he now introduced politics, surely Brodsky would be suspicious.

"Work into it slowly. You can use literature. Ask about a Marxist approach to your friend Congreve, for example. See where the discussion leads, and report back to me. In fact, I intend to call on him myself. Perhaps I can induce him to tell me about the people and ideas he admires. Some friends! They cost him his directorship."

All of Balyk had an opinion about Filatov frequently passing through Brodsky's gate and entering his cottage. Some hazarded that Filatov's visits were a warning to Brodsky to stay clear of trouble; others said he came to elicit information, which, if not forthcoming, could cost Avram his life. The teachers at the Michael School were particularly energetic in their suppositions and fantasies, each one advancing a different theory about the former director: that Brodsky worked for the secret police because his elderly parents had been threatened with exile; that he was secretly married to a Soviet agent or to a Trotskyist to whom he reported; that he and Sasha had made common cause to spy on the faculty; that he was an anarchist; that he was a Zionist urging Jews to leave the country for Palestine; that he had a shortwave radio that he used to stay in communication with the émigré communities in Paris and Berlin; that he could conjure spirits that conveyed his message to the netherworld; that he poisoned farmers' cattle and wells; that he preferred men to women; that he was a distant relative of Filatov; that he had escaped a longer prison term in Kolyma because the authorities regarded him as privy to traitorous plots, all of which he shared with the secret police. And so on. The one thing about which everyone could agree was the man was an enigma. Even though the teachers at the Michael School had served under him for many years, those same people now claimed that Brodsky had been a demon with supernatural powers, leading them to behave in ways they would normally have avoided. In a word, like all Jews, he communed with the devil. Had it not been for his occult powers and his chthonic connections, they would have denounced him when he was first appointed to direct the school.

"A word, Comrade Director." Sasha invited Vera Chernikova into his office. She sat across from him, with her skirt just above the knee, exhibiting handsome legs. Her perfume rose like incense, hovering in the room and clinging to his clothes. The scent followed her like a contrail. "I am not alone in my concerns." But before Sasha could ask their source, she continued. "Others, like Olga Oborskaia, share them. Nepotism has become a problem in our schools. This new woman, Galina . . . are you grooming her to succeed you? She will undoubtedly feel entitled if you make her your second in command."

"She is more an aide-de-camp than a school official or officer."

"When Director Brodsky left, we were led to believe that his successor would come from the ranks, a teacher who worked *and achieved* more than required, a sort of Stakhanovite teacher. But that never happened. Major Filatov felt new blood was needed, an attitude that I quite understand. But a new person has no knowledge of the school's history and traditions, as you are undoubtedly discovering. I would hope that one of your first official acts will be to designate the next in line."

"Have you any suggestions?"

"It would be forward of me to advance my own name. I leave that to others. But I would mention Olga Oborskaia and Semen Sestrov."

Sasha asked ironically, "Are directors so short-lived that before they even settle in, the staff prepare for their departure?"

"We in the Soviet Union are changing the world every day. One must be prepared for the coming Utopia. I am merely acting in the spirit of revolution and change. I'm sure you understand."

"Absolutely, and I thank you for your concern."

He saw her to the door and gave her a firm handshake.

Given Sasha's own specialty in Soviet history, he told Semen Sestrov, who taught a course in the Russian Civil War, he would like to observe his class. Semen was flattered to be the first teacher Sasha visited. The ten o'clock class had a full enrollment, and the students were exceptionally earnest and well behaved. One brave student asked about the role of various leaders in the conflict. When Stalin's name surfaced, as Sasha had hoped, he waited to hear Semen explain Koba's minimal contributions to the Russian Revolution.

"The Vozhd," said Sestrov, "was raising money from the Baku oil barons, and was fomenting rebellion in Georgia through his underground activities."

"Why," asked the same student, "does the traitor Trotsky and his ilk say that the Vozhd played no role, and that he may, at one time, have been in the employ of the Cheka?"

"As a double agent," replied Sestrov, skillfully evading the fact that Stalin played little or no role in the civil war.

Education was always a dicey affair. The Tsarist rulers, in need of bureaucrats to staff the many government agencies, had found it necessary to expose their servitors to modern Western ideas, and therein was the problem. A few of them, influenced by nonauthoritarian ideas, grew into disaffected radicals who challenged Tsarist rule. Sasha wondered how many among the current students at his school would become free thinkers, and what kind of changes would they clamor for? Despite his bitter disapproval, Sasha knew the Soviet reasoning for the vast surveillance system found in every school and university. In the Michael School, which classrooms were or were not bugged provided a wealth of humor, though it was no joke that some of the teachers were probably on the Cheka payroll.

One morning Sasha arrived in his office to find Goran Youzhny, his staged cell mate. He handed Sasha a letter with orders from Filatov to find lodging and a lab for "Comrade Youzhny, a friend of the OGPU," who was now honing his skills as a police photographer. The storyteller Bella Zeffina's house would fit the bill, but Sasha explained that the school had no room for a lab. Goran thanked him and replied that all he needed was a small space. And in the near future, would Sasha mind if he came to the farmhouse with his camera for a story he'd like to write about the school and the new director? Sasha agreed, and Goran left. But the idea of a falsely confessed killer, an OGPU friend, showing up with a letter from Filatov and the need for a lab troubled Sasha.

A few days later, on a chill autumn afternoon, with the daylight threatening to prematurely quit the sky, Goran drove up on a motorcycle with a sidecar holding a handsome box camera and tripod. He formally introduced himself to Galina and Alya, and immediately set up his camera on the grass, snapping a number of pictures of the farmhouse and barn, some just of the structures and some with Sasha and the mother and daughter. Inside the house, he arranged lamps and lights to allow him to photograph various rooms, again with and without the principals.

When Sasha asked wasn't the film prohibitively expensive, Goran conspiratorially replied, "We have a friend, don't we?"

"In a celluloid factory?" Sasha joked.

Moving into the barn for more shots, Goran observed that it wouldn't take a great deal of carpentry to turn one of the stables into a photo-processing lab. If Sasha agreed, and if money could be found for the remodeling, Goran volunteered to assume responsibility for maintaining the chemicals and equipment. He would even be glad to show Sasha and the Selivanovs how to develop film.

"I'll make inquiries," said Sasha, not at all happy at the prospect of being watched.

They were standing in the barn and Alya, as usual, was in the hayloft swinging on a rope that Sasha had doubled and fashioned into a swing. To exit the barn quickly, Alya frequently uncoiled the rope and dropped it from the hayloft door and repelled to the ground. Goran focused his camera on Alya swinging, but Sasha knew the light was insufficient for a good picture and the camera not good enough to capture an object in motion. Goran snapped it anyway, and then began to fold up his camera and tripod.

"The money?" asked Sasha.

"What?"

"It will take a large sum."

With a dismissive wave of the hand, he replied, "Our mutual friend will help."

Galina had silently watched the scene develop and asked enigmatically, "Tell me, Goran, will the pictures tell a story, one hidden in the film?"

Her question, which sounded innocent enough, discomfited Goran. He stuttered, fumbled with the camera, and tripped over the tripod, as he edged to his motorcycle and sidecar. Sasha stood amazed, but Galina, her arms folded across her chest, impassively watched the young man depart.

"A picture," she said, "is like a book. It lends itself to many interpretations. Now we'll just have to wait."

"For what?" asked a confused Sasha.

"The official reading."

Not surprisingly, money and a ukase materialized to build a photo-processing lab in the barn. Carpenters, electricians, and plumbers came and went silently. They arrived not from Balyk but from afar. Sasha knew a Muscovite just from his walk. Who had sent them and who was bearing the cost remained a mystery until Goran volunteered that his uncle was close to the Politburo and to Boris Filatov.

When Sasha related to Brodsky what he called "the Goran story," Brodsky said, "He'll denounce you." Then he lit a cigarette and leaned back in his chair.

"On the basis of what?" asked Sasha, sipping his tea.

"You really are credulous," replied Brodsky. "Lemon?"

"No, thank you."

"The photographs."

"They're perfectly harmless."

"Unless altered."

"To what end?"

"To incriminate you."

"I fail to see the purpose?"

"A purpose can always be found. Isn't that what the Soviets say, 'Everyone is guilty of some crime'?"

"I can't imagine . . ."

"Sasha, for all your education, you're still a country boy. Just look at the magazines and newspapers and periodicals. The photography is always being altered."

He then went on to explain the vast educational and ideological potential of photography. Daily and weekly publications issued idealized scenes of daily life in the Bolshevik paradise. They interpreted Soviet culture and shaped Soviet mass consciousness. Given the huge number of people in the country who couldn't read and write, the government was forced to rely heavily on pictures and photography. Although magazine design used different kinds of illustrations, photography was especially valued for its low cost and ease of reproduction.

"And one cannot overestimate the importance of the artist-retoucher," Avram added. "Given the poor quality of our photographic materials and the technical limitations of our developing processes, we need people to touch up the pictures. Our art schools turn out hundreds of these 'restorers.' They are expert at photomontage . . . and a major force in promoting Socialist Realism."

"I may be a country boy, but I know the difference between the real and the imagined. May I never see another article and picture about Russian motherhood, industrialization, state festivals, our beloved leaders, and the heroics of Stakhanovites. You'd think that Russia never accomplished anything before the revolution."

"This Goran fellow you mention," probed Avram, like a good scholar, "when you look at his photographs, check to see if he's combined parts from separate images and glued them together. Often you can see the joining lines. Also, see if the pictures were photographed under different lighting conditions. If they were, they'll look artificial."

His face etched in concern, Sasha nodded. He would ask Goran to show him the photographs, which he would study closely with Galina. Finding Goran would involve no more than stepping next door. Once the photo lab had been built, Goran spent most of his time developing film and mixing the chemicals and tinctures of his trade.

"Of course," said Goran, when Sasha requested to see the pictures, which he willingly passed on. Galina wondered why Goran hadn't volunteered to show them his work before now, and she crossly wondered why Sasha had waited until Brodsky had sounded a warning.

Sitting on either side of a floor lamp, Sasha and Galina pored over the pictures. Her literary training gave her an advantage in explication. He tended to ignore the details in favor of the broad sweep of the landscape. At first glance, none of the pictures looked incriminating, except perhaps one, in which Sasha's hand, unseen behind Galina's back, could be construed to mean that he was patting her derriere. But so what? Perhaps they had become lovers. Sasha's contract didn't forbid intimacy or, for that matter, marriage. In fact, he wished for the first and often thought of the second.

"Have you heard about all those photographs," asked Galina, "in which Trotsky has been expunged?" She placed a hand over an image. "Supposing I disappear from this picture and Brodsky replaces me?"

"He's never come to the farmhouse."

"Prove it!"

"Yes, I know. You can't prove a negative."

"And speaking of negatives, I suggest that one of these evenings we peek in the lab to study them for changes, if they're even there."

The lab had been constructed professionally, and the equipment, top of the line. At the time of its installation, Sasha had watched with envy, wishing that the school's chemistry and physics labs were this modern. Nothing like knowing the right people.

Ironically, the wall that now divided the farmhouse had brought Sasha and Galina closer. With their newfound privacy, they lived more communally than separately, glad that when the occasion warranted they could retreat to their own quarters. The dividing line between the two flats was, of course, no line at all to Alya. She treated them both equally. In a number of ways, Sasha was a better parent to Alya than was Galina, who mistakenly believed that good behavior rested on an adherence to rules. But Sasha knew, as did Alya, that some rules are simply fatuous, and therefore Sasha, to Alya's delight and Galina's initial annoyance, ignored them. But slowly the mother came to see that as the child's imagination bloomed, her manners improved. Appreciative of the liberties that Sasha extended to her, Alya rarely if ever abused them. Galina, noting the joy of her daughter in the presence of Sasha, observed:

"I think she prefers you to me."

"What she prefers," replied Sasha, "is what we all appreciate: freedom. She is a rare child because at her age she already knows the difference between freedom and license. And so should you."

"Me?"

"Just because you have the power to discipline her doesn't mean you should always exercise it. Independence is the flower of freedom and ought to be nurtured."

At the time, Galina's annoyance was palpable, as she asked herself, how dare this "stranger" tell her how to raise her daughter? But after some reflection, she realized that the word "parent" is merely a synonym for "authority," not "affection." Moreover, hadn't Sasha built Alya a swing in the barn, taught her to ride a bicycle, took her on nature hikes, and left licorice on the doorstep for her well-being? (He denied this last act of kindness, perhaps because Galina opposed herbal medicines.) In addition, he had made it possible for Galina to have a good academic position and comfortable living quarters. If nothing else, she enjoyed the intellectual energy that Sasha exuded. To be around him was to visit foreign places through the life of the mind. Even Alya experienced the thrill of living in ideas and other climes, especially when Sasha read her stories from Greek mythology.

The evening they entered the photo lab, Galina found herself clinging to Sasha's arm, for safety or affection. She herself didn't know which, but she liked having him next to her. A number of photographs stood in drying racks and some hung from clips attached to a wire. To one side rested a printer with two cables plugged into a socket. The workbench held chemicals and developing fluids of various kinds. Anyone could see from the bottles and equipment and bench that Goran was fastidious about his labors. In a four-drawer wooden filing cabinet, he had organized his prints according to people and places, and had distinguished between single and group photographs. Sasha mentally estimated the immense cost of the laboratory equipment and the film.

As well as school scenes, Goran had taken pictures of the village and woods, of the farmers and their animals. Here was a picture of a wooden plough, and here a woman giving suck to an infant. Sasha saw portraits of young and old, of drunks and dolts, of preening couples and pretty housewives, of vixens and veterans, of Galina and him, of Alya, and several, for whatever reason, of Devora Berberova. Goran had captured local scenes: the cemetery, tombstones, a cenotaph, the inn, a field of rapeseed, a haystack, a rutted road, a stately oak, a pond, a stream, a lake, a sunset and a sunrise, a gathering storm, a rain-spattered window. The number and types of photographs constituted an epic catalogue.

A folder titled "Metamorphosis" held altered photographs. People from different centuries were juxtaposed. Filatov, for example, was standing next to the late Tsar, and Pushkin, his visage taken from a painting, was peering around a curtain at a reclining naked woman, one of Rubens' nudes. Stalin was seated at a dinner table with a napkin tucked under his chin, a knife in one hand, a fork in the other, and on the plate in front of him rested the head of Leon Trotsky. A number of the original Bolsheviks who had played prominent roles during the revolution or in Lenin's government, for instance, Bukharin and Kamenev and Zinoviev, were posed in a chorus line, wearing tutus and kicking up their legs. The Lubyanka Prison had been redesigned to look like a fashionable apartment house.

Several full-body portraits of Trotsky and the recently disgraced head of the secret police, Genrikh Yagoda, had been cropped, perhaps waiting for some future juxtaposition. In one of the folders, Galina found a snapshot of several men at the Balyk pond. She put it on the zinc counter and reached for a magnifying glass, which she slowly moved until resting on a fixed point.

"What do you see?" asked Sasha, but she didn't respond.

He looked over her shoulder. From the position of the glass, she seemed to be scrutinizing some man standing alone and in profile.

Nothing unusual about the man attracted his eye. She adjusted the overhead laboratory lamp so that its narrow beam of light captured the subject. When she finally looked up, she stared past Sasha into the darkness, as if trying to locate a spectral being.

After a silence that felt like a thousand years, she said simply, "He's not dead."

"Who?"

"Petr."

"Petr Selivanov?"

"My husband."

"You must be mistaken!" he said with more alarm than he intended.

Sasha took the magnifying glass and, as Galina pointed, pored over the photograph. It was not the man he had slain and whose head he had severed. Having stared into its lifeless eyes, he could never forget the face. But he had no means of objecting without revealing his guilt. All he could do was ask if Galina was sure.

"Notice the licorice root he's sucking on. He was always touting its medicinal value. It's the same as the licorice roots I've found on the front steps of the farmhouse that I thought you had left. At the time, I found the coincidence eerie." She paused. "I suppose it's his way of saying he's back . . . he's returned."

Without weighing his words, Sasha blurted, "But if he's here, who was the person in the slicker?"

Galina moved the overhead light so that it shone on Sasha's face, temporarily blinding him. "What are you talking about?" she interrogated. "Which slicker?"

"The police said that Petr was wearing a rain slicker and Alexander was not."

Blinded by the light, he felt that she was eyeing him warily. It was vitally important, then, for him to tread carefully and not reveal information that only the murderer could know.

"What else did the police tell you?"

"Will you please put that light out! We can talk in the farmhouse or outside, if you prefer."

"Outside. I don't want Alya to hear."

Sasha returned all the folders to the cabinet and made sure that the premises showed no signs of their having been present. He then followed Galina into the cold moonlight. They were both shivering. This discussion would have to be brief.

"You never shared with me what the police told you about the murders. When I asked how Petr and Alexander were killed, I was told they were shot, and the killers got away. Is that true?"

"As far as I know." He tried to put an arm around her shoulders to keep her warm, but she shrugged him off.

Her next comment found him unready. "The secret police don't award plum positions unless they get something in return, or unless they are repaying some favor. Does one of those explanations fit you, and if so, which?"

It took him a moment to clear his head. In the moonlight, Galina's eyes reflected a crepuscular coldness. He suddenly felt pierced by silver shafts. "Neither," he replied.

Holding him in her gaze for a disquieting few seconds, she at last turned away and returned to the house. He gathered that her frigid behavior had something to do with Petr's return, which was clearly unwelcome. But had he actually appeared, or was she mistaking him for someone else? In the house, he cautiously asked if she had a photograph of her husband. Having seen the profile of the man in Goran's photograph, he would draw his own conclusion about their similarities. Galina went to her valise and removed a box that she used as a safe to store pictures and papers and the few valuable pieces of jewelry she owned. Extricating a small picture in a cheap wooden frame, she wordlessly handed it to Sasha. He studied it, nodded in agreement, returned the picture, and exited to his side of the farmhouse, where he opened a bottle of vodka, which he rarely drank. He sat at the kitchen table with a shot glass and, with shaking hands, threw back three glassfuls before he began to calm down. He could hear from the other side of the wall Galina crying. Tears filled his own eyes. He had killed a man whose life he was blind to. After two more drinks, he tried to analyze the dangerous situation in which he now found himself, but his mind was hazy from drink. So he slipped into his winter jacket and left the house for a walk in the bracing cold, now flecked with snow.

He stopped under an oak that still had its leaves, albeit wrinkled and brown. As the wet snow fell and quickly dissolved, he likened the flakes to a life span. From the moment of birth we are, with varying degrees of strength, falling, descending, heading in one direction. We escape dissolution, we escape, we escape, until . . .

Was the man Sasha murdered Petr's friend Martyn Lipnoski? Even Filatov thought the dead man was Petr Selivanov; or did he? And how had Selivanov escaped, leaving behind his diary? Sasha told himself to start with the facts. Although facts lend themselves to different interpretations, one must always begin with the known. The meanings or nuances will come later. Fact: Sasha had killed and buried two men, one with a wallet on his person and the other not. The man with a wallet had an identification card bearing the name Alexander S. Harkov. Everyone seemed to agree he was dead. His colleague and co-policeman, Petr Selivanov, owned a diary that said he'd given a slicker to a fellow policeman, Martyn Lipnoski, who had grabbed a ride with Alexander and Petr, after spending the night with a whore in an inn, where he had lost his wallet and papers or been robbed. At the time that Alexander and Petr gave him a ride, Martyn owned only his clothes, which were in a disheveled state. The three men remained together until the truck reached a rise above the Parsky house. Alexander and Martyn drank. Here the facts ended, and the suppositions began. If, for some reason, Martyn and Petr had changed places in the truck, and if Petr had set out for home on foot, neglecting to take his diary, how far had Petr proceeded before looking back? If he had not looked back, the next question was moot; if he had, how much had he seen?

At least Sasha now knew what Petr looked like, but did Petr know what Sasha looked like? The best course, if at all possible, was for Sasha to avoid meeting Petr. In pulp novels, witnesses to a murder are in danger of being "eliminated," but under no circumstances would Sasha entertain harming Petr. If Petr came forth and identified Sasha as the killer, Sasha would defend himself with the not-unreasonable argument that from such a distance as the rise in the road—a distance of at least fifty meters, in a heavy rain with a truck partially blocking the view—it would have been virtually impossible to identify the slayer. He would point out that from the rise, all that one could have seen was someone digging in the field and burying two large objects. At this moment, Sasha wished he had buried them in the barn, under the feed bin.

Strangely, Petr's return caused Sasha no jealousy regarding Galina; rather he felt that his closeness with Alya might be compromised. Licorice, indeed! Now he knew the source—and worried that Petr might not only alienate Alya's affections, but also incriminate him. Perhaps Petr could be bought off? But bribery, even when it worked, as it had so successfully for hundreds of years, required money or goods or land, and Sasha had none of these riches. Perhaps if Galina no longer wished to continue her marriage, she'd divorce him and send him on his way; but still there was Alya. Would Petr go gently into the night without the child? Not likely. Nor would Sasha, in his place. Some other means had to be found. He would speak to Brodsky. After all, hadn't the former director warned him about Goran and doctored photographs and photomontage, and hadn't that warning led to the discovery that Petr Selivanov still lived? Without telling Brodsky the whole story, merely that a wayward husband who had once deserted his wife had returned, he hoped to find a solution to the Petr problem.

"Denounce the bastard before he denounces you!" bellowed Brodksy, leaning forward in his favorite armchair and warming his hands at the fireplace. A cigarette burned in an ashtray at his elbow, and a cloud of smoke hung overhead. Sasha coughed, not at Brodsky's idea, but from the suffocating miasma. Brodsky, however, misunderstood. "So you don't like my idea. What's your objection?"

Without clarifying the confusion, Sasha merely said, "I've told you before. I abhor denouncers. The country is overrun with them."

Leaning back, Brodsky assumed an avuncular manner as he explained that most denouncers were self-serving morons who wanted their neighbor's apartment or their manager's job. "But think of the other side of it," he coaxingly said, "the transparent side. For a country to proceed without corruption and nepotism and sabotage, that is, for a country to protect itself against its enemies and defend its revolution, it must depend on loyal citizens to denounce the disloyal. Denunciation has an ethical aspect. Would you not warn your students if you found that a terrorist had planted a ticking bomb in the school? I trust that if you knew someone was intending to harm me, you would have the decency to tell me—and to identify the swine. It's that kind of denunciation I condone and call transparency."

Try as he might, Sasha could not think of some criminal behavior of Petr Selivanov that would justify denunciation, and he told Avram so. But Brodsky simply lit another cigarette and continued.

"Either you have misrepresented the situation or you are justifying it. Didn't you tell me that the man ran away from his wife and left a child behind? If that's not a crime, what is?"

Sasha bit his lip and said, "Perhaps I overstated the case. He actually loves his daughter. He even leaves licorice for her care."

"Aha!" said Brodsky, pouncing on that disclosure. "He sounds like a quack. As you know, licorice comes from a powerful root and has medicinal powers. People with heart problems and high blood pressure, for example, are told to avoid it. And here we have a father feeding a dangerous root, or what could be dangerous, to his daughter. It's malpractice of a sort, and the man isn't even a doctor. There are your grounds for denunciation! Trust me."

"I couldn't."

"Then why have you come to ask my advice? Either you want the man gone, permanently gone, or you don't."

Sasha shook his head and laughed dryly. "At this moment, I'm not sure. Let me think it over and come back."

Pulling on his cigarette and slowly expelling the smoke through both his nose and mouth, like a veritable dragon, Avram said softly, "As you like. I'm always here for you." Sasha was hardly out the door when Brodsky asked him to remain for just a second, went to a bookcase, and removed a thin book of collected essays. "Read this and tell me what you think. I value your opinion."

With the book in hand, Sasha left. It wasn't until he reached home that he looked at the title and author: *The Left Opposition,* by Karl Radek. He knew enough about Radek to hide the book in a stewing pot on the top shelf of his kitchen cabinet.

Late that evening, with the Victrola playing Beethoven, Sasha leaned back in his rocking chair and reviewed what he knew about Radek, a figure whom he had discussed in his history dissertation. Karl Bernhardovic Sobelsohn, born in Lemberg, Austria-Hungary (Galicia). Parents: Jewish. Pseudonym: Radek. Current age about fifty. Fluent in three languages: German, Polish, and Russian (perhaps even Yiddish). Profession: journalist. Agitated for Polish independence. Lived in Germany. Fled to Switzerland during the Great War and worked with Lenin as a liaison with the Bremen Left. One of the passengers on the "sealed train" carrying Lenin and other Bolsheviks through Germany to Russia. Exited the train in Sweden and worked as a journalist. Returned to Russia. Became a secretary of the Comintern (1920). Took part in the failed Communist revolution in Germany (1923). Expelled from the Party (1927) for siding with Trotsky; readmitted in 1930 after admitting his political errors. Currently at work, with other Bolsheviks, writing the Soviet Constitution. Appearance: short, nervous, wiry, pop-eyed, myopic (uses thick tortoise-shell spectacles), clean shaven except for a scraggly fringe beard, prominent lips, jerky body movements, and awkward walk. Personal qualities: devoted Communist, elegant writer, inveterate pipe smoker, genius at synthesis, sarcastic, viciously humorous, and never at a loss for an anecdote, often at the expense of Stalin.

Radek's book, which Sasha waited a few days to read, argued for worldwide revolution, and not socialism in one country, a major point of contention between Trotsky and Stalin. A social democrat in principle, if not name, he promoted the idea of local governance (Soviets) and rule by the workers. He admitted that the masses were uneducated, but placed his faith in the goodness of the people once they were imbued with a modicum of learning. In one essay, he stoutly defended the first head of the Cheka, Felix Dzerzhinski, drawing on personal friendship to defend the man as kind, modest, peace loving, and fearless. Hadn't Dzerzhinski told his comrades, when they were all surrounded by the Polish police, to give him their compromising documents, so that he would receive the blame and the prison term?

For the safety of the revolution, which Dzerzhinski regarded as the Supreme Law, anything was permissible. Sasha wondered if this absolutism explained why innocent people confessed to crimes they never committed. Was it for the good of the country and the revolution? It certainly wasn't for the survival of Stalin. To safeguard what people regard as the greater good, they are willing to confess to grievous misdeeds, of which they are innocent, and passionately swear to conform. Would the new Soviet Constitution protect free speech and the innocent? When Karl Radek found himself in trouble for his previous support of Trotsky, he recanted. How many recantations are enough; or is the "recanter" forever treated with suspicion?

No, Sasha decided, denunciation is behavior most foul, perhaps on a par with murder.

The death of Martyn Lipnoski haunted Sasha. Although the man had participated in the expulsion of his parents, he was an accidental traveler, an incidental surrogate. Did he, like his two companions, have a family? Despite his curiosity, Sasha knew that seeking answers might expose him. He would have forgotten the matter had he not found himself in Father Zossima's quarters. The boys at the Michael School were required to work in the community. Goran Youzhny had inexplicably volunteered. He and another lad were given the task of laying a wood floor for the ex-priest, who lived with a dirt one. Normally, only those in good standing with the local Soviet received favors from the Michael School, but Sasha had arranged for Father Zossima's name to make the list.

Although baptized as a Greek Catholic, Sasha knew little about the church and less about its clergy. Shortly after his birth, the Bolsheviks came to power and closed most places of worship. The priests were driven to find other work. His parents occasionally read the Bible to him, but as a child he preferred Russian fairy tales to those about desert marauders. Nevertheless, he did find himself wondering about existential questions during the college semester he studied "Philosophy of History," owing to his eccentric professor who enjoyed asking about free will, determinism, choice, freedom, guilt, and the origins of life. Many of these questions came to mind after the murders. Was his killing hand merely the instrument of a supernal avenger? How could he have acted against his own nature? Did he offer Galina a position to assuage his guilt or to live in the presence of a beautiful, talented woman?

When he arrived to examine the new floor that had been laid, he found himself alone with Father Zossima talking generally about matters of life and death. The priest lived behind a stable in a small room made possible through the goodness of the farm's owner, who had renovated a former storage area for tackle and tethers. A cross, the only religious symbol in the room, hung above the entrance. On either side of the door were hooks for overcoats and hats and scarves and other clothing. A Persian rug of handsome design and color covered one wall. The bookcases on another wall were the priest's handiwork. A third wall held framed photographs of his family: a deceased wife and two married daughters, each with a son. A cot, a small desk, two chairs, and an old steamer trunk composed his furniture. A sink with cold water and a Primus stove substituted for a kitchen and washbasin; his bathroom was an outhouse.

Sasha had once visited a monastery and seen inside a monk's cell, a scene that, except for the wooden floor, he was now reliving. Father Zossima knew better than to dress in clerical robes, given the antipathy of the government to religion, so he made it a point to wear a peasant *rubakha*, a long, coarse linen shirt that reached to his knees and cinched at the waist with a narrow belt. The shirt lacked a collar, but was high enough to reach his chin. Unlike most men, who dyed the linen, he wore his white and untrimmed at the cuffs. His gray trousers, made of thin wool, were tucked into felt boots. Never having seen the priest in any other garb, Sasha concluded that he owned only the clothes on his back. He therefore made a mental note to collect some used garments left behind by former students, and pass them along to the priest.

Heavily bearded, Father Zossima looked like a bear peering out of a thicket. At this moment, Sasha could reconstruct the priest's lunch. Bread crumbs and beet remnants clung to his beard. For all his austerity, Father Zossima indulged in one unseemly habit. He smoked, rolling coarse tobacco in any available paper, usually newspapers. Aware of Sasha's dislike of tobacco, the father refrained from lighting up, though Sasha could smell the nicotine on his fingers and clothes.

"Do you ever," asked Sasha, "question God's judgment?"

"For what reason?"

"To explain the ills of this world. Take yourself, for example. What have you ever done to deserve the treatment you've suffered?"

"God's ways are inscrutable. I would be guilty of unconscionable arrogance to question His will and works."

In light of his own crimes and their having gone undetected, Sasha had reason to believe that if God existed, He paid little or no attention to the affairs of men. So whether one believed or not hardly mattered. God seemed indifferent. But Sasha found it difficult to reconcile a Godless world with the untold sacrifices people had endured to worship Him and to study the Bible. Could God be so deaf to those who constantly beseeched Him? The promise of heavenly rewards counted for nothing with Sasha. People needed bread and butter and benignity now, not in a future paradise as a reward for good behavior. He finally summoned the courage to ask the one question he knew could cost him Father Zossima's trust.

"How can you really believe, given the world's evils and ills, that God exists?"

The priest exhaled in punctuated breaths, as if punched in the stomach. "That's the *quaestio maxima*. Can one ever disavow what he has spent the better part of his life believing? When one faithfully serves a higher cause, he has a stake in it. To disown it would be like disowning one's self. Even if God does not exist, we must continue to believe that He does, for the sake of moral courage and pity and civilized behavior. Given the frailty of man in the face of nature and the marauding and merciless conduct of others, we need to believe in something higher than us, some power capable of redressing the innumerable wrongs we suffer daily."

"But that's my point exactly, Father. Why isn't God slaying the wrongdoers and protecting the weak?"

"Then you don't believe He exists?"

Like Father Zossima, he was sitting hunched over with his arms crossed in his lap. "No," Sasha murmured.

"My response, I'm sure, will surprise you. I say He had better exist, because He has a great deal of explaining to do, and only He has the answers."

Rain sounded on the roof, and thunder moaned in the distance. The sky darkened and drained the light from the day. A serious storm threatened.

Shortly after this visit, Sasha received a terse note from Boris Filatov that read like a ukase.

Citizen Parsky,

The pioneering spirit of our students should be directed at those who wish to build a paradise on earth, not in heaven. Let Father Zossima call on God to build him a floor, not the Michael School. See that the priest receives no further favors.

B.F.

Sasha had been denounced, his name now added to the millions of others in Moscow's Archive of Denunciations. For safety's sake, he knew from Brodsky that it was important to discover the betrayer. Most informers, Brodsky had told him, were cowards and, once confronted, usually desisted, but not until they had tried to justify themselves with feeble explanations. In this case, the denouncer seemed apparent: Goran Youzhny. But when Sasha accosted him, not at school, which Goran frequented to chat with Devora Berberova, but in the photo lab at the farmhouse, Goran swore his innocence, deplored the cowardice of the one who reported Sasha, and swore to find the informer. A moment's reflection convinced Sasha that innumerable people knew about the priest's flooring, from students to farmers to friends. Finding the guilty party would prove virtually impossible, a fact that Goran had to know.

Then, too, there was that other matter.

A growing number of people feared that Father Zossima, a defrocked priest, was courting imprisonment or exile. They whispered, without proof, that he had, in violation of Soviet law, given asylum to a runaway soldier. Although numerous such military personnel roamed the countryside, having been inducted into the Red Army against their will, Sasha's fears led him to conclude that the man was Petr Selivanov. But whether he had come to Balyk to see Galina and Alya or to expose Sasha remained to be seen.

7

Poking his head into Galina's office, Sasha said, "Another day without my having to read a condemnation. Life is improving."

He was referring to the spate of announcements that had appeared outside her office on the bulletin board, which she could see through the window next to her desk. In an attempt to liberalize the school, Sasha had introduced numerous changes, among them an opportunity for students to post unsigned complaints outside the main office.

"You must not have looked very closely," she said. "There's an accusation that Semen Sestrov is engaging in revisionist history, with an eye to ingratiating himself with the Bolsheviks."

Sasha knew better than to ask who authored the statement. Galina had made it clear to him at the outset of the liberalized policy that she would never reveal a student's name. She was, she had declared, "no denouncer." "An admirable policy," Sasha had thought at the time, not anticipating that other teachers and students would accuse Galina of collaboration, a charge that Sasha dismissed with the observation that Koba himself had deplored the eavesdropping and searches that he had endured as a seminarian in Georgia. To quote Stalin was politically astute even if the Boss had instituted a police state where nothing was private, including a person's thoughts. In the public world of the Soviet state, one parroted the Party line; in the private world, the only safety was in silence.

Other reforms that Sasha instituted merely exacerbated the resentment that the faculty, all older than Sasha, felt at having been passed over for the directorship of the Michael School. Behind his back, they called him all manner of names: "upstart," "climber," "parvenu," "ass kisser," "bright boy," "Filatov's fellator," "God's gift to learning." Accustomed to the authoritarianism of Tsarist and Soviet schools, the teachers balked at the idea of students having a say, either to them or to the director. Sasha's open-door policy, which encouraged students to drop in and chat, was anathema to those who wanted their minions to remain strictly obedient. Most hated of all were Sasha's frequent observations of classroom teaching. Heretofore, the teachers had ruled over their classes with complete license. The classroom was as sacrosanct as the marriage bed; and fearful were the punishments visited upon students who took their complaints outside of class.

The faculty therefore treated the freedom of students to post unsigned comments on the bulletin board as a violation of trust on Sasha's part and a countenancing of public denunciations. Little wonder that Galina was besieged by faculty who insisted they tell her the name of the traitors. But having gained the students' confidence, she was not about to betray it to dispel the discontent of teachers who enjoyed tenured sinecures. The new Soviet order called for change. Well, here was change. Unfortunately, it threatened to rend the fabric of a famous school. When the complaints reached Sasha's ears, Filatov had already read them. They had come to him through denunciatory letters. No teacher would have risked posting a complaint on the bulletin board and having it seen by Galina, who was widely accepted as Sasha's "woman." Some even saw a resemblance between Alya and Sasha, and concluded that the child was a result of an earlier liaison, which would explain why Sasha gave her a position at the school. Other suppositions touched upon the child being the issue of Galina and Filatov, an indiscretion covered up by Sasha, for which he was amply rewarded.

Filatov's letter to Sasha came right to the point.

Citizen Parsky,

You have been accused of anti-Soviet behavior. As soon as possible please respond in writing to the following charges: laxity, indiscipline, formalism, subversion, bourgeois materialism, favoritism, wrecking, elitism, and Trotskyism.

B.F.

Ironically, these complaints served to strengthen the relationship between Sasha and Galina. If he had hoped to win Galina's affections through Alya or his giving employment and housing to her, he was mistaken. She seemed skeptical of his many kindnesses, but the moment he came under attack, the old warrior spirit in her genes came to the fore. As they sat together at the kitchen table in the common cause of answering his critics, they shared ideas, compared feelings, and treated each other as equals. It was she who said that general answers would not suffice and that, since the Soviets loved dialectical arguments, Sasha should parse every charge and use the favored "Although" opening to allow that his detractors might have some justice on their side.

Together they composed the following reply, with Galina taking the lead.

Comrade Filatov,

Although you must, given your responsible position, investigate grave complaints that come before you, and although their authors are well meaning, let me assure you that the charges issue from nothing more than discontent with the numerous changes I've brought to the school, in conformity with all that you wished. To enter the forest, we Soviets say, one has to be prepared to shoot wolves. To bring about pedagogical reforms in an institution long-accustomed to conducting business in the "old way" requires stern measures. You yourself directed me to raise the school's standards. I think that if you were to examine the students, you would find that their achievements currently surpass those of former classes.

As to the specific charges, permit me to observe that whether they refer to me or to the students is not at all clear; and yet the distinction is a vital one. Am I personally to blame, or are my policies creating an uncomfortable atmosphere in which the students are now demanding more of their teachers and taking control of their own learning? But since you have asked that I speak to each of the complaints, I shall do so.

Laxity. Have I been lax? Yes. I have allowed the students to escape the iron collar of rote learning and silent obedience. They are now allowed to speak in class, post their complaints on the school bulletin board, speak to the director, and spend time, if they wish, in a choir that performs music of their own choosing. So I would distinguish between my laxity toward the students and toward the faculty. The latter admittedly chafe at the new regimen.

Indiscipline. I suspect that this charge, like "laxity," refers to the new freedoms granted students. Students are now asking questions that heretofore were unthinkable. The result: Teachers have to prepare for class with more thought and depth. My own behavior has, I believe, been beyond reproach. I do not carouse; I do not smoke; I rarely drink. I read all the new directives that come from the Party; I study the works of Marx, Lenin, Engels, and Comrade Stalin; and, as you requested, I have befriended Avram Brodsky to learn what I can. At his request, I am currently reading a collection of essays written by Karl Radek. Some of the ideas are clearly subversive and, frankly, offensive to me, but I realize they were written before he was restored to the bosom of the Party.

Formalism. In all candor, I must admit that this term has never been entirely clear to me. The critics of formalism treat the term as synonymous with art for art's sake. But even the "purest" work of art speaks to the age from which it issues. No subject matter can escape class, and no style can hide its intentions. A work by Rembrandt can just as easily inform the masses as a painting about the great October Revolution. Speaking personally, I readily admit that my own literary tastes run to Restoration drama, which can be condemned as a courtier's literature, or it can be read for its insight into the pomposity and foibles of a class. I choose to do the latter.

Subversion. Once again I must ask whether I or my educational reforms are at issue? That I am reading Radek, I have already admitted. That I have undermined the previous system of teaching at the Michael School, I plead guilty. Am I a member of any political group? No. Do I write for any underground journals? No. Have I allowed the writings of Trotsky to enter our classrooms? No. I must therefore conclude that the complaint, like most of the others, bears on the new pedagogy.

Bourgeois materialism. Here, I suspect, the complaint has nothing to do with students and everything to do with me. Alya Selivanova wished for a pony. I arranged with one of our local farms for her to have one—on loan. In a year or two, the animal will be returned. I should observe that a number of students enjoy playing with the pony, which is the only pet at the school. If you wish me to return the animal, I will, of course, comply immediately.

Favoritism. Yes, I employed Galina, found a tutor for Alya, and allowed Goran Youzhny to build a photography lab in the stables. The first two actions cost the school little or nothing. The third had your blessing and that of the Politburo. But if Comrade Filatov wishes, I can close the lab. Ah! There was one other instance of favoritism. When I attended Leonid Astafurov's class in Latin, I praised the man for his cleverness. To help the students understand the peculiar syntax of Latin, he had them speak Russian in the same inverted way. Although I never learned Latin in that manner, I thought it effective, despite the carping of other teachers.

Wrecking. Have I wrecked the former way of doing things? Yes. Even Brodsky complains. As the former school director, he told me that he saw no reason to change a system that had stood the test of time. But that treasured past of his, as I explained to him, included Imperial Russia, Tsars, and serfs. Some would say that I wrecked the farmhouse by partitioning and renovating it to make two quarters from one. My view is that I improved the property—by means of barter. I admitted two students to the school free of cost because they did the work for nothing.

Did I wreck the school by admitting the two marginal students? They are children of the proletariat and can only improve the education of the masses.

Elitism. From its very founding, the school was dedicated to providing a first-rate education. By definition, then, it is elitist, especially when we compare the school to those others in nearby oblasts. Are the students selected on the basis of money or pull? No. We give preferential treatment to the children of poor, working-class parents. Are those students high achievers? Absolutely! Which only goes to prove that proletarian children are as gifted as the children of the privileged, even if the former take some remedial work to bring them up to speed.

Trotskyism. Having already admitted to reading the early essays of Radek, I would also include among my sins the belief that the world would be better served if the working classes in other countries took control of their governments. Surrounded as we are by Western hostility, and seeing the rise of fascism in Italy and Germany (which are not socialist countries, though they say they are), I worry for the safety of Russia, which would be less precarious if we had sympathetic neighbors and not warlike ones.

S. Parsky

After reading aloud a draft of the letter, Sasha sadly turned to Galina and observed that his colleagues had not taken kindly to his reforms, and that most of the complaints could be organized under a one-word heading: "Change" or "Reform."

"You can now understand," she said, "why progress requires constant struggle. The conservative, the self-satisfied, the inertial will always outnumber those who want change, particularly if the change means having to act in a different way. We are all creatures of habit, and once we get set in our ways, we don't want to trade the familiar for the foreign. To some people change is tantamount to learning a new language. In the Michael School, you have asked your faculty to speak a new tongue. Of course, they're unhappy. In a well-run capitalist society, they simply give the workers more money or additional inducements; in Soviet society, we appeal to the greater good. Material rewards are usually more effective than abstract ones, so if you can think of a way to bribe your faculty, I'm sure the complaints will end."

Mulling over Galina's advice, Sasha asked, "What if I introduced a sabbatical system? Every X number of years, a teacher receives a term off at full pay. Perhaps, then, vital saplings will grow from dead wood."

"Give me a day to think it over," said Galina.

The next evening they were sitting at the kitchen table, where most of their serious conversations occurred; and as always, they were sipping tea and nibbling black bread with honey. Sasha had come to depend on Galina's intuitive sense and reasoned advice. Not only intelligent, she was also cunning. He, less practical, still believed in the power of ideas to persuade. She knew better. Even the early church fathers learned quickly that homilies on good behavior meant nothing unless you could promise the faithful a reward: an eternal life spent in a celestial paradise. How the Jews managed to keep their people in line without the promise of heaven remained an enigma. Perhaps the absence of a bribe explained their fractiousness and their constant striving, although the Old Testament did make clear that God's rewards and punishments were visited upon one here and now, and not in some future Eden.

Galina opined she would have to ask Brodsky about Jews, though Avram rarely ever mentioned religion. He probably found it safer to say nothing, buried, as he was, in a Greek Catholic community, and serving a term of internal exile. Galina had met him only a few times, and always in the town square. She found his reminiscences of Kolyma captivating but felt uncomfortable when Bogdan Dolin would sourly ask him a question like, "What was the daily ration of bread?" The source of Dolin's skepticism remained a mystery, but Brodsky's ability to turn a Dolin question into a Brodsky one was undoubted. "The daily ration of bread, you ask? Are we talking about a political prisoner or a criminal, a man with or without contacts, a woman with or without her skirt pulled up?" Dolin would grumble and walk off. On the few occasions that Galina remained to listen to Brodsky chat with his "faithful," she detected a keen analytic intelligence. He had even graced her with his well-known wit when she asked him whether he thought that the astounding number of people accused of being "wreckers" were mostly innocent? His reply: "Has the government ever been wrong? Not to my knowledge." Everyone had laughed.

Brodsky, impressed with Galina's intelligence, had advised Sasha to put her in charge of the school library's French literature collection, even if it meant earning the displeasure of Anna Rusakova. Sasha had agreed, and to please her, even read some of the French masters: Hugo, Flaubert, Stendahl, and Zola. Of an evening, he'd invite her to stroll with him along one of the woodland paths, all the while talking about some book, for example, *Madame Bovary* or *The Red and the Black*.

Lively and engaging conversation, of course, can as easily ignite a romance as a pretty face. Slowly their talk of great literature and personal experiences led to more intimate disclosures and behavior, and finally coitus. Throughout, Sasha had behaved like an old-fashioned swain, courting his damsel with sweet words, kindliness, small gifts, and an avowal of his honorable intentions, knowing full well that she was married and her husband still living. In short, he wished to enjoy her both intellectually and physically in a state of freedom, not marriage. She, in turn, made it clear that even if she obtained a divorce, she didn't wish to remarry. With that agreement, they began sharing his bed, not hers, so Alya wouldn't know. Their lovemaking, even allowing for the hesitancy of the first time, was never a riotous stew. They sweated over one another, but not passionately. She occasionally cried when she climaxed, and he would ask why. But it took several months before she admitted the source: his gentleness. With her, yes; but the fact remained that two men were dead. Decapitated. By him. His gentle touch had hardened into a fist as it gripped the sickle. At the time, he felt not so much as a moment's hesitation or remorse. Gentle? Perhaps now, but not then. Galina's idea of gentleness did not include murder but tonguing. When she asked him to run his lips down her body and engage in cunnilingus, she climaxed immediately and then took him in her mouth, a new reality for Sasha, exhilarating and addictive.

For the sake of appearances, she never remained in his bed the whole night, but retreated to her own room, where she could hear Alya breathing in the adjoining alcove, which had been remodeled for her. The few times the child awoke and called for her mother, Galina instantly materialized, dressed in a robe and slippers that she kept at the ready. Initially, her only fear was pregnancy, given the paucity in the countryside of condoms. But that fear was eclipsed by another, her husband, who had emerged from a photograph and taken up temporary residence with Father Zossima. Yes, it was Petr. He had sent her a note; he would come to the farmhouse. But if he wished to engage in conjugal relations, would she insist, as she had before his disappearance, that he sleep on the couch? Just his presence on the premises would mean an end to the lovemaking with Sasha, a prospect that saddened her.

Late one night, she heard fingernails lightly tapping on her window. Pulling aside the curtains, she saw an emaciated, bearded man with long hair and sunken eyes. It took her a minute to recognize Petr, whom she admitted through a back door that adjoined the pantry. He looked sick, his eyes bloodshot, his skin covered with suppurating sores, his gait unsteady. Even his teeth were bad and his breath worse, which became apparent the moment he opened his mouth. They stiffly hugged, and he said without self-pity:

"I'm not well."

"I'll make you some soup."

Rather than use the kitchen she shared with Sasha and risk waking him, she resorted to the hot plate and kettle in her sitting room. Her small supply of personal provisions included tea, biscuits, and a few dried soups: leak, potato, and beet. Slowly stirring the potato broth, she looked not at Petr but at the pot, afraid that eye contact might reveal more than she wished. He was sprawled across the armchair she favored for reading. The slipcover she'd made to hide the chair's tattered state was now disarrayed, revealing the old sackcloth and rough stitching.

"Tell me," she said, without looking up, "where have you been? I was told you were dead. Killed. I even received a government stipend for your loss."

"Living with a priest in the village," he breathed laboriously. "A Father Zossima."

"No, before that. It's been well over a year since the murders."

"What do you know about that?"

"Only what I read in the police report."

"Never saw it."

"Were you even there?"

"Yes . . . and no."

She looked up. Her need to know was urgent. "Tell me!"

The story he conveyed came in starts and stops, and not always in order. He had been living with the priest because he feared that the police had learned of an army deserter in the area.

"The name 'Sasha Parsky' provided the scent I've been following to track you down."

"What does he have to do with you or the murders?"

"They took place at his parents' farm."

"I don't believe you! You must have the wrong Parskys. Besides, the police never told me the name of the family. How would you know?"

"Viktor told me."

"Viktor Harkov? I don't believe a word you've said. You've always been jealous of him."

"Ask Sasha Parsky. From what I understand you're living under the same roof."

A flustered Galina blurted, "But not in the same bed."

"That no longer matters," said Petr. "I met a girl in Ukraine, from Kiev. That's another reason I came looking for you. If I asked for a divorce, the authorities would know I'm alive and my whereabouts. If you divorce me—after all, I'm presumed dead—no one will be any the wiser."

Distraught, Galina slumped on the couch with her head in her hands, as if trying to keep the tears or the anger from leaking out. He didn't know which. "Tell me more," she mumbled. But he merely stared, as he often did in the presence of great emotion. Slowly, Galina raised her head. Only once before had Petr seen the fury in her face bulge the bones in her eye sockets. "Surely, there's more," she hissed through clenched teeth. "There always is in a world of murderous hatred."

Alexander Harkov and Petr had orders to expel the Parskys from their farm. They had been denounced as kulaks. As Galina knew, Petr had come to regret the "expulsion detail" assigned to Alexander and him. It was raining torrents. They—he and Alexander—had stopped at an inn before they reached the Parsky farm. A drunken Martyn Lipnoski, a fellow soldier heading home on leave, had spent the night in that wretched place with a whore . . . who had gone off with his wallet and papers. They greeted their comrade warmly and bought him a drink. In fact, two. He was broke. Alexander even paid to fill Martyn's flask and offered him a lift in the truck.

The kettle whistled. She poured the water into a mug, and then emptied the contents of the packet. "Here's your soup," said Galina, handing him also a tin of biscuits. Although she had brought the soup to a boil, he guzzled it. The biscuits he shoved whole into his mouth, wadding his cheeks, until he could flush them down with the soup. As she watched him voraciously eat, she could feel his hunger, resulting, no doubt, from the priest's meager stores.

He said that Martyn was delighted to join them, but the closer they came to the Parsky farm, the greater Petr's apprehension. When they stopped on a ridge above the farm, he exited the truck. Whether owing to the impending expulsion or to some intuition, he couldn't say, but he stood in the road refusing to get back in the cab. Martyn carelessly offered to change places with him, and Petr gladly accepted. Alexander fumed, told him it could cost him ten years in a work camp, begged him not to do this "stupid thing," and then drove down the hill in a huff.

Standing in the trees next to the road, he had watched. He knew from the expulsion papers given him and Alexander, the Parskys were elderly, but their farmhand, who must have been an illegal itinerant, looked young. Waiting for the rain to abate, he watched and then ran off in the opposite direction. Surely his eyes had deceived him. What he imagined he'd seen could not have been true. But to go to the farm was out of the question. He was now a deserter and had to find places to hide. That same night, he came to a barn that belonged to a collective. He found a pair of overalls and a coarse woolen shirt, which he exchanged for his uniform, and then continued walking. The back roads teemed with workers who had left their state farms and were heading in every conceivable direction, just so long as that direction did not lead back to Bolshevik control of the land.

A group of men heading to Ukraine invited him to join them. The number of wretched villages and hamlets he passed through were innumerable, and the suffering immeasurable. People had been reduced to cannibalizing their pet animals and even their dead friends and relatives. What he witnessed was a government-made famine, forced starvation, to punish farmers who fiercely resisted the confiscation of their land and livestock. After a year of wandering, he made his way back to Ryazan, where Viktor Harkov temporarily housed him. From Viktor he learned that Sasha Parsky had been at school when the murders occurred.

"You must be mistaken. You have the wrong Sasha Parsky."

"Not according to Viktor."

"How would he know? It wasn't in the police report given to us."

"He knew there was a son, and he knew his name. That's how I got here. Maybe you ought to ask Sasha about his parents, and don't forget the farmhand. Because if you don't ask him, I will. That's one of the reasons I returned."

"Viktor and I," said Galina, "were led to believe that the family and farmhand simply disappeared."

"For good reason."

"You saw it?"

"The rain, the truck, they made it hard to see, but I saw the farmhand bury two bodies, and the same man drove off with the couple."

"It has to be a different Parsky family."

"We can easily find out. In the morning, we'll ask."

Galina stared into space and mumbled, "Viktor never said anything to me, but then he hasn't written in ages."

"As usual, he's plotting."

"Vladimir Lukashenko?"

"Yes."

But Galina's mind was not on Commissar Lukashenko. It was on Sasha. She never slept a wink that night in anticipation of morning and the opportunity to confront Citizen Parsky. Petr had slept on the couch. Before breakfast, while Galina was asking Sasha questions, he played with Alya. His turn would come later.

No longer able to keep his secret, certainly not while staring into the large puzzled, tearing eyes of Galina, Sasha confessed—and lied—at the same time. "Yes, the murders occurred at my parents' farm. But I was away at school. So shocked was I by the crime that I volunteered to call on you and Viktor Harkov."

"Occurred at your parents' farm?" she dumbly repeated. "Then you must know who the murderer is."

"All I know is that after I returned to school, my parents were planning to hire one of the free laborers roaming the road to help with the farmwork. A day later the police were questioning me. Me! As if I knew anything. I would have gladly assisted them, but I was as shocked as they . . . as shattered as you."

"But surely your parents have friends and relatives in other parts of the country. Right?"

"Yes, and I made inquiries, but to no avail."

"When you first came to see me, you said nothing. Why?"

"I thought it would only increase your suffering."

"Even though you knew I was desperate for information."

"And once you learned where the crime had occurred, and that my parents owned the farm, what then? That information leads nowhere."

Incredulous that this man with whom she'd been sleeping was the son of accomplices to a crime in which two men were killed, one of whom could easily have been her husband, she lashed out sarcastically, "Do your parents always hire killers to work their land? They probably abetted the murderer."

He bowed his head, occasioning a muteness from Galina worse than her scalding words. Squeezing his eyes closed with such force that his nose wrinkled and his teeth clenched, he wanted to scream at the tangled web he had woven. Where would it end? To prevent discovery of his perfidy, he was leaving his parents unprotected, not only from the law, but also from the calumny of the victims' relatives. His parents, models of goodness, did not deserve to be thought of as criminals. That he had put them in that position, and that he now found himself suspected by a person he loved of covering up a heinous crime . . . of keeping from her information that she believed could lead to the apprehension of the murderer . . . introduced him to a thousand torments.

Obviously hurt, she challenged him with a question. "How could you have told Viktor and not me?"

"I told him nothing."

"You must have said something . . . maybe while playing chess, because he knew about you and passed the information to Petr. That's how Petr found out."

To persuade her, Sasha would have agreed to trial by ordeal—fire or water or both—but Galina remained convinced that Viktor could have learned about the Parskys and Sasha from only one person, and that person was sitting in front of her at the kitchen table. When he reached across the table, intending to touch her consolingly, she withdrew her hand. Defensively, he allowed that if he were Viktor's source, she could draw a knife across his throat; and he begged her to prove his innocence by contacting Viktor.

"He goes through moody periods. I suspect he's in one now."

Hoping to turn her attention from him to Viktor, he said, "Frankly, Galina, he must be privy to confidential police information, and that worries me. We know that conspiracies in this country are rife. Tell me about this obsession of his with Commissar Lukashenko."

She rose, looked down at him distrustfully, and replied, "You'll have to ask Petr." Then she stiffly strode out of the room, returning to her own quarters.

Through the kitchen window, Sasha could see Petr leading the pony with Alya atop the animal she called Scout. She had taken the reins to show him how well she could ride, turning, stopping, and backing up the horse. With each move, Petr clapped and ostentatiously tipped his hat to celebrate her equestrian achievements. She glowed. When she finally dismounted and came from the stable, they walked hand in hand into the house. Alya clearly adored him. Sasha exited the kitchen and returned to his own room, guessing correctly that Petr would make his daughter a cup of hot chocolate. He could hear Petr telling Alya a story, "The Tale of Stalin's Barber."

"As you can imagine," Petr said, "anyone entrusted with the job of giving the Vozhd a haircut would have to be expert with a razor and scissors, as well as with matches. Why matches? Because our Great Leader likes having Turkish haircuts."

Petr then went on to explain that a Turkish haircut is one in which the barber singes the auricle hairs, the unsightly black growth on the inside and outside of men's ears. A barber trained in this manner applies alcohol to the site, lights the liquid, and immediately fans out the flames with a towel—without burning the skin. Koba's barber, Georgian, like Koba, had learned his barbering in Istanbul, the former Constantinople, where the practice began.

"Now, as you can well imagine," Petr continued, "Stalin's barber had to have a steady hand, because one slip and he would be in big trouble. Also, the barber had to be trustworthy because anything our Great Leader said to him could not be repeated. What passes between a barber and his client is strictly confidential. Do you know that word, 'confidential'?"

"No."

"It means to keep a secret. Well, one day, when the barber was trimming Comrade Stalin's famous mustache, he found a mouse in it, a baby mouse no bigger than your fingernail. This discovery created a problem. Do you know why?"

"Because Stalin hated mice."

"You're close. Yes, he hated mice, but if the barber had said, 'Comrade Stalin, you have a mouse nesting in your mustache,' that would have suggested our leader never washed his face. Now no one wants to be thought of as dirty or unclean, especially not our leader. So what was the barber to do?"

"Secretly take away the mouse."

"And if Stalin found out?"

"He'd be glad the barber took it away."

"But then, every time he looked at the barber, Stalin would be saying to himself: That man found a mouse in my mustache and thinks I never wash my face, and what if he tells others about the mouse?"

"Then he should get a new barber."

"But the old one still knows the secret of Stalin's mustache. So would you advise Stalin to send his barber to another part of the country or maybe shoot him?"

"No, just ask the barber not to tell the secret to anyone."

"But even if the barber agrees to say nothing—ever—how can you be sure you can trust him?"

Alya's unresponsiveness indicated that Petr's question had stumped her. He had, in fact, touched upon a problem that pervaded the country. Whom could you trust?

"I have an idea," announced Alya triumphantly, "just leave the mouse where it is and don't tell Stalin."

"The barber still knows."

"Yes, but Stalin doesn't, and if our leader should find out, the barber can always say . . ."

"What? The moment he says anything, Stalin will have him dangling on the end of a hook."

"I give up," said Alya. "What's the right answer?"

"There is none. If the man is wise, and some men are not, he will tell Stalin nothing and keep the secret to himself. But even then the man isn't safe, because if Stalin discovers the mouse and asks the barber why he never told him about it nesting in his mustache, the man must admit either to ignoring the creature out of fear or to being a very bad barber. Which would you choose?"

"Fear."

"That's what most people choose."

"Then am I right?" she asked eagerly.

"You are certainly no more wrong than most of Russia."

Galina had asked Petr to dinner. A walk afterward provided the occasion for Petr to question Sasha. Galina remained at the farmhouse reading Alya a story. As the men crunched through the fallen leaves, recently golden and orange and red, Petr breathed deeply and commented that the countryside held far more riches for him than did the cities he'd seen in the last year. "Just look at that moon. Spectacular! Mind you," he said, "I never made it to Moscow, and everyone seems to want to go there."

"It's a lively city but not a beautiful one. Leningrad is the jewel. The Hermitage, the architecture, the canals. Dostoevski's city. It inspired him."

"The largest one I saw was Kiev."

"Never been."

"Not very interesting. Some old houses with charm. Wide boulevards. A few hills. The Ukrainian nationalists there are busy stirring up trouble. If I were Polish, Jewish, or Lithuanian, I'd get the hell out. That goes for the Romish, too."

"Stalin won't let Ukraine become independent."

"Agreed, but he won't lift a finger to stop the pogroms. They serve his purpose. In comparison to the nationalists, he looks good."

They walked silently for some time, each ostensibly lost in his thoughts. Petr stopped to collect some desiccated horse chestnuts.

"In their day," he observed sardonically, "they were shiny and hard. Now look at them. I feel the same way. Shriveled. So many young people in Russia feel used up, even though they have sixty and seventy years in front of them. I know that's how Viktor feels. He says he wants to do at least one thing for which he's remembered."

"Namely?"

"Before we talk about Viktor, I'd like to talk about you, if you don't mind."

Sasha broke off a branch for a walking stick, which he trimmed with his penknife. "Fire away!"

"Have you ever heard the name Martyn Lipnoski?"

Here was the first test. Should Sasha plead ignorance or admit to knowing the name? If he admitted to knowing it, the next question was naturally "how"?

"I can't say that I have."

"He's one of the two soldiers murdered on your parents' farm. He was a comrade."

Petr threw a horse chestnut, hitting a distant tree silvered by moonlight.

"Did you aim for it?"

"Yes," replied Petr.

"Then I'd better not enter into a shooting match with you," remarked Sasha casually, trying to suggest unconcern, all the while on the verge of exploding.

"Martyn's wife had left him for being a dissolute whoremaster. He was raising his six-year-old son, Konstantin. Whatever Martyn's vices, he loved his boy."

"Where is the son now?"

"With his grandmother. The wife disappeared."

"I hear similar stories wherever I go." Petr looked at him strangely. "I don't mean about fathers being murdered, I mean parents leaving their children behind to be raised by grandparents."

Petr skied all his remaining horse chestnuts and watched them fall. "With all the families sent into exile, there are millions of children parentless. You suppose Stalin ever worries about them?"

"Isn't that why the Bolsheviks adopt children—to show that they care for the homeless and orphaned?"

Sullenly, Petr replied, "Those kids would be a lot better off if they could live with their real parents."

"Is that how you and Galina came to adopt Alya?"

For a moment, Petr walked without answering. "How? Yes. Why? No. We knew the orphanage directoress, and once we saw the child . . ."

Given that untold orphaned children and their adoptive families were kept in the dark, Sasha haltingly asked, "Who were her parents?"

Petr's surprising answer rendered Sasha mute. "One of Stalin's barbers, he has several. A man from Tashkent, Yefim Boujinski. He and his wife, Maja, were sent first to Ryazan and then to a work camp. I have no idea of the charge, but given the problem with Muslims and other nationalities, I would guess he was exiled on religious grounds. The couple left behind a daughter, Alya, five, who was put in an orphanage. The director, Bella Platonova, knew Galina. We saw Alya, fell in love with her, and she with us. That's how it happened."

Sasha could feel the tears running down his cheek, and caught their glint in the cold light. He tried turning his head to keep Petr from seeing them. But why was he weeping? It was a question he would have found hard to answer. He knew Alya was adopted and simply assumed that her parents had fallen afoul of the government and been deported; wasn't that the fate of all enemies of the people? And yet Alya was cheerful and affectionate, playful and intelligent. Was it those qualities that had moved him to tears, her apparent triumph over madness? He fought for an answer, but none came. Petr filled the void, feeling at one time the same way.

"She *is* extraordinary, though at times lonely."

"I saw you with her when she was riding Scout. She loves you very much. If you're on the run, you'll have to leave her."

An uncomfortable pause halted the conversation.

"It'll be awful . . . as bad as you losing your parents. Worse, probably. You're an adult. They disappeared, right?"

At last they had come to the sensitive subject, the one that both men wished to dissect. Petr wanted to discover whom the Parsky's had hired as a farmhand, and trace Sasha's journey from the farm back to school. When had he left the house (the day, the hour), how did he travel to the station, which itinerant farmers did he pass on the road, who told him about the murders, why had he not returned to the farm to look for clues to where his parents had fled?

Sasha had an equal number of questions. How did Viktor learn about the deaths, who told him and why, and under what conditions? What did the police hope to gain? Why did Viktor tell Petr that Sasha might be the key to the crime? Was Viktor resentful that Galina had taken a position in Balyk and now shared a house with Sasha?

They began their discussion by agreeing that Viktor, a notorious malcontent, had numerous axes to grind. Sasha recounted his story yet again about leaving at five in the morning the day after Easter, boarding a ten o'clock train (he had carefully checked the rail schedule), and learning about the murders from the police who had come to his room at school. Sasha added only that he had met numerous workers on the road to the railroad, but none struck him as criminally insane. Hungry and in need of work, yes, but bloodthirsty, no. His failure to return to the farm could easily be explained. One, the state had confiscated it. Two, he had examinations to prepare for and a thesis to defend. Three, the site of his childhood house and the gruesome murders was too painful to bear. Surely, Petr understood his feelings.

As a matter of fact, Petr's expression was inscrutable. He listened without interrupting and seemed to accept Sasha's story uncritically, except for one thing.

"You have a driver's license. Most farmhands do not. And a police truck is more difficult to drive than a car. The murderer couldn't have been just any prole. Did you or the police give any thought to this fact? Also, no farm tools belonging to the itinerant were found, and none were missing."

Best, thought Sasha, to acknowledge Petr's perspicacity. "Damn clever of you, Petr. Although (the famous Soviet "Although") you are absolutely right about who's licensed to drive and who isn't, keep in mind that the collectives have been training the farmers to drive tractors and trucks. If the killer ran from a collective, he could have learned there. You are also wise to mention the tools. But it would be my guess that the killer took them with him, probably throwing his canvas satchel in the back. I've seen hundreds of farmers do the same."

Petr collected more chestnuts, but this time he pocketed them, murmuring they could spice his soup. For quite a while, they walked without talking. Sasha presumed that Petr was mulling over what he had said, at least he hoped so, since he wanted to pursue his own questions about Viktor.

At last, Petr remarked with a sigh, "I suppose you're right. Here I thought I was onto something, but what you say makes perfect sense. Now I'm no further along than before."

A relieved Sasha took Petr by the arm, and they walked on as comrades, into the night with the temperature falling. The trail was not unfamiliar to Sasha, but he knew that wild animals cavorted in these woods. He wondered, without asking, whether Petr was armed. A second later, he hoped not, lest Petr take it into his head that Sasha and Galina were lovers, and decide to settle matters. Releasing Petr's arm, he said:

"When the police questioned me about the crime, they made it clear I was not to say anything to anyone. By keeping the details secret, they hoped to trick the killer into revealing himself. So why would they tell Viktor?"

A rustling in the woods. They paused. Was it a boar or a deer or just a rabbit?

"Does that stick of yours have a point?" asked Petr. "If not, maybe you ought to sharpen it."

They waited. Nothing. Then they turned and headed home, passing a deserted hunter's shed that lovers used for trysts.

Petr said simply, "Perhaps they suspect Viktor. He and his brother were not always on the best of terms. Alexander didn't feel toward Lukashenko the way Viktor does. I think it likely the police were talking to Viktor about both men, Alexander and Lukashenko."

"Because of his diatribes against the commissar?"

"And his threats."

Sasha silently prayed that the police would link the two men. Perhaps then he could finally sleep the night through without waking up in a sweat. But was he prepared to see an innocent man hanged for his crimes? Whether he was or not, he now believed that Viktor was trying to save his own neck by casting doubt on Sasha, a clever ploy, particularly if Viktor fancied Galina and regarded Sasha as a rival. In addition, Viktor could divert attention from his hostility to Lukashenko by implicating Sasha.

"And the nature of his threats?"

"To kill Lukashenko. But Viktor wasn't alone. There was another. A policeman. The two of them were plotting."

This information frightened Sasha, and he suggested that Petr, whom he liked for his candor and treatment of Alya, no longer lodge with the priest, but in the farmhouse. There was a cot in the attic. In light of Galina's anger, it would be a while before she returned to his bed. For the nonce, he could determine whether the OGPU were actually in the area looking for Petr. Who better than Filatov to ask? By the time the two men reached home, the darkness had paled before the incipient light. Sasha would have little sleep this day.

On learning that Petr would be staying in the attic, Galina had more cause for anger. She interpreted Sasha's invitation as a devious means to keep Petr and her from making love. For this reason, the spirited Galina decided to behave all the more familiarly toward Petr. But her flirtatiousness merely strengthened Petr's belief that the woman he'd met in Kiev was more to his liking. The result: Sasha and Petr spent their evenings in animated conversation, forging a friendship, while Galina stewed on the other side of the wall.

Without the cunning Galina at his side advising him, the letter that Sasha sent to Filatov had taken more time to craft. After all, he had no intention of revealing that Petr was living—information Filatov would have valued—so he simply said that rumors were circulating to the effect that an army deserter had found his way to the area. Did Filatov know anything about the matter? If such a person was near Balyk, he might be desperate for food and shelter, and Sasha would therefore have to be especially vigilant in protecting the students and school supplies.

Filatov replied cautiously. Runaway soldiers were frequently on the loose, but patriotic citizens could be counted on to report them. Why did Sasha think that this particular soldier favored the Balyk area? Rumor, he counseled Sasha, was the enemy of clarity. He asked about Galina and her daughter, wished Sasha well, and reminded him that he had been asked to befriend Brodsky and report back to the major. He had yet to receive any information on this subject.

Lest he frighten Petr from frankness, Sasha took several days to reintroduce the subject of Viktor and the other plotter. This evening provided the ideal setting. A log burned in the fireplace, the wind outside shook the shutters, and the men, wrapped in blankets, slowly sipped mulled wine. Petr explained that after several months on the roads, he made his way back to Ryazan, thinking that after all this time, any police surveillance of Galina's apartment had probably ceased. But he learned from the Baturins that Galina and Alya had left . . . was it for Balakovo or Barnaul? Having lost her address, they pleaded uncertainty. Or were they simply, like millions of Soviet citizens, professing ignorance to protect themselves? Maybe Galina's destination was Belgorod or Beloreck or Bratsk. They couldn't remember. Ah, Briansk! That sounded right. But on the other hand maybe . . .

"You get the idea," said Petr. "So I called on Viktor. At first he was wary, but after he learned I'd deserted, he seemed to relax. We were two fellow pariahs. He knew that Galina had come to Balyk, offered a job by one Sasha Parsky, a young man who had come to Ryazan with condolences for Galina and him. The fellow worked for the police. The moment he told me about the visit, I was on the verge of asking him whether this Sasha Parsky was the son of the couple whose farm was the scene of the bloodshed. But I didn't know how much he knew, so I kept that information to myself. In this country, inquisitiveness is never a good idea."

"But Viktor did know where the murders took place."

"Not at that moment. He heard from an undercover police agent, when they met to talk about Lukashenko."

"You were there?"

"Viktor said that since I was a deserter, I could clear my record by cooperating with the secret police."

"Did you?"

"What? Clear my record or cooperate?"

"Are they different?"

"You decide."

In the best Russian digressive tradition, Petr spun a fantastic tale of deceit and duplicity. Born 1894 in Kopys, Vladimir Lukashenko, a former soldier, border guard, and farm-collective manager, studied at two universities, first history and then agriculture. He caught the attention of the Bolsheviks because of his outspoken contempt for the corrupt and illiterate peasants in charge of his oblast. Soviets must be pure, he said, and above reproach, frequently wrapping himself (figuratively) in the flag of the hammer and sickle. Patriotism may be the last refuge of a scoundrel, but it is the first stop of a rising politician. Decrying the venality of the local Soviets, he ran for mayor and promised that if elected, his would be the cleanest and most efficient oblast in Russia. No one had taken the time to interview his first wife or his second, both of whom divorced him for his skirt chasing and brutality. Nor did anyone speak to his old college mates, who knew of his fondness for vodka.

At first, the authorities in Moscow attributed his bad behavior to the need to clean out the Ryazan swamp of favoritism and nepotism. When state funds mysteriously began to vanish, his Kremlin apologists cited the expense of road building and apartment construction, both of which Lukashenko engaged in energetically. He wanted people to see his accomplishments and celebrate them. Then followed a series of mistresses who never failed to appear in public dressed in anything less than Paris fashions and sporting some conspicuous jewel, on a necklace or ring or pin. His confiscation of the top floor of an apartment building for his private penthouse and den of seduction (where aides brought teenage girls to be raped by the great man), he justified as standard practice for the directors of the secret police and commissars. No violation of decency was too great. He fashioned himself a man of iron in the tradition of Ivan the Terrible and Stalin.

Although Lukashenko's critics disappeared into jails and camps, Viktor Harkov remained. Ryazans, like most Russians, live and breathe conspiracies; hence Viktor's special status escaped neither their notice nor their theories, which included his brother Alexander Harkov served in the military police; Viktor was secretly in the employ of Lukashenko as proof that the mayor guaranteed free speech, even when it was critical of him; Viktor was in possession of secret documents that, if made public, would ruin Lukashenko; the OGPU, for some reason, had a special interest in protecting Viktor.

Petr himself had been undecided about which theory he favored until a man in an overcoat, with a scarf partially covering his face, arrived without warning in Viktor's flat and disappeared into the back room. Taking the hint, Petr immediately left. Stationing himself in the lobby of a building across the street, he waited for the man to exit and drive off in his black car. Only then did he return to the upstairs flat, where an abashed Viktor said:

"You probably guessed."

"They all dress the same, and divert their eyes in the same way. When I saw the black Zim at the curb, I knew for sure."

"In Moscow, I'm told, they drive Packards."

"If you want me to find other quarters, I'll understand."

"No, we need you. As a matter of fact, you were part of the discussion. In your capacity as a military policeman . . ."

"A deserter . . ."

"You accompanied my brother to the Parsky farm."

"I quit the truck before the killings occurred."

"Your desertion before the crime looks inexplicably suspicious."

The more wine Petr consumed, the more he disclosed. An orange glow from the fire inflamed his face and colored his anguish. Sasha imagined himself listening to St. Peter after his experience on the road to Damascus. Similarly, Petr was given a choice. Like Saul, he could serve the government and pursue the enemy, or he could listen to another voice.

Petr explained that according to Viktor, the OGPU remove their own kind, preferably with poison or a bullet, when they prove an embarrassment to the government. Lukashenko had exceeded that point. But the OGPU's hand could not be apparent in the assassination. An outsider, a hired gun, so to speak, had to arrange the details. In this case, it was decided that a land mine would be the best means to end the mayor's term of office. Lukashenko had ordered his lackeys to award him a medal for service to the oblast. The ceremony was to take place at the Ryazan Kremlin on the winter solstice. Outside the fortress, a ten-foot-high celebratory arbor of ferns would force Lukashenko's car to stop. The mayor would exit and acknowledge the display. A land mine planted at that point in the road would be detonated. The OGPU would provide the explosive and the equipment needed to set it off remotely.

"I had told Viktor, foolishly I now see, that the army had given me advanced training in the manufacture and detonation of mines. He wants me to return to Ryazan for what he calls the 'Fortress Plot' and hook up the explosive."

"Will you?" asked Sasha, who valued Petr's honesty and liked his gentle manner, which Sasha knew that Alya loved.

"I am being promised a full pardon, with my record cleared of desertion, and free transport to Kiev."

"Who will actually pull the trigger, so to speak?"

"Viktor. I am to be given the clothes of a construction road worker so I can plant the land mine and set the timer. By the time the mine goes off, I'll be in Kiev."

"When do you leave here . . . for the plot?"

"I'm expected in Ryazan by December 18."

"And what if the land mine fails to explode?"

"Oh, it'll work. Then, no more Lukashenko. A present to the people of Ryazan."

After spending the morning observing Pavel Glinski's class in world history and listening to him explain to a skeptical student that the North Pole was not discovered by the Russian Otto Schmidt, as the official Soviet line insisted, but rather by the American Rear Admiral Robert E. Peary, a civil engineer, Sasha spent the lunch hour with Pavel discussing the inadequacy of Russian textbooks.

"I wouldn't go so far as to use the word 'bias,'" said Pavel, "but omissions make my task all the more difficult. It would be one thing if the textbooks acknowledged other points of view, but in ours, we receive only the Bolshevik side of things."

"As you know, you have my full support to 'fill in the blanks.'"

Pavel stirred some sour cream into his steaming beet soup and sipped it slowly. The table had cold cuts and cheeses and a bowl with hard-boiled eggs. A loaf of black bread had been baked that same morning. Although Sasha had tried to dissuade teachers from taking a nip at lunch, a bottle of vodka stood within reach. Pavel never touched it, though he was known to be a tippler. He took a piece of brown bread, peeled and salted an egg, and remarked casually, almost apologetically, that he'd heard about Sasha having been denounced.

"We've come to a pass in this country," Pavel observed sadly, "where a man—or a woman—will denounce another for making eye contact. Suddenly, the evil eye has become a favorite complaint."

Sasha reached for an egg and stacked the shells like Chick-Chick, in the shape of a letter S. Pavel stared, as if expecting some magical effect to issue from the placement of the shells. But nothing unusual occurred.

"Do your students ever ask about Trotsky and his role in the revolution? As we all know, the subject is poison, and especially so for someone in my position, director of a school."

Holding up his hands, in a posture of surrender, Pavel replied, "Everyone—students and teachers alike—observe the unwritten but sacred rule that Trotsky is a disappeared person, never to be mentioned or even alluded to."

Sasha shook his head and said nothing. He reminded himself that Filatov wanted a report bearing on Brodsky. Galina had left the school office early. This afternoon was as good as any to call on the erstwhile director. Besides, he owed him a visit, having read Radek's essays. After his dessert of figs and yogurt, he would return to the farmhouse, remove the controversial book from his stewing pot, and set out for Brodsky's cottage. As a parting comment to Pavel, Sasha said, "If I can find less 'biased' textbooks—my word, not yours—I'll try to include them in your curriculum."

With the country now in winter, Sasha pulled up his fur collar, pulled down the ear flaps on his *ushanka*, and trudged home. Opening the door, he smelled a delicious odor. Petr was cooking a stew—in the very pot that Sasha used to hide Radek's book. Looking around and failing to see it, he stifled his fear and asked Petr casually, "Where's the book I stashed in the pot?"

Unruffled, Petr stirred the stew and replied, "I put it on the kitchen table, and Galina picked it up." He then ladled a spoonful of stew into his mouth and casually remarked, "Needs more spice."

Sasha knocked on Galina's door.

In a distracted voice, she asked, "Who is it?"

"May I come in? You have a book of mine that I need."

She opened the door and handed him Radek's collection. Perhaps because of the rupture between them, she stared at the floor. "You do know," she said, "that Radek's early essays are on the prohibited list?" Before he could respond, she added, "The bookplate says Avram Brodsky. For a man sentenced to internal exile, he's running quite a risk. And frankly so are you." She paused. "I thought you had no interest in politics." Lifting her gaze, she smiled wanly. "But if you are, I'm glad to see you reading the Left Opposition and not the Right, and especially not the Stalinists."

Over her shoulder, he could see into her bedroom. The door was ajar. He noticed that her bed, which she always made before leaving for work in the morning, was in disarray. His mind rapidly calculated. Alya had gone off to her tutor. Galina had quit work before lunch. Petr seemed unusually buoyant stirring the stew. The facts were few, but they all pointed in one direction: that husband and wife had engaged in a stew of their own. Sasha's first reaction was jealousy, but at once he reminded himself that the couple *was* married. Had he liked Petr less and Galina more, he would have felt betrayed. Without envy or anger, he pointed past her and said, "You forgot to make the bed."

He tucked the book under his coat and crunched through the light snow toward Brodsky's cottage. From a distance he could see smoke issuing from the chimney, and a minute later, he could smell the sweet scent of birch and maple, both of which, no doubt, were crackling in the fireplace. A single rap brought Avram to the door. Inside, Sasha immediately handed him the book, wishing to be rid of it. After stuffing his gloves in a pocket, he hung his coat and hat on a peg next to the door, and stomped on a mat to dislodge the snow from his felt boots. Then he followed Brodsky to a chair in front of the fire, rubbing his hands and gladly accepting Brodsky's offer of a shot of vodka, which he downed in the Russian manner, with one swallow.

"Well?" asked Brodsky. "What did you think?"

"I knew Radek's general view from the work I did on my history thesis. A Trotskyite."

"But not now."

"So I gather."

"He's helping write the new constitution," said Brodsky, adding mordantly, "A lot of good that will do."

"His help or the document itself?"

"The 1924 constitution provided liberties that this new draft will no doubt omit. Just wait."

An uncomfortable silence settled between the two men. Who would talk first? Brodsky was either trying to draw out Sasha or had carelessly stated his own view of current affairs. In either case, Sasha kept telling himself, "Keep your own counsel."

"Mark my words," continued Brodsky, "this new document is Stalin's constitution, not the people's."

Still Sasha said nothing.

"We were freer in 1924 than we are now," Brodsky added. "Don't you agree?"

Unwilling to take the bait, Sasha tried a diversionary tactic. He asked a question.

"You're asking me," said Brodsky, "what I did before I took over the directorship of the school? I thought you knew. Didn't the major tell you?"

Actually, Sasha did know, but feigned ignorance.

Brodsky went on to explain how his family had owned a chicken farm, and how he spent a great deal of his youth collecting eggs, cleaning them by hand with a rag dipped in a solution of vinegar, weighing them, and separating the white from the brown and the larger from the smaller for market distribution. He said that the chickens his family put on their own table were first ritually killed by a *shochet*, a rabbi of sorts, and that memories of those days drove him to excel at his studies to escape the life of a farmer. In his spare time, after classes, he liked to write. A kind teacher urged him to send one of his stories to a magazine. It was published, and the editor encouraged him to write a play. That experience led him at university to study literature and to write for the school theater. By the time he graduated, commissions had come his way from Soviet state radio for fifteen- or thirty-minute plays.

Now that Sasha had Brodsky reminiscing, he wanted him to continue. A few well-selected memories are the equal of a thousand photographs. The more he learned about Brodsky, the more selective he could be in his report to Filatov—and the safer. He hoped, therefore, that Brodsky would avoid self-incriminating statements and his year in Kolyma. To keep him away from politics, Sasha prompted him to talk about radio plays.

"My director—every writer was assigned one—behaved like a decent fellow. He treated the actors well, and he didn't demand too many script changes. The only thing that raised his hackles was tardiness. If an actor arrived late for rehearsals or taping, he would threaten to discharge the person and bring on another."

"Did you write science fiction, realism, fantasy, children's stories, fairy tales, what?"

Normally, Brodsky could talk and smoke at the same time, exhaling plumes from both nose and mouth. But Sasha observed that the more animated Brodsky became, the less inclined he was to light up. Before Sasha had posed his last question, Avram had reached for a cigarette, but on hearing the question, he put it down and launched into an aesthetic explanation of writing for radio as sight unseen.

"It relies on imagination, which is richer than any photographic realism. Your own mind sets the stage and pictures the action."

Avram said that most people prefer realism, with which they can identify. "They prefer feeling to thinking. Nonrepresentational art may work for painters, but not for writers, nor for Stalin. When characters represent ideas, as they did in classical and medieval drama, and fail to express their pain and suffering and confusion and happiness, listeners can't see themselves in the characters, an identification that most people want. Tearful stories rank higher than ethical dilemmas, unless the latter show the anguish that the characters feel from having to make a Hobson's choice. Admittedly, the best writers can describe sentiment without crossing the line into sentimentality, but there are more poor writers than good ones. The result: bathos, mawkishness, nostalgia, romanticism, mendacity. Just add music and you have melodrama and soap operas."

Sasha was well aware of Soviet realism, plays written to please the Vozhd. He remembered one in which poultry farmers lost their animals to diseases, like fowl pox, influenza, infectious bronchitis, and Newcastle's, until a Soviet veterinarian appeared on the scene and saved the day, that is, the animals.

Eventually, after talking about radio drama and the power of the unseen on the imagination, Brodsky asked whether Sasha had suffered any more denunciations. Having shared his fears at the time with the older man, Sasha appreciated Brodsky's concern. Avram hazarded that the truth-telling curriculum was probably no better than the Soviet one, and that the students, having been cowed in elementary school, were unlikely to ask embarrassing questions. Pausing to stroke his chin in a reflective attitude, he changed the subject. What did Sasha know about a Goran Youzhny who wanted to take Avram's picture? And what did he think of the Radek essays? Surely he had an opinion about them.

Equivocation in the Soviet Union had become a national disease, but Sasha had beheaded two men without hesitation. When he thought about this paradox, he shuddered at the bloodthirsty contradiction that ran through his veins. Perhaps he was one of the untold descendants of Genghis Khan. It certainly felt that way to him on occasion, like now. Summoning his courage and suppressing his suspicions, he went straight for Brodsky's last question.

"Like Radek, I would rather die *for* the country than *against* it. I admit that politics fail to arrest my interest. In Russia, they are either too unsophisticated or too ruthless. If at one time I believed that the best ideas eclipse the poorer ones, I no longer do. But I believe in the country. If at times I may wish to separate myself from it, I cannot. I am a Russian, even when my countrymen behave absurdly and abominably, and all too often barbarously. We live in a country where surgery is performed not with a scalpel but an ax. Radek would probably disagree, believing the Party is all, sick and degraded though it is. Frankly, I do not wish to die for it, as he seems willing to do. But he does recognize that the more the Party kills its critics and detractors, the more it kills itself."

As Sasha spoke, Brodsky devoured several cigarettes. Now he handed the vodka bottle to Sasha and said, "You are only partially right. Take a drink." He snuffed out his cigarette and immediately lit another. "When you have lived your whole life for the Party, as I have, you accept its judgments, even when those include exile or death." He paused to exhale a stream of smoke. "Not to accept is to nullify your whole existence."

Sasha warily noticed that Brodsky had said, "as I have," not "as I did." Was he saying, then, that he still supported the Party—after Kolyma, after all the innocent men and women who had frozen or starved to death, and the many yet to die in the future?

With the room growing dark and the embers fading, Brodksy's cigarette shone like a firefly. For a moment, Sasha imagined Brodsky not as a man but as a floating, bodiless red spot, a distant star, a Cyclopean eye. "The country has about it," said Avram, "the feel of a snowball gaining momentum and size as it hurtles to the bottom. One falsehood leads to another. Suddenly the Russians believe they have discovered the North Pole, and Darwin's theory of evolution has been eclipsed by Lysenko's theory of hybridization. We have already put Mandelstam and Akhmatova and Tsvetaeva on the black list. What will come next? Will Marx and Lenin replace Plato and Aristotle in the pantheon of philosophers? Or have they already? How many more people will be expunged from Soviet history and become non-persons? When we finish rewriting history, our textbooks will tell not of continuous human effort but only of Soviet exceptionalism." He threw back another shot of vodka. "As a teacher I cannot deny the facts. For better or worse, Comrade Sasha, the original snowball, which is now an avalanche, is hurtling toward us. A mountain is threatening to engulf us. Surely, you see that? We have been trained and educated to serve this regime. What else do we have? We are its creatures, its misbegotten children. Don't you understand what has happened—don't you see? That's why you, too, Sasha, must be loyal!"

Brodsky's appeal brought the discussion to an end. In the darkened room, the loudest sound was the crackling of dying coals. The pause gave Sasha time to think, and he suddenly regretted his outburst, knowing full well the cost in Russia of truth telling; but he also felt relieved. Brodsky said nothing.

On his way back to the farmhouse, Sasha stopped at his office. Turning on the hall light, he saw immediately on the bulletin board the large poster: "Trotsky Lives!" How many others had seen it? If no one, he was safe. The fat was in the fire if word got around. He removed the poster, folded it in four parts, and pocketed it to study later. Perhaps the handwriting would look familiar, though he doubted having such luck. The poster and the red crayon used to letter it might be traceable. Such supplies were not easily obtained in a country suffering from a shortage of paper and pencils.

Deep in thought when he arrived home, he almost missed seeing the light in the photo lab and Goran at work. Sasha stopped to ask him about his interest in photographing Brodsky.

"All the other directors of the school," said Goran, "have their pictures in the main hallway. Only Brodsky's is missing. I thought I'd add it to the collection."

According to Filatov, Avram's face had for many years been among those framed in the hall, but once he joined the Left Opposition, down came the picture. Oppositionists did not deserve remembrance. To replace his picture was tantamount to heresy.

"Perhaps not now," said Goran, "but in fifty years a new government might want a complete record. If no photographs of Brodsky exist, then the record can never be complete."

Sasha impatiently said, "I understand your point, Goran, but where do you suggest we store the picture until that rosy time in the future? Brodsky, you know, is considered a non-person. He is out of favor, so how can he exist?"

"In print and on celluloid."

"Not if his plays are banned and pictures erased."

An archive of the damned, thought Sasha, would make for remarkable reading, especially if it included not only what the pariahs had written, but also what others had written about them. Vice made better reading than virtue. Such a collection would be a gold mine. He wondered about all the people who had fallen out of favor with

Stalin. Did their photographs still exist? Perhaps one day, historians would find in old attics all manner of materials: diaries, letters, address books, manuscripts, photographs, paintings, wood carvings, metal works. The list of possibilities was virtually endless. Then, too, there were the radio and screen interviews and appearances. Where would those archives be kept, or had they already been destroyed? Again the question of history and what it means came to Sasha's mind. If you destroy the record of an event does that mean the event never took place? Were we back to the old philosophic chestnut: If a tree falls in the forest and no living person is present is there a sound? Sasha had heard that question asked innumerable times in school, but not until this moment did he have an adequate reply. There may not be a sound (if perception is reality), but there will certainly be a downed tree.

Goran handed Sasha a portfolio and invited him to look at the pictures. The first, taken in the Balyk marketplace, showed a dour Bogdan Dolin. "Did you know," said Goran, "I interviewed him. He's unusually reticent, but he's not stupid. His Kolyma tales are worth recording. As a historian, Director Parsky, I think you would find them valuable."

"I'm sure I would." Sasha pointed at a new piece of equipment. "What's that?"

"An enlarger. It brings out finer details, like the features of people in the background of pictures."

"From your uncle and our mutual friend?"

"Yes, they made it possible, and even had it delivered."

"By special courier?" asked Sasha ironically. "I never saw the postman deliver it."

Goran merely shrugged.

As he flipped through the pictures in the portfolio, Sasha had to concede Goran's artistic abilities. His sense of design and detail were impeccable, highlighting this man's beard or that woman's apron, thus giving definition and character to a picture. Sasha had heard indirectly that the townspeople loved being photographed, most of them issuing from peasant stock and never before being treated as persons of interest. Goran gave them copies of his photographic portraits, and they in turn blessed him, hung religious medals around his neck, and invited him to share their meals.

Without asking Goran, he pondered why Bogdan Dolin and Avram had captured his attention. Hearing the horrors of a work camp held no fascination for Sasha, but perhaps Dolin had more than Avram to offer about how abominably people treat one another.

Petr's delicious stew kept discussion to a minimum, as the party of four lost themselves in the savory tastes. Judging from Petr's diary, Sasha would never have guessed that the soldier loved to cook. His thoughts drifted to the locked chest in which he kept the diary, as buried as the unrecognized but meaningful skills of Petr Selivanov.

"Have you ever tried working as a chef?" asked Sasha.

"During the time I was gone, when the occasion warranted, I would fill in for an absent cook."

In jest, Sasha replied, "Ukraine could use you. From what I hear, the food there is awful: day one herring and borscht; day two borscht and herring."

"You forgot to mention potatoes," Galina added.

Suppressing a chuckle, Petr remarked that while he was traveling, he came across a great many peasants who believed that potatoes were the fruit with which Eve tempted Adam, and therefore they refused to plant or eat them.

"I gather," said Sasha, "that the government's attempt to stamp out religious ignorance hasn't been completely successful."

"Nor has their attempt to quash reverence for the Tsar."

Here was Sasha's opening. He took from his pocket the folded poster and opened it. "What do you think of this? I found it pinned to the school bulletin board."

Alya read the words out loud, "'Trotsky Lives.' What does it mean?"

"Good question," said Sasha. "I've been asking myself the same thing. Maybe someone here can tell me."

Galina immediately made it clear that she had left her school office early and had not seen the poster.

"Are you worried?" asked Petr.

"If others have seen it, yes. Otherwise, no."

Alya sat wide-eyed.

"It is either a prank or a serious protest," Sasha said. "But how can one know?"

Petr recounted similar experiences in the army. Drafted soldiers would post statements intended to embarrass or hurt senior officers. Hardly a single culprit was ever caught. "But," Petr added, "I can tell you what the officers did. They posted their own notices pointing out the error or malice of the first one. You might want to do the same. In these troubled days, defensive action is often called for."

"Who is Trotsky?" asked Alya. "I thought it was a swear word, like when one kid calls another a Trotskyite."

The three adults at the table exchanged glances before Sasha ventured an explanation. "Our Supreme Leader and Trotsky disagreed, so Stalin sent Trotsky to live and work in a faraway part of the country. But some people think that Trotsky's ideas were better than those of the Vozhd. And nobody likes to be thought of as second best. Right?"

Alya shrugged, but her indifference vanished when she asked excitedly, "Where did the person find crayons?"

Galina shook her head in agreement, remarking, "It might be a clue to the poster's author. Don't you think so, Sasha?"

For the first time since learning about the murders taking place at the Parsky farm, she'd called him "Sasha," instead of "you."

"So too might the poster cardboard, which is hard to find."

Petr nearly leapt from his chair. "Goran has thin cardboard."

"How do you know?" asked Galina.

"The other night, he was working late, so I strolled over to see him. You know I've always been interested in photography. He was using cardboard for backing on a picture he intended to frame."

Sasha mumbled to himself, "The uncle in Moscow."

"What's that?" asked Petr.

"Nothing."

Alya deepened the mystery when she remarked, "I sometimes see an old man go into the studio. He's from town, not the school."

"You know him?" Galina asked.

"No, but I've seen him in the village square. He's sort of scary." She waved her hands and described his mushroom-like hair. "You've seen him, too, Mamma."

Although Petr knew nothing of the "death cap," Sasha and Galina did. At that moment, Sasha knew whom to ask about Dolin: Brodsky. Goran had photographed Bogdan Dolin, and, in fact, had volunteered that he found him worth talking to. Bogdan had served time in the Arctic wastes, where many ex-prisoners married and remained, and yet he had returned to Balyk. Why? Was he from this town or area? Given his antipathy toward Brodsky, Bogdan may have crossed swords with Avram, in which case Brodsky could tell him about this man. Sasha leaned over the table and patted Alya's hand.

"You may have solved the riddle."

Gleefully, Alya said, "Have I?"

"I think I know the person."

"Tell me!"

"In this country, Alya, you never name names unless you are absolutely certain, and even then you have to think twice."

Sasha had come close to sharing his suspicions, but in the current environment the least said the better.

Wednesday nights, Galina conducted her male chorus in patriotic and classical songs. Four of the twelve young men actually had promising voices, two tenors, a baritone, and a bass. She had never learned music formally in a conservatory, but from her grandmother who played the balalaika and a beautiful accordion inlaid with ivory. The older woman had taught her granddaughter to read music, play a violin, and sing. Galina most enjoyed voice lessons because she could sing in virtually any venue, whereas she could hardly carry around a violin with her to play when she felt in the mood. Her pitch was perfect and her ear unerring. If a singer failed to hit the note perfectly, too sharp or too flat, she could immediately identify the offending voice.

Benjamin Korsakov, a countertenor, was one of the "tin ears." He keenly loved to sing and had a bellows for a chest, but he could never quite land on the note. "Benjamin Korsakov," she would say, "if you must sing flat, then sing softly." Although the other students snickered, they loved "Benjie" for his passion. They also loved him for his uncomplaining nature, despite a feckless father who treated learning as the devil's dung, and a sickly mother so thin you could see through her nearly transparent skin to her ailing arteries. An only child, Benjie stuttered, except when he sang; and then, as if to dispel his frustration, he sounded like Gabriel's horn. When the chorus performed for the public, Benjie's mother was sure to be found front and center. His father attended only once, dozed off, snored, and was led from the room objecting to having been awakened. Benjie's classmates pretended that the incident never happened.

Neither a slow student nor a particularly gifted one, Benjie had been admitted to the Michael School for mysterious reasons. His parents had no money, and, as Devora Berberova knew, the state wasn't paying. So who was? Benjie's father never worked, spending his days producing ash. He was a prodigious pipe smoker. Yet another mystery was who provided his tobacco money. The only saving grace was that the bronchitic and stenotic Ivan Korsakov suffered from narcolepsy, which meant that his habitual smoking was regularly interrupted by sleep. How he had found time to father Benjie was a standing joke.

Natalia Korsakova, Benjie's mother, who had once cooked and cleaned for Avram Brodsky during his tenure as director of the school, performed domestic duties around Balyk and worked as a midwife, a skill that had been passed down in her family from mother to daughter. It was rumored that she had delivered Benjie without assistance while her husband slept. Needless to say, Benjie was the apple of her eye, and she had sung to him from his first day in the cradle. As a young boy, he had a high-pitched voice that remained with him well into adulthood. Before the Balyk church had been closed and services banned, Benjie's soprano-like voice had gained him a place in the choir, and everyone in town looked forward to hearing his soaring countertenor, even though his pitch was frequently off. It was suggested by more than one person that the Michael School had admitted Benjie for his voice, but Galina knew that the townspeople had so little music training themselves that they wouldn't know a flat from a sharp. Tutoring him, as she often did, she treated him as a surrogate son, inviting him to dinner and watching him make loneliness less familiar to Alya, who never forgot him.

Alya's memory was remarkable for how much she could remember and from such an early age. In her adoptive home, she normally suppressed her memories and lived in the present, but on winter days, a certain slant of light brought to mind her parents and the happy times they'd spent together. The Selivanovs had kept her parents' names alive, Maja and Yefim Boujinski, and Alya had even managed to rescue a photograph of the three of them in a park, she on a swing, and they standing on either side of her. Her memories were always of places, phrases, and disembodied particulars. She remembered snowflakes disappearing in a river, a pair of yellow woolen mittens, a zippered bear suit dyed blue that she wore on the coldest days, a luge, a hill that children thronged to when the snow was right for sledding, a gully at the bottom of the hill that capsized more than a few of her friends, a woodland path in a birch forest, melodious birdsong, foxes with white tails, a pony ride in a nearby ring, a sliding board, a merry-go-round, a calliope, a man playing the accordion and leading a monkey on a chain, a bird seller, winter festival chocolates and choristers, Easter and painted eggs and the smell of incense, fasting during the day for Ramadan (she had insisted on imitating her parents) and stuffing herself in the evening on sweet meats and homemade bread and honey, her father's Koranic readings to the family, his barbering tools, and especially the silver comb and delicate inlaid brushes, her mother's shoes, which she loved to try on, neatly arrayed in the closet.

Unlike Alya's tutor, Ekaterina Rzhevska, a retired elementary-school teacher who had settled in Balyk to be near her son, Benjie had a way with Alya. Ekaterina came to the Michael School each day and tutored Alya and three other children, the offspring of teachers. Sasha had equipped a small room at the back of the school for this purpose. Katia, as the children called her, grounded her lessons in language and literature, and in the basic elements of arithmetic. What she lacked was a sense of humor and flexibility. She looked and acted like a ferule. Straight as a pole and thin as a pipe cleaner, she wore her gray hair tightly pulled back in a bun. Her face resembled a skin stretched to its limits, forcing her to speak out of a constricted mouth. Fastidious in her habits, she checked the children's fingernails each day. Not a naturally warm person, Katia could, when the situation demanded, embrace an ailing child. Neither Galina nor the other parents complained.

In comparison to Katia's stoicism stood Benjie, all mirth and merriment. He didn't tutor Alya but he brought out her playful qualities, introducing her to card and board games, sharing his scrapbooks with pictures of movie stars, and making up stories. Galina frequently observed that Benjie would one day write fiction. Given the stories he told, Galina predicted he'd become a teller of fairy tales. One "word" story that both Galina and Alya liked concerned a beautiful firefly, Gloriana, who often misbehaved and refused to come home at a decent hour, wishing to spend the evening making dazzling loops and turns and flips and dives and dips. When her mother chided Gloriana and said that her behavior was sinful, Gloriana merely performed another trick and replied, "I want to sin till late."

Everyone would laugh at the pun, but most of all Benjie.

Galina had assigned each singer a solo part and, in some cases, divided the part so that every member of the choir would have the opportunity to sing. For their next concert, Benjie asked if he could sing a soprano aria from *The Marriage of Figaro*: "Dove sono I bei momenti di dolcezza e di piacer" (Where are the beautiful moments of sweetness and pleasure?). The aria, one of Mozart's most poignant, seemed a strange choice—until his moment came. Then everything changed. In the opera, the countess is remembering the former happy days she spent with her husband, who is now running after other women. Benjie took a step forward on stage. The audience, composed mostly of students and townspeople, also included teachers, minor Soviet officials, school maintenance workers, Father Zossima, Sasha, Petr, and Alya. With the opening notes, Benjie dispelled Galina's fear that he would sing flat. He was right on key. But instead of the famous Italian words "Dove sono . . . etc." Benjie substituted the Russian words "Here sits my beautiful mother, who gives me pleasure and joy." Before the audience could react, he continued and concluded in Italian. At the end, the audience sat stunned. Was it from Benjie's audacity or the brilliant manner in which he had introduced Russian into the aria? In this moment of awe, Benjie bowed and stepped back into the chorus. Before the audience could respond, his fellow choral members, who knew never to applaud one of their own, clapped and stomped their feet. An instant later, the audience followed suit and demanded that Natalia Korsakova take a bow with her son. She slowly ascended the stage and embraced Benjie, both of them now in tears. The audience, equally moved, called for an encore. With his mother smiling and looking out over the heads of the audience, Benjie repeated his love song to his mother.

Sitting there, as affected as the others, if not more so, Sasha, thinking of his own mother, and perhaps all mothers, could not help but wonder at the Russian people's great store of feeling. At that moment, political parties, personal jealousies, poseurs, Stalin's paranoia—none of it mattered. What mattered was the music and Benjie, and Benjie was the music.

Although Brodsky kept up with news about the chorus—their performances and the music they'd sung—Sasha wished that Avram's exilic life did not exclude concerts. They could talk about the Mozart tomorrow night, when Sasha planned to ask Brodsky about Bogdan Dolin. Except for an occasional walk in the woods and his Sunday chats in the square, Brodsky remained at home. It was his study and cell. An elderly woman from town brought him food. Where he found the money to pay her was anyone's guess, but he never seemed short of food, drink, warm clothes, books, or cigarettes.

After the concert, Galina stayed behind to congratulate the students and to share some food and wine that Sasha had paid for out of pocket. Something about Benjie, other than his voice, had strangely moved him. He wanted time to think and volunteered to see Alya home—it was past her bedtime. Petr remained to help Galina. As Sasha and Alya tramped through the snow, he repeated to himself Shelley's line: "If winter comes can spring be far behind." Of course, Shelley had in mind more than the seasons. He was thinking of political change, as well. Perhaps Benjie's wonderful moment would be a harbinger of better things to come. Among those better things, he knew not to count Lukashenko's assassination. Sasha would have to dissuade Petr from abetting Viktor's madness, which could lead only to a life of bitter, black years.

Alya, who had understood the reason for Benjie's interpolation, asked whether other singers—professional ones—did the same. No, of course, they didn't, but her question made him think of those innocent men and women brought before the bar who subsequently change their stories. An interpolation of sorts. I am not guilty; I am guilty. A difference of one word, but a word powerful enough to decide life and death. If only an aria had that much authority.

10

"Magnificent, Avram! You should have heard the boy."

"I did."

"Where?"

"At the concert. I was standing at the back of the room next to the bookcase."

A skeptical Sasha looked at Avram in the dim light of the cottage and asked, "If you were there, then tell me what Benjie's mother was wearing in her hair?" Sasha knew that given Brodsky's contact or contacts, someone might have already told him in detail about the concert, but was unlikely to have described Natalia's headdress.

Avram had answered the door lipping a cigarette. He now lit it. "She was wearing two ribbons, one red and one yellow, which hung down her back, peasant style." He inhaled, and on the exhale said, "You would have no way of knowing, Sasha, but Natalia Korsakova was once a beautiful woman. In fact, she trained for the opera, until a botched tonsillectomy, which ought to have been routine, ruined her voice."

It wasn't until that epiphanic moment that Sasha realized what it was about Benjie that he had found so strange. Benjie resembled Brodsky, especially around the eyes. Of course, it all made sense. The beautiful mother had worked for Brodsky. They had had an affair. Natalia became pregnant. Brodsky somehow arranged a marriage between Natalia and Ivan Korsakov and promised to support the family. Hence the money for Ivan's tobacco and Benjie's schooling. It was Natalia who had fared the worst. She had to supplement the family's meager sums with housework and midwifery. Why had Brodsky not taken care of her? After all, she figuratively had him by the throat and could easily have exposed him. So why didn't she? Countless reasons ran through Sasha's head. If Brodsky had lost his job, which in fact occurred later, he couldn't have given the family any money. If Brodsky had married Natalia . . . impossible. The poor woman was barely literate, though she could read music. Perhaps, just perhaps, Brodsky had advised an abortion, and she had refused. That would certainly explain his selective support of Mr. Korsakov and Benjie. He thought again of Shakespeare's tangled web.

After his last visit to Brodsky, Sasha had intended to write to Filatov. He was now glad that he hadn't because further visits would give him reason to ask the OGPU officer for information about Brodsky's background. That Avram might still be secretly working with the Left Opposition meant precious little to Sasha. But by sharing with Filatov a few innocuous tidbits, he hoped to elicit a fuller understanding of this enigmatic Brodsky fellow: savant, pedagogue, enemy of the people, political prisoner (Kolyma), exile, nicotine addict, seducer (perhaps), and recipient of funds from some unknown source.

As usual, Brodsky invited Sasha to sit and share his vodka. But first he had to revive the fire. The dying one in the grate had already turned to embers. Stacking the kindling and logs, Brodsky proudly declared that he had a new idea, and that he wanted to run it by Sasha. He promised that his idea would not endanger Sasha, like the ones that had led to his own incarceration at Kolyma. Once the flames started leaping, Brodsky started explaining what he called the theory of exaggerated differences. Dressed in a woolen shirt that came to his knees and was belted at the waist, he also wore a pair of black flaring Cossack pants and high boots. He looked as if he were preparing to take part in a Hopak dance, though Sasha knew that the fifty-six-year-old Brodsky no longer had the stamina, strength, or knees to perform the Ukrainian national dance.

"My theory," he croaked, "is simple but elegant, the stamp of all good theories." He cleared his throat. "People poles apart in their thinking, without any chance of agreeing, present no threat to one another. Never the twain shall meet. But those people who belong to offshoots of political parties or churches, for example, religious sects, are just close enough to the core beliefs to represent a problem. A Left Bolshevik or a Right Bolshevik . . . they are both Bolsheviks. But they are just different enough from the prevailing orthodoxy that they need to be expunged, lest they draw others to their cause or corrupt the fixed orthodoxy. In addition, the sects have to exaggerate their differences from all the other sects to establish their identity; otherwise people are likely to say, 'I don't see any difference between you and them.' Among Protestants, you have Baptists, Lutherans, Methodists, Episcopalians, Congregationalists, Seventh-Day Adventists, and so on. How is one to tell the difference between them? Therefore they have to exaggerate their differences. But in fact between them there is little space. So the question becomes are we better off running around propounding our small differences or are we better off rallying around a single belief, a single church, a single political party that will be all the stronger for our allegiance and alliance? Differences invite comparisons, and comparisons lead to division. What do you think?"

Sasha wanted Brodsky to talk about Bogdan Dolin. So he tried to segue into his subject. "Did you figure out this theory in Kolyma?"

"The idea came to me when I was housed with a group of Christian missionaries. They fought among themselves more fiercely than the camp's criminal population."

"Then you were segregated at Kolyma?" he asked, knowing full well that the two groups were housed in different buildings, but hoping to wend his way to Bogdan Dolin.

"The usual separation was between the politicals and the criminals. And I can tell you, the criminals preyed terribly on the politicals, people like me. For one thing the criminals hated intellectuals, because they regarded all politicals as thinkers. For another, the criminals may have been moral cowards, but they were physical bullies, and the politicals had no stomach for a fistfight. For a third thing, the criminals regarded themselves as patriots. Oh yes, they had broken the law, stolen this or thieved that, but they were Stalin's true believers. The politicals detested the Vozhd, which was as good as telling the criminals they supported a madman."

"Why were you arrested?"

"I thought you knew of my outspokenness and my participation in the Left Opposition movement. My tongue and opinions cost me my job and earned me a year in Siberia."

"With Bogdan Dolin."

Brodsky scoffed. "My only convert. He used to come to the school auditorium to hear me speak. At one lecture, after I had been critical of the government confiscating farmland, he said, 'I agree with you.' That—and his other misdeeds—landed him in Kolyma. The government didn't take kindly to his forgeries and counterfeiting. His farm and fields were expropriated. They became part of the collective on the outskirts of Balyk. When Bogdan returned from Kolyma, he'd sit at the edge of the road and look at his lost land. People thought he had gone crazy, which I suppose in a way was true. Eventually he acquired the small cottage he now occupies. It was a bungalow belonging to a larger house. For a long time, it was boarded up. But Bogdan somehow managed to gain control of the place and has lived there ever since. Some people say he did a favor for a Soviet official, and in return was given the bungalow. I don't know."

"Why does he dislike you so?"

"He was housed with the politicals and suffered the tortures meted out by the criminals. He blamed me for introducing him to subversive ideas."

Sardonically, Sasha observed, "He's obviously clever enough to realize that ideas can be dangerous."

"He goes one step further. He tells anyone who will listen that a school is a dangerous place. Of course, he has in mind the auditorium, where he used to listen to my orations, as I immodestly call them." Brodsky refilled both glasses and threw back a shot of vodka. Sasha paused. No one spoke for a moment. Brodsky downed another. "Why do you think," he asked rhetorically, "Filatov or some other OGPU agent checks in here regularly? Unconventional ideas may surface and, as Bogdan says, inspire students to question the world around them. That's why I originally came here. I wanted to bring about change; I wanted to introduce new ideas, fresh ones. But most Soviet teachers are trained to be obedient and are expected to pass the lessons of obedience on to their students. But for yourself and perhaps Galina Selivanova, your entire staff has been schooled in obedience. You know it, and I know it, but they don't. Sadly, they have no idea that obedience is deadly. No matter what new idea, fact, or theory you share with your staff, they will ask themselves if it accords with Bolshevism. Why? Because of obedience. And if the idea is at odds with Bolshevism, it will fall on deaf ears. When I was director, I tried to speak to the staff about a liberal Bolshevism, the opposite of Stalinism. They patiently listened. Some of them I could tell even tried to understand me, but in the end, they adhered to what they'd been taught. They obeyed. The result: Your colleagues are automatons. They do not exist; they only obey."

Avram's discourse offended Sasha. He wanted to defend his staff, some of whom seemed to be trying to "modernize" their teaching methods. His reply was intended to counter Avram's pessimism. "Even when we obey, we continue to exist. And as long as we exist . . ."

Brodsky interrupted. "Yes, we exist as numbers and moving parts in a larger machine."

In his spinning mind, Sasha pondered the interchangeable parts the Soviets had put in place. With central planning, all a manager had to do when a person or part was needed was request a replacement. Someone on the other end of the telephone checked the rosters for each section of the country to see who was available. Ironically, because of the inefficiency of Soviet factories, people were easier to replace than mechanical items. He snickered to himself thinking that Russia had become a warehouse of human drones who could be sent through nine time zones to meet a need. They were the wheels and cogs and gauges and dials. If a plant or factory manager actually wished to see everything in working order—and not all of them did—broken machinery often required the presence of die makers and welders and skilled mechanics. But without a competent manager, the factories ground to a halt, sometimes simply for want of a gear or a flywheel or a washer.

If what Brodsky said about teachers and obedience was true, then were the government so disposed, everyone at the Michael School could be replaced by a compliant and complaisant cog from another area or school. No one was indispensable. Did this mean that Sasha had put his colleagues at risk by insisting on changes? Filatov had asked for modernization, but Filatov himself could be purged in a minute. Given that fact, a practical person could arrive at only one conclusion: better safe than sorry, better obedient than banished.

"You never said, Avram, whether you shared my opinion about Benjie's performance. Brilliant or not?"

"In voice, yes."

"Then I take it you disapproved of the homage to his mother?"

A large red handkerchief materialized out of Brodsky's pocket. He blew his nose loudly and stuffed the dirty linen back into his pants. Lighting a cigarette, he went to the bookcase. How he could see anything in the poor light was a mystery. But his hand knowingly reached above his head to a shelf with volumes of English works. He removed an enormous tome in Moroccan leather, Robert Burton's *The Anatomy of Melancholy*.

"The man was a genius. What he calls melancholy we call depression. You do read English, don't you?" Sasha nodded. "Good. Every educated Russian should know French, German, and English."

"Are you giving me this book because you think I'm depressed?"

"No, because if you want to understand the inner workings of Avram Brodsky, read Burton. We both use melancholy as the lens through which to view emotion and thought."

Sasha took the book and admired its leather binding. "I've never thought of you as melancholy or depressed, in fact, the opposite: irrepressible, committed, passionate, intellectually energetic."

"Since you arrived at the school, Sasha, we have become close, I would dare say good friends, and yet you don't know me. You don't know, for example, that I still retain a master key to the school, which I have kept among my belongings through thick and thin . . . kept it safe even in Kolyma. Just as we hold some memories dear, so too we treat some material things as talismans. The key to the school symbolizes to me the key to the world. It represents all that human beings are capable of achieving. But to achieve we must change. If our students leave the school the way they come—bigoted, provincial, superstitious—they will have accomplished nothing. The underlying assumption of education, the unstated premise, is that change is possible and desirable. To see a young man grow from sapling to tree is a miracle. In that sense, I regarded myself as a tiller of soil and a sower of seeds.

"I liked being a school director. I liked teaching classes. It's exhilarating to have an audience, particularly when you wish to share an idea. Actors play a role; teachers analyze ideas and argue points of view. I prefer the latter, even though I used to write radio plays." He paused for a moment, as if remembering something. "Some of the classrooms in the Michael School have a distinctive smell that comes from the desks and chalkboards and books. No two rooms are exactly alike. Blindfolded, I could tell you which one I was in. Occasionally, I make a nocturnal visit to the school, unlock the door, and just walk the halls and inhale the classrooms. The school floorboards are like maps. Without looking, I know which have soft spots and which are splintered. I know every creak. I even know the idiosyncrasies of the office typewriters, Devora Berberova's and Galina's. By the way, Galina dropped by here the other day and borrowed my French edition of Zola's *Nana*. We chatted briefly. She seemed interested in which of my opinions had earned me a trip to Siberia. I told her nothing. In this country, trust is impossible. But without trust we are alone. I have observed you closely and liked what I have seen." Then Brodsky made the most amazing request. "Let me put my life in your care."

Sasha held up his hands defensively and said, "I want no privileged glimpses into your heart."

In a deliberate and sober voice, Brodsky replied, "It is the only way I can make you my guardian, my judge and jury. If I die, so too does a part of you."

Unsure whether Brodsky was engaging in some kind of deceit, Sasha laughed self-consciously and said, "Fortunately, we don't share a life."

"Unless I make you privy to mine."

"I'd rather you didn't," pleaded Sasha, cupping his ears. "I don't want to be an accessory."

Lightly moving Sasha's hands, Brodsky gently coaxed, "To what, truth? I wish to promote honesty and not betray it. Just listen, and you decide who Avram Brodsky really is."

With this introduction, he told a convoluted story of treachery, double-dealing, and denunciation. Born in Lithuania to a herring dealer and a seamstress, he came to Russia at the age of five. His parents settled in a small fishing village north of St. Petersburg. The only Jews in the community, they worshiped in the dark, a condition to which Brodsky accustomed himself, with only a candle or two to light their way. Apprenticed to a tanner, he came to hate the sight of animal skins and the smell of tannic acid. His mother taught him to read and write, and his formal schooling did not begin until the tanner, Markus Schmidt, a kindly Bavarian whose family dated back to the German craftsmen who had helped build St. Petersburg in the eighteenth century, paid for him to attend the local school. By the time of the 1903 revolution, Brodsky was twenty-three, and he never forgot the sight of reformers and Constitutionalists strung up on lampposts, left to dangle in the wind until some brave souls in the middle of the night cut them down. The butchery and the Tsar's intransigence led him to become a revolutionary, first a Social Democrat, then a Menshevik, and finally a Bolshevik. Given his democratic leanings, he joined the liberal wing of the Party and opposed Stalin's ruthless rise to power, all the while subscribing to the socialist dream of a world in which wealth was shared, class and religion were abolished, and people worked for the greater good of the country and not greedily for themselves. His political group came to be known as the Left Opposition, and their leader, in spirit if not in flesh, was Leon Trotsky, born Lev Davidovich Bronstein (1879) and exiled by Stalin in 1929. Although Trotsky's hands were not free of blood, and though he had suppressed the democratic naval uprising at Kronstadt, he opposed Stalin's tyrannical rule and suppression of human rights.

The Left Opposition had a good friend in Avram Brodsky. In his mid-forties, when he became director of the Michael School (1925), he was fearless in sharing his ideas with his colleagues, the community, and anyone else who would listen. After Trotsky's exile, conditions for dissenters, on the left and the right, became dangerously precarious but not perilous. Then, in 1933, Stalin introduced terror as a political weapon. Kirov's murder in December 1934, like Hitler's "night of the long knives," ushered in mass arrests and shootings. Taking his cue from Hitler, Stalin purged his Party. The lucky ones were merely exiled, like Brodsky (denouncer unknown!). Uprooted from Balyk and in the company of Bogdan Dolin, he was transported in a Stolypin wagon—railroad cars divided into wire cages with shelves for sleeping quarters—to Siberia. The trip took two weeks. By the time they arrived, the slop buckets used for toilets were overflowing and the stench was unbearable. Those who had boarded the train in weak health worsened or died. Those who had boarded in good health often left the train diseased or defeated. Brodsky swore to himself that he would live, and that he would see the day that Russia subscribed to a humane socialism. In the camps and the gold mines, it was apparent that the only way to survive was to ingratiate yourself with some official and be assigned an easy duty, not cutting down trees or mining but working in the dispensary or cafeteria or camp post office. He immediately wrote his superior, the commandant, and disavowed the ideas that had cost him his freedom. He forswore the Left Opposition and wrote a scathing critique of Trotsky and his position on world revolution. Brodsky's paper urged his readers to support Stalin's theory of revolution in one country. That short treatise earned him a position in the dispensary administering morphine to dying patients.

Bogdan Dolin never forgave Brodsky his recantation and easy duty, having himself been brutalized by the camp criminals and having to serve a longer sentence than Brodsky. Dolin accused Avram of loving his torturers just to mitigate the conditions of his own sentence. So whenever Brodsky told stories in the town square about Kolyma, Dolin stood as a visual reminder to the apostate that he had led others to a near-death confinement and then saved his own hide by siding with the enemy. But Brodsky said that he and Stalinism were incompatible, and that his renunciation of his former beliefs had starved his conscience. When he returned to Balyk and took up his lonely residence, an old comrade contacted him to ask if he would become active in the underground of the Left Opposition. After much soul searching, he agreed. So although outwardly he was living as an internal exile and espousing the glories of Stalinism, he was secretly working for the democratic socialist opposition, writing letters, raising money from émigrés in Europe, anonymously denouncing orthodox Bolsheviks as wreckers and enemies of the people. Who was his courier? Here Brodsky paused, suspecting that Sasha would find it hard to credit the name he was about to confess. Natalia Korsakova. In 1920, during the civil war, they had fought together against the Whites and had sanctified their comradeship with an affair. Benjie was his son. But lest anyone suspect Natalia of working for Brodsky as his postal courier, he gave her no money. She was paid by agents of the Left Opposition. Her domestic work was a cover. And except for those occasions when they could meet at a deserted hunter's cabin in the forest to pass information or letters, and perhaps even make love (Sasha's extrapolation), he and Natalia had no contact.

What money came to Brodsky, which he shared with Benjie and Ivan Korsakov, came from . . . and again Brodsky paused knowing the effect his disclosure would have . . . came from the OGPU and Boris Filatov, to whom he was currently working as a double agent, spying on the Left Opposition, reporting to the secret police, and sharing what he learned from the secret police with the Left Opposition. Hence the periodic visits of Filatov or one of his associates to Balyk and to Brodsky's cottage.

"As a committed Bolshevik, I want a democratic socialism, not a totalitarian one. To continue working for the Left Opposition and to remain in Balyk, I have to keep on good terms with the Party, which means I have to be perceived as helping them. And helping them means reporting on others. So I pass along harmless information. In return, Filatov pays me. For what? For trivia. He thinks, like the poet William Blake, he can see the world in a grain of sand."

A wan Sasha, feeling as if he'd been skewed on the head of a pin, replied, "You realize, of course, that what you've just told me could cost you your life, as well as my own?"

"Why do you think I've opened my heart to you?" Sasha thought the diction rang false. "I'm not a madman hoping you'll expose me. I want you for our own. A Left Oppositionist."

"Of all the people to select: me! I detest politics."

Brodsky's coarse laughter was anything but mirthful, and in the light of the fire, the smoke issuing from his mouth and nose made him look demonic, an image that Sasha found as upsetting as the one of two decapitated men. At that moment, Sasha debated whether or not to tell Brodsky that Filatov had asked him to keep an eye on the former director. He decided against it, feeling certain Brodsky would reply that he too had been asked to spy—on Sasha. Such was life in the Soviet Union. But the one choice he could not escape was reporting to Filatov. He could repeat what Brodsky had said and thereby protect his own skin. Weren't all patriotic citizens expected to convey to the secret police information that might prove detrimental to the state? Not to convey it made you equally guilty. For the nonce, he decided that silence was better than being a knave.

Although he had decided after the murders that he would make every effort to ingratiate himself with the law, using every linguistic and lexical trick in his toolbox—neologisms, indirection, double meanings, obfuscation, euphemism—he refused to employ the national disease of the Soviet Union, denunciation. Some means vitiated the ends.

No, denunciation was too repulsive. Although Sasha couldn't swear to Brodsky's trustworthiness, he knew his own. If a good conscience is a soft pillow, as the Russian proverb says, then Sasha intended to sleep peacefully. Besides, he knew that the type of information people traded in and how they represented it could reveal as much about the trader—or did he mean traitor?—as the person being denounced. There were other difficulties. Even if Brodsky had told the truth, had he told all of it? Based on what he had heard, Sasha wanted to ask him innumerable questions. Without answers to those questions, he felt that Brodsky's narrative was incomplete. Why, for example, would Filatov continue to pay him for worthless gossip? Then, too, other people were involved, in particular, Natalia Korsakova. Sasha therefore decided that for now he would simply recount for Filatov the interesting literary discussions in which he and Brodsky frequently engaged. "Interesting" was normally a safe word when you wished to avoid a direct question: "How did you like the play?" Reply: "I found it interesting." In short, information was a slippery business. Either you knew too much or too little. Both conditions rendered one vulnerable.

But the one truth he knew for sure was that he had unwittingly become Brodsky's creature.

11

The Michael School, under Galina's energetic supervision, began to plan for the Russian Winter Festival that would take
place for two days in the school auditorium on the weekend prior to
the winter solstice. Everyone was encouraged to participate or lend
a hand: students, faculty, and staff. Even some villagers pitched in,
contributing to the carpentry and stitchery. The auditorium became
a beehive of activity, as the seats were carefully removed and stored
to create a large, open area. Saws and planes, hammers and nails,
chisels and screwdrivers converted the drab space into a colorful
bazaar with student booths featuring different foods, a dart game,
a palm reader, a crystal gazer, a shell game, a book sale, artwork,
and photographic exhibits. The center area was reserved for music,
dances, and songs; and the stage would hold a vaudeville routine,
poetry readings, short dramatic scenes, and a play. Until Petr departed to meet Viktor in Ryazan, he worked alone in the farmhouse
on sketches for the stage set, and Natalia Korsakova and Ekaterina
Rzhevska actively contributed to the costume design.

The festival was scheduled to open at two on Saturday afternoon
and the play, advertised as a surprise, was to begin at eight. Sunday
would be dedicated to winter sports. All of the indoor activities
were taking shape within sight of the organizers. Rehearsals, however, were held in another part of the school. No one but the actors

and the director, Galina Selivanova, knew which play would be staged Saturday night. Whether it was a Russian masterpiece, written by Chekhov or Ostrovsky or Tolstoy or Turgenev, or an original play composed by one of the students or staff, remained a well-guarded secret. Galina would say only that "it will be quite amusing." Not even Sasha had read the play, but knowing the author, he had expressed some reservations.

In the period leading up to the production, Galina was a whirling dervish, appearing everywhere. Her ambient electricity fired up others as they swung into action preparing scenery, sets, lighting, and props. Leading her charges, Galina, with her sleeves rolled up, seemed especially attractive and sexually alluring to Sasha. At the end of each day, he had a fierce desire to bathe with her, fondle her breasts, and then make love. But not until Petr left for Ryazan would that be possible. He rarely left the farmhouse, lying low, afraid that at any moment a policeman would come knocking at the door. Except for an occasional nocturnal walk in the woods with Sasha, he stayed close to home, so close that a few people began to ask questions about his reclusiveness. Goran, for one, wondered about this guest and often invited him into his photo lab to see some of his work.

Following a particularly satisfying rehearsal, Sasha asked Galina to remain after the others had left. Backstage, he took her in his arms and begged to make love. She agreed. As they lay on a pile of costumes, she traced her finger along his mouth and told him about Petr: his girlfriend in Kiev and Petr's wish for her to divorce him. Alya would remain with her, of course, but Petr swore to stay in touch with his daughter. Galina then remarked on Alya's affection for Sasha, and how well the two got along. "It's the child in you," she said, "and when I see that playfulness, I am reminded of my grandfather's zest for games and fun. He and my father never saw eye to eye, but he was special to me. It was he who taught me to ride and handle horses. When he died, I was devastated." She pressed her lips to Sasha's and said, "Never abandon me. I would find it too painful." Then they slipped out of their clothes and, more than ever before, made passionate love.

On opening day, booths lined the auditorium except for the stage. By early evening, strolling minstrels appeared in the middle of the room making music on puff accordions and violins and castanets. At the same time, students dressed in Tartar robes and turbans sang and danced in a manner reminiscent of Scheherazade. A few of the more athletically gifted boys juggled and tumbled and somersaulted and stood on their hands. After this introductory number, which concluded with young men dashing around the room with lighted torches, four students took the stage for a vaudeville skit. Dressed as American hoboes, with black cork smeared on their faces, they engaged in a rapid give-and-take.

FIRST: This may be a circus, but git away from that thar elephant.
SECOND: Aw, I ain't hurtin' him.

The next two students step forward with a chair, a scissor, and a cardboard cutout of a dog. One student sits while the other pretends to snip his hair.

CUSTOMER: Your dog seems very fond of watching you cut hair.
BARBER: It ain't that; sometimes I snip off a bit of the customer's ear.

The four boys engage in a rapid patter.

FIRST: This dog cost us virtually nothing. He was a real bargain.
SECOND: Oh, that's nice. Because a bargain dog never bites.
THIRD: He's a kleptomaniac.
FOURTH: What's he doing for it?
THIRD: Oh, he's taken everything.
FIRST: My wife is so irritable, the least thing starts her off.
SECOND: You're lucky. Mine's a self-starter.
THIRD: When did your husband lose his inclination for work?
FOURTH: Don't ask me, we've been married for only six years.
FIRST: Do your daughters live at home?
SECOND: No, they're not married yet.

The third student removes a tape and starts to measure the fourth student.

THIRD: In my line of tailoring work, sir, I must ask you: What
about a small deposit?
FOURTH: Just as you like. Put one in if it's the style.
FIRST: Where were you born?
SECOND: Moscow. Why?
FIRST: I don't know why. I was asking you that.
THIRD: He never did a thing in his life; and he didn't do that
well.
FOURTH: I guess you might say that he belonged to the No-
ability.

The audience guffawed. At the end of the teaser and before the
play began, the guests descended on the food booths and stuffed
themselves with cold meats and cheeses and bread and herring and
cooked potatoes. During the commotion of eating, Filatov and two
aides entered the room in civilian clothes. Sasha was aghast. What
if the play was provocative or, worse, subversive? Who had invited
them? Boris greeted Sasha warmly and introduced his two colleagues, Larissa Pankarova and Basil Makarov.

"Larissa's a doctor who works for the service, and Basil gave up
a promising career as a lawyer to work with us."

Calling for attention, Sasha introduced his guests. A slight ripple
of applause followed. He knew not to leave them unannounced, lest
he be accused later of insinuating the secret police into the audience.
They declined Sasha's offer to bring them folding chairs for the play,
insisting that they would join the others on the floor, cross-legged.

When the lights dimmed, Galina appeared on stage and introduced the play. "Our fare for tonight is called *Summoned*. For the
moment, the playwright shall remain anonymous. I will return to
that point after the completion of the play." Galina exited the stage.
After a pause, the lights in the auditorium dimmed and came up on
a living-room set that served as the centerpiece for most of the play.

IVAN (*downstage*): You can't trust anyone these days . . . not
anyone. The name is Ivan Goniff, and I'm here to tell Nicholas
Ostroff, "Nicky" for short, that his time has come. But please

don't confuse me with the OGPU; I take my orders from a higher source. The people I work for don't enforce the law; we *are* the law. We are the nation's brain and conscience. Everyone needs leadership, what with enemies of the people everywhere. In fact, conditions are so bad, I lock up the silver if my local commissar comes around. You can't be too careful. Safety! That's the point of government. Which is why Nicky has been summoned. He's the chief document shredder for the Politburo. Right now, you can see him sitting in his living room, in a leather chair with a Victorian floor lamp at his elbow, an inlaid teak table at his feet, and a Finnish couch against the wall.

Anyway, until today, Nicky was an important man. After all, chief shredder of top-secret documents is an enviable position. The only trouble is, you can never be sure the shredder can be trusted. What if he squirrels away an incriminating piece of paper or two? Like a memo from you-know-who about some important political issue. Well, a paper like that could bring down the government. That's why it's best, if you have any doubts, and we do, to remove the shredder. Consequently, the Boss has put out an order to terminate Nicky's association with the Politburo. When I tell him he's been summoned, he'll say, "Just give me a little time." Sure, so he can run to his friends for help. Friends like Miroslav Mirnov. But I can't give Nicky any time. His term of office is over. And now, excuse me while I knock on his door.

Ivan enters Nicky's living room.

NICKY: Good to see you, Comrade Goniff.
IVAN: You're looking well.
NICKY: Feeling pretty good. And you?
IVAN: Not bad.
NICKY: Why are you wearing a service revolver?
IVAN: I'm on assignment.
NICKY: Looking for enemies of the people?
IVAN: They're everywhere.
NICKY: Sit down, Ivan. You said you wanted to see me.
IVAN: Just long enough to . . .
NICKY: A shot of vodka?
IVAN: A good idea.

NICKY: Here's your drink. I'll leave the bottle here. Take as much as you want.

They throw back their drinks.

NICKY: Why are you removing your service revolver?

IVAN: Nicky, I have some bad news for you.

NICKY: What are you talking about?

IVAN: A summons . . . for your arrest.

NICKY: You can't be serious! Why me?

IVAN: You know too much.

NICKY: I've never violated a trust. Never gossiped.

IVAN: Admirable behavior, Nicky.

NICKY: I love the Leader and all my superiors. .

IVAN: You'll have your day in court.

NICKY: Who's behind this? I know it's not the Dear Leader.

IVAN: You know how these things work, Nicky. A sealed envelope arrives. Inside is an order, a summons. As for the rest . . .

NICKY (*interrupting*): Listen, Ivan, you and me, we went through the same training together. We play tennis. You wouldn't, would you? Why just the other day I was saying to Comrade Ufa, "Of all the people I know, the one person I most admire is Ivan Goniff." (*stands*) Look at that! You have lint all over your jacket. Just turn around. I'll brush it off.

IVAN: Sit down, Nicky. You don't think I'm going to fall for that old trick, do you? (*pause*) Nice apartment you have here. First floor. Elegant furniture. Outside the window an old elm tree shading the terrace. You're lucky you don't live in capitalist America, where the elms are being cut down. I suspect it's the fault of their foreign policy.

NICKY (*laughs immoderately*): Dutch Elm disease! The fault . . . (*laughs harder*) of their foreign policy. That's rich. (*laughs harder still*)

IVAN (*breathing deeply*): I love the scent of lilacs in the spring. You have several lilac bushes outside your window.

NICKY (*serious*): Planted them myself, four years ago.

IVAN: I didn't know you liked to garden.

NICKY: You ought to look at my communal plot next door. It's ripe with vegetables.

IVAN: Good try, Nicky. But I have things to do . . . here and now. Get your coat. You've been denounced.

NICKY: Believe me, Ivan. There's been a mistake. You have the wrong person. I can prove it. Just give me a little time. A few days . . . so I can find out who's at fault.

IVAN: Who's at fault? Nicky, you can't be serious? What a sense of humor! (*laughs*) Who's at fault? (*laughs harder; then notices a frame on the wall*) Where'd you get that?

NICKY: The needlepoint? My blessed mother made it for me.

IVAN (*reads*): "They serve best who never question." Well-chosen words. Classic. Sounds like Cicero. Hand me the bottle, will you, Nicky? One for the road.

NICKY: Sure, Ivan, here it is.

Nicky strikes Ivan over the head. Ivan falls to the floor.

Sorry, comrade, but when denunciation is in the air, it's dog eat dog.

The stage is quickly cleared. We are now in Miroslav Mirnov's office.

NICKY (*stage whisper*): Psst! Psst! Miroslav! Comrade Mirnov. It's me, Nicky. I came in the back, so no one would see.

MIRO: You look ill, Nicky. Something wrong?

NICKY: I've been summoned, Miro. Somebody's trying to get me out of the way. I need your help.

MIRO: Why me?

NICKY: You're my lawyer, aren't you?

MIRO: I'll be happy to draw up a new will for you.

NICKY: Forget the will. I've got an incendiary document stored in a safe place.

MIRO: You didn't shred it?

NICKY: Kept it for security . . . for a moment like this.

MIRO (*whistles*): Whew!

NICKY: Believe me, it'll finish off the Boss if I make it public.

MIRO: Think of the danger, Nicky.

NICKY: I can't be worse off than I am now.

MIRO: Do you know what it means to expose the Boss? You'll be charged with slander and have to stand trial. Crowds will howl at you. The prosecutor will ask personal questions.

NICKY: For example?

MIRO: For example: (*assumes the voice of the prosecutor*) Citizen Ostroff, what do you do for a living?

NICKY: I work for the Politburo shredding top-secret documents.

MIRO: Please be specific.

NICKY: The Beloved Leader's notes to his aides.

MIRO: What else?

NICKY: Some of Lenin's personal papers.

MIRO: On whose orders would you shred a document that once belonged to Comrade Lenin? That's a capital crime.

NICKY: On the Boss's orders.

MIRO: Well, that's different.

NICKY: Oh, I could tell you a thing or two.

MIRO: Didn't you once work for the secret police?

NICKY: It was the worst experience of my life.

MIRO: Please explain.

NICKY: The former Cheka head was shot, also several of his aides. A member of the investigative office was caught bank-rolling a drug operation. The new Cheka head is a rapist and, to boot, a dwarf.

MIRO (*normal voice again*): Forget it, Nicky. Court's no place for you. The judge will order you put up against the wall.

NICKY: Is there no justice in this country?

MIRO: If I were you, I wouldn't ask questions like that. What about seeing Teodor Tolstoi, your old army mate. Maybe he can help you.

NICKY: Of course, Teodor! I saved his life once.

The stage is quickly cleared. We are now in Teodor's flat, where he is pedaling a stationary bicycle.

TEOD: Comrade Ostroff! How are you? It's been too long since we last saw each other. Sit down. I have to do my forty miles a day on the exercycle. So don't mind me, I'll just pedal while we talk. What brings you here? Are you in a mood to crush some heads, like before?

NICKY: I'm in trouble, Teodoro, and I need some assistance.

TEOD: Whatever you need, just say it. You can always count on Teodoro. He'll never let you down. After all, you did save my life when you dragged me to safety under fire.

NICKY: You're a noble comrade, Teodoro. I knew that of all my friends, you'd be the most steadfast.

TEOD: What are comrades for? Old army men. I hate a man who's all talk and no action. What's your problem?

NICKY: You won't believe it. After all my years of faithful service, instead of giving me a gold watch, they gave me a summons.

TEOD: Who delivered it?

NICKY: That apparatchik Ivan Goniff.

TEOD (*pedaling slower*): My old friend, Ivan . . . an apparatchik?

NICKY: A snake in the grass.

TEOD (*stops pedaling*): A snake!

NICKY: A viper. Now here's what I'd like you to do for me.

TEOD (*pedaling again*): I'm listening.

NICKY: Hide me, let me sleep in the spare room, until I can get to the bottom of this business.

TEOD (*alarmed; stops pedaling*): The spare room?

NICKY: Why not?

TEOD: You're asking a lot, Nicky.

NICKY: Just for a little while.

TEOD: You'd need sheets and pillowcases and blankets.

NICKY: A pillow and a blanket would do.

TEOD (*stops pedaling*): Like the time in the Crimea when we stayed at Irina's place?

NICKY: Exactly.

TEOD: Remember the women at the beach? They knew what a good time was, right?

NICKY: If not the spare room, maybe the basement.

TEOD: I can still see those two dames from Minsk. They were great. Blonds! Bam! Bam! Two scores in one night. What dames!

NICKY: Maybe the toolshed.

TEOD: And afterward we got roaring drunk. And then we went to the other side of town and cracked a few heads until the military police came. What a night! (*pedals quickly*)

NICKY: Teodoro, I don't think you're listening to me.

TEOD (*pedals slower*): You were really something, Nicky. The women loved you, and the men feared you.

NICKY (*ironically*): Yes, that's me, a man with a chest full of medals.

TEOD: As much as I'd like to help you, Nicky, my mother's coming to stay with me. Tomorrow. So the spare room is out. Also the basement and toolshed. They're already occupied with drifters from the countryside. If I could, I would but . . .

Nicky exits. The stage is quickly cleared. We are now in Sergei Tangenital's flat. His secretary/girlfriend, Dina, sits on his lap.

TANG: Nicky, what a surprise. You know my secretary, Dina. What can I do for you?

NICKY: When a man's in trouble, the first person he thinks of is relatives. Right? And I said to myself who better than Cousin Sergei Tangenital to come to for help.

TANG: Get that down, Dina. You don't mind, Nicky, if Dina takes down our conversation? You know, just for the record.

NICKY: No . . . go right ahead.

TANG: So what is it you need? As you know, I . . . well, I've always been overly fond of you, Nicky. Your father and my mother . . . brother and sister. Blood is thicker than water. Relations, that's what counts.

DINA: That's . . . what . . . counts.

NICKY: Cousin Tangenital, I've been summoned.

TANG: Summoned? What in the world for? You have a chest full of medals.

NICKY: I have no idea. I've done nothing.

TANG: That's the trouble with this modern generation. They always want something for nothing. (*to Dina*) Get that down.

DINA: Some . . . thing . . . for . . . nothing.

TANG: No regard for hard work and decency. They think they can just walk into your house and strip the medals from your chest.

NICKY: I need travel money to get out of Moscow. I'll pay you back. You can trust me.

TANG: Trust. Now there's a fine word.

DINA (*stage whisper*): Ooh, Serge. Your hand!

TANG: Who can we trust? That's the question. Your wife?

DINA: Or your secretary! (*stage whisper*) A little lower!

TANG: Which one matters most?

NICKY: You know very well I've been divorced for two years. I couldn't stand Eva's nattering.

TANG: That doesn't for one minute lessen the need for someone who can give you good advice about trust.

DINA: Good advice. (*whispers*) That's better.

TANG: Remember Socrates, henpecked of the historical Xanthippe. Remember Job, whose wife had nothing to offer for his carbuncles but violent doses of profanity.

DINA: Remember those two. (*moves Sergei's hand to her derriere*) And remember *this*.

TANG: I can think of a thousand such men married to unworthy wives, termagants, who scold like a March wind. On this sea of matrimony, where so many have wrecked, am I not right, Nicky, in advising expert pilotage?

NICKY: Are you advising me, Cousin Tangenital, to take a wife? The last one laughed at any inanity.

TANG: Nicky, I think our choices are so many and so varied, it's no wonder we are swindled. Consider Adam for a moment.

DINA: Consider Adam.

TANG: Adam, as you know, did not have a large group of women from whom to select a wife. It was Eve or nothing. And judging from the mistakes that Eve made afterward, I think nothing might have been the better choice. All sorts of mistakes occurred because Eve was made out of a rib from Adam's side. Nobody knows which of his twenty-four ribs was taken for the nucleus. Which means, Nicky, that if you depend entirely upon yourself in this matter, the possibilities are twenty-three-to-one that you have selected the wrong rib.

DINA: The wrong rib.

NICKY: You know, Cousin, you've given me an insight. Perhaps I picked a bone with the wrong person.

TANG: Just wait here a few minutes, Nicky. Dina and I will be right back.

NICKY: Cousin, why are you and Dina going into the bedroom?

TANG (*from afar*): Just a minute, Nicky, I've got my hands full.

Nicky exits. The stage is quickly cleared. We are now in Father Kadaver's flat.

KADAV: Nicky, I'm surprised word hasn't already gotten out. I denounced my calling as a priest, denounced the church, and took a job with the Ministry of Religious Affairs.

NICKY: I need some advice, Father Kadaver, but if I'm interrupting . . .

KADAV: Sit down, Nicky. I remember you as a child. Your mother used to bring you to church. Before you knocked, I was reading the story of the Good Samaritan—in a Soviet light.

NICKY: I'm only vaguely familiar with it.

KADAV: Although some old believers treat ignorance of the Bible as a grievous sin, I do not. My own opinion in the matter is that given the Soviet attitude toward religion, the less a person knows about the Bible, the less chance he has to be arrested. Don't you agree?

NICKY: You're looking at a man on the run, trying to avoid arrest. That's why I need your advice.

KADAV: Of course, what's the problem?

NICKY: I've been summoned, so I'm trying to get to the countryside. Can you let me stay a few nights?

KADAV: You want advice? Here, let me read to you from the Good Samaritan. "A certain man went down from Jerusalem to Jericho, and fell among thieves, which stripped him of his raiment, and wounded him, and departed, leaving him half dead." Et cetera. "But a certain Samaritan, as he journeyed, came where he was; and when he saw him, he had compassion on him." Do you see the point, Nicky?

NICKY: Not exactly. If you try to help the stricken man and you make things worse, he's liable never to forgive you. But if you walk away, he'll probably hate you. Either way you lose. So what are you supposed to do?

KADAV: It's a difficult moral question, one not easily answered.

NICKY: Now, if you help me, Father, isn't that like the Samaritan helping the man attacked by the robbers?

KADAV: Not at all, Nicky. Let's look at the text again. It says: "Which . . . of these three, thinkest thou, was neighbor unto him that fell among the thieves? And the lawyer said, 'He that showed mercy on him.' Then said Jesus unto him, 'Go and do thou likewise.'" Although some Bibles use the word "pity," and others "mercy," the meaning of the story is clear. We must pity those less fortunate than we, and have mercy on those who would ignore us in our hour of need. Therefore: It is for *me* to show pity and for *you* to be merciful.

NICKY: It sounds to me as if you've already started working for the Ministry of Religious Affairs.

KADAV: I certainly have.

NICKY: Then tell your head commissar to pass the word along. If the summons I received is not withdrawn, I intend to tell what I know about everything. And as the official shredder for the Kremlin, I know a lot.

KADAV: Nicky, you wouldn't!

NICKY: And why not?

KADAV: It would be uncharitable not to turn the other cheek.

Nicky exits. The stage is quickly cleared. We are now in Eva Giardina's flat.

EVA: Hard feelings, Nicky? Not at all. Our getting divorced was the best thing that ever happened to me. I got a job in the Soviet housing ministry, a job that puts me in a good position to help others. So what brings you here? Tell me. Perhaps I can be of assistance.

NICKY: I've been summoned.

EVA (*laughs*): What a sense of humor.

NICKY: My intention is to head east, but I'll need a place to stay for a few days and some money.

EVA (*laughs*): You always did have a good sense of humor. East! You'd die from the cold and the lack of culture.

NICKY: You don't know what I've been going through, Eva. I've been breaking my neck trying to find someone to help.

EVA: Speaking of breaking your neck, Nicky, reminds me . . . (*laughs immoderately*) of that joke you told when our neighbor Isaak Steinberg was summoned. Remember?

NICKY: No, I must have forgotten.

EVA: The one about the man who hanged himself on an apple tree? And the woman from next door asked the widow for a graft from the tree because, she said, "You never can tell, but it may bear the same fruit for me."

NICKY: Funny. (*doesn't laugh*)

EVA (*laughing*): It's hysterical! (*pause*) You don't look good, Nicky.

NICKY: I'll be all right . . . if I can stay with you and get some ready cash. My flat has some valuables worth selling. With your contacts . . .

The telephone rings; Eva answers it

EVA: Yes, Mrs. Tukhachevsky? (*pause*) Yes, I promise. The flat will be available in two or three days. All we have to do is sell the furniture and knickknacks. Of course I'll ring you. Good-bye. (*hangs up*)

NICKY: I'll make you a deal. Walking the streets, as I've been doing, is no pleasure.

EVA: No pleasure! (*laughs*) That's a good one. (*laughs immoderately*) It reminds me of the joke you told after Isaak Steinberg's funeral . . . the one about the widow who was walking behind the bearers at her husband's funeral and cried out to them: "Don't go so fast; there's no need to make a hurry of such pleasure." (*laughs*) I never heard anything so funny before. (*laughs immoderately*) It's hysterical.

NICKY: Hysterical is what I am at the moment. I've been denounced.

EVA (*still laughing*): No need . . . to make a hurry . . . of such a pleasure. (*suddenly serious*) What's the deal you want to make?

NICKY: Give me an advance against the sale of my belongings and you can send the rest to me later.

EVA: But that's unethical.

NICKY: I need the money!

EVA: When you work for the Ministry of Housing, you can't afford to let friendship get in the way. If I do this for you, I'd have to do it for everyone.

NICKY: Come now, Eva, all I'm asking for is a simple favor. You know the flat inside and out. You lived in it for three years. Whatever you think the furnishings are worth, I'll take. No questions asked.

EVA: Nicky, I'm doing you a favor by not getting involved. If I sell your possessions *secretly*, and the ministry finds out, it will only be harder for you.

The telephone rings. Eva answers it.

Mrs. Tukhachevsky, I told you. I know every stick of furniture in the flat. You needn't go out and buy a thing. It has everything you and your husband have been looking for: a leather sitting chair, an inlaid coffee table, a Victorian floor lamp, a Finnish couch. (*pause*) Unusual? Not at all, Mrs. Tukhachevsky. Circumstances. Uh huh . . . called away. Summoned, you might say. (*pause*) Dirt cheap. The owner's in no position to bargain. (*pause*) Don't thank me, thank the denouncer. Right. (*pause*) Well, you could do one thing. Contact the Ministry of Housing and tell them that the previous tenant and I are going over the details at this very moment. Not at all. Good-bye. (*hangs up the telephone*)

NICKY: That call?
EVA: A friend of a friend . . . Mrs. Tukachevksy.
NICKY: The flat . . . with the leather chair and Finnish couch.
EVA: It belonged to a former acquaintance of mine.
NICKY: Former?
EVA: Deceased . . . you might say.
NICKY: I ought to shoot you.
EVA: Wa-a-ait a minute, Nicky. Don't blame me for what's happening to you. After all, when Isaak Steinberg was taken away, you didn't say anything. Not a word. So you can't very well complain now.
NICKY: You're right. I should have helped Isaak. But what about you?
EVA: What do you mean?
NICKY: I'm standing here right now. I'm not next door.
EVA: Believe me, Nicky, if I let you stay here or give you money, it will only make matters worse.
NICKY: They can't be any worse.
EVA: They can, Nicky, believe me: they can. By bringing me into this situation, you could cause the loss of something far more important than *your* life.
NICKY: What's that?
EVA: *My* life.

Someone is knocking on the door and shouting "open up!" Ivan Goniff and others burst into the room as the curtain falls.

To enthusiastic applause and laughter, the cast took several bows and then cleared the stage of props and scenery. Filatov's face was ashen, as his two colleagues whispered to him earnestly. Sasha had gone backstage to help strike the set. From his vantage point behind the curtain, he could see the three police officers huddled so closely that their heads nearly touched. Galina had promised to say a few words about the play, and Sasha urged her not to keep the audience waiting, most of whom remained in the room, either to frequent the stalls, or to chat, or to hear Galina. The three secret police officers disengaged and came to the foot of the stage.

Galina's public explanation differed only slightly from what she had told Sasha. The play had originally been written in 1933 for the Moscow State Radio, but during rehearsals the censor had shelved it. A member of the Politburo close to Nikolai Bukharin had made the script available to his nephew, whom she failed to identify as Goran Youzhny. She likewise failed to mention that the play had been commissioned by the Leningrad Communist Party. "The play-wright," she said candidly, "was none other than the former director of the Michael School, Avram Brodsky, who at my request adapted it for the stage."

The audience quickly glanced around and, no doubt owing to the presence of the OGPU, failed to call for the author. When Sasha emerged from backstage, Filatov summoned him. Confronting the three police officers, he counterfeited a smile. No response. Larissa, broad faced and blond, with pale blue eyes, looked stoically Ukrainian. Basil's narrow face, sunken cheeks, dark eyes, and yellow teeth, brought to mind a wolf in search of a bone. Certainly, thought Sasha, a former lawyer could afford a dentist.

"If I'm not mistaken, you owe me a letter," said Filatov calmly.

Debating whether to plead overwork, Sasha decided the less said the better and answered laconically, "Correct."

"Then why haven't I received it?"

"My contacts with Brodsky, which are frequent enough, haven't turned up any information worth passing along." Trying to anticipate Filatov's next question, he added, "He even failed to react to my censorious comments about Radek and the Left Opposition."

Filatov shook his head with a jerk, as if trying to dislodge water from an ear after swimming. His expression read, "I'm tired of waiting."

"We can talk now, if you wish," Sasha politely suggested.

Pause.

"This play," Filatov asked suddenly, "whose idea was it?"

"The playwright's."

Filatov looked at the floor and then slowly raised his head. "I will listen to an intelligent argument in opposition, but I will not tolerate insolence."

At that moment, both Larissa and Basil, their faces blank, were penning notes on similar flip-lid, pocket-size pads, official OGPU issue. Apparently protecting the country required one to relinquish all feeling and transmogrify into stone. Filatov was the exception. Sasha knew, therefore, not to abuse the feelings of this officer, feelings that were all too rare in the secret police.

"My apologies. I was trying to protect the innocent."

Filatov ran his thumb from his lower lip to his chin, a gesture that he had used during their first interrogation. "Name them!"

"The director, the actors, and the writer."

A second later, the policeman in Filatov smartly went to work. He directed Larissa to interview Galina, and Basil to question the actors. As the two officers went their separate ways, Filatov gently touched Sasha's arm and patiently explained, as if talking to a child, that the tensions between the Leningrad Soviets, the home of the Right Opposition, and the Moscow Soviets had been and still were tense, especially in light of Kirov's murder.

Boris lowered his voice and asked, "Did you hear about the assassination attempt on Lukashenko's life? This morning . . . in Ryazan. It failed." Then in a normal voice: "No need to protect the identity of the person who selected Brodsky's play. I'm pretty certain I know."

Clever man, this Filatov, mused Sasha. But if he thinks I'll ask him to share his thoughts, he'll wait for the rest of his life.

An unduly long pause on the part of Filatov followed. He was apparently waiting for Sasha to take the bait. When he realized that his ploy hadn't worked, he remarked rather sharply, "You've been denounced yet again. This time for calling our Soviet textbooks biased, and for allowing a wall poster to go undetected for almost a day, a poster in praise of Trotsky. Are you utterly without sense? On these two accounts alone, I could have you jailed."

Convinced that Filatov was a consummate actor who wished to render him defenseless, and therefore had just played the part of the outraged but compassionate cop, Sasha decided to try boldness instead of submission, an approach that surprised Filatov.

"You say you'll listen to a reasoned argument to explain the production of the play, good." With more daring than he'd exhibited ever before, Sasha declared that they both knew that if the OGPU hoped to pin anything on Brodsky, they needed Sasha to draw out the ex-director. Had Filatov forgotten how Hamlet used the same technique, a play, to discover the guilt of his uncle? Through the production of the play, Sasha had hoped to achieve a similar effect. Brodsky might reveal himself. But Brodsky had not attended the performance, a miscalculation that Sasha owned up to.

For the first time in years, Filatov found himself speechless.

Sasha took it as his cue to continue. "Although, as you saw for yourself, Brodsky was not in the audience, he knew it was to be acted and seemed exceedingly pleased. Now you can draw your own conclusions. Is he serving the Soviets or the Left Opposition? If the latter, then he would want his play to elicit sympathy, not laughter; if the former, he would expect to hear execrations. Did you hear the audience? Laughter. So what do you conclude?" Sasha paused. "Laughter lends itself to contradictory interpretations. The audience may have been tickled or teased to reflect. Which? Who knows? And as for Brodsky, what he thinks is anyone's guess."

The shine on Filatov's shoes had faded. He kneeled and rubbed them with his handkerchief. In that position, he noticed that Sasha's footwear was badly worn. Shoes had played an important role in Filatov's life. He and his brother had shared a pair so that in winter one or the other could attend school. In his closet at home, he had fourteen pairs stored in a neat row. Some people thought that clothes or uniforms or epaulets made the man. Not Filatov. Shoes.

"I judge from your shoes, Comrade Parsky, that your expenses are so great that they have kept you from a new pair."

A knowing smile crept across Sasha's face. He had given his best shoes to Petr Selivanov when he had left for Ryazan. The poor man had been reduced to putting strips cut from old tires into his torn boots. Once Sasha realized that he and Petr wore the same size, a fact that he found strangely comforting, he gladly parted with his black dress shoes, which he had little or no occasion in Balyk to wear.

Sasha played on sentiment. "Alya's pony is costly, but the child's smile is worth it. Shall we eat?" At one of the food booths, he asked for two plates of blintzes with a generous dab of sour cream.

Filatov insisted on paying. "Your boots! Remember?"

Maneuvering the policeman through the milling crowd to a quiet spot, Sasha tried to redirect the conversation to the school. "The students are reluctant to return to cold rooms with inadequate light. What we need is a dormitory. Living with the locals has its disadvantages; the students are constantly subjected to superstition."

"Yes, but their having to share the houses of farmers and craftsmen also has a good side. The experience teaches them to value education. They appreciate all the more their good fortune in being enrolled here."

"You are an intelligent man, Comrade Filatov. Tell me: Why is it that Soviets think hardship, hunger, abuse, and even beatings are useful prerequisites for a formal education?"

Savoring a blintz, Filatov replied, "Because there is no better teacher than pain. I once heard Stalin explain that in the Georgian language one of the meanings of 'beatings' is to educate."

When Larissa and Basil returned, Boris thanked Sasha for the typewritten invitation and told him he expected a "full report" sooner rather than later. He then excused himself and exited with the comment, "I want Larissa and Basil to meet Comrade Brodsky."

His last night in Balyk before leaving for Ryazan, Petr Selivanov had made a special meal for the four of them: duck a l'Orange, rice pilaf, steamed asparagus with butter, and, of course, strong black tea. The meal had begun with shots of vodka and Petr's succinct but heartfelt speech of appreciation for Sasha's hospitality, which included a pair of shoes. Alya cried, and Petr promised to return, though he never said when. Sasha knew that after the Fortress Plot, Petr would be leaving for Kiev and his new girlfriend, and that he was unlikely to pass this way again. During the course of the meal, he distributed gifts: for Alya a riding crop, for Galina a zircon bracelet, and for Sasha a collection of handwritten poems that had been passed from one person to another (*samizdat*).

"One day, the Lord willing, these banned poems will see print, but probably not until Stalin dies, which can't come soon enough."

So blasphemous were Petr's words that before Galina and Sasha could thank him for their gifts, they instinctively scanned the room, terrified that someone might have heard.

The next morning, Alya crawled into the attic to say good-bye, but Petr had already left. Sasha had reason to suspect that in the early hours, Petr had quit his attic aerie and crawled into Galina's bed. Although Petr had taken great care not to make any noise, the wooden ladder leading to the attic loft squeaked. Sasha had pretended not to hear.

As the train clickety-clacked toward Ryazan, Petr mentally pictured priming the dynamite sticks made from nitroglycerin, soaked in diatomaceous earth or powdered seashells, but not sawdust, which was unstable. Two sticks, he thought, would do the job nicely, assuming they were each about 8 inches long and 1.25 inches around, and each weighed about half a pound. He trusted that he would have available to him reliable blasting caps and fuses or electrical cable. An elderly woman, across the aisle, opened her chestnut-brown rattan picnic basket. Her jaws moved in anticipation of her savory snack. Eyeing Petr's new shoes, she concluded, though he hungrily smiled at her, he had no need of a handout. When the food porter pushed his wagon through the car, he too noticed Petr's shoes and nodded approvingly. Petr bought a cup of tea and a roll. Before long, he realized that others in the car were pausing to stare at his shoes, which had become objects worthy of admiration among all these badly shod people. Before the train reached Ryazan, Petr carried his military service bag to the men's room and slipped into his old boots. On his current mission, he certainly didn't need to be calling attention to himself.

A tram took him to within walking distance of Viktor's flat. But instead of walking directly to the building, an ugly cement slab, one among many, he circled the block to make sure he wasn't being followed. The front door stood slightly ajar, and the elevator wasn't working. It was as if time had stood still. Nothing had changed since he last saw Viktor. The hall still reeked from cooking odors and urine. Given the paucity of public toilets, people simply took it upon themselves, when walking down the street and feeling the need to pass water, to duck into a building hallway.

Petr nervously knocked on Viktor's fourth-floor flat. The peephole in the door moved and an eye appeared. Viktor mumbled some undistinguishable words, opened the door, and quickly closed it behind Petr. Without speaking, Viktor led his guest into the back room and unlocked the closet. Inside was a wooden crate stamped with German words. Not even pausing to take off his overcoat, Petr kneeled and asked for a claw hammer; then he carefully pried loose the top boards.

"Who gave you this crap?" he asked, slipping out of his coat.

"The secret police."

"It's from Austria. Date: 1934. The shelf life is usually one year. You're damn lucky the stuff hasn't gone off, killing you and bringing down the whole building."

"But if the dynamite can still be ignited . . ."

"Tell your police friends to discard this stuff immediately—before it goes off accidentally."

An agitated Viktor ran a hand through his hair and paced. "That's your job! That's why we brought you back."

"I never agreed to undertake a suicide mission."

"And what if they say, use what we gave you—or else?"

"Or else what?"

"We'll sling your friend into prison and throw away the keys."

"If that's the case, I'm leaving right now."

Viktor sounded like a braying mule. "From the moment you approached the building you've been watched from the building across the street, and I wouldn't be surprised if an OGPU man is already stationed down the hall. Look for yourself."

A skeptical Petr grabbed his bag and said good-bye. He opened the door and looked. To his left, he saw a man lounging against the wall and smoking a cigarette. Bold as brass, Petr approached him and whispered, "The dynamite is so old it's bound to be unstable. You shouldn't be around it. If it goes off, the building and you are rubble. Is that what you want?"

"Just do your job, and we'll do ours."

"Do you plan to stand here all night and tomorrow and the next night?"

"Someone will."

Defeated, Petr returned to the open door of the flat, from which Viktor had watched and surmised from Petr's downcast look that his request, whatever it was, had been denied. Pulling off his coat, Petr said simply:

"Let's get started. The first thing I want to do is dismantle one of the sticks to see which absorbent substance they put the nitro in." He just hoped it wasn't sawdust or wood pulp.

"Nitro!" Viktor exclaimed. "Those bastards told me the dynamite was perfectly safe. Even an idiot knows to shy away from that stuff!"

"What did you think dynamite was based on, shoe polish?"

With Viktor eyeing the door, wishing to distance himself from the danger, Petr said, "Let me check the electrical cable and fuses." He carefully unpacked the crate. "We'll need extra fuses and blasting caps, just in case. But whether any of it will work, who knows? By the way, ask your friends," said Petr irascibly, "who will be digging the loading holes in the road for the sticks."

A second later, Viktor was gone. In his absence, Petr looked through whatever personal papers he could find in the flat. He still harbored the suspicion that Viktor and Galina had been lovers. Although he no longer cared, given his girlfriend in Kiev, he still wanted to know. From the top shelf of Viktor's clothes closet, Petr removed a brown accordion file that held letters from friends and associates. Among the letters were two from Galina. In the first, she agreed to help him distribute leaflets and complained about Petr's working for the secret police. The nature of the leaflets was never mentioned. In the second, she deplored Petr's political timidity and wished she and Viktor could live together instead of having to "steal a few minutes when conditions permit." For a second, Petr entertained the idea of rigging a small charge of dynamite and a timer to Viktor's bed, but he knew that the dynamite was so unstable it might kill him in the process or might not ignite at all; and then too there was the agent in the hall. Petr would not be free until the day the explosives were buried in the road.

Several hours later, Viktor returned. Over dinner, which, given Viktor's culinary incompetence, Petr prepared, he brought up the subject of Galina, but not before prefacing it with the admission that he and Galina planned to divorce, and that he had met another woman. "For all your professed lack of interest in women, you did have a yen for Galina. I admit she's extraordinary." He paused and waited for his statement to seep into Viktor's ventricles.

"Good soup," said Viktor, clearly trying to decide how to respond. "We had a great deal in common. I suppose we still do. It began as a political alliance and ended . . ."

"In bed," Petr interrupted.

"You know the Soviet attitude toward such things. No one owns another. We were simply living like . . . liberal Bolsheviks."

Petr made no reply. If he decided to settle the score with Comrade Harkov, it would be on his terms, not Viktor's, and Petr had time before that moment arrived. Perhaps with the same thought in mind, Viktor remarked:

"I don't see your service revolver, the faithful Nagant M 1895. You had it the last time you were here. The secret police now carry TT 33 pistols."

The OGPU had obviously introduced Viktor to bullets and bombs. "I left the gun with Galina. If a military patrol had stopped me on the way here, I didn't want to be armed. Desertion is one thing, a revolver, another. People with guns are tempted to use them. I didn't want to be tempted."

The telephone rang. Viktor answered it, and looked sick. Then he grabbed his coat and excused himself, saying he had to meet someone. But before leaving, he made the same loud alveolar clicking noise that he had often made when approaching or seeing someone he knew. He would pull the tip of his tongue down abruptly and forcefully from the roof of his mouth. In college, Petr had read about click languages in Africa. Viktor knew myriad sounds. And why not? He had taken a degree in linguistic anthropology and had always rued that his middling academic record had prevented him from doing fieldwork in Africa. As Petr carefully sorted and organized the dynamite sticks to his liking, he wondered how extensive a vocabulary "clickers" could have. The larger the selection, the more subtle the sounds. Did click language precede words? Infants and young children respond excitedly to clicks, as if the sounds were lodged in their genes.

Out of the vaporous night, a car quietly came to a halt. From the window, Petr saw a man hurriedly exit, and Viktor emerge from the building to greet him. They entered the building together. A few minutes later, the two men materialized in the flat, neither of them looking pleased. Viktor introduced Petr to an unsmiling OGPU officer, Comrade Kirill Razumov, who wasted no time in laying out the "new" assassination plan. On the kitchen table, he spread a map with all the roads leading to the Ryazan Kremlin clearly outlined. Pointing to an X, he said:

"Here's where you need to plant the dynamite."

The spot differed from the one originally agreed upon. It was a hundred yards farther from the Kremlin, on a section of road that ran between a line of trees. Razumov, a squat brawler, whose bushy hair and eyebrows gave him a wild appearance, suddenly burst forth with a diatribe about traitors and Lukashenko lackeys. As if for effect, his powerful arms and large hands visually reinforced his angry words. A dumfounded Petr listened to Viktor explain that Lukashenko's bodyguards had somehow learned of the arbor plan.

"So forget the ferns and the car stopping and Lukashenko's being blown sky high," Razumov added. "We have to recalibrate. There's an informer in our midst, but he'll eventually tip his hand, and then . . ."

Dismayed, Petr asked, "If the secret police can't keep a secret, who can?"

Without responding to Petr's indictment of the police, Razumov wiped his runny nose on his coat sleeve and removed his black gloves, which he folded neatly and put in a pocket. "Our new plan is probably safer. We'll run the cable under the road and place the detonator behind the trees. Then you can make a dash for it down the hill. We'll have a car waiting for you. Don't even consider the river. Half the city would be watching from the hill."

From Petr's expression, the two conspirators saw something was amiss. But before Petr could speak, Viktor said:

"I promised Comrade Selivanov I would be in charge of the detonator, and all he had to do was plant the dynamite and wire it."

Razumov shook his head in disagreement. "Your man here digs the bore holes, plants the sticks, wires the explosives, and sets them off. He's the professional. You," he said to Viktor, "are just an amateur. We're not going to alter our plans again."

Clearly annoyed, Petr said, "Explosives are my territory, road digging is yours."

Comrade Razumov coldly eyed Petr. "I understand you're particular about the loading holes, their width and depth. Well, since we can't conduct a trial or test shot, I am merely suggesting," he said archly, "that an expert make the bores: you!" Petr responded with a grimace. Razumov lit a cigarette. "Comrade Selivanov, I have the impression you regard me as a country bumpkin, a member of the secret police who can't keep a secret. But I'm knowledgeable enough to know that in matters of explosives, you leave the details to the expert. If I'm not mistaken," he said, proud to show he was hardly a fool, "in hard ground the hole is tamped at the top about the charge, and when you tamp the hole, you take great care to see that no dirt or pieces of sod get between the primer and charges below." He smiled triumphantly. "In the service academy, we learned how to plant charges." He then said that the OGPU would provide Viktor and Petr with the clothes and tools of a road worker. "Not even the local police will give you a second look."

The road to the Ryazan Kremlin, like most secondary roads in the city, was only partially paved. Viktor drove a repair truck to the site on the map marked with an X, parked, and from a toolbox removed a pointed bar, sledge, and crowbar. The truck bed held shovels and wooden horses, which Viktor and Petr carried to the designated place in the road. Positioning the wooden horses in a circle, Petr began shoveling the thin layer of snow that covered the ground. The men were dressed in overalls, fleece-lined jackets, and rubber boots of the kind that all ditch diggers were issued. Once Petr had cleared the snow and bared the icy ground, Viktor went to work with his sledge and pointed bar.

"The ground's like cement," Viktor groused.

"Keep digging. I need the hole at least a foot deep."

When the two holes were dug, eighteen inches apart, Viktor started to run a trench toward the woods. A patrolling police car stopped. Two of Lukashenko's henchmen exited and asked to see the work order. Razumov had provided Viktor with all the necessary documentation for a new drainage line.

"On this stretch of road, it ices up bad," said Viktor, affecting a laborer's diction. "Then what you got is a toboggan run, with cars slippin' this way and that. Why just last week I seen . . ."

While one policeman questioned the digging, the other poked his head in the truck. Opening the toolbox, he found dynamite, blasting caps, and electrical cable. He immediately drew his pistol.

"How do you explain the dynamite sticks in the toolbox?" he asked, tapping the barrel of the gun against Viktor's chest.

Had the Ryazan city police and the local OGPU not hated each other, Viktor could have pulled rank and displayed his OGPU courtesy card entitling him to special treatment. He would have to fashion another escape. "This ain't the only drainage line we're layin'. We're layin' others and also buildin' a holdin' pond for the runoff. That's where the explosives come in. In this weather and with this rock-hard ground . . . and since we ain't got no rock drills, we got to do the work with dynamite. If you wanna watch, we'll be blowin' the hole later." He pointed to an open spot through the trees. "Right over there. But it'll take several hours to get set up. Like I said, you're welcome to watch."

Given the chaotic state of Bolshevik files and records, the policemen knew it was fruitless to telephone the office of roadworks to inquire about drainage lines and a holding pond. The best thing to do was simply return to the office and sort through the construction permits. The policeman holstered his pistol and, copying Viktor's ID card number, said, "We'll check in with headquarters. If there's a problem, we'll be back."

Watching the police car drive off, Viktor said, "No use hanging around here. Let's find Razumov. We need a new site. Those guys just ruined this one."

A furious Razumov stomped around Viktor's flat. "We can't blow up the bridge. Too many innocent people might get killed. Besides, he might not take that route. There's only one other course. We do some minor damage to Lukashenko's official car, and while it's being repaired, Comrade Selivanov will fit it with an explosive device."

"That's far more complicated than detonating a road bomb," said Petr. "For a start, you'll need batteries, the right circuitry, transceivers, connectors, nonelectric igniter tips, a dependable clock, and more."

"Whatever it takes to rid ourselves of that bastard . . . I'll get it for you. Just give me a list. Unlike the nitro, this stuff will be current. I promise."

Razumov made it clear that the black Packard sedan that Lukashenko used was bulletproof. So neither a sniper nor a hand grenade could do the job. They would have to plant the bomb in the car, but not in the trunk or under the hood, which would be the first places that Lukashenko's bodyguards would check.

"Is there a clock in the dashboard?" asked Petr. "If there is, I can rewire it."

Razumov asked Viktor to pour him a drink, which he threw back the moment his hand touched the glass. His body trembled from the effect. "I've never seen the inside of that vermin's car, but others in the service have. We'll arrange to have it serviced."

"And if it doesn't have a clock, what then?" asked Petr.

"Let's not jump to conclusions," said Razumov. He took another shot of vodka. "Leave everything to me. I'll see that his car ends up in the shop by tomorrow."

The winter festival would be ending in a few days, and, as Viktor pointed out, Lukashenko often used the occasion to take his mistress to a Swiss spa, his favorite retreat.

Razumov vociferously declared, "I don't care if it takes from now until the Second Coming—pardon my heresy—to kill that bastard, I'm going to finish him off." With that statement, he departed.

Why, Petr asked, was Razumov treating the killing as personal? Viktor explained that Razumov, like a great many others, had once trusted Lukashenko for his denouncing corruption, but that was before he became a sleazy mayor. A niece of Razumov had participated in the Ukrainian independence movement. Betrayed, she fled to her uncle, even though he was a Bolshevik and opposed to Ukrainian separatism. Razumov hid her in his flat for a few weeks, until her presence proved dangerous, particularly since Razumov at the time was training to be an OGPU officer. He wanted to spirit her to the East of the country, where she could work in one of the Siberian cities and establish a new identity. Having cooperated with Lukashenko on his anticorruption campaign, Razumov felt here was a man whom he could trust. So he told Lukashenko about the presence of his niece and his wish to arrange her escape. Lukashenko assured Razumov that he would help get her out of Ryazan, and asked for her particulars: name, age, height, hair color, and a general description. When Razumov questioned the need for such information, Lukashenko said that it would be safer if Razumov did not accompany her to the train. Lukashenko would personally show up at the station and lead her to safety. Hence his need for the details. The day of the rendezvous, Razumov saw an unusually large number of city policemen guarding the platform—the very policemen whom Lukashenko and Razumov had been exposing for their venality. He told his niece they'd been deceived; they should leave in separate directions and meet again at his flat. But Lukashenko spotted the niece crossing the street and ordered her to halt. She started to run. A shot rang out, and the girl bled to death in the road. Either from fear or shame or deceit, Lukashenko swore the killing was a mistake.

The obvious question, and the one that Petr immediately asked, was what did Lukashenko have to gain?

Hardly able to contain his own hatred for the man, Viktor replied, "That mendacious maggot played both ends against the middle. He ingratiated himself with the local constabulary, who, he heard, were a step away from arresting him, and he earned the gratitude of the OGPU for fingering a Ukrainian nationalist. The

OGPU, to their later regret, helped bring him to power. Now they want to depose him, having recognized their error."

"And we've agreed to help," said Petr walking to the window. On the street, a horse with a yoked collar was straining to pull a canvas-covered wagon. The horse's steamy exhalations, which looked like silver shafts, came in spurts. Then the horse stopped in the middle of the street. The driver climbed down from his seat and swore at the animal, but to no avail. Reaching into the wagon, he removed a whip and fiercely applied it to the horse's rump. The horse buckled and fell to its knees. Petr could see stripes of blood running down its legs. The driver immediately unharnessed the horse, lest it topple the wagon. Without turning to face Viktor, a distraught Petr asked, "I know what I get, a clean record, but what do you get?"

Viktor came to the window and looked at the scene below. What he saw was a horse quiver and roll to one side, apparently dead. He silently watched for a minute, as the driver kicked the animal in the back. When the horse failed to respond, the driver strapped the harness around his shoulders and waist and started to pull the wagon himself, leaving the horse behind. "What do I get, you ask? I'll tell you. I rid this oblast of an odious creature, I ingratiate myself with the OGPU, and best of all I savor the sweet taste of revenge."

In the ensuing silence, Petr was thinking, as one often did in Stalin's Russia, of other motives and possible machinations. Revenge for what? He glanced around the room, looking for a family photograph. Not a one, not even of parents or brother or sister. The flat was devoid of any evidence that the Harkov family had ever lived, except of course for Viktor's presence. How very strange. Or was the explanation that Viktor's head, teeming with plots, conspiracies, intrigues, and stratagems, had shriveled his heart? Petr wondered, remembering Alexander's photograph of the Harkov family and his beautiful sister.

"Your brother," ventured Petr, "once showed me a snapshot of your parents seated in a garden, with their three children around them. What was your father's occupation?"

"He owned a general store, which the Soviets confiscated."

Petr felt confused. If Viktor was telling the truth, why would Alexander have joined the OGPU, and why would Viktor lend himself to their black deeds? A second later, Viktor uttered the reason. "I despised my alcoholic father for mistreating my mother and sister."

"What happened to them?"

"We'd better think about dinner."

Petr went straight to the stove. "If you can stand soup again, I have a nice potato recipe."

"It's just as well, because we're out of beets and cabbage. But there's a lamb shank, which you're welcome to use. I need to shop."

Petr wrapped a dish towel around his middle and started slicing potatoes. "Tell me," he said offhandedly, "about your mother and sister."

"What's there to tell? My mother died of typhus and my sister— she was older than me—she died for a revolutionary cause."

"Your mama's name?"

"Celia, and my sister's was Relitsa."

Now was the moment, Petr decided, to advance his hunch. "Did Comrade Razumov know your family?"

Viktor's discomfort could be felt across the room. "He lived in the same apartment building and hung around with Alexander."

"How old is Razumov?"

"Early forties, I would guess."

"About the same age as your sister. Right?"

Grabbing Petr from behind by the shoulders, Viktor spun him around so they stood face-to-face. "Out with it! What are you trying to worm from me?"

Uncertain whether to be candid or not, Petr hesitated. It was just long enough for Viktor to tell him what he wanted to know.

"Razumov was in love with my sister. There, now you have it."

But Petr knew he didn't have it all. He felt certain that Razumov's niece whom he hid from the police was actually Relitsa Harkova. Presumably he loved her. Was his ardor returned? And where did Lukashenko come in? Did he also have a yen for the lovely Relitsa? It wouldn't be the first time a thwarted lover killed the object of his affections. Petr's head was spinning with scenarios and scenes right out of a Russian romance novel. But was he right or simply nesting ideas, one inside the other, like a matryoshka doll?

A morning telephone call from Razumov alerted Viktor and Petr that Lukashenko's official car, with its tinted windows, was now in the repair shop, and that the two mechanics, by prior arrangement, would be absent from two to three. The car had a clock, and they had an hour to rig it.

The garage, situated in the basement of a government building and reached from the street by a ramp, was a dark and grimy affair. Petr had stored the dynamite and all his attachments in a canvas bag that he cradled ever so carefully. A sleepy porter nodded at the two men and then returned his gaze to a soiled newspaper. The door to the work area stood slightly ajar, and the interior lighting was poor. In under ten minutes, Petr disengaged the clock from the dashboard and wired it to two sticks of dynamite that he deftly lodged behind the glove compartment, so that when the explosion took place, it would occur directly in front of the passenger, Vladimir Lukashenko. By the time the porter looked up from his paper, all he could see were the backs of two men making their way up the ramp to the street.

The next step was to decide where to position themselves along the road to the Kremlin. Petr had serious reservations about taking the life of the innocent driver, but Viktor said that the "incidental damage" couldn't be helped. "Cold-blooded" was the word that came to Petr's mind, but he could not disguise the fact that he was not only party to the crime but also the bomb designer. He tried not to think about his participation, but unbidden reflections came to him, like concentric circles that radiated out from a fixed center called "assassination." What if Lukashenko's car was flanked by other automobiles or mobbed by admirers? Would they too be incidental damage? And could Razumov assure him that the only people in the Packard would be the driver and Lukashenko? The mayor was fond of appearing in public with average citizens and their families. Supposing a child was in the backseat? And not least was the fear that whoever replaced Lukashenko would be worse. Hadn't the killing of Tsar Alexander II derailed reforms and enthroned his hateful son?

Returning to the area of woods where the police first encountered Viktor and Petr was out of the question. A new hiding place had to be found. But where? You could hardly set off a remote control device in a crowd. In an open space, the conspirators would be seen. After their last encounter with Lukashenko's men, the woods undoubtedly would be patrolled. Razumov finally decided to have an OGPU car officially parked along the highway, ostensibly for the mayor's protection, with Petr in the back operating his equipment. When Lukashenko's Packard passed, Petr would signal the clock, which in turn would ignite the dynamite sticks. At Viktor's suggestion, Petr had briefly considered setting the clock to explode at a certain time, but decided against that plan because, as Razumov pointed out, Lukashenko's movements were notoriously erratic.

The night before the winter festival, Razumov invited the two men to dine with him at a restaurant frequented by OGPU agents. For all the candles and glitter and lights, it was a depressing place where secret policemen brought their mistresses and girlfriends. Viktor disliked coming here because the clientele drank too much and spoke too loudly, but Razumov, for some reason, had a soft spot for this cookhouse. Petr's feelings were a mystery. Perhaps his mind was elsewhere: on the next day's activities.

During the course of the meal, Razumov, who had a high threshold for alcohol, consumed nearly half a bottle of vodka. To look at him, you wouldn't have known that his eyes were losing their focus and his mind its clarity. Even when drunk, he kept his physical balance. His head never lolled; his feet never shuffled; his hands never shook. The only sign of drunkenness was his maudlin remembrances: of family, friends, a pet dog, a forgiving schoolteacher, and Relitsa Harkova, a subject Viktor would have preferred to avoid.

"God, she was lovely," Razumov intoned, to the discomfort of her brother. "Only a poet could do her justice, and I'm no poet. Far from it, just a cop with rough hands."

"I think we ought to leave," said Viktor.

"Hell, the night is young and tomorrow . . . tomorrow dawns a new day. For all of us. Thanks to our friend here, Tovarish Selivanov." Forgetting Relitsa for the moment, Razumov shared his vision for the country. "Free of want and privilege. A place of equality, fairness, and justice. Are we there yet? Not by a long shot." He quickly looked around to see if any of his colleagues might have heard him. But his fellow agents were seated at a safe distance. "The walls have ears," he said. "You can never be too cautious." He suppressed a burp. "I can just see that oily prick being thrown through the roof of his car and landing in pieces, a leg here, an arm there. His face no longer recognizable. He's a murderer. You do know that, don't you, Petr Selivanov? He's a murderer. Ask Viktor here. Or maybe he's already told you. He shot and killed the beautiful, lovely, and wonderful Relitsa Harkova. In the back, when she tried to run from that filthy rapist."

"I think that's quite enough," said Viktor. "I'm going home. Petr, will you join me? We have to be up early tomorrow."

But Razumov laid a heavy hand on Petr's arm. "Let him go, I haven't finished my story, and it's one that haunts me daily." Viktor reached for his wallet to pay for his share of the dinner. "Forget it," said Razumov, "it's my treat."

Without another word, Viktor stood, went to the coat stand, slipped into his jacket, and left, while his friends watched.

"Well, that's that," said Razumov, though Petr had no idea to what the "that" referred. "Where was I? A dismembered Lukashenko. Yes, how much pleasure that will give me. But the real point of the story is not about our soon-to-be-buried mayor . . ." This time he did belch, and loudly ". . . but about Viktor's sister. The Harkovs lived in the flat above us. I was an only child. Breach birth. Mother couldn't have any more kids. We could hear Viktor's father, upstairs, beating the hell out of his wife and daughter. When Relitsa left for school in the morning, I walked with her. She was always bruised. I think the old man hated her because she was so pretty. You know how ugly people can often resent beautiful ones."

Petr listened raptly. The more Razumov drank, the more Petr learned. Razumov admitted his fondness for Relitsa, "the only girl I really ever cared for"; and he defended her when other children threw snowballs or disparaged her drunken father. They had both studied at the college in Ryazan, she, philosophy, and he, accounting. Their different disciplines led them in opposite directions, both literally and figuratively. She departed for Ukraine, and he went into the secret service as a statistician and then an analyst. He hadn't seen her for several years when he crossed her path in Geneva. Razumov had been sent there on an undercover mission, and she was fleeing a Soviet crackdown against Ukrainian nationalists. They had spent several days together, and had even enjoyed a boat ride on Lake Geneva. As they parted, she confessed that she would shortly be leaving Switzerland and stealing back to Kiev to continue the fight for independence, a cause that Razumov warned her would fail.

The next time they saw each other was in his flat, to which she had gained admittance by telling the building superintendent that Razumov was her brother. She was wanted for "espionage" and had been labeled "an enemy of the people." After a week in his flat, the "super" started to nose around and ask questions about the stunning blond Razumov was "keeping." It was she who first suggested moving east and assuming a new identity in Siberia. Unbeknownst to Razumov, Lukashenko had met her on one of his holidays to Andeer in Switzerland, where he went to enjoy the mineral waters. Relitsa had traveled to the spa to meet a comrade, a fellow nationalist, who was apprehended at the Swiss border and never made it into the country. While she was waiting, Lukashenko, who had an eye for the ladies and was already in the company of another woman, approached her and, in his charming Russian accent, tried to inveigle her into a rendezvous. She resisted and returned to her room. That night, posing as a hotel employee, he knocked on her door and, when she opened it, tried to rape her. Had she not screamed so loudly, he would have succeeded.

Why had Relitsa not taken refuge with Viktor in his flat? Razumov had asked her the same question, and she had told him about the bad blood between them. The cause? She had never forgiven Viktor for failing to stand up to his father and protect his mother and sister from the drunken man's abuse. She related an incident in which she had taken refuge behind Viktor and had begged him to keep her from a certain beating. But Viktor pleaded neutrality and stepped aside. After Viktor had learned from Razumov the details of her death, he swore to kill Lukashenko—with the help of the OGPU, and from a distance, with a bomb.

By the time that Petr led Razumov from the restaurant, the fog of cigarette smoke and the humidity from the sweating windows had made breathing nearly impossible. The cold air of the street was tonic. Razumov seemed to shake off his intoxication like an old snakeskin. Petr stood gulping oxygen and only slowly recovered his senses.

"Well, tomorrow's a red-letter day," said Razumov. "Get some sleep, comrade. I'll collect you at eight in the morning. The car will be parked at the curb outside your building. In the evening we'll celebrate."

Promptly at eight, Petr and Viktor entered Razumov's car, a black Skoda, which was not official OGPU issue. They were dressed in the same working clothes they had worn when they had tried to dig a hole in the road. Petr was carrying his canvas satchel with all the necessary equipment, and Viktor seemed intent on disguising himself with a peaked cap and dark sunglasses. Wordlessly, Razumov turned into the street and made his way slowly toward the main artery that Lukashenko's car would follow to reach the Ryazan Kremlin. No secret police units, in their black Zim cars, were in evidence. This killing was not to have OGPU fingerprints. Razumov had brought his lunch.

"You never know how long you may have to wait."

Petr asked, "What if you need a toilet?"

Razumov chuckled. "In the service, you learn to go once a day, in the morning, and once before bedtime. Good sphincter muscles . . . that's what you need."

Shortly after ten o' clock, an escort of motorcycles appeared leading the black Packard with the tinted glass windows.

A second or two after the car passed, Petr set off the blast. The car seemed to rise off the ground, return to earth, and then fly apart, with windows and doors acting like projectiles and taking down everything in their path, including a few onlookers and motorcyclists. He had gauged the distance correctly. The assassins were untouched. Razumov backed up and sped off, taking numerous side and back roads to return to Viktor's flat. Viktor and Petr exited the car, and Razumov drove away to hide the car in a barn on the outskirts of town.

Once the two men entered the apartment, Viktor turned on the radio. A lugubrious male voice interrupted a program of martial music to announce an explosion on the highway leading to the Ryazan Kremlin.

"The city police have already declared the incident an assassination attempt on the life of our beloved leader, Vladimir Lukashenko. But owing to the vigilance of devoted bodyguards, our precious mayor's life was spared."

Petr looked at Viktor and said, "Not a chance. More official lies." Viktor calmly poured himself a drink and sank into his parlor chair, the one in blue slipcovers, the one he used for reading.

The announcer continued. "At this very moment, a river launch is docking below the Kremlin, and Mayor Lukashenko, to thunderous applause, is ascending the steps leading up to the fortress. All of his admirers, who have braved the cold and the wind, are on hand to see their adored leader. As for the bloody murderers, the police are looking for them at this very moment, rounding up Mensheviks, Social Democrats, dissident priests, monarchists, and, of course, Trotskyites. Once the villains are identified, they will be tried and shot. The victims of this terrible bombing have yet to be identified, but ambulances are on the scene."

Martial music resumed. Viktor wordlessly entered his bedroom and returned with two traveling bags, both packed. When he put on his overcoat, Petr asked him where he was going.

"It's time to leave," he said. "For you, too."

"Why's that?"

"Are you deaf? Didn't you hear? Lukashenko escaped. That means his bodyguards were tipped off. This job was assigned to Razumov and me. Ergo, some senior OGPU officers knew about it. But no one's going to touch a senior official. That leaves the three of us: Razumov, you, and me. So start packing—and get out!"

A bewildered Petr asked, "Where?"

"You said you had a girlfriend waiting for you in Kiev. Me, I'm going to bury myself, as you did, in Balyk . . . with Galina. While the mayor's men are looking for the bombers, the OGPU will be looking for the snitch. It's time to clear out."

"Police and secret agents will be watching every train and bus leaving the city. Did you think of that?"

Viktor opened the door, shouldered his two bags, and said, "I have a transit permit—and a promise to keep my name out of it. Comrade Razumov's OGPU membership will insulate him from suspicion. That leaves you."

Before Petr's mind came into focus, Viktor was out the door and descending the stairs two at a time. "I'll tackle the swine and choke him to death," thought Petr, and sprang to his feet. But by the time he gained the stairs, the fleeing double agent had reached the street and entered a waiting car that roared off. "I must warn Galina," he told himself. Returning to the flat, Petr quickly packed, leaving behind the satchel with its incriminating evidence. When he entered the hall, two armed policemen were already on the stairs. Unseen, Petr climbed the narrow ladder to the roof, where the building superintendent maintained a greenhouse. No one was inside. He hid behind the potting table.

Shortly, the greenhouse door opened. Pause. Then he heard a man's voice say, "He must have gone down the fire escape." Petr remained frozen for well over an hour, until cramping forced him to stand and stretch. It was already dark outside when he stole from the greenhouse and made his way to the street and then to the rail yards. Still dressed in the same work clothes, he saw a freight train unloading coal. He clambered inside and rubbed his hands and face with coal dust, to blend in with his landscape. The train's next destination was a mystery. He didn't care, just so long as it left Ryazan. Slowly moving down the track, the train attracted two other itinerant travelers, who hoisted themselves into the car at the last second. By this time, Petr knew not to trust anyone and merely grunted when the two men extended their greetings. After several hours, he felt certain the men were not city police or Lukashenko bodyguards or OGPU. Only then did he hazard a laconic word, or rather a question:

"Where we headed?"

"Last stop, Minsk," replied one of the men.

The reply suited Petr. It brought him that much closer to Kiev. He leaned back against the wall and closed his eyes, trying to make sense of what had just taken place. Viktor had originally been allied with the OGPU to rid the oblast of Lukashenko, and he had induced Petr, with his training in explosives, to join him. In return, Petr would have a clean military record. Razumov was Viktor's OGPU contact. Both men had personal reasons for wanting to see Lukashenko dead, but aside from the personal, both men also had political motives. Razumov and his colleagues in the secret police wanted to see the oblast governed by one of their own, and Viktor had an unimpeachable reason to see the man dead: Lukashenko had killed his sister. The accusations of corruption and bribery were merely cosmetic. But in the end, Viktor Harkov was the most ruthless of all, and the most venal. He knew that Razumov would find protection in the spacious folds of the OGPU gown, and that Petr would be the likely suspect, a deserter on the run. A lingering question was whether Viktor's behavior had anything to do with Galina? Petr had already indicated that he intended to unite with a woman in Kiev. He and Galina would divorce. So if Viktor had designs on Galina, Petr presented no threat. Then why set him up? It made no sense, unless it was a pure and simple monetary transaction and someone had to take the fall. Of the three men, Petr was the dupe.

As soon as he arrived in Minsk, he would find a public bath and a safe doss house. He would then write Galina to warn her of Viktor's treachery. But his epistolary endeavors took a few days, by which time the Ryazan OGPU had received a letter from Viktor in which he named Petr as the one who had warned Lukashenko of the intended assassination and praised Razumov for risking his life in support of the plan. Of his own role, he said nothing. When Viktor reached Balyk, Sasha offered him Petr's former attic room (at Galina's urging). Two days later, Viktor intercepted and destroyed Petr's letter. He then grew a beard, let his hair reach his shoulders, and dyed it, making him look like an old believer who had lived with monks in the forest.

13

Although initially Viktor rarely showed his face in the village and never at the school, he spent days on end in the attic, working on a treatise or apologia of some kind. Galina seemed pleased with his presence, and Alya had expressed delight at seeing him but really preferred Petr and Sasha. She found Viktor aloof, even when he played with her. Horses had never appealed to Viktor, so he could not appreciate her joy in riding around the corral on her pony, Scout. What he did enjoy was making Goran Youzhny's acquaintance and being introduced to the fine art of photography. As for Sasha, Viktor treated him as a nonentity. Anyone earning his keep as a teacher or school director was, by his definition, feckless. People with real talent became writers and journalists and engineers. Nothing but failures who couldn't do anything else became professors and teachers.

Underlying Viktor's anti-intellectual attitude toward pedagogues was the simple fact of his failure to do graduate fieldwork in linguistic anthropology. Although he had attended college at the expense of the state, he expected the state's largesse to extend to a year in Africa, despite his dull academic record. When the state balked, Viktor grew disconsolate and then resentful. Denouncing all scholarship as fatuous, he became a polemicist, living at first on the money his brother earned and then, so long as he raged against

Lukashenko, on an OGPU subsidy. No one denied that Viktor had the intelligence and writing skills to compose a first-rate treatise or book. But what he wrote in the attic was a full and false account, sent to the Ryazan OGPU, of his and Razumov's efforts to keep Petr from revealing the planned attempt on Lukashenko's life.

Unbeknownst to Viktor, Razumov had been suspended without pay and put on the "Watch" list. His career as a secret policeman appeared to have ended in disgrace—until Viktor's long and detailed history of events arrived. Using every literary device, including the favorite Soviet "although" opening, he had composed a narrative that exuded the very essence of truth. It acknowledged mistakes (small ones) and blamed himself for overreaching (a prerequisite of Soviet apologies). But he forcefully argued that the botched assassination was owing to the treachery of Petr Selivanov and to his "minders" (he and Razumov) not watching Petr closely enough. He apologized for his and Razumov's failure, and insinuated that he would never inform Lukashenko's people of the OGPU's hidden hand in the matter. The implication, of course, was that in return for his silence, he could always count on OGPU support.

Why Viktor had gone to such lengths to exculpate Razumov was a different story. For all his own anger and self-serving conduct, he had long felt ashamed of his failure to protect his sister from his drunken father. Razumov's fond regard for Relitsa, probably the only person Viktor had ever truly loved, was a debt he needed to repay. This letter would settle the account.

Sasha disliked Viktor from the moment he'd read Petr's diary. He thought then that Petr's suspicions were entirely justified. In Ryazan, he had found Viktor self-absorbed and consequently selfish. Now that they were living under the same roof, he disliked him even more, regarding him as underhanded and unscrupulous. Sasha and Galina had resumed intimacies after Petr's departure, but with the arrival of Viktor, she became distant. Her previous passion returned only briefly when Viktor and Goran retired to the Balyk Inn, on the edge of town, to carouse. The inn was a converted barn that an enterprising farmer, Fyodor Kolchak, had fitted out as a tavern. The police periodically shuttered the place because private enterprise

192   LEVITT

was illegal; but as soon as they left, usually with their fill of vodka, Kolchak reopened. Here, at a corner table, Viktor and Goran liked to huddle, ostensibly talking about photography, though Kolchak whispered that the talk often focused on politics.

Sasha gathered that Goran's Leningrad family had ties to the Right Opposition, influential ties that reached to the inner sanctum of the Politburo. If Goran's family had been fishing in those conspiratorial waters, they might find themselves snagged on their own hooks. But why would Viktor, always ready to change sides, find any appeal in a losing cause? And the Right Opposition was certainly a lost cause. Perhaps Viktor had in mind getting his hands on personal property and selling it for a profit before the government made all such activities illegal. Or perhaps the Right Opposition didn't even come into his thinking, but rather he saw in Goran's photography a way of advancing his own interests, whatever they might be; or perhaps he was merely trying to appropriate Goran's lab. He did buy a number of artistic photographs from Comrade Youzhny, all bearing on some physical aspect of the school: a broken chimney, a cracked window, a roof missing a few slates, unpainted siding, water-stained books in the toolshed, a withered apple tree, a weather-beaten bicycle pump lying in the grass.

Shortly after Viktor's arrival at the farmhouse, Sasha heard him steal into Galina's room late one night and her say, "Not here! Are you mad? Alya's sleeping in the alcove." Then Sasha had the impression that Galina, who often entered the kitchen before bedtime to make a cup of hot milk, had returned not to her bedroom but to the attic. He dared not spy lest he invite her disdain for such conduct, which she called "Bolshevik behavior." But with each passing week, his suspicions grew, particularly since he had overheard Viktor tell Galina that he didn't trust Sasha, and that something about Comrade Parsky wasn't right. The conversation included the following:

"I felt uneasy when he first came to Ryazan bearing condolences. The man is hiding something."

"What might that be?" asked Galina.

"I don't know, but no one is innocent."

Then he had made his signature clicking sound, the same one that he had made on the beach below the Kremlin—by pulling the tip of his tongue down abruptly and forcefully from the roof of his mouth.

Sasha tried to imitate him. Click, cluck, clack. He sounded like a lame chicken. But he continued trying and eventually realized that to increase the effect he had to pucker his lips. Retracted lips muffled the sound. Before long he had become quite adept.

Overhearing that conversation had led Sasha to burn Petr's diary and to ask Brodsky's advice. But there was a difficulty: How could Sasha represent the situation without incriminating himself? He wished that Petr were present to give him some insight into Viktor. But given Petr's absence, all Sasha could think of telling Brodsky was that he suspected Viktor of trying to seduce Galina, an embarrassing admission and a weak excuse for wishing him ill.

"Has she complained to you?" asked Brodsky.

"No, but then she wouldn't because he's an old friend."

After smoking a cigarette and lightly running a hand along his bookcase, as if absorbing the wisdom of the ages through his fingertips, he stopped behind Sasha's chair. "Denounce the bastard!"

"For what?"

"Make up something, like being involved in that Ryazan mess. You said he hated Lukashenko."

With Viktor at the farmhouse, Galina clearly felt compromised. She had no interest in marrying Sasha, but she found that their lovemaking had enriched her fondness and deepened her appreciation of his concern for her future and Alya's. Not long after Viktor arrived, Galina confided in Sasha that Viktor had told her that he wanted to share her bed, and hinted at more, though what the "more" amounted to, he had failed to spell out, merely dropping hints, all of them pointing to Sasha.

With the fall term winding down, Viktor expressed an interest in quitting his isolation in the spring and becoming a teacher, without pay. He proposed a linguistics course. Sasha had his reservations, knowing Viktor's views about teaching. More important, would such a position be a signal to Viktor that he could remain at the farmhouse? He could hardly live elsewhere when he was a wanted man. To remain off the books as an unpaid teacher would raise eyebrows and perhaps lead to an investigation. And how was Viktor supporting himself? All that Sasha or anyone else knew was that fortnightly, Viktor received a packet addressed to Ivan Goncharov, clearly someone's idea of a jest, since Viktor was no novelist. Sasha knew that his best interests would be served by refusing Viktor a teaching position and sending him packing. If not for Galina's objections, he would have done both. She begged Sasha, in light of the death of Viktor's brother, to give Viktor a temporary appointment and permit him to remain at the farmhouse until he could find other lodging.

"He has no papers," Sasha objected.

"Since he arrived, he has made friends with Goran, who introduced him to Bogdan. And Bogdan . . ."

Sasha interrupted. "Is a forger!"

"Then you know."

"May I ask where your information came from?"

"The locals. And yours?" she asked.

"Avram."

"You ought to get out more often," she said conspiratorially. "The villagers have a lot to say about Bogdan Dolin."

"Such as?"

She told him that Bogdan was known to have a healthy dislike of authority, and always acted alone. A silent man, and a sullen one, he had previously owned a printing press that churned out counterfeit passports and rubles. At the time of his arrest, one of the officers was heard to say that Bogdan's rubles were nearly perfect. The only thing lacking was the right kind of paper, which Bogdan had no way of buying since it was the preserve of the Soviet treasury. A high wall of his making, that surrounded his bungalow, had led to speculation that, as before, he supported himself by forging documents for wealthy people and government officials in flight from the country.

"Soviets!" exclaimed Sasha. "The story grows more bizarre with each passing minute. It makes no sense."

"That's what I said, until Viktor reminded me that apparatchiks regularly fall out of favor. If *you* needed travel papers to disappear in the East, say, where would you go? The government wouldn't oblige you. So you'd find someone like Bogdan. It makes perfect sense."

"Now I know where Viktor will get his new papers and passport."

"And Goran will provide the photograph."

"What does he gain out of it?"

"Good question. Viktor hasn't said, but I intend to find out."

With box camera and tripod in hand, Goran continued to beg Brodsky to sit for a photograph, but Avram refused his requests. The result was an ugly scene that took place in the town square, where Goran had set up his camera in the back of a covered wagon and covertly snapped pictures of Avram, who was watching with dozens of others as two men led a couple of male lambs, each a year old and without blemish, into the square to be slaughtered in anticipation of Easter. The men, accustomed to killing, were dressed in rubber aprons and galoshes. Father Zossima was present and could be heard, by those at his side, mumbling Easter prayers. Brodsky was thinking of another holiday, one that he alone among the villagers knew by its proper name, "Korban Pesach" (Passover). As a child he had read in the Old Testament from Numbers 9:1–2, "And the Lord spake unto Moses in the Wilderness of Sinai, in the first month of the second year after they were come out of the land of Egypt, saying, Let the children of Israel keep the passover at his appointed season." The men and women of Balyk, formerly observant Greek Catholics and now forbidden to practice their faith, still maintained certain traditions, whether or not they even knew their sources. How many Christians, mused Avram, have any idea that Easter began as a Passover service? The locals certainly knew what it meant to be passed over, in every sense of those words, since the most prosperous villages were those free of Soviet control, and free of illiteracy and illness. At the back of Avram's head echoed the words he'd been made, as a child, to memorize: "For the LORD will pass through to slay the Egyptians; and when he sees the blood on the lintel and on the two doorposts, the LORD will pass over the door, and the plague shall not be upon you."

The crowd circled the two men who pulled the lambs by ropes attached to their necks. One of the lambs stumbled and fell to its knees. The shorter of the two men grabbed the lamb by its neck hairs and forced it to its feet. The other man produced a sickle that caught the glint of the sun. A minute later, both lambs lay dead in a pool of blood, as an excited howl rose from the crowd and then faded. A farmer, standing only a few feet from the wagon, heard the click of a camera. Thinking that his own picture had been taken, and superstitiously believing that photographs stole a man's soul, he cried out that a devil was lodged in the back of the wagon. With Goran's exposure, Avram insisted he relinquish the photographic plates or destroy them on the spot. Goran refused. An argument ensued. When the older man reached for the camera, Goran fled the scene leaving behind his tripod and jacket. Avram swore to bring a charge against Goran but instead asked Sasha to expel the young man from his lab. Caught between the two warring parties, Sasha asked Goran to erase the plates—in his presence. Goran complied, complaining that the destruction of a valuable photographic record was a state crime. Sasha scoffed and reported back to Avram that the matter had been settled amicably. For the nonce, no more was said, though Avram continued to complain and Goran kept his lab.

By now, Viktor and Goran had become kindred spirits. Only a few steps from the farmhouse, the lab provided Viktor an oppor-tunity to learn photography, an emerging field. To Sasha's dismay, Goran bragged that he was teaching Viktor about hidden cameras and altered photographs. Perhaps worse, Goran had introduced Viktor to Bogdan and to the art of what . . . forgery? The three fellows, frequently seen together, seemed a strange trio, ranging in age from twenty-one to fifty-eight. Viktor had just turned thirty. When Sasha asked Viktor about his interest in photography, Viktor replied he could take pictures of the lip and mouth formations that created alveolar clicking sounds, and that such images would prove useful in the linguistics course Sasha had agreed to his teaching in the spring. Then Viktor placed his tongue on the roof of his mouth and made a loud click, as he habitually did on entering and leaving a room or punctuating a point. Was it his way of saying "I know click languages," or did it have some personal meaning that only Viktor could fathom? Sasha found his enigmatic behavior vexing, but Galina often seemed blind to Viktor's social maladroitness.

Shortly before the start of the spring semester, Viktor showed up in Sasha's office to tell him that he had papers and a passport in the name of Ivan Goncharov, and that Sasha needn't worry if the secret police came snooping around. "I'm now official," said Viktor, "so you can safely introduce Ivan Goncharov to the other faculty members." Given that Viktor had never appeared on campus, he was a stranger to the other teachers; and Goran, at Viktor's request, had sworn to keep his friend's real name unspoken. Although the teaching staff and students had often whispered about the "new" man staying at the farmhouse, no one had had the courage to ask. In fact, shortly after Viktor's arrival, it was bruited about that the new man was Galina's brother and that the director would also find him a place in the school. So when Sasha announced that Viktor would be teaching a course in linguistics, the other teachers, assuming that their own salaries would suffer from the addition of another person, made known their displeasure. But when Sasha explained that Comrade Goncharov was teaching for nothing, smiles replaced sneers.

Viktor set out immediately to ingratiate himself with the other teachers, a task that he accomplished handily with the help of Goran's camera and tripod (eventually returned), and Goran's painstaking instructions. Posing each of the teachers in his or her favorite setting, Viktor flattered the staff with his portraits, which in fact were handsomely done, owing to Goran's lessons and artistic flare for developing and framing. The teachers nearly swooned. In no time, Ivan Goncharov was a favorite of his colleagues, who chuckled at his name but never dared to call him Oblomov, the title of the famous author's novel and a name associated with laziness.

Students took to Viktor at once, fascinated by his subject and his skill at producing click sounds of every tone and variety. For all his natural reticence, he came alive in front of a class. The school soon buzzed that the hot new topic and teacher were linguistics and Ivan Goncharov. Galina was pleased that Viktor had a new view of teaching. Sasha was less enthusiastic, not because of any failing in Viktor's classroom performance, but because he worried that the man would never decamp from the farmhouse. At the end of the first week of school, however, Viktor surprisingly announced, with a click of his tongue, that he was moving in with Bogdan Dolin. He retreated to the attic, packed his belongings, and exited with another alveolar click.

"No good will come of this move. Mark my words. You'll see," Sasha observed.

"I thought you wanted him gone," Galina replied. "You ought to be delighted."

"The next thing you know, we'll hear that Goran has left his digs at Bella Zeffina's house and joined Viktor at Bogdan's." Galina said nothing. "I tell you, they are an unholy trio."

With a puckish smile, Galina said, "We'll have privacy again."

"Not entirely," he corrected her. "There's still the lab, and you can bet Goran and Viktor will be spending a lot of time there, up to no good."

"You are entirely too suspicious. One would think that *you* had something to hide."

"It's the times."

"Well," she said, making for the door, "I can't argue with that."

A prolonged period of rain plagued Balyk, causing cellars to flood, roofs to leak, and roads to become boggy. The horse-driven sleds that glided so easily on the winter ice were useless in the ankle-deep mud. Then, too, there was the fog that marinated the countryside. Thick clouds hung in every valley, and the sky overhead seemed low enough to touch. Unlike the rains of April and May, February precipitation was a cold harbinger of the uncomfortable months ahead. Clothes took days to dry, even when hung near a stove; electrical circuits, never dependable at best, short-circuited; and the generator at the Michael School sputtered and frequently plunged classrooms into darkness. Any motorist foolish enough to drive his vehicle in such wet weather was sure to experience an electrical failure. Only the local storyteller appreciated the foul conditions, which made her tales of mermaids, water sprites, and demons all the more present. Bella Zeffina invited the local children to come to the elementary school on Saturday afternoon to hear her tell the tale of the water snake. In the meantime, she said, "Be careful. Bad dreams are related to water." Alya begged to attend. Galina shrugged and said, "Why not?" and Sasha told her to dress warmly and take her galoshes.

Bella Zeffina, considered by the locals as something of a sorceress, loved children, kept a clean house, cooked Polish dishes for her husband, Max Zeffin, who had come from Lvov, and had an inexhaustible supply of folktales that she shared with the children on special occasions. The current forty-day rainfall qualified as an unusual event. With her dimpled cheeks and elbows, round face, pale blue eyes, and flaxen-gray hair done up in a coiled hank, she rested her heavy body on a stool, rolled up her wool socks, pulled her knitted shawl tightly around her shoulders, lowered her eyelids, and began.

Once upon a time, an old woman like me had a daughter. (Bella, in fact, had lost a young daughter to smallpox.) Her name was Abigail. While she was swimming in the local pond, a snake, who introduced himself as Vikenti, which means "conquering," came out of the water and rested on her clothes, which she had spread on a bush. When Abigail left the pond, she discovered the snake, who said, "If you want your clothes back, you'll have to marry me." Well, Abigail couldn't walk home without any clothes on, so she agreed, thinking that it was nonsense that a girl and a snake could wed.

Arriving home, she told her mother what had happened. Her mother scoffed at the very idea of a human being and a reptile being joined in marriage. And there the matter stood, because both the mother and daughter forgot all about it. But several weeks later, the snake wriggled up to Abigail's cottage. Finding the windows and doors locked, Vikenti stole into the house through the chimney, which left him covered with soot and resembling a demon. Abigail tried to run out of the house, but Vikenti caught her, carried her back to the pond, and dragged her into the water. On the bottom of the pond, he miraculously turned into a well-spoken young man, explaining that out of the water he became a snake but under the water he was a human. Abigail and Vikenti lived submerged for several years and had one daughter, Alina, which means "bright and beautiful." One day, Abigail said that she wanted to visit her mother and show off her daughter. Vikenti agreed. Abigail asked him how she could return to the bottom of the pond after she returned from seeing her mother. Vikenti told her to call his name three times. Abigail spent a week with her mother and related how good her life was at the bottom of the pond. One day, her mother asked was there some secret to reentering the water? She said she need only call her husband's name three times.

Then Abigail's mother stole from the house, went to the edge of the pond, and called "Vikenti, Vikenti, Vikenti." When he surfaced, he appeared as a snake. The mother, who had brought with her a sharpened axe, cut off the head of the snake, causing the water in the pond to grow dark with blood. On learning of her mother's betrayal, Abigail took her daughter to the pond and wept and wailed, calling Vikenti's name. But all she heard was the silent lapping of the water among the lily pads. Knowing some of Vikenti's magic, a sorrowful Abigail turned her daughter into a wren and herself into a nightingale, and they both flew off on the wind, never to return.

For some reason, Galina felt uncomfortable listening to Alya retell the story. She had always feared snakes, but was that the reason for her discomfort? That night, she recounted to Sasha the story and her response to it. Perhaps he could provide some insight into her feelings. He pondered her words and after a long pause, remarked gnomically, "The earth and snake alike renew their skins, and that is when the world's new age begins."

Trouble arose before the rains ceased. A note appeared on the school bulletin board saying cryptically, "Sasha Parsky's time is over." The author of the note was a mystery. Had it come from a teacher, a student, a parent? No one knew. If it constituted some kind of cabal, Sasha thought he'd better learn more, if possible. He spoke individually to his teachers, but though all of them had seen the note and it had become a source of whisperings, the staff disclaimed any knowledge of the writer. Perhaps in fear of inviting the director's suspicions, the teachers never met in groups, but rather entered into colloquy two by two. A week passed and nothing further untoward occurred. But in the second week, another note appeared: "Director Parsky OUT!" It was then that Sasha glimpsed the intent behind the two notes. They were not intended to scare him but to get him to relinquish the directorship of the school. Brodsky had experienced similar events, so he might be able to tell Sasha which teachers were acting behind his back to expel him.

As usual, Brodsky sat reading and smoking. On hearing Sasha's story, he skeptically said:

"It doesn't sound like one of the old-timers. They'd complain directly to the secret police. Have you heard from Filatov?"

"Nothing."

"Then I would assume that someone is trying to organize an internal coup." He paused just long enough to light a new cigarette from the old one. "What about this new fellow you've told me about?"

"Viktor Harkov is quite capable of rabble-rousing, but why would he want to plot against me?"

Brodsky, wearing a worn cardigan covered with food stains, shook his head in disbelief. "Simple. He wants your job."

Sasha noticed that Avram's sweater was missing a button. For some reason, he wondered where it had gone. His mind wandered. Only slowly did he bring his attention back to what Avram had said. Viktor would be the last person to want the directorship. It would mean being vetted by the secret police. In no time, his betrayal in Ryazan, and his connection to Lukashenko, would be known. Surely Viktor wasn't foolish enough to think that a forged passport with the name Ivan Goncharov would pass scrutiny by the OGPU, renamed the NKVD. Perhaps Viktor had someone else in mind to become director, someone who would defer to Viktor and treat his support not grudgingly, but devoutly, unlike Sasha's attitude. If so, who would that person be?

"Which of the teachers," Sasha asked, "was particularly bitter over your original appointment and wanted to replace you?"

Brodsky laughed, bringing on a coughing fit. Spitting into the fire, he hoarsely replied, "All of them, but especially Olga Oborskaia. She felt that teaching physics entitled her to a higher academic position, since physics and math are harder to master than the other disciplines, except perhaps for chemistry. But I long felt that Vera Chernikova, for all her surface sweetness, would have been glad to join Olga in a palace coup. There has always been among the staff an undercurrent of rivalry: those trained in the physical sciences against everyone else."

"You're telling me that Olga or Vera or both would conspire to gain my position? If Viktor is stirring the pot, he presumably has most of the staff on his side. I seem to have lost this game."

"Then strike first."

"How?"

"I've told you before: Denounce him."

Although he abhorred snooping, Sasha used his passkey after hours to enter the classroom-offices of his teachers. In almost every instance, the filing cabinets and desks were securely locked. Where a drawer was accessible, nothing of importance was found. On the desk of Vera Chernikova he found a diagram of a mouth, designating the various parts of the oral cavity: lips, gingiva (gums), hard and soft palates, uvula, papillae of tongue, palatine tonsil, tongue, and the teeth. At the bottom of the page in small script were the letters "c.c." He came away from his nocturnal endeavors disappointed.

Without telling Galina about his unsuccessful search, he asked her help to locate the person behind the notes. Her own distaste for surveillance of any kind rendered her reluctant to do anything more than keep an eye on the bulletin board. Sasha felt that given all his favors, at the least she could ingratiate herself with the staff and try to find out if a plot was afoot. Galina refused. Her open disdain for becoming what she called a "mole" reinforced Sasha's fears that she and Viktor were lovers. He told himself he had cause for concern. On one occasion, he had found them in the farmhouse alone, after Viktor had taught his one class and Galina had returned home for lunch. When he walked in, they averted their eyes and stuttered through explanations that Sasha found unconvincing. His original impulse had been to enlist Alya's help, but he could not bring himself to induct a child into the filthy business of spying. Now he wasn't so sure. With Galina refusing to cooperate, his thoughts once again turned to Alya. He might just use her after all, but he would have to be subtle in his approach. She was much too clever to fall for some obvious ruse.

"We have to find out Viktor's birthday so we can prepare a party for him. Wouldn't that be nice, Alya?"

"Why not just ask him?"

"That would give the whole thing away."

"Maybe Mamma knows."

"She and Viktor are such good friends, I think if she asked he'd know in a minute."

"But what if she already knows?"

"Well, that's different."

"But we must keep it all a secret."

"I'd never tell. There are a lot of things I know that I never repeat. Mamma says I'd make a good soldier."

"Really? I would never have guessed that you knew secrets."

"A lot of them."

"Well, maybe someday you'll tell me one or two of them."

She reflected for a moment and said, "Maybe."

This conversation took place shortly after Galina rejected his plan as unsavory. Sasha and Alya were in the barn brushing Scout, she on one side, he on the other. Each had a strong-bristled brush that came with a handstrap. As they stroked the pony, he punctuated his comments about animal husbandry with his questions. She seemed intent on the job at hand and gave no indication that he was trying to use her. In fact, when she had said that she knew "things," he had let the conversation trail off so that his wordlessness would sink in, providing an impulse to talk. As she brushed the animal's mane, she ran her hand through the hair and let it fall lazily off to one side.

"I once saw Viktor do this with Mamma."

"Do what?"

"Run his hand through her hair."

"Well, he is, after all, a good friend."

"I think he loves her."

Sasha smiled at Alya but deliberately failed to respond. After a long pause, she added: "That's why I stayed with the Baturins when she went to see him."

"Oh?"

"She didn't want me along. I know that."

"Well, I get the impression they must have quarreled, because they're not so friendly of late."

Alya blurted, "Yes, they are!"

"When I see them at school," Sasha lied, "they hardly speak."

"I can sometimes hear them at night."

"Talking?"

"One of the boards in the attic is loose."

"Where? I must fix it."

"Over our bedroom, near the closet. I sometimes crawl into the closet and listen. The time Benjie ate with us, he listened too."

"Alya, you really shouldn't . . . unless it's important."

She made no reply. They put away the brushes, swept up, and returned to the farmhouse. Alya said nothing more about it for the rest of the day; but on the following afternoon, after returning from her tutoring lesson, she coyly said to Sasha:

"My teacher taught us the meaning of the word 'discreetness.' She said discreetness is a kindness, and its opposite can hurt people. But she also said sometimes it's right to report what we know."

"Know what?"

"What you were talking about: important things."

Galina's untimely entrance put an end to the discussion, except for Alya telling her mother that she had learned several new words, and one of them was "discreetness."

"It's a good word to know, my dear Alya, and an even better one to put into practice," Galina advised as she went to her room.

The child shook her head and ran off. Sasha sighed in relief, immensely glad she was not indiscreet.

A few minutes later, a loud click outside announced Viktor's presence. He had made an appointment to see Galina and hoped that Sasha would excuse them while they talked.

"It's about a memorial stone for my brother," said Viktor.

Sasha started for the barn to find Alya. But he caught a glimpse of Goran and stopped at the photo lab. Goran had several wooden packing cases in which he was carefully loading his equipment.

"Are you moving?" asked a surprised Sasha.

"The rains have made the walls sweat and I see evidence of mold. So I plan to transfer the lab to Bogdan Dolin's bungalow. He's offered me a dry spot at the back of the house."

"Do you plan to move in or will you continue to board with the Zeffins? She's quite a storyteller," said Sasha, hoping to dissuade Goran from leaving the Zeffins high and dry without a boarder.

"Oh, I have no intention of living elsewhere. It's just the lab that I'm moving. But thank you for allowing me to use this space and disrupt the routine of your house. I have some good portraits of you and Galina and Alya. I'll crop and frame them by May Day."

"Can I give you a hand?"

"No thanks, I'll be fine. I've even arranged for a car to transfer the cases."

"A car?"

"My uncle."

"Of course."

They shook hands and Sasha continued into the barn. As expected, Alya was grooming her pony. Wordlessly, Sasha picked up a brush and joined her. After a temporary lull in the rain and a brief burst of sunshine, dark clouds moved in again. Several minutes had passed, and neither he nor Alya had spoken. He often felt that their silent times together were more affectionate than their spoken ones. Silence, he had concluded, speaks more fondly than words. Although it can serve ill, as when one person won't speak to another owing to anger, it can also serve good, as when people are spellbound in the presence of some wondrous moment or thing; or when strong feelings render one mute. The examples were endless. Why, he asked himself, didn't he write a treatise on the subject and root it in some historical event? Such a paper might advance his career. Too many teachers and academics with fruitful ideas never shared them in print. Why did so many in his profession find it hard to write? Their ideas, when spoken, often revealed first-rate minds, but their unwillingness to take up pen and paper argued . . . what? Lassitude? Indiscipline? A busy life? Fear of rejection? He had read enough scholarly papers in his young life to know that not all ideas or arguments were transcendent. Did self-doubts inhibit the profession?

"You're not listening," said Alya. "I just told you something."

"Sorry, I was daydreaming."

"Mamma tells me to pay attention and not go wool gathering."

"She's quite right. Now what were you saying?"

"The last time I hid in the closet I could hear Mamma snipping at Uncle Viktor. She told him to find another place to live."

"Really?"

"Aren't you glad?" She smiled devilishly. "I am."

"I know what you mean."

"She also was mad at him because of someone called C.C. Those were the letters she used, C.C."

"And what did he say?"

"That he had been teasing."

Sasha weighed the wisdom of asking what he wanted to know most. After a few false starts, he said, "Does the floor creak a lot? I mean the loose board. Does it sound as if I should fix the floor so the bed doesn't fall through?"

Alya shrugged. She no longer had any interest in the subject.

Returning to the house, Sasha heard Viktor's familiar click as he left. Asking Galina to join him for tea at the kitchen table, Sasha filled the kettle and waited for it to boil. Touching her hand, he slowly gave voice to his fears.

"I have a feeling—mind you, it's only a feeling—that Viktor would like to see me replaced as director of the school."

"Replaced by whom?"

The water boiled. As Galina mutely watched, Sasha filled their cups and spooned in generous portions of honey.

"By Olga or Vera."

"You must be mad!"

"I can't prove it, but I feel it."

"Since when have you put so much reliance in feelings? You're always advising your staff to think before acting."

"I'm not acting on my feeling, I am simply sharing it with you to get your reaction."

"Well, you have it. You're letting your dislike of Viktor lead you astray."

"You're probably right," he replied and slowly stirred his tea. Galina looked off into the distance and only occasionally let her eyes settle on Sasha.

"He's a difficult man, I know, but he's not a bad man. After the murders, we became very close."

"Even closer than before?"

"What does that mean?"

"Galina," he said, with as much sincerity as he could command, "I gather that before you'd been told that Petr had died, you and Viktor were lovers."

She impaled him with her eyes, which began to tear. Without uttering a word, she left the table, entered her bedroom, and quietly closed the door. A minute later, Alya came bounding into the farmhouse. Sasha, with a bent finger, summoned her to his side and whispered that her mamma was ill and not to be disturbed. The child made no response. Sasha hugged her, slipped a few coins into her hand, and told her to buy some candy at the country store in

Balyk. He even helped her into her raincoat and galoshes, and gave her his black umbrella. At the window, he watched as she opened it and splashed through some puddles. Her free spirit made him think that only a child's resilience could save the world.

He waited several minutes before he knocked on Galina's door. No response. He looked at his watch and told himself he would wait five minutes and then knock again. But Galina's door slowly opened and she appeared red-faced and disheveled. Her tears were no longer in evidence, but her uncombed and wild hair bespoke her emotional state. She wordlessly made her way to the kitchen table, where she rejoined Sasha. He waited for her to speak first. When she did, it felt to Sasha as if an age had elapsed.

Galina said simply, "We were lovers once, yes, but now it is over." She paused. "I told him about us, and said that I wanted to make a life with you." With undisguised derision, she added, "Comrade Click or C.C., as he's taken to calling himself, told me that he had found another."

"Vera Chernikova."

"Then you know."

"I didn't until you said C.C."

"It's all part of his cloak-and-dagger posturing," she said in a tone of weary resignation. "That's Viktor through and through."

"And yet you don't believe he wants to discredit me."

"I do admit that he's a capable slanderer. But once he's achieved his end, which is usually to ruin some person or group, he moves on. Most likely, he would like to see Vera Chernikova take over." Pause. "What he sees in that string bean is anybody's guess."

That night Sasha and Galina made love. But this time it was different from anything they'd ever experienced. The sexual heat was there, as well as the gentleness, but in addition there was a genuine affection. In the morning, Sasha had the strange sensation that he was married, and that everything between him and Galina was understood. They were no longer tense, and they behaved as if they had been relieved of some burden. An unfortunate side effect was that Sasha now felt fiercely protective of Galina and became aggressively jealous if some man even paid her an innocent compliment. His chemical reaction was similar to the day of the murders. He acted instinctively, a throwback to primitive hominids.

With Viktor out of the farmhouse and Goran's photo lab now removed, Sasha, Galina, and Alya fell into a domestic rhythm that pleased them all. Even the weather seemed to shine on them. The rains abated, the sun shone, Alya rode Scout in the paddock and along a short trail that circled the farmhouse, and birdsong and blossoms were a harbinger of spring. Among the religious farmers, preparations began in earnest to celebrate Easter, which Father Zossima would celebrate in some hidden cellar. The Three Musketeers, as Sasha called Bogdan, Viktor, and Goran, seemed to spend most of their time in the walled bungalow. Did they present a danger? Avram, whom Sasha still visited and watched, was the person who could best advise him. When Sasha knocked and identified himself, Avram shouted that the door was unlocked. A cigarette dangled from his mouth, and a writing board rested on his lap. He was putting away writing materials, and papers peeked out of a black leather folder. Sasha quickly came to the point, and Avram prophesied that no good would come from the Three Musketeers.

"Men with grievances feed on filth," he warned.

"Tell me about Vera Chernikova."

A wry smile suffused Avram's face. He clearly knew a great deal about the chemistry teacher. "So you think she and Viktor . . ."

"I do."

"She has an engine."

"How so?"

Brodsky explained that Vera had prospered under the Soviets. A good student from a poor family, she was given a college scholarship and showed great promise as a chemist. She came to teaching late, after working in a lab trying to increase plant growth. She knew that the genes regulating growth were found in the cell walls of plants, but she could never gain enough knowledge to manipulate them. She had hoped to win a state prize, like the Order of Lenin or the Red Banner of Labor, but the only prize she won was a teaching position at the Michael School.

"As you know," Brodsky mused, "she's an attractive woman, albeit a skinny one with an unduly small head perched on a thin stem of neck. Men are drawn to her. Glinski liked her. So did one or two others."

"It appears that Viktor fancies her."

"She's no fool, and once she gets the bit in her mouth, she never lets go. I warn you, she's relentless."

"Relentless is one thing, ruthless another. Which is it?"

"Definitely the first and occasionally the second."

"If she wanted the directorship . . ."

"I'd watch my back. I suspect she was one of the teachers who denounced me, and when she was passed over for the directorship, I know for a fact she was outraged. Before you arrived, she was sharpening her knife."

That evening, after school hours, Sasha pulled Vera's files. They confirmed Brodsky's word. She came from a background of want. Her father had worked in the shipyards at Archangel until an industrial accident left him lame. Her mother took in sewing. Two brothers never returned from the Great War, and a sister died of diphtheria. On graduating from a technical college, Vera had been assigned to an agro-factory, dedicated to increasing food output through fertilizers and plant mutation. The cellular walls of plants proved her undoing. She could not crack the genetic code, though she tried every conceivable means to tease it out. Had she not made exaggerated claims, she might have remained at the factory lab, but when her work could not be duplicated, she was pointed toward the Michael School. In her estimation, teaching was a demotion, and she, like the last leaf of fall, hung on, using the school lab to continue her research, until she finally admitted defeat. To sweeten the bitter pill of secondary teaching, she apparently hoped to rise to the role of director.

"I know you say she's relentless," Sasha said at his next encounter with Avram, "but she's not young anymore."

"With an admirer as a goad, she's twenty again."

The two men were drinking apple-flavored vodka. "I know what you're going to say next," Sasha replied with a wave of his hand. "I should denounce her."

"You can be sure that if she hasn't already, she'll denounce you by Easter or May Day. It's a Russian tradition to enliven those holidays."

Brodsky's grim irony was not lost on Sasha.

"I'd prefer a colorful Easter egg or *kulich* or *pashka*."

"For May Day," Avram added, "the locals will put together a ragtag march waving red banners and photographs of Stalin. They'll congregate in the town square and sing patriotic songs. It's not Red Square, with the Boss and his cronies standing atop the Lenin Mausoleum, but it's the best that Balyk can do."

Fearing the worst, Sasha asked whether Vera might be working for the secret police.

Avram's sardonic reply was unhelpful. "Why not? All of Russia reports to the police."

"So you think it's a possibility?"

"How would I know? In this country nothing is what it seems. There are always other levels and layers of meaning. It would take a Nostradamus to negotiate the labyrinth. But that's just the point. None of us have the powers of prophecy, except of course the Boss. So any law, any edict, any ukase, any line in the Soviet Constitution can mean a different thing depending on the need for a certain interpretation."

"Then words and facts are meaningless."

"*Precisely* meaningless: the great oxymoron."

14

A week before Easter, three soldiers drove into town and billeted themselves at the Balyk Inn. They had been sent to make sure that no religious observances took place on Easter. Presumably, Balyk had been singled out because of the presence of Father Zossima. Wherever an ex-priest was resident, particularly a popular one, the police or army could be found on religious holidays. The government had dedicated itself to stamping out all vestiges of religion. None other than Father Zossima had told Sasha that he understood why and that the reason wasn't merely theoretical. Sasha and the priest had recently strolled through the woods near Father Zossima's quarters. For his tutoring, Father Zossima received a monthly payment. Sasha always made it a point to settle their accounts in cash and away from prying eyes. On this day, with Easter approaching, the priest grew reflective, observing that the state of the church before the 1917 revolution was ignorant and cruel. He candidly admitted that the priesthood had exploited the peasants gullibility by feeding their superstitions, advertising absurd miracles, and trading in relics—the toe of a saint, a hair from the head of St. Peter, a splinter from the true cross.

"They shamefully," said Father Zossima, "extorted money and food from the poor and kept them uneducated, uncritically served the Tsar, and fomented awful pogroms. I won't even speak of their sexual depravities, which are too numerous to count. Their churches dripped gold, and their priestly vestments shone with jewels. In truth, they were self-serving devils who would have gone down in history as the most unsavory scoundrels in Russia had the Communist apparatchiks not eclipsed them with their cold-blooded betrayals and mindless genuflecting before Stalin."

But even these sentiments could not have saved Father Zossima if he had been caught celebrating Mass. Although former believers were only too willing to volunteer their cellars for services, Father Zossima held his Masses in a cave, a choice that had led believers to include him among the many catacomb priests illegally conducting church services in forest retreats.

Normally, Sasha took his lunch at school with the students, but when the secretary, Devora Berberova, told him that Galina had come down with a migraine and left school in the company of Viktor Harkov, he returned home to check on her health. He deliberately entered the farmhouse through the back door, the pantry door, the less conspicuous entrance. He heard voices coming from Galina's bedroom, hers and Viktor's. His chest tightened, gripped with jealousy. Was Galina's headache a ruse, and had the two of them resumed their affair? If so, the recent closeness between Sasha and Galina was a sham. But why would she feign affection; to achieve what? Once again he found himself in the uncomfortable position of suspecting Galina and searching for clues. He hated such conduct. Inching toward the bedroom door, he stood close enough to listen and far enough to leave unobserved. Galina was talking.

"Don't deny it!"

"Why should I?"

"If not for me, you wouldn't be teaching at the school."

"I admit it: You positioned me brilliantly."

"For betrayal."

"You're being melodramatic. Just look at the facts."

"I have, and what I see is ingratitude and deception."

"She . . ."

"Is unworthy."

"Compared to you . . ."

"Stop! I won't hear of it."

"Will you tell Sasha?"

"Not if you promise to end it."

A minute of quiet ensued, rent only by Galina's deep breathing. "I promise." Pause. "Have you heard from Petr since he left?"

"No."

"Strange."

Sasha heard Viktor's click, his signature sound upon leaving, and took the clue. He eased out the back door and waited for several minutes behind the house to make sure that Viktor was well on his way back to school; he then came through the front door, making no attempt to hide his presence. Galina was leaning back in bed, her head resting on several pillows. On the nightstand rested a bottle of medicine. Her eyes were closed. She knew by the footsteps it was Sasha. He gently knocked. She smiled and invited him to come sit beside her. He asked how she felt. She ignored his question and inquired if he had passed Viktor on the path.

"I came from another direction," Sasha replied. "What did he want?"

"He took me home when I developed a migraine. We chatted briefly and he left."

Before Sasha could gently ease into the question haunting him—had she any romantic interest in Viktor?—he heard knocking at the door. Two soldiers, clean shaven and moderately literate, politely asked if he knew of any religious services planned for Easter, either at the Michael School or in town.

"Certainly not on the part of the school," replied Sasha.

"And your friend, Father Zossima?" prodded one of the soldiers, obviously schooled by Filatov.

Sasha's first impulse was to say that he and the priest hadn't talked in months, but if someone had seen them entering the woods, he would be a suspect himself. "I speak to him occasionally, but I know of no planned religious activities. Besides, it's against the law."

The soldiers laughed sarcastically and departed.

Easter came and went. No church bells rang, and none of the faithful indicated that they had secretly celebrated Easter Mass in a cave. Within days, the school and village began making plans for May Day. Balyk had no official mayor, but the townspeople had decided among themselves to hold a parade, honoring not only the working class and its labors, but also Lenin and Stalin and those who took part in the Great War, the October Revolution, and the civil war. Although most of the students at the Michael School took a keen interest in the marching events, to be overseen by Viktor, Sasha had limited his role to arranging a dinner for the evening festivities. Filatov was footing the bill and composing the guest list. He had been less than candid about his motives, telling Sasha that he preferred enjoying the day in the beautiful countryside of Balyk and dining with friends to standing in a Moscow crowd cheering the Vozhd and others on the reviewing stand over Lenin's tomb. He was, in fact, deeply troubled.

According to reports from his mole, the school seethed with intrigue. His agent had described a situation in which the teachers were compiling a dossier on Sasha in the hope of replacing him. One of the new teachers was leading the band of brigands, Ivan Goncharov, who had materialized in Balyk, it seemed, out of nowhere. A college graduate, he taught linguistics and was especially keen about click languages. Reclusive, bearded, long-haired, he claimed to have blood ties with the famous novelist, although Filatov's agent doubted it. His loyalties were unclear. At first, he bestowed his attentions on Galina Selivanova, then befriended one Goran Youzhny, and then fell in with the internal exile Bogdan Dolin, who gave all indications of having resumed forging passports for those who wished to flee the country, though Filatov need not worry that Father Zossima was among them. He was not.

Although he had taken a university degree in engineering, Filatov did not regard himself as an intellectual. He was suspicious of people who lived in what he called the world of airy thinness. A life of the mind was not subject to scrutiny. How could you ever know for sure what one was thinking? Teachers and professors and priests were all of a kind. They argued over nothing; the stakes, inconsequential, unless they were plotting counterrevolution. Then their thoughts became dangerous. The good thing about intellectuals, Filatov had decided a long time ago, was that they treated action as beneath them. They would generate the ideas, but implementation was the province of others. Intellectuals didn't dirty their hands. If this fellow Ivan Goncharov, undoubtedly a pseudonym, was indeed behind the plot to replace Sasha, then he must also be responsible for all the letters of denunciation Filatov had been receiving.

"What exactly," Sasha asked Brodsky, "do you think is the point of the dinner? I know the NKVD values surprise. If you're unprepared, you can't escape or resist. I know how it works."

Brodsky, as was his wont, gilded the lily. "A knock in the middle of the night. A car pulls up alongside as you are returning from work. A public denunciation at the very moment you are surrounded by your so-called comrades. That's their modus operandi."

Not surprisingly, the Michael School preparations were subject to Major Filatov's wishes. With fascism in Italy and Germany becoming increasingly militant, the Politburo had directed that all May Day celebrations take for their theme the anti-proletarian nature of these regimes. Accordingly, Filatov had ordered that the school emblazon their banners with the following international slogans.

- For irresistible unity of the working class.
- Down with fascist aggression and war makers.
- For bread and freedom for all.
- Down with German fascism—the leading warmonger of Europe.
- Out of Ethiopia with the Italian invaders. Long live the Italian people from the yoke of fascism.
- Down with fascism. Down with capitalism.

- Long live Soviet power in all the world, under the flag of Marx-Engels-Lenin, forward to the victory of the Socialist World Revolution.
- Expose reactionaries and fascist sympathizers who are sowing enmity among the working classes.
- Let us be vigilant in protecting the peace that has been won.
- Prevent reactionaries from provoking war with the Soviet Union.
- Workers of the world unite.

To honor the patriotic spirit of the Michael School, the Soviet flag with the hammer and sickle hung from every window. Goran and Viktor's excitement was palpable. As the self-appointed group in charge of banners and bunting, slogans and signs, and placards and posters, they had festooned the school grounds and would march at the head of the parade. The Soviet oblast for Balyk had sent pictures of the Great Leader, looking avuncular, yet strong. Of course, Stalin's image showed none of his imperfections, like pock-marked skin and bad teeth. Viktor's portraits of the teachers of the Michael School would be displayed by appreciative students. And Goran had mounted his photographs of the school buildings and environs. Sasha wondered what Bogdan, as a member of the Three Musketeers, would contribute.

Viktor's exertions noticeably advanced the school's preparations, which were beginning to take on a professional look. He seemed to be everywhere, and his clicking noise echoed through the halls. By this time, his alias (Goncharov) had been superseded by Comrade Click. Whether to gain a reputation for faithful Party work or for some other reason, Viktor became maniacal about every detail of the celebration. Even Goran sighed at his friend's fanaticism. Sasha believed that Viktor and his two companions had an ulterior motive, as yet unknown. It was Brodsky's idea to have Filatov ask the Ryazan NKVD if they had a file on Viktor Harkov. But, although Sasha had read Vera's file, he had always found the relationship of family history to current behavior questionable. The country was rife with spies, and he had no intention of adding his name to the number of people writing letters that famously began: "Dear Comrade, I have reason to believe that X has something to hide and suggest you look into this person's past."

"You asked my opinion," Brodsky shrugged.

"In the end, your advice might produce some useful information, but I don't trust the means."

"One man's means are another man's ends."

"I don't follow."

"Beginnings and endings are impossible to discern. Consider. I assassinate a political leader for the purpose of bringing my own man to power. The killing provides the means to change the prevailing order, my ends. The new leader then turns around and orders me killed for murder. Execution provides him the means to remove all witnesses or opponents, his ends. And so it goes, here and elsewhere. Where does the circle begin and end?"

Sasha had the distinct impression that more was being implied than said. Brodsky continued.

"You say you have seen Viktor at the farmhouse and have heard about his presence from others, like Alya. From this information you have decided he is up to no good, and though you are vague about the nature of your fears, I gather you think he and Galina are making the beast with two backs. Right?"

Sasha lowered his head and stared at his feet. The two men were, as always, seated in front of the fireplace in Brodsky's cottage. But on this occasion, Brodsky was not enveloped by smoke or alcoholic fumes. He was wrapped in a blanket and treating a bad cold with cups of hot tea. An occasional sneeze and cough punctuated Brodsky's musings. From the kitchen stove came a terrible odor, a home remedy that some herbalist had recommended.

"You're not really going to drink that awful stuff?"

"Marina Cheslava swears by it."

"It smells like excrement."

"That's because you have dung on the mind. You think someone has fouled your nest."

"And what if the report from Ryazan were to come back negative?"

"It won't. No one, as the secret police say, is innocent."

"But what if the evidence is false?"

"The secret police and the church think the same way. If a person isn't guilty of one thing, then he's guilty of another. Does it matter for which murder a killer is hanged or for which sin we're condemned?"

"Justice would demand . . ."

Brodsky interrupted. "The only thing justice can determine is length and quality of life. In the end it's all the same."

On those depressing words, Sasha left the odorous cottage and tramped back to his office. He wanted to think. In the clean, clear air, an idea came to him; it danced like a dervish, arresting his attention and becoming the focus of his imagination because of its seductive simplicity. Best of all, it dispelled his moral ambiguity. "Yes, that's what I'll do," he decided. In the meantime, he would keep practicing his alveolar clicks.

Lest anything go awry during the celebration, all the principals had to appear before a three-man board of Filatov's men. The background check took place in the confines of the abandoned town church, which had been hastily swept but still exhibited cobwebs and clusters of dirt. The filthy windows, particularly those with colored glass, attenuated the light. Hence the examiners were reduced to using candles, which gave the proceedings the look and feel of a medieval inquisition. The soldiers were there to check each person's passport and identification papers. A few local men, all devoted Bolsheviks, stood apart prepared to unmask any impostors. Since false passports and papers were a booming business, thanks to forgers like Bogdan Dolin, the government found it necessary to keep in attendance fact-checkers. Although Sasha had distanced himself from the parade organizers, as the school director he was compelled to appear before the examiners to take part in the chistka. Well aware that Soviet bookkeeping was more often than not erroneous, he approached his questioners with some trepidation.

Two long tables had been placed end to end. An implacable military typist, with a flat Asian face, her black hair pulled back tightly and tied in a bun, sat mutely, her hands curled over the keyboard preparing to spell out a man's fate.

"Parsky, Sasha," said the chief examiner. Clickety-clack went the American Royal typewriter. "Director of the Michael School." Clickety-clack. "Parents, enemies of the people. Missing. Presumed dead or in hiding." The examiner, sporting a bright-red glass eye, paused over the record for a minute or two, a favorite trick of the secret police to instill fear in the person being questioned. He then popped his glass eye out of its socket, wrapped it in a dirty rag that might have once, but no longer, passed for a handkerchief, looked at Sasha with his one eye, and said, "We have no record of a formal denunciation of your parents. Did you not sign such a document?"

"Comrade Filatov said it was unnecessary."

This remark caused some confusion among the three examiners, who immediately huddled and whispered excitedly. When they emerged from their scrum, the second man, bespectacled and bemedaled, opined that although Major Filatov had cleared Sasha for his current position, the record showed various complaints and denunciations since Sasha had assumed the directorship. What did Comrade Parsky have to say for himself?

Knowing that Filatov's endorsement made him immune to arrest, Sasha let the charade continue. A person exhibiting a chest full of medals, Sasha reasoned, needed an opportunity to preen, especially since the man had a medal for bravery during the civil war in the Crimea.

Comrade glass eye prodded, "Speak up!"

"Those of us in positions of authority are always fair game, comrade. I didn't catch your name."

"Captain Himalayski," said glass eye.

Suppressing amusement at the presumptuous name, Sasha remarked that he had answered the charges against him to the satisfaction of Major Filatov. He watched Himalayski tap his pencil on a pad and knew what to expect next, the murders.

"According to the file, a tragedy occurred at your parents' farm. Two murders."

"I was questioned and found innocent of any wrongdoing. But I, like you, carry that record with me and hope someday to expunge it by finding the felons."

Himalayski, surprised by the absence of a puling response, sputtered something to the effect that he indeed hoped that the malefactors would be found, mumbled to his adjutants, directed the typist to take down what Sasha had just said, and called the next person for questioning. As Sasha left the dilapidated church, he could hear the clickety-clack of the Royal immortalizing his words for storage in some ominous archive.

With a number of gawkers, Sasha stood on the church porch and watched through the open door as others suffered the chistka. In particular, his attention was drawn first to Vera Chernikova and, a few minutes later, to Viktor Harkov. After a few preliminary questions, the chief examiner asked Vera what role she would play in the coming celebrations.

"I have been asked to sing the 'Marseillaise.'" She coughed self-consciously and added, "I've been told I have a good voice."

"Your passport lists your age as thirty-two." Himalayski tilted his head birdlike and with one eye studied her skeptically. Sasha knew that Vera was at least ten years older, but if Viktor was courting her, she had every reason to alter her passport. Bogdan had probably done her a good turn. What he had done for Viktor remained to be seen.

"Given all the deaths in my family, I have not had an easy life."

"Yes, yes, of course," said Himalayski, clearly embarrassed. "I just wish I could be present to hear you sing."

She thanked the chief examiner, took a few steps backward, seemed to bow, and left.

When Viktor Harkov was called, Sasha pressed forward to hear every word. While Sasha wished to see Viktor exposed, his supporters murmured prayers for Ivan Goncharov's deliverance.

"Passport, please."

Pause.

"Ivan Goncharov! Are you related to . . ."

"I am. He's a distant cousin."

"Really?"

"A poor one. Another side of the family made off with the inheritance. But then you know how kulaks behave."

"All of them . . . enemies of the people. Wreckers."

"I trust my papers are in order. And also my passport."

"Yes, quite. Absolutely. No further questions, unless you'd like (a nervous cough) to exchange a few words about *Oblomov*. It's a favorite novel of mine."

"My friends used to call me Stolz, Oblomov's German friend."

"For good reason, for good reason. A relative of the great Goncharov. What do they call you now?"

"Comrade Click."

"And why is that?"

Viktor made several loud clicks, one after the other, sounding like a machine gun. "That's why."

Himalayski tried to imitate the clicks, but sounded like a plodding horse. "Not so easy," he said. "I'll have to practice."

"I learned how to do it in Africa."

"Yes, yes, I see from your passport that you studied . . . where was that . . . he turned a few pages, ah, yes, in the Kalahari among the Bushmen. Very impressive."

So the trip that Viktor had wanted to make for graduate studies had become a reality with Bogdan's help. As he made his way back to the school, Sasha wondered how many others had resorted to forgeries to alter their lives? In a country where history determined one's fate, the Soviets had become expert at changing the past. A new name gave a person a new reality that could include a different history. In effect, a new passport enabled one to be born again.

Two days before the start of the parade, with patches of snow still lurking in shaded areas and the lilacs not yet in bloom, a military cargo truck rolled into Balyk. From under the tarp in the rear emerged several soldiers who immediately swept the square, drilled pole holes in the ground, installed red flags that languidly moved in the breeze, whitewashed the buildings facing the square, and covered the entire front of the church with a two-story-high canvas portrait of Stalin. They then set to work improvising a grandstand with a raised speaker's platform, the spot from which Major Filatov would address the crowd. The locals gathered to watch, commenting on the fact that although they were often told that wood and nails were in short supply, when the government wanted a structure built, materials miraculously appeared.

The soldiers had brought tents and spent the first night billeted outdoors. But by the second day, the hospitable people of Balyk insisted the soldiers lodge with them. In short order, the uniformed men had made common cause with Goran and Viktor to organize the most splendid May Day celebration conditions allowed. Sasha could hear the hammering and smell the paint. Excitement infected the school, which became a whirligig of movement, as students repeatedly practiced marching from the school to the square and back. The citizens of Balyk had never before paid particular attention to May Day, though appreciative of a holiday that gave them a day off from work. But with the feverish activities around them, they began to fall in with the rhythm and communal spirit of the endeavor. From attics and old trunks surfaced old Tsarist military uniforms and fancy dress clothes, which the locals would proudly display during the festivities: the march, the speech, and the fireworks planned for later that night.

Alya and her good friend Benjie were beside themselves with joy. It was rumored that none other than Major Filatov might ask Benjie to sing, but as we all know, rumor is nothing more than many mouths playing on a pipe. Nonetheless, he prepared a song just in case, "Dark Eyes." Alya would have liked to accompany him on her recorder, a Christmas gift from Sasha, but she was still struggling with the fingering and stops. Galina tried to downplay the importance of the day, lest her daughter be disappointed, but Alya, like most children, was intoxicated by the colors, the movement, the high spirits, and the anticipation of the students and locals. Here was a special event. There would be music, peasant dancing, finery, a parade, celebratory shouts, salute by gunfire, a speech, and thirty minutes of fireworks. Best of all, Alya had been selected as one of the drummer girls, and Benjie as a flag waver. After the festivities, the two of them would be left to their own wiles, because Galina and Sasha would be attending Filatov's dinner, and Benjie's mom, for some unknown reason, was also a guest.

An overnight rain had left the leaves sparkling and the earth redolent of spring. The Michael School students lined up early with their red armbands and scarves, and their white shirts newly washed and starched. Although a chill hung in the air, the students would march without jackets or coats, impervious to the weather in the service of socialism. Viktor and Goran would randomly distribute the placards and banners and signs just minutes before the start of the march, when the school orchestra struck the first notes of "The Internationale," which Galina had been asked to conduct.

From the sidelines, Sasha watched Viktor and Goran hurry to the shed that held the poles and banners and such. When the first notes of the anthem sounded, they scooped up the results of their weeks of labor and carried them to the assembled body of students, who snapped to attention when handed a pole with an attached sign or poster. Few of the students even knew the people featured on the pictorial placards. The anthem was followed by the thump-thump and rat-a-tat-tat of several drums; then the students began to make their way from the school grounds to the road and then to the village square, where the early arriving Filatov and his two faithful agents, Larissa and Basil, stood on the reviewing stand, with Boris positioned slightly in front of his aides. Sasha and the teachers walked behind; hence they could not understand the reason for the disturbance and agitated finger-pointing on the reviewing stand as the two marching groups—the students and townspeople—merged in the square. It did not bode well for Sasha that the reviewers were pointing not at the Balyk citizens but at the students. As Sasha scurried toward the reviewing stand, he glanced fleetingly at a few of the placards. One said, "Fascism Means War," another "Peace and Brotherly Unity Among the Workers of All Nations," another "Victory Over Capitalism," another "Rescue People from Hunger and Want"; one photograph, titled "Enemies of the People," exhibited three adoring men flanking Leon Trotsky: Genrikh Yagoda, Karl Radek, and Avram Brodsky. Below each man was his signature. Given Stalin's hostility toward Trotsky and Yagoda, and Radek's recent arrest, Brodsky could not have been pictured in worse company. The question that flashed through Sasha's mind was whether the photograph had been doctored and the signatures forged. If so, he knew whom to accuse.

The dismay of the reviewers was not shared by the hundreds of people, few of whom had any idea about the internal struggles of the Politburo and the jockeying for power. On seeing Sasha, Filatov ordered him to his side.

"Is this some kind of ill-mannered joke?" he barked. "That Trotsky, Yagoda, and Radek should appear in our sacred May Day parade is an offense to all good Bolsheviks. And Brodsky: Why is he being celebrated? For writing a scurrilous play? I certainly hope not."

"I think your first supposition is correct. It's a bad joke."

"Perpetrated by whom?"

"My guess is Bogdan Dolin and two of his friends."

Filatov fell silent. After scanning the crowd, he replied, "Make sure all three of them are at dinner tonight. Do you understand? It will be their last supper."

15

The table was set for thirteen places. Sasha offered to seat Filatov at the head, but the major refused, choosing to sit between his two aides across from Brodsky, Galina, and Viktor. Also present were the school secretary (Devora Berberova), Vera Chernikova, Bogdan Dolin, Natalia Korsakova, Ekaterina Rzhevska, Goran Youzhny, and an NKVD agent from Moscow (Polkovnikov). What in the world, thought Sasha, can such an incongruous group have in common? Undoubtedly, Filatov had interrogated groups of people before, but in such a narrow room, a furnished teacher's lounge on the upper floor? If your aim is subterfuge, he'd heard it said, then act calmly. Filatov certainly fit the bill.

The menu included fish and lamb and wine, with fresh-baked loaves. A special cook had been employed to prepare the dishes. Student monitors served the food. Filatov sat regretting his May Day speech, which he knew missed the mark. He should have ignored it and spoken of Party loyalty and the dangers of dissent. Instead he had talked about the current crisis in Europe and Asia. How many of his listeners even knew of civil wars in those places? Most of Balyk's citizens couldn't read. And the speech had been diffuse and pretentious. He wished to call back those stilted, repetitive words.

We call for a common front of the workers of the world to oppose fascist aggression. We deplore the failure of Great Britain,
France, and the United States to stop international fascist brigandage in Spain and China and Austria. The English, French,
and Americans cynically lie when they say they cannot check
such aggression. All they need do is accept the proposal of the
Soviet Union for joint action against the warmongers by all
states that are interested in the preservation of peace. The Western countries must reinforce action by measures of economic
pressure. Let the fascist bandits be deprived of credit; refuse
them the raw materials that are necessary for conducting war;
close the channels of trade to them.

Cease blockading republican Spain. Open the borders and let
the Spanish people buy armaments freely. Such action would be
enough to make fascism retreat like a whipped dog. We must
arm the republicans. The proletarians of France—renowned
descendants of the Paris Communards—must demand immediate removal of the blockade from republican Spain. Workers of
England must force their ruling classes to end their policy of supporting fascism and of hostility to the land of socialism. Proletarians of the United States must demand a policy that outlaws the
fascist violators of universal peace, a policy worthy of the tradition
of Lincoln and Washington. Demand immediate removal of the
embargo on the export of arms to Spain.

And so we celebrate this May Day filled with proud consciousness that the magnitude and sublimity of the goals we fight for
inspire us, and with the feeling of profoundest solidarity and
union with the proletarians of all lands and peoples.

A conflicted Filatov shook his head. What the government
called "unity," he called "lockstep conformity." Every village in the
Soviet Union had been issued the same speech to be read from the
reviewing stand. He was merely a mouthpiece for some apparatchik
in Moscow who had been told what to write. Couldn't they have
asked a poet to craft the speech? Probably not. Most of the writers—poets, novelists, and playwrights—had been imprisoned or
exiled. Pasternak was still free. Why hadn't he been asked to write
the speech; or was he, too, on his way out? What a country, thought

Filatov, such a beautiful country. It was all so sad. And considering the business ahead made him sick.

"A toast," said Filatov, reclining at the table and holding up his wine glass, "to Mother Russia, to socialism, and to Stalin."

"Hear! Hear!" the diners cried and clinked their glasses.

As if to steel himself for what was coming next, Filatov swallowed his wine in one gulp, and then twice more filled his glass from the decanter, each time draining it with a toss of his head. He unfolded his linen napkin, blotted his lips, paused, and folded it. The others watched. Had Filatov spread it on his lap or chest, the guests would have followed suit. But since he seemed to have more to say, they sat motionless in their chairs anticipating the major's explanation for why they had been summoned to this Faustian feast. Filatov knew that everyone among them had sold his soul, in fact, many times over, and that there is no witness so dreadful, no accuser so terrible, as conscience.

The decisive time had come, the minatory moment when he'd have to accuse wrongdoers and make arrests. He detested these occasions.

Allow me to say, at the outset, I joined the police not to apprehend people, but to maintain order in these troubled times. Given all the different languages spoken in our vast land, and the many religions, and the myriad views, the Vozhd found it necessary to go back on Lenin's promise that every nationality would be allowed to observe its own culture. As the Great Leader pointed out, that way lies madness. Similarly, we cannot allow different views of socialism: those of the Social Democrats, of the Mensheviks, of the Constitutionalists, of the Left Opposition, of the Right Opposition. A farrago of political theories is not a country. A mélange is not a government. The Soviet Union rests on a body of incontestable principles, and those who would seek to undermine those principles sow discord and confusion. They are enemies of the people. To keep our glorious revolution from being undone by self-serving factions and oppositionists, we must remain eternally vigilant.

It was to that purpose I joined the police and dedicated myself. As you all know, police forces throughout the world depend on informants to keep anarchy at bay. Better, of course, to prevent a crime than to punish it. That's where you, my dear guests, enter the picture. All of you labor in the service of one opinion or another. Harmless opinions the government ignores, reckless ones we try to neutralize. How? By acting before our enemies act. To accomplish this task, we must obtain information that enables us to know what our enemies think and where they intend to strike. Some of you here tonight have earned the gratitude and rewards of working with the Soviet state. Woe to you who persist in the error of your ways. If Stalin is right about how to proceed—and I think he is—then why do some resist? Is it because of culture, religion, foreign money, obstinacy to truth? In our experience, those who oppose us are either mad, in which case we put them in mental institutions, or brigands bent on feathering their own nests. It is they who must be rooted out and . . . dealt with by the courts. Do I make myself clear?

The twelve guests sat transfixed; they dared not even move their eyes to gauge what others might be thinking. The student monitors had left the serving door ajar and looked like peeping gargoyles, each one peering over the shoulder of another. No one even turned his head to see the heavy rain spattering the windows. No one even moved a fork or a muscle or an eyelid. Some mouths remained shut, others agape. All breathing seemed to have stopped. Filatov inhaled deeply remembering the excitement he felt when walking in the rain through the forest adjoining his village. He could see the white birch and alder and cedar and pines, and hear the squishy sounds of leaves underfoot. When he ran barefoot through the forest, the leaves felt like moist cushions and stuck to his feet. He loved spring rains, the water rolling off his beaked Lenin's cap, the earth's attar, the perfumed pine scents, the drops, which in the splintered light resembled crystal earrings, dripping into the undergrowth of ferns and ivy from the overhead canopy of cedars, whose roots turned the local rivers brown.

"You're not eating," said Filatov, breaking the spell. "Eat the bread and lamb. The fish is river trout. Feed your bodies. Drink the wine. It is a good wine, aged, the color of blood."

One of the student waiters took the decanter and tried to refill Filatov's glass. "Allow me, Comrade Major."

Putting his hand over the top of the glass, Filatov said, "I will not drink again of this fruit of the vine until the wreckers and enemies of the people identify themselves. It would be better for you not to have been born than to take refuge in silence." No one moved and no one spoke. Filatov ominously continued, "The hands of the traitors rest on this very table. I repeat: Woe to you."

With downcast eyes, the guests began to ask themselves who among them might fit the major's accusations of violating the covenant, namely, of betraying Soviet rule?

"I tell you," repeated Filatov, "that betrayers sit among us."

Larissa touched Filatov's arm and said, "Surely not I?" Basil did the same.

Then, taking their cue from Larissa, everyone else at the table repeated, "Surely not I."

Filatov responded to the chorus of voices with a knowing smile. As if staged, he assured his two aides of their innocence. To which of the guests, then, was the major referring? The sound of silverware ceased. The eating came to a halt. Quiet reigned.

"You put me in the unenviable position of having to name names. I would rather not bear this cross, but if I must . . ."

Devora Berberova spoke so faintly, one had to strain to hear. Some heard her say, "I have loyally reported"; others heard, "comported" or "deported" or "resorted."

Not until Filatov responded was her meaning clear. "You have served your country well. We have appreciated all your reports and learned a great deal from them."

Sasha immediately began to catalogue mentally all the sources of information that the secretary could have accessed. The files, of course. Rumor, yes. The bulletin board, no doubt. But what else? She hardly left her office and rarely spoke, even to Sasha.

"I shall pass over not only my two aides," said Filatov, "but also Citizen Berberova and Comrade Polkovnikov from Moscow."

Sasha said, "That leaves eight of us."

"I commend your arithmetic," Filatov replied, sarcastically adding, "Comrade Director Parsky."

"Surely not I," repeated Vera Chernikova. "My students have never complained."

Removing a paper from his vest pocket, Filatov conspicuously unfolded it and turned to her. "Have you not been conspiring to replace the director?" asked Filatov.

Here was a subject to which Devora Berberova might have been privy, thought Sasha. The information had to have come from her, in which case, she would also know Vera's fellow conspirator, Viktor Harkov (aka Ivan Goncharov). Sasha watched Filatov's eyes move from Vera to Viktor; but before the major could speak, though he'd rested an arm on the table and raised a forefinger, a habit and harbinger of forthcoming remarks, Viktor said urgently:

"Surely not I!"

"Viktor Harkov, you have much to regret and . . ."

"My name is Goncharov, Ivan Goncharov," he said, reaching into his shirt pocket and removing his passport. "Here, see for yourself."

"A forgery," said Filatov. "I needn't look."

"Government issue," declared Viktor.

"No," Filatov corrected, "Comrade Dolin issue."

Viktor sat speechless, looking first at Filatov and then at Bogdan. His mouth opened and closed like a fish pulled from the sea. He obviously wanted to speak, but instead lowered his head to his chest and nervously fingered his shirt buttons.

That Filatov knew about the forged passport could mean only one thing: Goran had told him. Or was it Bogdan? The Three Musketeers indeed! Apparently, when the secret police came calling, the honor among thieves disappeared. But after further thought, Sasha wondered if he hadn't unduly restricted his list. Every person in Balyk knew about Bogdan the forger, though they didn't know precisely what he was forging. Galina knew about the passport, and Devora Berberova might have overheard Sasha call Viktor by his given name. Depending on how intimate Viktor had become with Vera, he might have told her. Then, too, Brodsky knew about Bogdan's printing press, and what Brodsky knew Natalia Korsakova was

232   LEVITT

likely to know. Ekaterina Rzhevska, Alya's tutor, may have heard gossip from any one of the children. Even Polkovnikov, the Moscow agent, might have exposed Viktor, given that the NKVD had files and photographs for everyone. The more he thought about who might have informed, the more Sasha decided the possibilities were virtually endless, particularly in a police state.

"Your real name is Viktor Harkov," said Filatov calmly. "So let us not fence with one another. We haven't all night to drain the cesspool. The truth saves time."

To Sasha's amazement, the major dropped Viktor and moved on to someone else, Avram Brodsky. With Brodsky's complicated history, divided loyalties, and different patrons, he was a cauldron of conspiracy. Almost anything that Filatov touched upon would be true. But he wasn't prepared for Brodsky's answer to his question, "Which side are you on?"

"All sides. It's the only way to keep current and to support myself. Which side do I favor? None of them. They are all equally bureaucratic and nepotistic."

Filatov shot a glance at Polkovnikov, not knowing how much the Moscow agent knew. For just a second, the major's calm exterior seemed to crack, but a moment later, he looked as unruffled as ever, asking Brodsky how he could prove his loyalty to the Soviet state.

"Secret intelligence comes in two forms. One is real information; the second is disinformation. I traffic in both, the first for the preservation of our glorious state, and the other for those who would betray us."

At that instant, Sasha realized the difficulty of unmasking a double or triple agent. Unless Filatov had access to the information that Brodsky had transmitted to the Left Opposition, he had no way to disprove Avram's loyalty. No wonder Filatov's next question was directed to Natalia Korsakova, Brodsky's former or maybe even current lover. The Soviets must have known that she was Brodsky's courier to the Left Opposition. But did the Soviets know whether the information she took from him was important or not? If they didn't, she was in the clear; but if they had intercepted any of the transmissions and found them to be traitorous, then the game was up.

Brodsky's flippancy evaporated. He looked genuinely worried. Could Natalia be trusted? She certainly had reason to turn on Avram. He had impregnated her and then married her off to an imbecile.

"Citizen Korsakova, you recently traveled by train to Ryazan. Comrade Polkovnikov arrested the man whom you met on the platform. In that man's possession was falsified information bearing on the relations between the Soviet Union and Germany. The documents could have come from only one person, Avram Brodsky, because it was I who left them with him the last time we met. I specifically warned him they were top secret. We wanted to test him—and you."

The gasps in the room were palpable.

Without looking at Brodsky, Natalia said coolly, "Yes, the documents came from Avram. But he didn't give them to me. I stole them from him."

All eyes were now on Filatov, who patiently replied, "Then Avram must have told you he possessed them."

"Not at all," she said, equally unperturbed. "He was out, I entered the cottage, saw a folder with a government seal, read the contents, and put the papers in my purse. It was that easy. The rest you know."

Brodsky stared at her so intensely that the veiny blue worms in his neck and temples threatened to burst their bonds. Sasha couldn't decide whether Avram was surprised or alarmed. Had Natalia told the truth? Perhaps, as before, she was merely protecting him. Only Brodsky could say. If he didn't speak up, Natalia would undoubtedly be exiled to some work camp. But he said nothing, and the longer he did, the greater the tension in the room. Exploiting the dramatic effect, Filatov finally spoke:

"Come now, Natalia, we all know you're protecting Avram."

"I have every reason not to," she answered.

"And the same reasons could be educed for aiding him."

Filatov gave no indication of how he had learned about Brodsky and Natalia and Benjie. But then the secret police, except for rare occasions, never publicized the source of their information. Perhaps the cottage was bugged. Filatov had also said that Natalia was followed, perhaps not for the first time. Anything was possible in a world where even one's private life appeared in the archives.

"You do realize, Natalia Korsakova, what you are condemning yourself to?"

Courageously she answered, "I'll be joining Russia's finest."

The rain had increased, and the lights occasionally flickered. The electrical generator needed replacing, which provided the occasion for Sasha to say, "We could use a new power source."

Seeing the possible irony here, Filatov remarked, "I trust you are referring to the generator and not the Vozhd."

A trickle of laughter briefly lightened the mood, which Filatov and the others took as a signal to continue eating. At one point, the lights went out, and Sasha wished that in the dark the guests would escape.

"Citizen Rzhevska," said Filatov, "you have been tutoring Galina Selivanova's daughter, correct?"

"Yes, Major."

"We all know that children often unwittingly reveal truths that adults would never utter."

"Quite so."

"Have you learned anything from Alya that might help us determine whether the director and Galina are harboring a nest of spies?"

From her cardigan, she removed a piece of paper and then put on her spectacles. "First, Alya's adoptive father stayed at the house."

A shocked Filatov leaped to his feet. "Do you know what you are saying?" Then, making no attempt to hide his consternation, he exclaimed, "You must be mistaken. Petr Selivanov is dead."

"Not according to the child. Oh, I do remember her saying at our first tutoring session that her father had died. But then she said he came back. Not so long ago. She was overjoyed."

"And you failed to report this information?"

"I had no way of knowing that *you* assumed he was dead."

Ekaterina Rzhevska continued making her way through the list, mentioning Viktor and Goran's lab and a few other overnight guests, but Filatov was still fixated on the first name, Petr Selivanov. When his head cleared, he turned to Galina and said:

"Can you explain this turn of events?"

Of course the other guests had little or no knowledge of what was being said. They sat looking on as if attending a badly made Russian film. Although they could understand the words, they had no context for them. Shrugging at one another, they stared, hoping for a key to the mystery.

Galina looked pale, but as always she controlled her emotions. "I learned of his survival only recently. He turned up here in Balyk and then left for Ryazan."

"Did the Moscow office know of this, Comrade Polkovnikov?"

"Nothing. The tension in Ryazan between the mayor, Vladimir Lukashenko, and the local secret police has undermined our lines of communication. My deepest apologies."

Filatov pulled his napkin loose from his collar, squeezed it into a ball, tossed it on the table, and started to pace. Had the room been larger he might have ignored the small storage chest in the corner that held some old framed pictures, dating back to the last century. On his opening the lid, one in particular caught his attention: a painting of an eyeball surrounded by a square and a compass. In the allegorical background was King Solomon's temple. He knew that the painting symbolized Freemasonry, depicting the wisdom and tools of the medieval stonemason. The Freemasons regarded themselves as speculative masons, building not real structures but philosophical and moral ones: "Brotherly Love, Relief, and Truth" or, in France, "Liberty, Equality, Fraternity." Trotsky had been a Freemason, also Marx and Lenin.

He studied the picture and saw staring back at him the eye of political heresy. In 1922, the Freemasons had been forbidden to practice their mumbo jumbo, which they called a system of morality veiled in allegory and illustrated by symbols. Communism had done away with religion. Why had this picture not been burned in a bonfire of the old superstitions? What other pictures and persons had escaped detection? The eyes of the law must be ever vigilant. His lucubrations led him to wonder who had died, if not Petr Selivanov, and might Petr be the killer? He would personally have to contact the Ryazan NKVD to sift through their information. Suddenly, his long-standing suspicions of Sasha Parsky disappeared. Petr Seliva-nov had to be the killer, and Galina probably knew his whereabouts.

Turning from the window, he stepped forward with his arms folded across his chest. "Galina Selivanova," he commanded, "where is your husband?" Before she could reply, he added, "I will not stand for obfuscation. The truth and only the truth will do."

Galina swiveled in her chair to face the major. She showed no signs of guilt or remorse. "By now, he must be in Kiev."

"What do you mean 'by now'?"

"He left several months ago. One night he showed up at our door. We let him stay in the attic. Since the murders, he has been living as an itinerant farmhand. During this time, he met another woman, one more suited to him, he said. He asked me to divorce him so he could marry her. She comes from Kiev. If I initiated the divorce, he could keep out of sight and not appear in court. He was afraid of being arrested as an army deserter."

Filatov held out his arms with the palms up, as if imploring Galina to explain away the obvious. "Did you give no thought to the possibility that he had committed the murders?"

"Yes, but he explained that a transient farmworker was to blame."

"And how did he know that?"

"He had exchanged places with an army mate and exited the truck on a hill overlooking the Parsky farm. Although he said the rain and truck obstructed his vision, he saw the farmhand bury two bodies. He also saw the couple drive away in his company, with him at the wheel."

"That's what he told you?"

"Almost word for word."

The major walked over to Sasha and put a hand on his shoulder. "Do you have any idea who the transient laborer might be?"

Without weighing his answer, Sasha merely reinforced Filatov's new theory by saying, "My parents rarely employed hired hands."

"Petr Selivanov . . . he's the one. I will call Kiev at once."

But he remained in place, with his hand on Sasha's shoulder. "Tell me, Comrade Parsky," the major said in a voice overflowing with friendliness, as if he had dispelled all his doubts, "did Selivanov speak to you about the murders?"

"He told me what he told Galina. That's all."

"Did he mention the name of the woman he wishes to marry?"

"Just that she lives in Kiev."

He squeezed Sasha's shoulder in an affectionate manner. "Don't worry, Comrade Parsky, we'll find him and once we do, we'll learn where your parents are hiding. If I had seen two grisly murders, as they did, I would also run away. But now it's time for them to come home. Perhaps they can even join you here in Balyk." He snapped his fingers and said, "Now let's properly enjoy the meal."

Over dinner and three bottles of vodka, Filatov recounted the killings. Those guests unaware of the story sat entranced. Sasha hoped that Filatov's newfound buoyancy would shorten the inter-rogation. But after several shots of vodka, he turned to his aides and asked them to continue with "the small matter of disloyalty at the Michael School."

Larissa Pankarova spoke first. Opening her black briefcase she removed a folder, opened it, adjusted her glasses, and fixed her eyes on Goran. "Your uncle in the Politburo, as you may have heard, has fallen out of favor. But then," she said without a trace of irony, "changes occur frequently. As Comrade Brodsky said earlier, nepotism is a problem. And so it is. We, that is, Major Filatov, intends to end it. You will, in the future, find no succor with us. We suggest you find productive work, relinquish your photographic equipment, and avoid Viktor Harkov. Understood?" The color drained from Goran's face. He looked like a child chastised for wetting his pants. "Well?" asked Larissa. He hung his head and murmured yes.

Filatov then added, "You will also turn over all your fabricated photographs to our office and denounce both Citizens Dolin and Harkov for their nefarious attempts to discredit Comrade Brodsky."

Sasha could hardly believe what he heard. Brodsky, for all his scheming, had escaped arrest. But what of Natalia? Would he let her take the blame for his misdeeds? Apparently he would. So that's what the system did. It turned intellectuals into apologists and cowards willing to let others suffer unjustly. He knew what Brodsky would say, "What's the alternative?" And he would have answered, "Truth, exile, and even death." But then it was easy enough for him to take the high moral ground when he had escaped the hot seat. Heroism and valor emerge not from words and fancy phrases but from the crucible of pain. What pain had he experienced?

Basil Makarov spoke next. He had a file on Bogdan Dolin. "Didn't Kolyma teach you anything?" Basil asked. "Are you so anxious to return that you continue your forgeries and fabricated documents? We have left you untouched for all this time because Balyk is a provincial town with little connection to the larger world. But when enemies of the people come to you for passports to escape the country, we cannot turn a blind eye. The odious Leon Trotsky slipped through our grasp, and now look at the price we are paying. Every counterrevolutionary is headed for Mexico. It is intolerable. Do you deny that you forged a passport for Goran Youzhny's uncle, who was stopped at the Finnish border?" Bogdan's sullen look said nothing and everything. "You will be remanded into police custody for trial and probably deported to Siberia. Your home and possessions will be confiscated and your identity papers stamped invalid."

Filatov thanked his assistants and, to Sasha's delight, resumed his questioning of Viktor. But after a few minutes, Sasha rebuked himself for his schadenfreude. He felt as if he'd become part of the Soviet apparat, taking pleasure in seeing others suffer. Viktor may have been personally reprehensible, but to see him interrogated in front of all these people reminded Sasha of what Chekhov had said: Never humiliate a person in public; it leads to lasting hatred. And yet, at this moment, Viktor's eyes radiated unconcern, neither fear nor enmity.

"Then you readily admit," Filatov summed up, using repetitive flourishes, "that you have colluded to replace Sasha Parsky with Vera Chernikova as director of the Michael School, that you have assisted Bogdan Dolin in defaming Avram Brodsky, that you have used Goran Youzhny's contacts to obtain information about the school's teachers, whose portraits you have donated to the archives of the Moscow NKVD—to what end, who knows?—and that you have, in violation of the law, changed your identity papers and forged a new passport. Am I right?"

Without the slightest hesitation, Viktor admitted his sins. Surely, thought Sasha, this man must feel he's untouchable. But what was his invisible shield? The answer came swiftly.

"If you have finished," said the secret agent from Moscow, Polkovnikov, "I would like to have a word in private with you, Comrade Filatov." He then folded his eyeglasses, lifted his briefcase, and followed the major out of the room.

In their absence, nothing was said, but the contagion of suspicion spread from one person to another like a deadly bacillus, smothering any impulse of generosity or charity.

When the two policemen returned, Polkovnikov perceptibly smiled at Viktor. Filatov looked grim. His colleague Larissa, seeing his discomfort, whispered to him, but he dismissed her with a wave of his hand, clearly out of sorts at the prospect of sharing what had just taken place. But with others facing arrest, he felt that he owed the assembly an explanation. He began with an astringent and terse apology to Viktor Harkov for questioning his loyalty and motives.

"Had I known," he said, "that you enjoyed the protection of the Ryazan NKVD, I would have been more circumspect. But I still find your behavior, in the instances I've cited, to be unworthy . . ." He trailed off.

Unworthy of what, he never said, leaving his guests to fill in the blanks: unworthy of an honest man, of a Soviet citizen, of a comrade, of a friend, of a colleague, of an intellectual, of a lover. Filatov took no pains to cloak his intense dislike of Viktor. He sneered at his smarmy behavior and decided that before crucifying the guilty in the room, he would, in his own way, expose Viktor.

Suddenly, Sasha leaped to his feet, coughing and spitting. He bolted from the table, choking on a fish bone. He could be heard in the kitchen, gagging. Filatov directed Larissa Pankarova to look in on him. Then, as if no interruption had occurred, he continued:

"I don't suppose, Comrade Harkov, that you know the whereabouts of Petr Selivanov, whom you have roundly denounced as a traitor? It would be interesting to compare his views with yours. But on one point we're agreed: No traitor should go unpunished."

Galina's expression was one of confusion. It seemed to say: Could I have possibly heard the major correctly? Did Viktor really denounce Petr; did he actually label him a traitor? Surely there's been a mistake. At that moment, she would have protested had not Larissa and a pallid Sasha, full of apologies, returned. For a moment, no one spoke. Rain pelted the windows, a sound that Bogdan mentally likened to the flogging of convicts. Then Polkovnikov stood and asked Viktor to join him in bidding the guests adieu. As he went out the door, Viktor threw Galina a kiss and made a loud clicking noise, his familiar sound. A suspicious Sasha, absent during Filatov's revelation of Viktor's treachery, took Viktor's gestures to mean, "I'll see you later."

Filatov told his two aides to arrest Natalia Korsakova and Bogdan Dolin, and to hold Goran Youzhny and Brodsky for further questioning.

That night, with Alya and Benjie planning to sleep at the home of Ekaterina Rzhevska, where Benjie would sing his May Day song for family and friends, Galina undressed alone, put on her flannel nightgown, and climbed into bed. The storm had shorted the electricity. She lay awake in the dark thinking about the evening's events, tortured by questions. Would Brodsky let the mother of his son be exiled without trying to free her? Would he join her in exile if he could not obtain her release? Would Bogdan Dolin be transferred (most likely in chains) to Magadan, the major transit center for prisoners sent to labor camps, like Kolyma? Would Goran be exiled to a work camp now that his uncle had fallen from favor? Would Filatov or Polkovnikov be promoted for their work? Would Vera Chernikova continue teaching at the Michael School, as if nothing had happened? Would Devora Berberova resume her position in the front office now that everyone knew she reported to the secret police? Would the other teachers wish to remain at the Michael School once they learned about the evening's proceedings? Would Petr escape arrest or would the police track him down in Ukraine? Would anything ever be the same? Would she ever be the same? She feared not. Like most purges, this one did not clean or cleanse. If you add too much bleach to the water, the colors fade. Balyk and the school would be colorless after this chistka. The Soviets, of course, would repeat, as they did ad infinitum, that you can't make an omelet without breaking eggs. But measuring progress by the number of people purged accomplished little and damaged the country. Was there not a shortage of engineers, teachers, scientists, doctors, and poets? Where were they? Purged and locked up!

Filatov's aides, Larissa and Basil, had already left with their suspects tucked away in the back of a Black Maria, which they had brought to Balyk in anticipation of the purge. The major had decided against spending the night on the school cot in the nurse's room. The rain was increasing, and with the school generator down and all the outlying buildings lacking electricity, he would sleep at the Balyk Inn. The next morning he and Sasha could decide on the school's future. He would return to Tula on the afternoon train. Sasha had remained behind to oversee the students who were tidying up after supper.

As Galina lay in bed, alone and unseen under a moonless sky, she wondered whether Viktor and Polkovnikov had already left in the latter's car, a black Zim, and if they had, where were they headed? Ryazan? Probably. All was still, except for the clock on the windowsill. Then she heard the back door open and close. But she couldn't hear footsteps. Instinctively, she knew that the person had removed his shoes. Only a thief would do such a thing. She reached for Petr's service revolver, the faithful Nagant M1895 that she kept in her nightstand, at the back of the drawer, wrapped in burlap. Petr had taught her how to use his revolver, and as a young girl, she had accompanied her father on pistol shoots, though never on hunting trips. Straw targets were one thing, animals another. The revolver was loaded, just the way Petr had left it. He had told her that should she ever need to ward off thieves or drunkards, always afoot in the countryside, the pistol was ready. She had warned Alya never, never to touch the gun. Not even Sasha went near it. The intruder slowly opened her bedroom door, but waited to enter, as if listening to determine whether she was asleep or awake. Although unable to see in the dark, she trained the revolver on the door and waited. When the dim outline of a person appeared, accompanied by an alveolar click, she fired one shot. The body hit the floor without so much as a groan. She waited to see if he moved. Perhaps he was only pretending. Slipping out of bed, she kneeled next to the body and ran her hand over the face. It was beardless, not the face of Viktor Harkov. She couldn't believe the features she felt; they were those of Sasha Parsky.

How could such a mistake have occurred? When Sasha left the school building, he'd caught sight of Viktor and Polkovnikov standing next to the policeman's car. Why hadn't they left yet? Consulting his fears instead of his reason, he concluded that Galina was in the house waiting for Viktor's final embrace—and perhaps more. Gripped by an instinctive jealousy and primal possessiveness, he decided to do the unimaginable. He would test her. If his and Galina's recent lovemaking truly mattered, she could easily prove it. He entered the farmhouse through the pantry, removed his shoes, and tiptoed to Galina's door. In the few seconds before he eased it open, a thousand fears raced through his mind. Everything would depend on her first reaction to his address. His was a life in the balance. He opened the door and heard Galina's soft breathing, but was unable to see her. Given his hours of practice, he sounded a good imitation of Viktor's alveolar click. He knew that if Galina greeted him warmly and invited him into her bed that all their recent affection was a sham and that she could never again be trusted. A pistol sounded and he sank to his knees, unable to speak. He rolled to the floor. A moment later, he felt her hand on his face. With his dying breath, he whispered the fond and fugitive words that made everything clear.

Coda

Before sunrise, Galina packed a few belongings, collected Alya at Benjie's house, and caught the morning train for Ryazan. She left Alya with the Baturins, who were delighted to reunite with their former charge. Knowing Viktor's haunts and habits, Galina had no trouble finding him. She ascended the steps of a bleak building to the top floor. The nameplate was devoid of a card. She listened for a moment. On hearing movement inside the apartment, she knocked. At first, Viktor opened the door only a crack, but on seeing Galina, threw the door open and spread his arms wide. Several minutes later, he was found on the floor in this cruciform posture, with a bullet hole in his forehead. Galina had made no attempt to escape. The neighbors on hearing the report of the gun had called the constabulary. She was casually reading a magazine when the police arrived.

Alya remained with the Baturins during her mother's trial, at which Galina was found guilty of having been driven to murder because of jealousy—her lawyer argued that Viktor, her former lover, had abandoned her—and sentenced to ten years in a work camp. With the outbreak in 1939 of the Russian-Finnish war, she volunteered for nursing duty at the front. In February 1940, after a massive Russian push breached the Mannerheim Line (the Finns' southern defensive barrier stretching across the Karelian isthmus), the Red Amy moved north to the Finnish city of Viipuri (Vyborg), where Galina died of typhus.

Petr Selivanov, although a deserter, and denounced as an enemy of the people, made his way undetected from Kiev to Ryazan, where he rejoined his daughter and took her back to Bogdanovka, in Ukraine, where he was living with his second wife, Tatiana, and his young son, Benedikt. In October 1941, Bogdanovka became the site of an extermination camp, run by Rumanian occupation authorities. At one point, fifty-four thousand Jews were held there. Petr and his wife hid a local Jewish couple and their two daughters. When discovered in the attic of the Selivanov's house, the Jews, as well as Petr's family, were marched to a nearby forest, ordered to remove their clothes, and kneel. They were shot in the back of their necks. A plaque, honoring all the murdered, now marks the spot of the extermination camp.

Bogdan Dolin was sentenced to ten years in Kolyma. At the end of his sentence, he chose to live in Magadan, working for a printer.

Goran Youzhny escaped punishment but was forbidden to work as a photographer. He apprenticed to a tinsmith, eventually gravitating to a metal shop in Leningrad. The shop, however, published its own newspaper, and Goran quietly oversaw the photography department.

Vera Chernikova was appointed temporary and then permanent director of the Michael School and immediately invalidated all of Sasha Parsky's reforms, returning the school to its former curriculum and pedagogy.

Major Boris Filatov had hoped to find a new director for the school, but before he could do so, he was transferred from Tula to Moscow, to work in the disinformation section of the NKVD.

Avram Brodsky escaped imprisonment, but was placed under house arrest, forbidden visitors, and subject to the whims of a police "minder," a state of affairs that he regarded as tantamount to capital punishment. During Stalin's purge of "cosmopolitans" (read: Jews), the government rescinded his food-ration card. Rather than depend on the handouts of neighbors, he slowly starved himself to death, perhaps in part because of what had happened to Benjie's mother.

Natalia Korsakova was transported to the Vorkuta Gulag, located in the Pechora River Basin, twelve hundred miles from Moscow and one hundred miles above the Arctic Circle. She died of starvation in the service of the state, digging coal.

Devora Berberova continued as the head secretary of the Michael School and quickly became a favorite of the interim director, who now knew that Devora reported directly to the NKVD.

Father Zossima, because of Comrade Berberova's benign reports of him, was left to his hovel and humble life, dispensing aid when he could.

Ekaterina Rzhevska, Alya's tutor, adopted Benjie, following the Soviet custom of adopting waifs and the orphaned children of exiles.

Larissa, Basil, and Polkovnikov remained with the NKVD. They felt that they had played an important role in unmasking the Three Musketeers and exposing the "wreckers," and that the medals they received, like the many they'd earned in the past, were not sufficient recompense for their unstinting work. But they said nothing and merely increased their vigilance for the good of the country.

And the innumerable denouncers, what of them? Did they too have medals pinned on their chest? As far as anyone knows, they received the government promise that they would live in a prosperous and glorious land, a paradise, in the life to come. Sadly, the government neglected to say, "only not yours."

FINIS

Glossary

apparat: literally: apparatus. The Bolsheviks began as an underground movement. To survive, the Party machine demanded solidarity and discipline. Members were known as apparatchiki, that is, men of the apparat. The term eventually came to mean the Soviet bureaucratic system and had a distinctly negative connotation.

apparatchik: a member of a Communist apparat; a blindly devoted Bolshevik official, follower, or member

Cheka: the secret police under the Tsar. After the Russian Revolution, although the Bolsheviks formed their own secret police with its own acronym, people still used the old name.

chistka: literally: cleaning or cleansing; a political purge

kulich: from the Greek: a roll or loaf of bread. It is a sweet yeast-risen bread with raisins, almonds, and candied orange peel. The recipe for kulich is similar to that of Italian panettone.

Nagant M1895: a seven-shot, gas-seal revolver designed and produced by Belgian industrialist Léon Nagant for the Russian Empire. The gas-seal system allows the cylinder to move forward when the gun is cocked, to close the gap between the cylinder and the barrel. This feature provides a boost to the muzzle velocity of the fired projectile and suppresses the sound of the weapon when fired, an unusual ability for a revolver.

nepman: businessmen and women in the early years of the Soviet Union who took advantage of the opportunities for private trade and small-scale manufacturing created by the New Economic Policy (NEP), which was instituted by Lenin as a response to revolts against meager rations in the USSR during the early 1920s under Lenin's policy of War Communism. NEP encouraged private buying and selling even to, as one official put it, "get rich."

oblast: county

OGPU (Joint State Political Directorate or All-Union State Political Board): the formal name of the secret police, it operated from 1923 until 1934, when it was replaced by the NKVD, the People's Commissariat for Internal Affairs

oprichnik/oprichniki: originally: a member of an organization established by Tsar Ivan the Terrible to govern the division of Russia known as the Oprichnina (1565–1572); modern usage: a functionary, a toady, a flatterer, a sycophant

pashka: a rich Russian dessert made of cottage cheese, cream, almonds, and currants, set in a special wooden mold and traditionally eaten at Easter

proletariat/prole: from the Latin: a citizen of the lowest class. In its long or short form, the term is used to identify a lower social class, usually the working class.

samizdat: an important form of dissident activity across the Soviet bloc in which individuals reproduced censored publications by hand and passed the documents from reader to reader. This underground practice to evade officially imposed censorship was fraught with danger as harsh punishments were meted out to people caught possessing or copying censored materials.

Stakhanovite: a worker in the Soviet Union who regularly surpassed production quotas and was specially honored and rewarded

tovarish: comrade (especially in Russian Communism); American equivalents: associate, companion, comrade, fellow, yokefellow

TT 30: a semiautomatic pistol, developed in the early 1930s by Fedor Tokarev as a service pistol for the Soviet military to replace the Nagant M1895 revolver

ukase: a proclamation by a Russian emperor or government having the force of law; an edict, an official order

ushanka (hat): literally: "ear hat"; also known as a trooper, it is a Russian fur cap with ear flaps that can be tied up to the crown of the cap, or tied at the chin to protect the ears, jaw, and lower chin from the cold. The hat provides some protection to the head should one fall on the ice.

zek: an inmate; a Russian slang term for a prison or forced labor camp inmate